#1 *New York Times* Bestselling Author

DEBBIE MACOMBER

Something About Her

Heartsong **and** ***Love Thy Neighbor***

Recycling programs for this product may not exist in your area.

ISBN-13: 978-1-335-00215-0

Something About Her

All Illustrations by Paula Miquelarena.

For questions and comments about the quality of this book, please contact us at CustomerService@Harlequin.com.

TM is a trademark of Harlequin Enterprises ULC.

Harlequin
22 Adelaide St. West, 41st Floor
Toronto, Ontario M5H 4E3, Canada
Harlequin.com

HarperCollins Publishers
Macken House, 39/40 Mayor Street Upper,
Dublin 1, D01 C9W8, Ireland
www.HarperCollins.com

Printed in U.S.A.

Praise for the novels of #1 *New York Times* bestselling author Debbie Macomber

"Popular romance writer Debbie Macomber has a gift for evoking the emotions that are at the heart of the genre's popularity."

—*Publishers Weekly*

"It's clear that Debbie Macomber cares deeply about her fully realized characters and their families, friends and loves, along with their hopes and dreams. She also makes her readers care about them."

—*Bookreporter.com*

"Debbie Macomber is one of the most reliable, versatile romance writers around."

—*Milwaukee Journal Sentinel*

"Readers won't be able to get enough of Macomber's gentle storytelling."

—*RT Book Reviews*

"Bestselling Macomber . . . sure has a way of pleasing readers."

—*Booklist*

"It's impossible not to cheer for Macomber's characters. . . . When it comes to creating a special place and memorable, honorable characters, nobody does it better than Macomber."

—*BookPage*

"Macomber is a master storyteller."

—*Times Record News*

Debbie Macomber is a #1 *New York Times* bestselling author and a leading voice in women's fiction worldwide. Her work has appeared on every major bestseller list, with more than 170 million copies in print, and she is a multiple award winner. The Hallmark Channel based a television series on Debbie's popular Cedar Cove books. For more information, visit her website, debbiemacomber.com.

Also by Debbie Macomber

Blossom Street
The Shop on Blossom Street
A Good Yarn
Susannah's Garden
Back on Blossom Street
Twenty Wishes
Summer on Blossom Street

Cedar Cove
16 Lighthouse Road
204 Rosewood Lane
311 Pelican Court
44 Cranberry Point
50 Harbor Street

Visit the Author Profile page at
Harlequin.com for more titles.

Contents

Heartsong

Dear Friends,

Although it's been many years now, I remember with vivid detail the day I got **the call.** It was September 29, 1982, at 3:49 in the afternoon. Mary Clare Susan, an editor with Harlequin, phoned to make an offer on my book, *Heartsong*. I believe I said five words in total: *Hello. Yes. Thank you. Goodbye.* I scribbled down her phone number and then called her back the following day to be sure it hadn't all been a dream.

The sale of my first book couldn't have come at a better time. My husband, Wayne, a construction electrician, had been out of work for several months. He was staying in Alaska, hoping to get work on the pipeline, while the four children and I lived on his $150-a-week unemployment check. Those were bleak days in our household. The sale of my first book is what carried us financially through that difficult winter. When published, *Heartsong* was dedicated to my parents, Ted and Connie Adler. They were so proud and excited about the sale of my first book. I would be remiss if I didn't mention Wayne. My husband has been my hero from the very first. It was because of his encouragement and support that I am a published author.

Now on to the book. In order to get *Heartsong* ready for republication, I read through the manuscript, updating it where I could. If anything, this first novel will show how much I've improved as a writer in the past few decades. It's a book sold into the Christian market with lots of references to faith and God.

My hope is that you enjoy this vintage story. It is the book that launched my career and started me down the path to where I am today. I'm grateful for Harlequin's faith in me and to my first editor, Mary Clare Susan, who saw my potential and nurtured me along.

Please check out my website at debbiemacomber.com or look for me on all the social media platforms.

With warmest regards,
Debbie Macomber

For my parents,
TED AND CONNIE ADLER,
who were afraid that if I used my married name,
no one would know I was their daughter.

Chapter One

Slowly, silently, the heavy fog began to rise. The brisk offshore breeze set the thick moisture stirring around the Golden Gate Bridge. Gradually the sun broke through the low-lying vapor to display the wonders of the beautiful city of St. Francis.

Releasing a sigh of appreciation for the natural beauty around her, Skye Garvin leisurely strolled toward the hospital. A freshness seemed to flow through her. Usually by the end of the day the demands of teaching a classroom full of enthusiastic kindergartners left her physically and mentally drained. But even knowing she would be volunteering several hours at the hospital this afternoon couldn't dampen this new exuberance. The fresh air and brilliant sunlight brought a bounce to her step, and she hummed a catchy tune.

Once on the children's ward she paused to resecure the thick, honey-colored chignon the brisk wind had ruffled about her oval face. Her bright blue eyes sparkled, and her cheeks were whipped a rosy hue.

"You're here at last." Sally Avery, the head pediatric nurse, smiled in greeting. "Billy's been waiting impatiently all afternoon. I think he's ready to collect on his bet."

Skye pulled a wry face. "Oh, dear, I was afraid of that."

The corners of Sally's mouth curved upward. "You realize you're hopeless, don't you? Anyone crazy enough to race that child down the corridor in a wheelchair deserves what she gets."

Skye disguised her own amusement. "Kindly remove that snicker, Sally Avery. How was I to know Billy would practice day and night? You're the one who told me he wouldn't even sit in the wheelchair, and then on the day of the race he takes off like Parnelli Jones."

Sally laughed, but her eyes grew serious. "All kidding aside, thank you. I don't know if Billy would ever have voluntarily accepted the wheelchair if it hadn't been for you."

"Oh, nonsense, he just needed a little subtle encouragement," she said, refusing the credit. "I'd better go see the little rascal and discover my forfeit."

"While you're there, see if you can do anything to cheer up his new roommate."

"I'll do what I can." Skye paused, thinking she'd detected a gleam of mischief in Sally's expression. "I'll be back with Billy in a few minutes." She flashed a quick smile to the short brunette, who had been her good friend for several years. Skye and Sally were strikingly different in looks, but not temperament. Sally, with her short, stylish curls and slightly plump build, was perpetually dieting, while Skye, tall and slender, never needed to worry about her weight. But both were the impulsive, fun-loving type.

"Good afternoon, Sprout," Skye greeted her favorite ten-year-old.

"Hello, Skye!" Billy's young face lit up with eagerness. "You haven't forgotten our bet, have you?"

"I doubt that you would let me," Skye said a little drily.

"You said I could choose anything I wanted."

"Within reason," she added quickly, wondering how she could have been so rash.

"We'd better whisper," Billy warned, and gestured to the hospital bed beside his. The heavy white curtain surrounding the area prevented her from looking at his new roommate. "He's asleep, I think."

"Then let's go before we wake him," Skye whispered.

"I know what I want for my prize," Billy said loudly, forgetting his own advice in his enthusiasm.

An impatient oath came from the unknown occupant of the room.

"Oops, sorry, Mr. Kiley," Billy apologized.

"Either be quiet or get *out* of here." The hard voice breathed heavily in irritation.

Involuntarily Skye moved closer to Billy. There was no need for the man to be so impatient and brusque. Billy was having a rough enough time. A tragic victim of a hit-and-run driver, he was facing the possibility of spending the rest of his life in a wheelchair. Billy was special, always offering others a ready smile, even when in considerable discomfort. Other children came and left the hospital with amazing briskness, but Billy had remained for two months, and Skye had become devoted to the courageous youth.

Gently she lifted him into the wheelchair and wheeled him from the room.

"Your new roommate is a man," she said a bit incredulously. No wonder Sally had been so eager for her to meet him. From the beginning of their relationship Sally had assumed the role of matchmaker, intent on finding Skye a husband. Skye had resigned herself to Sally's schemes but had never allowed any male relationship to develop beyond a light flirtation. Her life would have been so different if Glen had lived. She immediately cast the unpleasant memories from her mind. It did no good to brood over the might-have-beens in her life.

"Of course Mr. Kiley is a man," Billy said, laughing. "Nurse Sally says he swears like a trooper, and she's right."

"What on earth is he doing on the children's ward?"

"The hospital must be full. I heard someone say my room had the only available bed, but I think Nurse Sally is going to get rid of him fast." His young mouth twisted into a lopsided grin. "Mr. Kiley knocked his lunch tray on the floor this afternoon."

Skye shook her head disapprovingly. Sally and the other nurses on the children's ward were gentle and patient. They certainly had enough to do without having to deal with an ill-tempered, oversized juvenile.

"It seems your new roommate needs to be reminded of his manners," Skye retorted crisply.

"I don't think you should blame Mr. Kiley for being in a bad mood. He's just in pain and hungry," Billy said with a maturity beyond his years. "You said for my prize I could have anything I wanted."

"Yes, but—"

"Well, I've decided what I want." He turned in his chair to look at her, his eyes full of boyish enthusiasm. "I want you to get Mr. Kiley to eat. He's only a grouch because he won't let anyone feed him, and his hands are bandaged so he can't feed himself."

"Oh, no, you don't, Billy!" Skye protested, waving her finger back and forth urgently.

"Please, Skye," Billy pleaded. "Remember how you coaxed me? I bet it would work with Mr. Kiley. If anyone can do it, you can."

"Oh, Billy." She sighed, hating to disappoint him. "It just

won't work. A man isn't going to get excited over a button that says I ATE THE WHOLE THING."

Sally joined them in the wide hospital corridor. "Did you tell her yet?" she asked Billy.

"Yeah. I think she'll do it." He gave a reckless grin.

"No way!" Skye said instantly. "I'm sorry, but your request is beyond reason."

"It sounds fair enough to me," Sally interjected, a glint of laughter shining in her eyes.

"Sally!" Skye glared at her friend, her look speaking volumes.

Unaffected, Sally laughed. "You'd best be on your way, or Billy will be late for his physical therapy session."

"Come on, Skye." Billy's hands hurriedly rotated the large wheels of his chair as he pushed himself toward the elevator. "If we don't hurry, I might be late for dinner."

"And we wouldn't want to miss dinner, would we, Skye?" Sally taunted.

"Come on, you guys," Skye pleaded helplessly.

But Billy refused to be persuaded otherwise, although Skye made repeated attempts as they rode the elevator downward. Leaving him with the physical therapist, she returned to pediatrics.

"I'm glad you're back," Sally said when she saw Skye had returned. "Pastor Johnson phoned and asked if you could visit Mrs. Montressor when you get the chance. There's nothing pressing here. Go now, if you like."

The hospital chaplain often requested that Skye visit certain patients. Her duties entailed reading scripture aloud, writing letters, or just visiting with a Christian brother or sister. Mrs. Montressor was a sweet, elderly woman from Skye's church who was being transferred from the hospital to a nursing home. Skye realized the older woman was anxious about the move and just wanted a reassuring chat.

The visit lasted nearly an hour, and Skye returned to pediatrics only a few minutes before Billy was due, so she hurried to put his bed in order. Nervously she entered the room. The curtain around his roommate's bed was open, but the man's face was turned away from her. She said a quick prayer that she wouldn't wake him and worked as quietly as possible.

"Well, if it isn't little Miss Pollyanna." A gruff voice thick with amusement spoke as she completed making the bed. A grin twisted the corners of his mouth as he regarded her volunteer uniform. He paused to read the button attached below her name tag, which said: I BELIEVE IN MIRACLES.

"Oscar the Grouch, I presume," she said without her usual warm smile, hoping to show her disapproval of his behavior.

Their gazes met and held. Cool arrogance returned her study. As Billy had explained, his hands were bandaged in thick white gauze resembling makeshift boxing gloves; his left arm was propped at an awkward angle in traction. He wasn't strikingly handsome, but he was compelling, with a sense of self-assurance. His eyes were a deep gray, widely set, and lent his face a look of intensity. His jawline, proud and strong, was ruggedly carved.

His eyes darkened under her scrutiny, as if he deeply resented her or anyone seeing him as incapacitated. Not that it was likely she would view this unnerving male as weak. He exuded an easy strength and confidence, but Skye could sense his frustration and impatience.

His helplessness stirred something within her, and she realized she wanted to help this man. Common sense quickly intervened, however. She was out of her element, and there was little she could do.

Their gazes remained locked until Sally wheeled Billy into the room.

"Okay, young man, let's get you into bed; dinner is on the

way." Reverting her attention to Billy's roommate, Sally added, "And, Jordan Kiley, you'll be pleased to know you're being transferred to another ward first thing in the morning."

Amusement returned to the intense gray eyes. "Couldn't wait to be rid of me, could you?" his husky voice challenged.

"Certainly pediatrics will miss your wit and charm," Sally lied, and Billy giggled.

"Just as long as we understand each other." The voice fit the man: low-pitched and demanding. "And as for dinner, either give me something I can eat myself, or forget it. I'm not a baby, and I won't be hand-fed."

Billy's eye quickly caught Skye's, and she shrugged in a gesture of defeat, but Billy's eyes widened imploringly.

The large cafeteria cart had arrived from the kitchen, and glancing from the hall to her patient, Sally said, "I'll see what I can do, but it's doubtful."

Skye tucked Billy's sheet in and brought the vanity around from the side of the bed before leaving the room.

"Where are you going, Pollyanna?" Jordan asked.

His question surprised her. "I'll be back," she promised, and offered him a tentative smile.

"Remember, I want to collect on my bet *tonight*!" Billy shouted after her.

The dinner trays had all been delivered . . . save one. Skye stood beside the large cart deep in thought. She knew Jordan Kiley represented a far greater challenge than any child she had ever worked with. It wouldn't be easy to spoon-feed him and salvage his pride at the same time.

"Hello, Skye. I haven't seen you in a while." Joyce Kimball, one of the younger high school volunteers, addressed her warmly. "Do you like the new me?" She turned, allowing Skye to study her appearance. It was unmistakably the Carin Cain look. The sleek, high-fashion image was sweeping the country.

It seemed everyone was imitating the famous model: the Carin Cain hairstyle, the Carin Cain designer jeans, the Carin Cain cosmetics.

Skye's eyes widened as an idea began to form. "Joyce," she cried, "you're a genius." Obeying the impulse, Skye began pulling the large pins from her hair.

Several minutes later the latest Carin Cain imitator approached Billy's room. Silky, honey-blond curls cascaded over her shoulders. Normally Skye applied her makeup modestly, but now her mouth was liberally coated with gloss, and blush had been added to accentuate the natural color of her rosy cheeks.

She found Billy enjoying his meal and cast him a secret smile. He returned her wink in silent communication.

Jordan watched dispassionately as she set the dinner tray on the vanity and rolled it to the side of his bed.

His gaze traveled leisurely over her, measuring her. Skye's face grew hot under his slow appraisal; her courage nearly failed her.

"You must really believe in miracles if you think I'm going to let you feed me," he announced caustically, sending a shiver of apprehension up her spine.

The words seemed lodged in her throat as his look penetrated through her.

"I learned a long time ago that when it comes to miracles, I have to pray as if everything depended on God—and work as if everything depended on me." She was surprised at how composed she sounded.

"Just how do you propose to work *this* miracle?" He sounded cynical.

"I'm prepared to offer you a little inducement."

His thick brows arched in curiosity.

She offered him a warm smile. "You must understand, the

nurses are held to a certain code of ethics. But I'm not a nurse, I'm a volunteer. And I'm prepared to offer you a small reward if you let me feed you."

His eyes showed interest. "What kind of reward?"

"More of a dessert."

Interpreting his silence as consent, she rolled the vanity closer to the bed and dipped the fork into the potatoes. But Jordan's mouth remained defiantly shut, his dark eyes brooding.

Skye's spirits sank; her ploy wasn't going to fool this intuitive male.

Unexpectedly a faint smile formed at the corners of his mouth. "Feed me," he sighed with self-derision. "I always was a sucker for a pretty face."

Her thick lashes fluttered down to conceal the triumph in her expressive blue eyes.

Jordan continued to watch her, his eyes sharp and intent. Skye knew it was all Billy could do to keep from applauding.

"Do you find fulfillment in life as a hospital volunteer?" Jordan asked between bites.

"I'm responsibly employed. As a matter of fact, I hold a highly respected position." His smile brought a marked defensiveness to her voice. "As it happens, I enlighten, train, and discipline."

"She's a kindergarten teacher," Billy supplied laughingly.

"I also button coats, pour juice, and kiss away hurts . . ." Again she was interrupted by Billy.

"She's not married, either."

"Billy!" Skye snapped, her cheeks flushed crimson.

"It happens that way sometimes," Jordan explained to Billy. "She's pretty enough but has probably been jilted or hurt. It'll take time before she's ready to love again." It was an open dare for Skye to contradict him.

Instead she laughed lightly, shrugging off the challenge. "I see that the psychiatrist is *in*. Thank you for your analysis, Doctor." The curve of her mouth softened into a smile.

His gray eyes held her look; he seemed to know she would not be easily provoked.

Now it was her turn to satisfy her curiosity. Putting down the fork, she asked, "How did you manage to get yourself into this fine mess?"

"Car accident." He sounded annoyed, though his anger wasn't directed at Skye but at himself. "Besides totaling my car, I managed to ruin my first vacation in years."

"What happened?" she asked, chilled by the memory of another accident long ago.

"Lombard Street." He groaned at his own stupidity. "I'd heard so much about San Francisco's famous curved street and decided to take it as fast as possible. I didn't make the last curve."

Skye had read an account of the accident in the morning paper. The crazy fool was lucky not to have been killed—or to have killed someone else. Lombard Street, with eight consecutive turns at ninety-degree angles, was difficult to maneuver at the best of times. "Did you enjoy the novelty of reading about yourself this morning?" she asked, hiding her disapproval of such irresponsible behavior.

Some emotion flickered in his eyes, and for a brief second Skye thought it might be alarm.

"Are you a teacher, like Skye?" Billy interjected his own curiosity.

"No. I work for a radio station."

Billy's voice rose eagerly. "Are you a disc jockey?"

The pause was only momentary. "Among other things," he remarked absently. "You say there was an accident report in the morning paper?"

"Would you like a copy? I'm sure there's an extra paper in the lobby. I can get it if you like."

"Please." He sounded grateful.

Skye returned a few minutes later with a section of the paper. It was only a short account of the accident, a few sentences that didn't give his name.

Jordan seemed to relax and joked, "What does a man have to do in this town to get his name in the paper?"

Gently Skye placed her hand on his arm. "Has your family been contacted?"

The slant of Jordan's mouth became cynical. "As there is only my mother, I can't see much point in distressing her over a few scratches."

A badly broken arm could hardly be considered a scratch. Nonetheless, Skye laughed lightly. "Obviously the poor man has been jilted, Billy. He just hasn't learned to trust again. Or as Sally would say—you're either separated, divorced, or just plain unmarriageable."

"At thirty-six, I suspect she's right." But Jordan didn't enlighten her about which category he fit into.

Betty Fisher, Billy's mother, arrived as Billy finished his meal, and she wheeled her son into the large recreation/visiting room at the end of the hall.

"You coming, Skye?" Billy asked, eager for her to join the children and play the piano.

"Not until later; I'll only be a few minutes," she promised.

Giving Jordan the last bit of his dinner, she asked, "Now, that wasn't so bad, was it?"

"When do I get dessert?"

"Soon," she said. "I'll take your tray to the cart and be right back."

Skye lingered outside the room for several seconds gathering her courage. The I ATE THE WHOLE THING button was clenched tightly in the palm of her hand. Unsteady fingers looped a long strand of honey-blond hair behind her ear. Jordan Kiley wasn't going to find humor in her little deception.

His eyes probed her as she entered, but she purposely avoided eye contact with him.

"I didn't think you would come back." His voice was cool.

"Of course I was coming back. I always keep my promises," she said, finding it difficult not to smile. "Now, close your eyes," she whispered, and bent over him.

He complied and she quickly attached the button to his hospital gown.

Jordan caught his breath and reached for her. The attempt to catch her was ludicrous, and Skye stood only inches from his reach, her blue eyes triumphant. A certain pride at having outwitted him prompted her mouth to curve into a Mona Lisa smile.

Jordan looked at the button and grinned. "Clever trick, Pollyanna, but have no doubts I will collect what is due me."

Skye realized he was the type of man who ultimately got what he wanted. His words were more of a promise than a threat. Disguising the effect of his statement, she put on a smiling façade and handed him the pie on the hospital tray while gaining control of her racing heartbeat. "I told you, I keep my promises," she said with far more confidence than she felt.

Gradually the tension began to fade, and she relaxed. Combing her fingers through her long hair, she said, "Good-bye, Mr. Grouch."

The sound of his low laugh followed her into the corridor.

She had escaped Jordan Kiley this time, but she realized she wouldn't be so fortunate a second time.

Billy and his mother, along with the other children and their visitors, were waiting for Skye when she entered the recreation room. An upright mahogany piano rested against the outside wall, and when she sat on the padded bench, the happy chatter grew silent.

Skye's slim fingers flew across the ivory keys in a light, catchy tune, and soon the small audience was clapping in time to the happy melody. The uplifting beat of the music eased some of the worry etched so clearly on the faces of the children and their families. It was for this reason Skye came week after week, year after year. If she could help others forget their own unhappiness, even for a short while, then her time was well spent.

Although everyone enjoyed the piano playing, it was the songs Skye composed that the children loved the best. The clever descriptions of make-believe dragons, castles, and children's dreams brought smiles and giggles to cherubic faces.

Skye's closing number was a soft lullaby she had composed using Psalm 62:

My soul rests in God alone.
My salvation is from Him.
He alone is my rock, my salvation,
and my fortress.
I will never be greatly shaken.
Find rest, O my soul, in God alone;
my hope comes from Him.

Rich and melodious, her voice rang clear and true through the passageway, and as she hummed the final notes several children yawned, ready for sleep. Hoping to place homesick patients in a familiar family routine, the hospital encouraged parents to put their children to bed before leaving.

As Betty wheeled Billy toward his room she asked Skye hopefully, "Do you have time for a cup of coffee tonight?"

Alone and young, Betty Fisher needed someone as a sounding board for her worries over Billy's uncertain future.

"I always have time for you, Betty," Skye assured the young mother.

"Are you coming tomorrow, Skye?" Billy asked the same question after every visit, as if he were afraid she would disappear someday, just as his father had.

"No, Sprout, but I'll be here Thursday," she whispered, hoping not to wake Jordan. The white curtain had been replaced, and the nurse had put a finger to her lips when they had entered the room, indicating that the man was asleep. Skye had given an unconscious sigh of relief.

Just as Betty and Skye were ready to kiss Billy good night, Sally stuck her head in the door. "Do you need a ride home tonight, Skye?"

"Not tonight, thanks, Sally."

"Okay, I'll see you Thursday."

"Good night, Sally." She smiled a friendly farewell. "Sleep tight, Sprout," she whispered tenderly, and lovingly kissed his brow.

Halfway across the darkened room a clear male voice taunted, "Good night, Pollyanna."

Chapter Two

School didn't go well the next day. Skye had difficulty concentrating on her teaching and several times found her troubled thoughts drifting to Jordan Kiley. In the light of the new day she felt no sense of triumph over her deception or in having bested him, only a guilty uneasiness. Sally had mentioned that Jordan was being transferred to another ward as soon as possible and would probably be discharged by Friday. There was little likelihood she would ever see him again. She couldn't understand why this restless feeling persisted.

Skye welcomed three thirty and the dismissal of her kindergartners. Her students had picked up on her mood as well. It didn't help that there were only a few days left before spring break. Anticipating the vacation, the five-year-olds were antsy and hyperactive.

It was after four when she finally left the school for home. Her apartment, a rare find in the Marina district, had large bay windows that presented a sweeping panorama of the water. Healthy, abundant plants hung in the window, flourishing under her tender care and in the warmth of the sun. It was a homey apartment, decorated with cushioned bamboo furniture, and possessed the appeal of simplicity.

The lock on her front door clicked loudly as she turned the key; then she paused momentarily to replace the key inside her purse.

"Howdy, neighbor." The apartment door across the hall opened at the sound.

"Hello, John." She gave him a deliberate, casual smile. "Nice day, isn't it?" She didn't wait for his reply before pushing open her door.

"No need to rush away. I've been wanting to talk to you. We're neighbors; we should get to know each other better."

"Not today," Skye offered, apologetically but firmly. The last thing she wanted was to become trapped in John Dirkson's apartment for the rest of the afternoon. Strikingly handsome and charming, John didn't lack female companionship, but Skye found his sleek good looks and huge ego unattractive. Unfortunately, he refused to accept her rebuffs as sincere; her refusal to become involved made her a novelty.

"It's not going to work, you know," John said, affecting disinterest.

"What's not going to work?"

He hooked his thumb lazily in the belt loop of his designer jeans and leaned against the open door frame. "This playing hard to get."

"I'm so pleased to hear it." She adopted a lighthearted, bright smile. "I was worried for a minute."

"I'll get you yet," he added confidently, not in the least discouraged by her attitude.

"No, you won't," she said quickly, then stepped inside her apartment and firmly closed the door.

She placed her purse and mail on the entryway table and hung her hooded raincoat in the closet. After slipping off her shoes, she walked barefooted into the tiny kitchen to put on water to boil for tea. Obeying habit, she flipped the switch on the radio in her bedroom while changing clothes. The air was crisp and chilly, and she chose a winter outfit that had been a birthday gift from her brother. The red plaid pants slipped easily over her slim hips, and the matching turtleneck sweater made a striking contrast to her golden hair.

A slow and soothing romantic ballad filled the room. Unbidden, the music conjured up a mental image of Jordan's taunting smile, and Skye bit into her lower lip, nibbling on it unconsciously.

"Go away," she said aloud, and irritably turned off the radio.

A few minutes later she stood before the bathroom mirror, pulling the pins from her hair.

"Rapunzel . . . Rapunzel . . . let down your hair." She laughed, and wondered at her strange mood. The thick curls shimmered down like liquid gold upon her shoulders and back. Its length was a nuisance; a shorter style would have been far more practical, but she couldn't summon the courage to have it cut. Glen had always loved her long, thick hair, and in a way its length was a symbolic memory of his love. She brushed the curls vigorously until they crackled with electricity. On impulse she left her hair down, the length curving attractively about her shoulders. In reality she was much too tall to be wearing it up all the time, but she had long ago quit worrying about her height. Accustomed to seeing her hair away from her face, she did an automatic double take, surprised at how good she looked, when she happened to glance in the mirror on her way out the door.

The teapot was whistling, and soon the aroma of cinnamon and spice perfumed the air. The mail contained a newsy letter from her mother in Florida, and Skye sat with her cup of tea, propping her feet on the large wicker chest that served as a coffee table, while immersing herself in the letter.

She needed this time to relax and unwind from her day but instead found herself fidgety and restless. Perhaps she should do some shopping and even splurge and have a meal out before attending the Wednesday-evening church service and choir practice.

The idea proved to be a good one. She bought herself a new pair of shoes, plain but comfortable ones she could wear to school. Impulsively she stopped in a toy store to browse around. Billy had been so unselfish in his choice of a prize that she picked out a small electronic game he was sure to enjoy. Since it was on sale, it was easy to rationalize the expense.

Pleased with her purchases, Skye decided to deliver Billy's gift to him instead of waiting until the following evening. And while she was at the hospital maybe Sally would join her for a light meal in the cafeteria.

As usual pediatrics was a hub of activity. Nurses and the other staff members moved with purpose. Skye stopped by the nurses' station to leave a message for Sally, then lightheartedly headed for Billy's room.

Entering the room, she froze midstep. Billy's bed was empty, but Jordan Kiley was very much present. The force of his personality filled the room, compelling and totally male. He viewed her shock with a half smile that touched the corners of his mouth.

Suddenly the smile left his eyes, and he grimaced as his rugged face twisted with pain. Her surprise quickly receded into concern, and she haphazardly deposited her packages on Billy's empty bed before rushing to Jordan's side.

"What's the matter? Should I get Sally?" Alarm coated her voice.

Before she could protest, she found herself roughly jerked against the side of the bed. The strength of his right arm was unbelievable, and the unyielding muscles of his upper arm flexed as he held her firmly in check. A slow, satisfied grin spread evenly across his face.

Panic erupted within Skye but it was useless to struggle against his superior strength. Frantically she whispered, "Please, don't."

Jordan studied the terror in her eyes, and gradually his merciless grip relaxed, but his bandaged hand remained around her waist.

"This is just to let you know I can claim what is mine anytime I want. No more games, Pollyanna."

Numbly, Skye nodded; her voice seemed to be locked in her throat, and she was breathing unevenly.

His arm fell, freeing her. "You're really nervous, aren't you? Has it been so long since a man kissed you that you tremble at the possibility?" His voice was smooth and teasing.

"Of course not," she denied stiffly, backing away from him. Her hands were still shaking when she bumped against the rail of Billy's bed. "I brought this for Billy," she said, her hands groping for the smaller package. "Would you see that he gets it?" she asked in what she hoped sounded like a normal voice.

Jordan ignored her request, his eyes studying her astutely. "You've been badly hurt, haven't you?" His words were soft with discernment. "How long have you managed to hide behind that easy laugh and witty personality?"

Despite herself Skye's head snapped up, and what color remained quickly drained from her face. His perceptions were unnerving. Automatically she swallowed back a denial; as for her quick wit, where was it when she needed it so desperately?

"I should have remembered Billy wouldn't be here," she said, ignoring his question. It was a struggle to keep her voice even. "Please tell him I'll be back later."

"Oh, no, you don't," Jordan interjected quickly. "I'm not letting you go now, not when I pulled every string I could to remain on this floor until I got the chance to see you again."

His disclosure halted Skye's flight from the room. "You wanted to see me again?" she asked incredulously. Slowly a smile meandered across her face as she realized what he was saying. "Ah, you just wanted to collect another 'dessert'."

He answered with a lazy grin. "True, but thinking of a way to even the score helped pass the long day." He shifted slightly and grimaced with a rush of pain. "Darn this arm," he swore harshly.

Again Skye found his discomfort greatly affecting her, but she forced herself to stay where she was. "That trick won't work a second time," she said, although she realized his pain was genuine.

"Pity," he murmured with a forced smile.

"Isn't there something I can do?"

"No, it'll pass in a moment." His breathing was hard and labored.

"Please," she whispered, her gaze resting on his strong face. "Let me do something to help." The compassion he evoked in her was almost physical. "I'll get Sally."

"No," he shouted.

His anger shocked her, and she stepped back as if burned.

Jordan made a savage gesture. "I didn't mean to snap your head off, but the nurses can do nothing." He relaxed against the pillow, the pain easing. "The doctors placed a pin in my arm, and every now and then a pain shoots through it like fire." His eyes darkened defiantly. "But I refuse to be constantly drugged."

Skye's legs felt shaky; it was ridiculous to be so affected by this man.

"Skye," he said, using her name for the first time. "Will you stay awhile?"

"I . . . can't." Nervously she moistened her dry lips. "I'm meeting Sally for dinner." She had only left a message for Sally to meet her if she could, but Skye knew if she were to remain with Jordan it would only enhance this unsettling effect he had upon her.

His eyes narrowed. Too late, Skye realized her excuse had dented his pride. Jordan wasn't the kind of man women would easily refuse. She had already tried his vanity before with her deception; to provoke him again would be unkind. Jordan wasn't like her neighbor who saw her as a conquest to be made. Billy's roommate was in pain and lonely.

"Afraid?" he mocked.

"No, of course not," she denied instantly.

"How about later tonight then?" he said, surprising her by pursuing the subject.

"I don't think so . . . I sing with the church choir, and we practice on Wednesday nights," she hurried to explain. She was making a mess of this. Her whole purpose as a hospital volunteer was to help others. Surely it went against his nature to even ask her to stay, and she knew she was denying him only because of the strange feelings he stirred within her. Right away she felt guilty. "I suppose I could stop for a few minutes afterward, but it might be late."

"Don't worry, I'll be awake." He sounded like he was silently laughing at her.

"It's spring vacation next week, isn't it?" Sally asked as the late-afternoon sunshine filtered through the hospital cafeteria.

"Praise God, yes," Skye rejoiced openly. "I could do with a vacation." Maybe all this turmoil with Jordan was just the result of a bad case of spring fever.

Eyeing Skye's meager dinner, Sally demanded, "How can you survive with just a bowl of soup?"

Skye couldn't very well admit that her confrontation with Jordan had robbed her of her appetite. "I ate a little something before leaving the house." A small deception; she'd had only tea.

Sally pushed the remainder of her salad aside. "I hate dieting," she declared vehemently. "I could kill for a pizza."

Skye couldn't keep from laughing. Sally had been dieting with no real success ever since Skye had known her.

"Losing weight would be easier if you exercised more often," Skye advised with an encouraging smile. "Why not run with me, Sally? It'll help."

Sally rolled her eyes expressively. "Thanks, but no thanks. I'm not that desperate. You've forgotten I've seen you run. I couldn't keep up with you if I was pedaling a bicycle." Absently her hand smoothed a nonexistent crease from the skirt of her uniform. "If you weren't so easy to like, I could be jealous of you."

"Me?" Skye was genuinely shocked. "I can't believe that. I'm the one who steps into a cold apartment every night. I don't have a loving husband or a precious baby like Anne Marie. I should be the envious one."

A full smile teased Sally's mouth. "You don't have twenty extra pounds to lose, either. I guess it's just a case of the grass being greener on the other side of the fence. But honestly, if you're lonely, let me introduce you to Andy's new accountant."

"Sally, no!" Skye interrupted brusquely. "I'm a big girl now and quite capable of finding my own dates."

"Jordan Kiley has been asking questions about you."

"Oh?" Skye took another sip of her coffee, hoping to appear nonchalant and hide her interest.

"You know me," Sally said, grinning. "By three o'clock in the afternoon I'd sell my soul for a chocolate chip cookie, and Kiley offered me the whole bakery." Her eyes sparkled with impish delight. "I spilled my guts."

"Sally!"

"Oh, all right. I hardly said a word." She paused, mumbling something under her breath.

Skye couldn't let the matter drop. "Pardon me?" she asked firmly.

"I said, I didn't have to say a word. Billy told Kiley everything."

"Heaven help me," Skye groaned.

Glancing at her wristwatch, Sally stood. "I've got to rush, or I'll be late. By the way, Kiley is being transferred to the third floor after dinner. You might stop by and say hello; it's the only way you'll be able to clear away any untruths."

Sally looked surprised at Skye's laugh. "I just might do that." Not for the world would she relate what had happened that afternoon, but by her own admission she was interested in Jordan Kiley.

Flashing Skye an approving smile, Sally said, "You should wear the new blue dress we bought not long ago the next time you come. You're quite a knockout in it."

Skye had no such intention. "Yes, Mother."

Unaffected by the heavy sarcasm, Sally laughed. "See you tomorrow."

The church choir was practicing an Easter cantata, and several members of the group were already present when Skye joined them.

"Here's our little songbird." The male director smiled and handed her the sheet music.

"At five foot ten, I can hardly be described as little," she joked with the ease of familiarity. Others joined in the teasing banter, and the sound of laughter echoed across the empty church.

The practice proceeded with only a few minor interruptions.

Skye's solo came before the final reprise; her rich, clear voice vibrated through the room with brilliant bravura.

"I get chills down my spine every time you sing," Mrs. Peterman, the organist, said as the choir was dismissed. "Have you ever considered singing professionally, dear?"

Skye had been asked the question before and considered it a supreme compliment. But singing for money was something she'd never consider. She was perfectly content with the uncomplicated pattern of her life, and had no aspirations for fame and glory.

"Some of us are going out for coffee. Will you join us, Skye?" the director asked.

"Not tonight," she apologized ruefully. "I'm visiting a . . . friend." By now she thoroughly regretted the promise she'd made to stop by the hospital. Any contact with Jordan Kiley was asking for trouble, and it would be far better to avoid him.

Walking swiftly to the hospital elevator, Skye didn't consider stopping to visit Billy; it was after nine o'clock, and he was sure to be asleep. Besides, she didn't feel up to Sally's curiosity.

Visiting hours had ended an hour earlier, and since she wasn't well known by the third-floor nursing staff, they were sure to ask her to leave after only a few minutes anyway. She sighed in relief and stopped just long enough at the nurses' station to ask Jordan's room number and be sure they knew she was there.

"It's past visiting hours," the nurse informed her disapprovingly after relaying the information.

"I know. I'll only be a few minutes," Skye said, and beamed her one of her brightest smiles before starting down the silent corridor. About halfway down, raised voices could be heard. The most prominent, deep and rich, rumbled angrily with a cutting edge. It didn't take Skye two seconds to recognize the voice as Jordan's.

"I can see you're up to your persnickety ways, Oscar the

Grouch." She stood stiffly in the open doorway. Both the nurse and Jordan turned their attention to her. A furrow of painful frustration lined the forehead of the red-faced nurse.

The corners of Jordan's mouth lifted in a half smile, thawing the cynical curve of his features. "Welcome, Pollyanna."

"Good evening, miss." The nurse flashed Skye a grateful smile. "I'm afraid visiting hours are over." The older woman calmly stepped to Jordan's bed. "But I feel we can make an exception tonight *if* Mr. Kiley can be convinced to accept his medication."

The line of Jordan's mouth tightened in grim disapproval. "I refuse to be blackmailed!" he spat.

"In which case I'll have to ask your friend to leave," the nurse returned just as sharply.

"Good-bye, Jordan." Skye turned away from the door.

A disgusted sound of exasperation came from his throat. "All right, I'll take the darn pill, but I don't like it."

Smiling, Skye unbuttoned her coat and laid it across a chair while the nurse handed Jordan the pill and a glass of water. He had been transferred to a private room. It was spacious, containing two comfortably upholstered chairs and an end table with a lamp. Skye wondered at the expense. This was probably the only bed available, and she murmured a silent prayer that his insurance would cover the additional cost.

The nurse winked on her way out the door, and when Skye turned to Jordan, his face was transformed from the heavy scowl to a welcoming grin. Her unsteady fingers looped a long curl of hair around her ear.

"You should always leave your hair down. It's lovely," Jordan said, and watched with amusement as color suffused her face.

Why had she ever let it down? It seemed to welcome comment; several people had mentioned it during the course of the evening, and by now she was thoroughly sorry and vowed it would be a long time before she did it again.

"Thank you," she replied stiffly, self-conscious and unsure. "Are you eating?" Her gaze followed the pattern of the linoleum floor.

"No one has offered me any rewards or desserts." The teasing quality of his voice was a mocking reminder of her game the night before.

Her deep blue eyes crinkled in amusement and bounced away from the strong lines of his face. "Trickery and extortion seem to be the only effective means of dealing with that arrogant pride of yours."

"Ah, but if the food were better, your scheming wouldn't be necessary." His eyes held a dancing light. "What I wouldn't give for a thick pizza and a cold beer."

Skye's gaze was drawn back to him. The light dinner hadn't satisfied her, and now her stomach growled hungrily. "Pizza does sound good, doesn't it?"

"Like heaven," Jordan returned wistfully.

"Italian sausage, mushroom, and black olive, covered with a thick layer of mozzarella cheese?"

"Anchovies," Jordan added.

"Okay, but only on your half." She sat, unzipped her boot, and pulled a small, flat plastic card from the bottom of the boot.

"What are you doing?"

"Getting out the card to pay for the pizza," she replied, as if he were dense.

"What pizza?" He sounded like an amnesia victim.

"The Italian-sausage-mushroom-and-black-olive-with-anchovies-on-one-half pizza—the one I am going across the street to order and sneak inside this room," she explained in one giant breath.

His rueful smile became a soft chuckle. “Of course, I should have known—*that* pizza.”

Skye laughed and limped on one shoeless foot to the door to peek down the hallway.

“Now what are you doing?” he demanded in exasperation.

“Checking the entrance to the stairs. I can’t use the elevator since it opens directly in front of the nurses’ station, and the only way I can avoid their eagle eyes is to take the stairs. That wasn’t a sleeping pill she gave you by any chance, was it?”

“No, one of those blasted painkillers.” Anger reverberated in his husky voice.

Zipping up her boot, Skye smiled reassuringly. “I’ll be back before you know it.”

“I’ll be waiting.”

Skye returned in far less time than she expected. She opened the door to Jordan’s room and closed it quietly behind her after she hurried inside, hoping to avoid attracting anyone’s attention. She was breathing hard from the exertion of running up three flights of stairs.

“That didn’t take long.” Jordan’s head was drawn back, poised and alert.

“They weren’t very busy.” She set the square cardboard box on the vanity.

“Boy, that smells good,” he said, sighing, as she lifted the lid to the steaming pizza. “I think I’ll be able to manage on my own if you give me the pieces in a napkin.”

“Okay, but if it’s awkward, I don’t mind feeding you,” she offered.

The silence between them was serene as they ate. Skye smiled to herself a couple of times as she watched Jordan’s attempts to eat the pizza with his bandaged hand. Actually he was doing very well, and it surprised her. Perhaps she was making too much of this attraction. What harm would result from a budding friendship? What did she have to fear?

"I hope you won't find me unduly nosy," Jordan said, his voice cutting into her thoughts, "but I was wondering if you always carry your money in your shoe."

"Do you think I have a foot fetish?" she questioned with a laugh, her tone matching the lightness of his. "Actually it's a precautionary measure against muggers."

His thick brows arched.

"San Francisco is one of the most beautiful, romantic cities in the world, but that doesn't make us exempt from crime. I carry several single dollar bills in my wallet, and anything larger in my shoe. Brad, my older brother, worries about my living alone and advised me always to carry money in my purse just in case I do get mugged. Then the robber won't beat me in frustration over an empty purse."

"You're kidding."

"No, I'm not," she said, defending herself. "A girl alone in a big city, even a city as beautiful as San Francisco, is forced into a defensive stance. Crime is a fact of life, and after some of the stories my brother has told me, I'm ready to play it safe."

"Why do you do it then?" he mocked openly.

"Do what?" She glanced up from her pizza.

"Live alone. You're an attractive, enticing blonde. Surely there's some man standing on the sidelines just waiting for you to say the word."

His inquisitiveness quickly resurrected the barrier of humor she hid behind, and she responded with a hearty laugh. "You make my life sound like a football game. I hate to disappoint your curious nature, but there is no one waiting for my punt return."

Jordan raised a dubious brow, but smiled into her laughing eyes. "You think you're pretty smart, don't you?"

"Without a doubt." She wrinkled her nose and fluttered her eyelashes wickedly. She was having a good time, and smiled, unable to remember when she'd enjoyed an evening more. Perhaps she was enjoying it too much.

"It's after ten. I think I'd better go. I'm a working girl, you know, and there would be Hades to pay if I was found out now." She was referring to the nurses.

"I don't want you to leave." He studied her with a disturbing light in his eyes. "I don't think there are many women in the world who would spend an evening visiting a demanding, ill-tempered invalid."

"There's no need to thank me. I enjoyed it; it's been fun."

"I owe you for the pizza." His expression became strangely brooding, as if it were a great insult to his pride to have her pay for their meal.

"Oh, no, please, it was my treat. You're the one out of work—"

"I can afford a pizza." His mouth twisted with irritation.

"I'm sure you can." She sighed, drawing a deep breath. If anything, her insistence was doing more harm than good. *Please,* her eyes implored, *let's not ruin our time by arguing over something so petty.*

He flashed her a tender smile, his eyes holding hers magnetically. "You are very lovely."

Her eyes widened in surprise and her heart thundered against her ribs as her mind searched for some witty retort, but it was as if her senses had been struck numb. Self-consciously she lowered her head, the long, golden strands of hair falling forward, wreathing her flushed face. Just a few seconds before they had been teasing and joking; now, disconcertingly, they were on intimate terms.

"Don't, Jordan, please," Skye whispered shakily.

"Why not?" he asked quietly. "You're a beautiful woman, inside and out."

Skye drew a steadying breath and quirked her eyebrows suspiciously. "I thought you broke your arm in the car accident. I didn't realize you had also suffered brain damage. Your tongue may be smooth, but you won't have me believing out-and-out fantasy. I am no raving beauty." Her voice shook slightly. "Besides being a virtual Amazon, did you happen to notice my schnozzle?" She placed her index finger on the tip of her nose, and crossed her eyes as if examining its extended length. "Good night, Mrs. Calabash, wherever you are." With a theatrical gesture typical of Jimmy Durante, Skye stepped across the room to where her coat rested on the chair.

A low, gravelly laugh shook Jordan's shoulders. "Skye—" His laughing gray eyes suddenly became serious. "—come here," he requested softly.

"Not on your life," she retorted.

His round eyes feigned innocence. "You don't trust me?"

"No!" She finished buttoning her raincoat.

"I'm still hungry," he insisted.

"Then ring for the nurse," she suggested. "The hospital keeps a supply of snacks available."

"I was thinking more along the lines of dessert." He smiled. "I seem to have developed a sweet tooth lately."

Skye's heart lodged somewhere near her throat at the suggestiveness of his tone. "In which case I suggest you go on a diet," she countered smoothly, belying the uneven beat of her heart.

Jordan chuckled softly. "Good night, my frightened little bird."

It was an accurate description. Her heart hammered fearfully against her ribs like a trapped, wild fledgling. Why she should experience such alarm was a mystery. Jordan Kiley was just a man. Rugged and compelling, but nonetheless a man not unlike a hundred others she had successfully parried in the past years.

"Good night, Jordan," she whispered, quietly closing the door after her.

"Are you coming tomorrow?" he called brusquely.

His sharp question brought her back inside the room. His eyes were directed solely upon her, and she frowned, confused by his barely concealed anger until she understood. His pride resented the necessity of asking her to return. She hovered uncertainly, just long enough for his face to twist into a scowl.

Skye found herself incapable of meeting his gaze. "All right," she said, nodding. "I'm working on the children's ward until about eight. I'll stop in after that."

Jordan nodded. "I'll see you then."

Chapter Three

Everything went better on Thursday. Not that her kindergartners behaved any differently, Skye realized, but her attitude had changed. Instead of finding herself constantly on edge, she was more relaxed and at ease with the children.

Skye decided to stay after class and tie up a few loose ends. As part of the educational budget cutbacks, the janitor cleaned the classrooms only twice a week. But a high sense of neatness drove her to sweep the floors once or twice a week herself.

After she'd swept and straightened the small desks into even rows, Skye cut out the letters for the bulletin board she had designed for the month of April. There would be plenty of time to do it during vacation week, but she knew she wouldn't rest easy until the project was finished.

She was sitting at her desk cutting jaggedly shaped letters from brightly colored paper when a gruff voice interrupted her. "Need any help, little sister?"

"Brad!" she exclaimed. "What are you doing here?"

"What's the matter, aren't I welcome?" Brad Garvin was a

taller version of Skye. Lean and angular, he had blond hair and vivid blue eyes that mirrored those of his sister.

"Of course you are." A certain amount of curiosity entered her eyes. Brad had been unemployed for several weeks, caught in the economic slump of the construction trade. New housing starts were at a record low; because he was a carpenter, things didn't look promising. But from the smile on his face, whatever news he had must be good.

"I tried to phone you last night, but you weren't home. Don't tell me you were on some hot date."

"You're right, I'm not telling," she teased lightly, and threw a dusting cloth at his mocking grin. Five years separated them, but throughout their youth and into adulthood they had remained close.

Without so much as a flinch Brad neatly caught the rag. "Be careful, little sister. I could pull your pigtails."

"In case you haven't noticed I don't have pigtails any longer." A smile lit up her face. "If you weren't so infuriating, I'd admit it was good to see you. What have you been up to?"

"Not much." He sat on her desk, one leg dangling over the edge. "I talked to Mom last night. Moving in with Aunt Vi has been great for her. Janey is counting the shopping days left until her ninth birthday and, oh, Peggy's pregnant."

"Pregnant?" Skye breathed in disbelief, her blue eyes widening. "You're not teasing, are you?"

Brad and Peggy had given up hope of having another child even though the doctors assured them there was no medical reason for their difficulties. Certainly Janey, born a year after their wedding, proved they were capable of having children.

Brad didn't need to answer her doubts; his laughing blue eyes said it all.

With a burst of joy Skye stood and enthusiastically hugged

her brother. "Oh, Brad, I'm so pleased. When is the baby due? How is Peggy feeling? Is Janey happy?"

"Slow down. One question at a time." He laughed at her enthusiasm.

"You've had time to get used to the idea, and don't tell me you weren't just as excited when Peggy told you." A knowing look flashed from her eyes.

Brad shook his head. "I'm still having trouble believing it. We've tried so hard for so many years, and now, when we can least afford it and haven't got a penny of insurance, Peggy gets pregnant."

"Listen, count your blessings. Wasn't it you who told me God's timing is always perfect? Besides, if you need help . . ."

"No," he said, raising his voice with pride. "Don't even offer, Skye. You've done enough for us already. The baby's not due until November, and I'm sure to have found some kind of employment by then."

"All right, but I'm going to pray up a storm . . . Remember, the effective prayer of a righteous *woman* availeth much."

"That seems to be a slight misquote of that verse. But for heaven's sake, don't let that stop you: Pray! By the way, where were you last night?" he asked.

"Out." She batted her eyelashes wickedly. It wasn't like her to hold back anything from her brother, but to explain about Jordan would be pointless. Skye had decided not to see him again, and with the decision came a relaxed freedom. Jordan had the uncanny ability to stir awake feelings she had long considered dead. He was too astute, too perceptive. Her simple defenses would easily crumble under the force of his personality. The uncomplicated pattern of her life suited her, and there was no reason to openly invite disruption.

Playfully her tightened fist punched his upper arm. "A baby after all these years. You had it in you after all, you big brute."

Brad was a wonderful husband and father. He had been a solid rock supporting her in a dark world after Glen's death. If anyone deserved happiness, it was Brad.

The children's ward was bustling with the pre-dinner rush, and after a hasty visit with Billy and Sally, Skye resumed her volunteer duties. As was her custom, the piano playing and singing followed dinner. Several of the children dissolved into fits of laughter over Skye's cleverly worded jingles. Cheers and applause filled the recreation room as parents and staff joined the merriment. Skye's own elated mood became infectious, and even the most cynical could not help being drawn in and touched by the joy shining from the eyes of the children.

Her closing number was one that held deep meaning for Skye. She had composed it herself, and it spoke of darkness and light, sorrow and joy, the contrast between the valley and the mountaintop. The final words brought huge smiles of awe and appreciation from the audience.

Don't let the song escape from your life
For every life must have a song
A song to ring out loud and long
Let Jesus be your heartsong.

"Sometimes I think I know you so well, Skye Garvin, and then there are times like these and I realize I don't know you at all." Sally looked at Skye, her brow marred by a puzzled frown.

"What makes you say that?" Skye questioned.

"I'm not exactly sure. The quality of your voice when you're especially happy." She shrugged. "There are times I have the impression that one reason you are able to communicate so well with these families is that you've walked through some deep valley yourself. And yet you're so outgoing and positive, it's almost as if you've never known a minute's worry." They slowly continued down the hall. "Like Betty Fisher." Sally paused. "There's a communication, an understanding between you that's beyond compassion."

If Sally was seeking confidences, Skye wasn't going to share them. Glen, his death, and all that followed was in the past. Reliving those terrible months would be like tearing open a half-healed wound. And yet Sally was her friend, and she didn't wish to offend her.

"Things are not always as they appear," Skye admitted cryptically. "But I do know that one has to walk through the valley to know the exultation of a mountaintop."

Sally looked far from appeased but changed her line of questioning. "What did you bring for dinner?" she asked. "Yogurt and sunflower seeds again?" she teased lightly, and added, "I certainly hope you're not planning to wear that outfit to visit Jordan Kiley."

"What?" Skye exploded. "Who said I was visiting him?" Her suspicions immediately bobbed to the surface. How like Jordan to try to outwit her. He must have guessed she would change her mind and back out of her promise. But involving Sally seemed underhanded and unfair.

"*You* said you were visiting him."

"I most certainly did not," Skye denied hotly.

"It seems to me I distinctly recall you saying you'd visit him and clear away any half-truths Billy and I may have inadvertently spread about you," Sally insisted, annoyed.

"Oh." Skye sighed in relief. "I guess I did say something to that effect."

"Well, are you going?"

Skye knew from past experience there would be no appeasing her friend until she conceded. If she made a quick stop on the third floor and left a message for Jordan saying she couldn't make it after all, she'd be satisfying him and at the same time satisfying Sally.

"I suppose a few minutes wouldn't hurt," she said with a twinge of guilt.

A bubble of elation rose from Sally. "You're not wearing that, are you?"

Skye's gaze slid down over the cream-colored silk blouse and caramel wool suit. She hadn't changed clothes, coming directly from school to the hospital. "What's wrong with what I'm wearing?"

"Have you got a year?" Sally asked with an exasperated sigh. "You really should think about going home and changing."

"You're being ridiculous," Skye said with a bit of disbelief. The outfit was one of her best. Although plain and practical, it suited her.

"Well, we'll just have to make the best of what we've got."

"Sally"—Skye expelled the name in a long, drawn-out breath—"I look fine. I'm going exactly as I am." It was easy to read the disappointment in Sally's eyes.

"Unfasten the top buttons at least," Sally entreated.

"No." Skye shook her head but couldn't help smiling at her friend's insistence.

"Okay, but at least let your hair down. I never have understood why you insist on wearing it up when it's so pretty down."

"I very seldom wear my hair down." Skye flushed slightly, remembering she had done so the day before. No, it would be far safer to keep her hair in its tightly coiled chignon. "Another time maybe." She smiled gently.

The large doors of the elevator glided open silently, welcoming Skye to the third floor. The nurse she'd met in Jordan's room the night before nodded in recognition.

"Hello," Skye said, and smiled. "I wonder if it would be possible to leave a message for Mr. Kiley in room 324."

Dark eyes stared back at Skye blankly for a moment. "I'm sorry, dear, but Jordan Kiley was discharged this afternoon."

"Oh." Skye felt at a sudden loss for words.

"It's my understanding he's returning to Los Angeles." The nurse continued, "Perhaps the hospital can relay his address if you care to contact administration."

"No, that's fine." Well, that was that, she mused. A confused mixture of relief and disappointment settled over her. "Thank you," she said, and smiled weakly at the nurse before turning back to the elevator.

By Friday evening Skye still hadn't shaken the feeling of melancholy; instead of being pensive and a little depressed, she should be grateful. She'd never intended to continue seeing Jordan and should be counting her blessings instead of dealing with this deep sense of disappointment.

She was mixing together a chicken salad for dinner when her doorbell rang. Sighing heavily, she abandoned the salad, wondering what John wanted to borrow this time. Did the man ever do any grocery shopping?

She crossed the living room, wiping her hands on her apron as she went. When she opened the door, the good-natured, tolerant smile froze on her face. Shock closed her mouth, and for the life of her she couldn't utter a single word.

"Hello again." Jordan smiled, not in the least affected by her obvious surprise. His arm was in a cast and supported by a sling, but that did little to mar his compelling features. Skye had always considered herself statuesque, but he stood four or five inches taller, seeming to dwarf her.

"Jordan," she whispered incredulously as the shock slowly dissipated.

"The very same," he told her mockingly. "May I come in?"

"Oh, of course." She hurriedly stepped aside and closed the door after him, leaning against it for support as he leisurely walked into her apartment. "Can I get you something?" she asked somewhat stiffly, unable to gain her poise.

"No, I have a car and driver waiting."

Knowing that relaxed her slightly. He certainly wouldn't be staying long then.

"I'm happy to see you haven't eaten." His gaze left her flushed face momentarily, and he eyed the lettuce and chicken on her kitchen countertop. "I made the dinner reservation for eight, so you have plenty of time to change if you wish. However, what you're wearing is fine."

"Dinner?" She swallowed uncomfortably. "Oh, I couldn't. I mean . . ." Her mind searched frantically for an excuse to refuse. She immediately knew why he hadn't contacted her in advance. Apparently he knew her well enough to realize that given time, she would have somehow extricated herself from the date. Now she was trapped.

"I won't take no for an answer, Skye." Determination narrowed his eyes.

"All right," she agreed weakly. "Just give me a few minutes to put the food away in the kitchen." She wouldn't change clothes, not with the practical side of her nature adding the toll of the waiting car and driver.

She glanced at herself briefly in the hallway mirror as she reached for her earth-toned blazer. The jacket went nicely with her rust-colored pleated pants.

"I'm ready." She paused, feeling gauche and insecure. "Are you sure this outfit is okay?"

His dark brows lifted, and a smile touched the corners of his hard mouth. "You might want to wear shoes."

Her face flushed a deep shade of pink, and she nodded. She

had always had a ridiculous habit of walking around the apartment barefoot. It was second nature to slip off her shoes the minute she walked in the door. Luckily her pumps were in the entryway. Turning her back to Jordan, she slipped them on slowly, giving her racing heart a chance to quiet. But when his hand settled on her shoulder and his husky voice sounded in her ear, she found her pulse rate anything but normal.

"The apron," he reminded her. "I'm taking you out to eat. I don't expect you to cook."

Her trembling fingers immediately reached behind her back to untie the knot. She wished she knew what it was about Jordan Kiley that turned her into a bumbling, forgetful idiot.

The restaurant was one Skye had never heard of before. The dining area was small and contained only a few elegantly set tables. The interior was dimly lit by flickering candles. A single long-stemmed rose set in a crystal vase served as the centerpiece of each table.

Once they were seated and studying the menus, the waiter arrived. "Would you care for something to drink?" Jordan asked.

"A drink?" Skye realized she sounded like an echo. "No . . . I don't think so . . . not now, anyway."

Jordan ordered wine, and the waiter returned with the bottle, complimenting him on his choice. It was when he was testing the wine that she noticed his right hand. He now enjoyed the freedom of his fingers, although a thin layer of gauze covered a major portion of his hand.

His gaze followed hers, and he flexed his fingers for her benefit. "The doctor changed the dressing the day I was discharged. I imagine you're relieved to know it won't be necessary for you to cut my meat."

"I wasn't worried." She smiled, beginning to relax.

"Have you decided what you'd like to order?" His menu

was folded beside his plate; apparently he had made his decision already.

The menu ran the full gamut, but the prices were outrageously high, and Skye chose the least expensive item.

"I'll have the chicken Florentine." She closed her menu, and as if on cue the waiter appeared.

"I'd like to propose a toast," Jordan suggested, tipping his wine goblet to gently tap her water glass. "To Pollyanna, whose radiant smile could melt a polar ice cap." His own smile, directed at her, left Skye feeling weak.

A few minutes later their salads were served. Skye was grateful for the diversion; the atmosphere was quickly becoming intimate.

"I ordered dessert for us," Jordan announced, his gray eyes briefly meeting hers. "I hope you have no objection to flaming Baked Alaska."

"Baked Alaska." She swallowed, a smile trembling at the corners of her mouth. "I'm surprised you forgot the violinist." It was important to maintain this lighthearted banter; only when she could laugh and tease did she feel at ease.

Throwing her a sideways glance, Jordan reached across the table and rang a small bell. Almost immediately two violinists strolled into the room.

Against her will Skye burst into helpless laughter. The palm of her hand covered her mouth to hide the outburst.

A full smile tugged at Jordan's mouth. "Is any romantic dinner complete without music?" He quirked a brow in question.

"Jordan Kiley, I don't think I've met anyone like you in my entire life," she managed, shaking her head at him. "You're hopeless." But she didn't question why he'd gone to such lengths to create a romantic atmosphere for her.

The chicken was succulent and tender, and as long as Skye concentrated on the meal the intimacy was held to a minimum.

"Do you know all the volunteers on the children's ward?" Jordan inquired lazily as the waiter replenished his glass of wine.

"Of course; I've been a volunteer for several years," she replied.

"Who plays the piano and sings?" His dark eyes watched her closely.

Skye was mildly surprised Sally and Billy hadn't supplied him with the information. She felt strangely reluctant to reveal herself. She hesitated momentarily. She didn't want the evening to center on her, nor did she wish to answer the inevitable question: *Why don't you turn professional?*

"That's Jane." It wasn't a lie. Jane was her name; she had been dubbed Skye after a growth spurt in the sixth grade had shot her head and shoulders above every boy in class. The name had stuck and now most people knew her by her nickname.

Skye was certain Jordan wished to question her further, but she hurriedly stood, asking to be excused. The ladies' room offered a quiet moment so she could compose herself. She couldn't deny her attraction to Jordan, but at the same time she realized how pointless and dangerous the attraction was. He obviously felt he owed her a dinner and had very possibly delayed his return to LA to settle his debt. Now she must be gracious enough to allow him to satisfy his sense of obligation.

When she returned to their table, Jordan had ordered coffee.

"Have you ridden the cable cars yet?" she asked before he could pursue his questions.

Jordan glanced at her a bit suspiciously. "Not yet."

"You really should," Skye insisted. "You haven't truly savored San Francisco's uniqueness until you ride the cable cars."

"Oh?" Jordan's smile was mocking, and, swinging his broken arm outward, he added, "I think I've had enough of a taste of San Francisco."

Skye loved her city and was undeterred by his lack of enthusiasm. "I bet you didn't know that the cable cars were invented by a horse lover."

"No, I didn't." His gaze lifted from his coffee to study her.

"It's true. A man by the name of Andrew Hallidie felt sorry for the horses, who sometimes slipped on the steep hills and were badly injured. So Hallidie invented the cable car. By 1890 San Francisco had eight major systems operating within the city limits. The idea caught on elsewhere, too. I bet you didn't know that Los Angeles also used cable cars for a while."

"When was that?"

Skye realized she must sound very much like the teacher she was, but his eyes expressed interest. "Back in 1887. Now are you ready to ride a cable car?"

"After a history lesson like that, I dare not refuse." His returning smile was full and warm and had a crazy effect upon Skye.

Friday evenings were always a busy traffic night for the cable cars, and Jordan and Skye were forced to wait a few minutes before boarding.

"Where are we headed?" Jordan asked indulgently as they stepped aboard.

"Fisherman's Wharf." Skye laughed, her smiling features profiled in the moonlight. "You really must see the wharf before you leave."

"You've missed your calling." Jordan's eyes also smiled. "You should have been a tour guide."

The ride was exhilarating. Jordan's good arm cradled her around the waist and gripped the wooden column behind her. Skye didn't object to the intimate hold; she felt warm and secure with the strength of his arm around her.

Colorful and amusing, the cable car operator chatted loudly

with his customers, calling out the street names and interesting bits of information.

"These boys seem to be a unique breed," Jordan said with a throaty chuckle, watching the gripman push and pull the long lever that connected to the cable running underground, towing the car.

"We're unique all right," the cable man replied. "You have to be to take a job like this one."

All too soon the invigorating ride had ended. Crowds were thick on the wharf's wide sidewalks, even though it was well into the evening. The permeating aroma of salt water and fish drifted pleasingly to their senses. Hundreds of vessels making up the fishing fleet were docked at the pier.

They strolled hand in hand, not speaking until Skye pointed to the boats. "Over three million pounds of fish are caught every year by our industrious fleet. Sardines account for most of that, with crabs running a close second."

"Do you enjoy crabmeat?" Jordan asked unexpectedly.

"Far more than I like sardines," she joked lightly.

Several vendors had set up shop on the sidewalks, and a lovely seashell necklace caught Skye's attention.

"Look." She stopped to examine the tiny, delicate shells. They lay gently across the palm of her hand. "It's my niece's birthday soon. This would be perfect. Janey's just the right age to appreciate something this lovely, and she has a seashell collection."

"I'll buy it," Jordan offered immediately.

"Oh, no." She gently laid a restraining hand against his arm. "You can't. The gift would be from you then, not me."

"All right," he agreed reluctantly. "But one thing."

"Yes?" Her eye sought his.

"Are you going to take off your shoe in order to pay for it?"

A corner of her mouth twitched upward as she fought to suppress a smile. "No, I think I can manage it."

They decided to stop for a cup of coffee at a small restaurant beside the bay. Fish, crab, and other delicacies were displayed on a bed of crushed ice outside the restaurant doors. An old seaman, a stained white apron hugging his chest and waist and black rubbers on his feet, smiled up at them before they entered.

"Good evening, folks. Enjoy your dinner. It's a night for young lovers." He looked into the clear sky. The stars shone like jewels on a blanket of black velvet.

"It is a beautiful night," Skye admitted, her face flushed with embarrassment.

"Yes, beautiful." Jordan added his agreement, but he wasn't looking into the sky.

The coffee was dark and strong. Skye was grateful for its potency. She needed to be reminded, in a down-to-earth manner, that this little excursion was a onetime experience. It would be too easy to allow herself to fall under Jordan's spell. He was a rare kind of man, both confident and totally masculine, and she didn't doubt he used his charm to achieve whatever he wanted. She faked a subtle yawn.

"You're tired?"

Skye had difficulty meeting his look. "It's been a long week . . . Maybe it would be best if I did head home."

Skye would have willingly caught the bus that took her directly to her apartment, but Jordan wouldn't hear of it and insisted on calling for the car. Her heart hammered frantically when they arrived at her building.

"You weren't going to invite me in?" He looked into her confused eyes.

"Well, actually . . . no. I generally don't." She spoke bluntly.

She knew she sounded very prim and proper, but that couldn't be helped. His laughing eyes riled her. "I'm glad you think it's so funny," she burst out irritably.

He ignored her outburst and took the keys from her trembling hand. "And as a proper gentleman, I consider it my duty to escort you safely to your door."

Skye was forced to follow him and did so ungraciously. The hallway outside her door was well lit, and Skye offered a silent prayer of thanksgiving that her landlord had recently installed brighter lightbulbs.

"I enjoyed the dinner. Thank you, Jordan," she said as soon as he had unlocked the door. She extended her hand, ready to accept her keys, her knees suddenly weak at his close proximity. The cold metal felt good against her outstretched hand as he placed the chain there and gently folded her hand closed. With his forefinger tucked beneath her chin, he raised her downcast gaze to meet his. Forced to meet his eyes, Skye felt a flood of warmth sweep over her. His eyes were no longer laughing but warm and sensuous. She wanted to back away from him and break the spell, but the attraction was so strong, she couldn't blink.

The pressure of his hand moved from her chin to the back of her neck, his fingers sliding into her hair. Slowly his mouth descended to hers. Skye could have protested, but she didn't utter a sound. Caught in the powerful pull of her senses, her eyes closed slowly, the curiosity to discover his kiss overpowering.

His mouth was warm and gentle, the pressure light and sweet, as if he understood her need for tenderness. Fighting the clamoring of her nerves that had suddenly burst into life, Skye remained frozen, unable to respond and equally unable to break away.

When the pressure of the kiss ended, Skye remained caught in the sensations, her eyes shut. Only when Jordan's hand pulled away from her hair did she find the strength to look at him. Moving aside, he turned the knob of her door and pushed it open for her.

"Good night, Skye," he whispered huskily.

She stared at him blankly for a moment.

"Don't look at me like that," he groaned. "Now go inside before I change my mind."

His words quickly broke the spell, and Skye hurried inside.

Chapter Four

Saturday morning the skies were overcast, leaden-gray clouds gloomily foreshadowing a day only a true San Franciscan could love.

Skye woke in good spirits; she had enjoyed herself last night. Unwillingly she admitted that Jordan was good company, but made no attempt to analyze her feelings regarding his kiss. It had been her moment of reckoning; she had wanted that kiss. As for his surprise visit and the dinner, it had just been his way of settling a debt, she supposed. She had bought the pizza, and he was simply returning the gesture. He was probably on his way back to Los Angeles by now, and she could close the door on this short episode, remembering him fondly.

The Saturday-morning housework took almost two hours, and with the last load of wash folded, Skye sat down with a good book. The latest study on child behavior she had purchased had come highly recommended, and she had been looking forward to reading it.

Yet despite how hard she concentrated hardly a word filtered through her thoughts. Somehow the picture of the violinists strolling into the restaurant kept flitting through her mind. Skye couldn't refrain from laughing all over again. No wonder Jordan had looked so pleased when she had teasingly said all they needed were violinists. She had fallen right into his trap.

The old seaman had thought they were lovers. Jordan Kiley probably had lots of lovers; he was definitely a man of the world. She wondered why he had never married, but suddenly realized that for all she knew he could have a wife conveniently tucked away. Somehow the idea wasn't feasible. No, he was too straightforward and candid to cheat on his wife. She didn't doubt he was an experienced lover, but believed that for all his experience he didn't know love as God intended it to be. Jordan Kiley was like so many others, seeking to fill a void in his life that could only be satisfied by a relationship with God.

Reading was useless; setting aside the book, Skye changed into her jogging clothes. It looked like rain, but that didn't bother her. She often jogged in the rain; the cool drops splashing against her face were refreshing and invigorating.

She followed her usual route, running around the green at the Marina. The sultry breeze rolling in from the Pacific teased her. The ironic thing was the wind seemed to be whispering Jordan's name. As if to free herself, she tossed her head back. Her long hair, driven from her face, flowed gracefully behind her. Yet the action did little to dispel Jordan's presence from her mind. If she listened carefully, she could almost hear his husky voice calling her.

"This is silly," she said aloud. To allow this one unnerving man to throw her now was like succumbing to a temporary kind of madness. She had long before accepted God's plan for her life and didn't regret being single.

As if to outrun her thoughts, Skye jogged twice as far as normal and was exhausted by the time she stopped to walk the remaining blocks home. Walking the last few blocks home gave her body a chance to cool down after the long run and was as vital as the warm-up exercises she ritually performed before taking to the streets. Yet she didn't feel herself cooling down. It was as if her body and her mind were working against her at a fever pitch. Memories of Glen bobbed to the surface of her mind, happy ones that she'd long ago locked away. Skye couldn't help wondering if the short time she'd been with Jordan had done this to her. From past experience she realized she needed to keep herself busy, push the memories away.

After a short shower back at home Skye changed clothes and left almost immediately, although she had no real destination in mind.

"Anyone home?" Skye knocked loudly on the varnished door before letting herself in.

"Skye?" Peggy Garvin came from the kitchen, a large terrycloth apron tied around her slim waist. Bursting with the news of her pregnancy, Peggy threw her arms around her sister-in-law.

"Brad told you, didn't he?" she said, hugging Skye close.

"Of course. He never could keep a secret for long," Skye said, returning the affectionate hug. She stepped back and carefully studied the happiness in Peggy's eyes. "You show already."

Peggy's hand automatically rested against her flat stomach as her gaze swept downward. "Do you really think so?" she asked.

"Not there, silly," Skye chided. "It's that radiant gleam."

"I know, I know. I don't think I've been more pleased about anything in my life. What are we doing standing here? Let's go into the kitchen. I'm baking cookies. Chocolate chip—your favorite."

"These smell good. Mind if I help myself?" She didn't bother to wait for permission but bit into the melting morsel, savoring the chocolate flavor.

Peggy pulled another sheet from the oven and carefully lifted the cookies with her spatula onto a waiting rack. "This is the last of the batch. Let's have some tea; I picked up a new flavor at the store the other day. How does cherry almond sound?" Stretching her petite frame to reach the top cupboard, Peggy brought down her china cups. "Only the best for us," she declared.

The aroma of the tea pervaded the room as they chatted.

"It's so good to see you, Skye. How have you been?"

"I should be asking you that question. How are you feeling?" Although her attention was directed to Peggy, her fingers were making lazy circles around the rim of her teacup. "You're taking good care of yourself, aren't you?"

"Heavens, yes! Oh, Skye, the Lord is so good. I'm still having trouble believing I'm really pregnant, after all these years." Some of the enthusiasm left Peggy's eyes. "Now, if only Brad could find a job."

"Speaking of my dear brother, where is he?"

"He told me he was going to help a friend move, but I know differently." Peggy shifted uneasily. "He's out again looking for a job, any job. With a baby on the way Brad feels such a sense of urgency." Her fingers tugged nervously on her bottom lip. "I guess I do too. My moods swing from elation and ecstasy to doubt and worry."

Skye had the same feelings herself. Although very pleased for her brother and his family, she couldn't chase away a sense of unease. She realized her family was in God's hands, but reminding Peggy of this sounded trite and overused.

"Do you remember the Joyce Landorf series we saw at church last year?" Skye asked.

Peggy nodded.

"I guess this is what she meant by being stuck in a waiting room."

"Yes, with both exits covered."

It was Skye's turn to smile. "You know, I'd do anything in the world to help you."

"We know, Skye, and thanks, but Brad's pride is at stake now. You've done too much already."

Skye studied her sister-in-law seriously. "Don't let pride get in your way, Peg."

She paused, searching Skye's face. "You've met someone, haven't you?"

Taken aback by Peggy's directness, Skye flushed slightly and lowered her gaze. "What makes you say that?" she said, trying hard to hide any telltale inflection of surprise in her voice.

"You look, well . . ." Again Peggy hesitated, as if searching for the right word. "Happier . . . brighter, as if some spark has been ignited again. Brad mentioned something, too. He said you'd obviously been dating someone because you closed up like a clam the minute he asked about it."

"I guess you could say I've met someone," Skye admitted reluctantly.

"And?" Peggy probed.

"It's someone from the hospital. He was in a car accident and has a broken arm. It was in traction for a while, but he's been discharged now."

Peggy's eyes rounded at the information and twinkled with delight.

"It's no big deal, Peggy. Honest," Skye stressed. "I enjoyed his company, but it's not what you think. He's from LA and has returned home."

"Is he handsome?"

Skye tilted her head thoughtfully and shrugged noncommittally. "I'd say he was, but not strikingly so." Unconsciously she stiffened; this was dangerous territory. Her own feelings for Jordan were a mystery. How could she explain them to another?

Peggy seemed to understand her indecision and smiled in

return. "Anytime you show this much interest in a man, I can't help getting excited. I don't mean to pry, but honestly, Skye, Glen's been gone a long time. Too many years for you to continue on the way you have been."

A guarded expression came over Skye's face. Glen's name was rarely mentioned. Brad and Peggy had always been sensitive to her grief. "What are you saying?" she asked brusquely.

Peggy sighed, almost as if she were unwilling to continue. "You've been living your life in a shell. For eight years there hasn't been anything or anyone who has been able to bring you back to reality, and it's time you realized that."

It was unlike Peggy to be so blunt. "That's not true," Skye said defensively, the tiny hairs on the back of her neck bristling. "Glen and I shared something unique. Our life together would have been very special, but for you to insist I've built a wall around myself is totally false." She paused, gathering the strength of conviction. "I have to think very hard to clearly remember what Glen even looked like."

Peggy was watching Skye with concern. "We seem to have gotten off the track, haven't we?"

Swallowing determinedly at the tight lump in her throat, Skye gave a wavering smile. "We certainly have. I came to congratulate you and discuss Janey's birthday present. I bought her a shell necklace, but how would you and Brad feel if I got her a puppy?"

"A puppy?" Peggy echoed, sounding aghast.

"Sally's dog recently had a litter, and she's offered me first choice. You remember Sally, my friend from St. John's."

"Of course." Peggy's eyebrows arched thoughtfully. "You know, it might not be a bad idea. With the baby coming it could be just the thing for Janey. I'll talk to Brad."

The remainder of the visit was strained, with both women pretending an ease neither felt. Skye left shortly afterward.

Confused and unsettled, Skye drove home in a thoughtful mood. How could Peggy have been so blunt? Skye had worked hard to overcome her grief. It was true that for a while she had lost her will to live. Something deep within her had died with Glen. But she was a free spirit now, free to love and be loved. Hadn't she always been? Peggy had never hurt her this way before. It was true Skye seldom dated anyone for long, but that wasn't because she was carrying a torch for Glen. There were very few men who interested her. Certainly all the dates Sally had arranged over the years should prove that to her sister-in-law. Nonetheless Peggy's attitude stung.

About a mile from home the car coughed and sputtered. Skye tensed. "Not again," she said, groaning inwardly. Suddenly the buzzer to her seat belt began to hiss, although it was connected. The radio began making eerie, high-pitched screeches, fading in and out. She had purposely turned it off in order to think. Quickly she pulled her small Ford to the curb before it gave one final cough and died.

"Blast it." Her hand banged the steering wheel impatiently. First Peggy's comment and now this! She tried turning the ignition key but was met with silence.

"I can't believe it!" She opened her car door, climbed out, and in a burst of frustration slammed the door shut. She didn't even bother to look under the hood, knowing it was useless for her to try to figure out what was wrong.

It began to rain about halfway home, an angry torrent that added fuel to her bad mood. She was drenched by the time she arrived at her apartment building. Heavy drops of rain ran off her hair and face as she paused to unlock her door.

John Dirkson stuck his head out of his apartment and greeted her with a flashy grin. "I see you got yourself all wet and cold. I'm perfectly willing to warm you up," he offered, with all the subtlety of a serpent.

"Oh, shut up, John," Skye stormed, and shut her door in his surprised face. Feeling chilled, she started a bath.

No more than two minutes later her doorbell rang impatiently.

Stamping her foot irritably, she turned off the water. Luckily she hadn't gotten around to undressing.

"Don't hassle me, John, I'm in no mood to—" She stopped dead in midsentence. It was Jordan. What was he doing here? Oh, no, not him. Why hadn't he returned to LA? Why didn't he just get out of her life?

"Do I detect a note of anger?" he asked, amused, letting himself in.

Skye gave a short sarcastic laugh. "Angry? Me? That's my problem: I don't have the common sense to get good and mad every now and then. People think they can take advantage of me, that I won't fight back. They think of me as Holly Holiness."

Irrationally she paced the floor, waving her hands.

"A Pollyanna?" Jordan inserted.

"Exactly!" She stopped and looked at him momentarily. "I'm as even-tempered and coolheaded as the next person. But I'll only be driven so far."

The amusement left Jordan's eyes. "What's wrong?"

"You know what my problem is?" She didn't wait for his answer. "I never let loose. I let people walk all over me. Well, I'm good and loose now," she said as she continued pacing. "I don't smoke. I don't swear. I've never marched in a protest rally. I didn't even burn my bra when it was the popular thing to do." She stopped to take a quick breath. "Well, I've had just about as much as I'm going to take."

"Skye?"

She ignored him.

"Skye?" He spoke louder.

"I'm taking the mechanic to court. I'll sue him for every penny. He'll . . ."

She didn't get the opportunity to finish. Jordan swiftly caught her arm and pulled her flush against him. Before she could protest, his mouth captured hers.

Taken completely by surprise, Skye felt the anger drain away, replaced by a budding awareness. She was frightened that she should respond to him like this, all consideration of her anger and her plight erased by a single action.

She broke the contact, raising her questioning eyes to his. His look trapped her, warm and sensual. Slowly his hand slid over her back, drawing her closer to him.

Taking an uneven breath in confusion, Skye made a feeble attempt to break away. Undaunted, he continued the gentle caress, slowly drawing her into his protective embrace. When he lowered his mouth to hers, her lips parted in anticipation.

Why does it have to be him? her mind questioned unreasonably. His very touch seemed to bring her suddenly back to life. She was caught in the sensual awareness and yet felt frightened and unsure. If this continued, Jordan Kiley could easily become a weakness she might not be able to overcome. Forcefully she tore her lips from his and, taking a deep breath, struggled to regain her bearings.

"Jordan, please, this is important," she insisted.

"I know," he said, his voice thick and husky as he explored the side of her neck.

"Please, stop." She was breathless yet fervent. "Kissing me isn't going to fix my car."

He straightened, his mouth curving into smiling grooves. "Ah, but my arm aches considerably less."

She broke contact, moving purposefully away from him. "I . . . I think aspirin would work far more effectively."

He shrugged, his glance focusing on her lips as if to say it wasn't aspirin he was interested in.

Her pique rose. "Darn it, Jordan Kiley, don't look at me like that. I'm stuck with a useless piece of junk, and you want to play spin the bottle."

Promptly he pulled her back into his arms and placed a quick kiss upon her unsuspecting lips. "Settle down, or I'll be forced to take drastic measures."

She stared up at him wordlessly, swallowing tightly.

"Now, what's wrong with your car?"

She couldn't answer. Her heart was hammering so wildly, it made clear thinking impossible. She lowered her head, not wanting Jordan to see the effect he had on her.

His free hand gently lifted her face. "Your car?"

"It's not running again." Her voice didn't sound right, even to herself. "It stalled last week, and I couldn't get it started. I phoned the car dealership where I'd bought it, and they put a new battery in. The mechanic said since the car is three years old, that probably was the problem."

"Who's the mechanic?"

"George somebody. He works for Olsen Ford, where I bought the car."

"And?"

"Well, it died again the other day, and this George said it needed a new alteration."

"Alternator," Jordan supplied with a grin.

"Whatever!" she said irritably. "Anyway, the car did it again today. That's why I'm drenched. I had to leave it and walk home."

A flickering light of anger entered his eyes. "I'll handle it for you."

"No," she challenged sharply. "It's going to give me a great deal of pleasure to talk to these people."

A light rap on her door stiffened her instinctively. She wasn't expecting anyone.

A tall, well-dressed man of towering bulk greeted her.

"Jordan here?" He placed heavy emphasis on *Jordan,* his expression alive with amusement.

"Bill." The name was spoken with no welcome as Jordan moved toward the man. "I said I'd only be a minute."

The huge man shrugged. "I got tired of waiting" was the only excuse he offered. "Aren't you going to introduce me?"

"Bill Malloy, Skye Garvin." The introduction was issued grudgingly.

Bill Malloy smiled warmly at Skye, and his strong hand closed firmly over hers. "You're everything Jordan said and more." He released her hand slowly. His eyes, trapping hers, possessed a mocking gleam.

"Weren't we on our way to a meeting?" Jordan asked curtly.

"We were." Bill smiled. "I know how Dan hates to be kept waiting."

"Then let's get moving." Jordan's voice sounded thin and brittle.

"It was a pleasure meeting you, Skye." Jordan's friend's gaze continued to hold hers.

"Yes," she said in some confusion. Her attention darted from one man to the other. Bill was finding something highly amusing, but what? Jordan was recognizably upset. His lips were firmly compressed, as if he was holding his anger tightly in check.

"I'll phone you," he promised Skye, ushering his friend out the door. Gently his hand touched her cheek.

Skye watched them go, thoroughly bewildered. Jordan had never mentioned why he'd stopped by. Although he hadn't said he was returning to LA, Skye had gotten the impression he was. She honestly hadn't expected to see him again.

A shiver danced over her skin, reminding her she was wet. She didn't care to ponder the question of what exactly had caused her skin to quiver.

The bathwater steamed up the bathroom mirror. It was a luxury to linger in the tub. Skye could actually feel the hot water chase away her chill. Scooping the moisture over herself with the washcloth, her thoughts drifted back to her visit with Peggy. It was almost unbelievable that her sister-in-law would talk to her like that. And because the things Peggy said were so untrue, it hurt all the more. Skye had come so far, considering that the grief had been overwhelming at first. It was as if the pieces of her life had crumbled before her. But simply because she was a living, breathing soul, she found herself forced into a resilient, elastic world. Although others cared, they couldn't know the emotional torture she had endured. Suddenly a gnawing pain swelled inside her until her eyes burned with tears.

Resting her head against the back of the tub, she stared sightlessly at the ceiling, tears streaming unheeded down her face. Could it be that Peggy was right? Had all this grief lain just below the surface, not really being dealt with at all? Skye examined the last eight years of her life. Had she really made a martyr of herself? Deflecting male relationships and commitment to another man? But Glen had been so special. He was the only man she'd ever loved, ever wanted. Loving another would betray what they had shared. It had been cruel and heartless to take him from her.

It came to her then. Profound and deep. The shock raised goose bumps over her pale skin, although she lay in a tub of steaming water. *She blamed God for taking Glen.* Over the years she had yielded other areas of her life to her Lord but had stubbornly withheld this one facet of her Christian walk. Her faith had been smaller than a mustard seed. Instead of looking upon his death and all that followed as having worked together for her good, Skye had never forgiven God.

Rising from her bath, she wrapped a towel around herself and faced the bathroom mirror. With jerking movements she wiped away the steam to examine herself. Sally was right; her hairstyle—the coiled bun—was harsh and purposely unattractive. With troubled eyes and her heart hammering, she pulled the pins and watched her hair tumble down. It needed to be cut to a more manageable length. Her pale cheeks looked bloodless and waxen. How long had it been since she'd purposely made herself attractive? But perhaps she looked wan because she was seeing herself with new soul-searching eyes.

She dressed quickly, an urgency driving her. Throwing open the doors to her closet, she critically examined its contents. Her clothes were outdated and unappealing—beiges, grays, browns, and blacks. The exceptions were a few colorful outfits her family had given her for Christmas and her birthday.

Perhaps most profound was how she'd maintained her wit and sense of humor. Her natural good taste in clothes and style had wavered dramatically over the years, but not her enthusiasm and vitality. Instinctively she knew if she'd allowed this bizarre grief to infiltrate the core of her personality, she would have shriveled up and died in a unique form of suicide.

"Oh, Father," her soul cried out, "forgive me, forgive me." She fell to her knees beside the bed and buried her face in her hands. A peaceful silence filled the room as she surrendered this part of her life to her Lord. Time lost meaning as Skye poured out her heart, and when she rose she felt as if a heavy burden had been lifted from her, an eight-year-old yoke she had bound to herself. She was free to love and be loved . . . at last.

Later that evening she idly flipped through the pages of the *TV Guide,* a smile playing at the corners of her lips. She felt like a new woman and stood to examine herself again . . . A smiling stranger was reflected back. She had spent most of the afternoon on a one-woman crusade to create a new image for herself, and she was pleased with the results.

Her first concern had been her car. She had called the dealership expecting to do battle, but the mechanic stumbled all over himself apologizing. He didn't know what the problem was, but he would look into it immediately. He worked so quickly, Skye was stunned. He stopped at her house for her keys, had her car towed to the shop, and returned, all within forty-five minutes. It had been a cut wire, he explained with chagrin. There was no charge.

Her first stop had been at the beautician's, who'd cut only an inch or two from the length of her hair. An overall treatment added body and vitality to the silky gold strands.

Now it curled beautifully around her shoulders like a gilded wreath highlighted by beams of moonlight. In her closet hung three new outfits in attractive colors. The old clothes were packed away in sacks, ready to be donated to charity. A warm smile quivered at the corners of her mouth as she remembered Sally's reaction that afternoon.

"Skye?" Sally had asked in a questioning tone, almost as if she didn't recognize her friend. "I like it, I like it." Enthusiastically she circled Skye, nodding approvingly. "Holy mackerel, what happened to you?" Sally laughed gaily. "No, there's no need to answer that, I already know . . . Jordan Kiley happened to you. I knew it was coming someday, I just never thought I'd live to see it." She clapped her hands with the enthusiasm of a young child.

"Come on, you're embarrassing me," Skye said, grinning. "But *no*—" she waved her hand to press her point "—it's not Jordan Kiley." It was only a partial lie. The transformation had come as a result of her talk with Peggy, Skye told herself.

"Oh?" Sally sounded skeptical. "Is there someone else I don't know about?"

"Have you met John Dirkson, my neighbor?" Skye asked coyly, instantly regretting the implication.

"You know darn good and well I haven't." Sally wrinkled her nose in suspicion. "Tell me about him."

This was becoming more than a half-truth, and Skye lowered her head guiltily, hoping to hide her discomfort by picking up one of the puppies chewing at the toe of her shoe. "There isn't much to tell." She prayed for a nonchalant, devil-may-care attitude. "The reason I stopped by is to tell you I would be taking one of the puppies. It's Janey's birthday soon, and I thought this fluffy little rascal would make an excellent gift."

"My dear friend, you know the path leading directly to my heart," Sally noted dramatically. "Are you certain you wouldn't care for another one as well? It would be a shame to separate these brothers. Besides, if you took both of these well-behaved, royal-blooded mutts, all my problems would be solved."

"Dreamer," Skye said pointedly, and laughed as Sally hung her head in despair.

Several hours later, the apartment felt lonely and lifeless. Loud rock music blared from the party across the hall. Involuntarily Skye tapped her foot to the beat of the slower ballads, which blared in equal volume. For the first time in years her feet yearned to dance. Without warning the image of dancing with Jordan rose to her mind, and she bit her lip at the appeal the image conjured.

When the phone suddenly began ringing, Skye jerked around, caught off guard by the unexpectedness.

Two rings.

It had to be Jordan. He'd said he was going to phone, and he was a man of his word.

Three rings.

She stared mutely at the ringing phone, frozen in her chair.
Four rings.
She had made such a fool of herself this afternoon.
Five rings.
How could she have ranted and raved like that?
Six rings.
How could she have said those things?
Silence.
Skye breathed again.

Chapter Five

Hauling her guitar, Bible, and purse from the parking lot to the church, Skye found Peggy waiting for her in the foyer.

"Skye," Peggy said, looking troubled and uncertain, "I like your hair. When did you have it cut?" she asked haltingly.

"Yesterday afternoon . . . And thanks, I like it, too." She accepted the compliment but wondered how long it would take Peggy to notice the real change.

Tears shimmered in Peggy's eyes. "I want to apologize for yesterday. I was blunt and rude. Will you forgive me?" It was apparent from her hurried speech that their conversation had weighed heavily on her mind.

Tears misted Skye's deep blue eyes as well. "Of course I will, Peg. But there's no need to apologize. Most of what you said was true."

"Perhaps, but there were nicer ways of saying it." Her fingers wiped away the moisture from her cheek, and she gave a half laugh. "We better get to class before we turn into Water Works, Incorporated, right here in the church foyer."

Skye was touched by the thoughtfulness of her sister-in-law.

"I'll talk to you later." Impulsively she set her guitar down and gave Peggy an affectionate hug before making her way to the Youth Department downstairs.

Working with the youth Sunday mornings offered Skye a challenge completely different from her kindergartners, one Skye enjoyed. She was the Sunday School teacher for the eighth-grade group and was also in charge of the opening Sunday services.

She was met in the large room by several enthusiastic hoots. The youths had always been known for their liveliness, and Skye responded with a ready smile.

The songs she led were some of the standard ones the teens enjoyed. She wandered around the room, her fingers moving agilely over the guitar strings. She paused, seeing two of the younger teen girls passing notes. Past experience had taught her that if she brought pressure from within their own peer group, any behavior problems cleared up quickly.

She stopped the song. "All right, girls." She didn't mention names but pointedly fixed her gaze on the offending class members. "This isn't the *Woody Woodpecker Hour.*"

The whole class burst into laughter.

"Yeah, girls, shape up," one boy shouted, and several girls responded by sticking out their tongues.

Skye resumed the song before things got out of hand, and soon everyone was singing again. And there was no more note-passing.

Skye left church feeling elated and cheerful. The pastor's sermon had reinforced the insights revealed the day before, and she was amazed at how persistent her blindness had been.

The aroma of meat and vegetables slowly cooking in a Crock-Pot met her as she entered her apartment. Skye usually ate her main meal at lunchtime on Sundays, a tradition her family had followed. Sundays were centered on the morning and evening worship services, and it was convenient to eat the main meal of the day at lunchtime.

Skye had lingered over the morning paper and was changing her clothes when the phone rang.

"Hello," she said cheerfully, expecting Peggy.

"Good afternoon," Jordan responded.

Instantly her heartbeat accelerated. She needed to explain yesterday's outburst, and it wasn't going to come easy. She so seldom lost her temper like that.

"Hello, Jordan." She hardly knew where to start. "I'm glad you phoned . . . I feel I owe you an apology."

"Good." His crisp voice seemed to mock her. "I'll take you to lunch, and you can tell me all about it. I'll be there in twenty minutes."

The connection was broken, and Skye was left listening to the hum of the dial tone. Skye shrugged. He hadn't even asked her. Jordan Kiley could be the most infuriating man. What if she had already made plans for the afternoon? She often did with her niece, Janey. Apparently any arrangements she'd made were of no consequence. She wasn't angry, but bemused. Jordan's personality was commanding and forceful, as if he was accustomed to giving orders and having them followed. What an enigmatic man he was.

The doorbell rang well within the allotted twenty minutes. His smile was warm and lazy when she opened the door.

"Are you ready?"

"Ready?" Her round blue eyes feigned ignorance.

"I thought we were going out to eat." His gaze narrowed slightly.

"I don't remember your asking," she said matter-of-factly.

Catching a glimpse of the table set for two in her tiny kitchenette, Jordan expelled his breath. "You're expecting someone." It wasn't a question but a statement of fact.

"Yes, I am. You."

His gaze swiveled back to her, his thick brows knit in confusion.

"If you'd have asked me, Jordan, I'd have told you I had a meal ready in the Crock-Pot. You're welcome to join me if you like."

He seemed to relax. Had the suspicion she was expecting someone else bothered him? The pleasure this bit of evidence brought overrode any sense of outrage at his presumptuous behavior.

His free hand gently caressed the soft flesh of her upper arm before he placed a tender kiss on her forehead.

"I'll be right back. I have a car and driver waiting."

Skye watched him leave. She didn't know what it was about his touch that brought her senses to life. A kiss, the feather-light stroke of his hand, gave her undeniable pleasure.

Steaming bowls of Irish stew had been placed on the table by the time he returned. The smell of fresh sourdough bread filled the apartment as she drew it from the oven.

"Lunch is ready," she said, feeling awkward.

Once they were seated, Jordan paused, waiting for Skye to begin eating.

"Do you mind if we pray?" she asked unsteadily.

He arched his brows expressively. "I suspect you want more than the prayer my father taught me." His eyes were smiling. "You know the one: *Good bread, good meat, good God, let's eat.*"

Skye couldn't help laughing. "Yes, I guess I do."

"You do the honors then."

Skye bowed her head, her hands folded. "Father, thank you for this meal and for abundantly supplying all our needs. Bless Jordan and the time we spend together. In Your precious name. Amen."

When she lifted her head, she discovered Jordan was watching her intently, and she shifted uncomfortably under his scrutiny.

"Before we eat," she began haltingly, "I think I'd feel a whole lot better if I could explain about yesterday."

The smiling sparkle returned to his smoky gray eyes. "Bothers you, does it?"

She lowered her gaze, pretending to study the thick bowl of stew. "The car breaking down was a culmination of several other things. I'd had a rather disconcerting conversation with my sister-in-law, and I got caught in that cloudburst . . . and, well, I feel I overreacted. I don't often blow up like that, and . . ."

He reached across the small table and gently squeezed her trembling hand. "It's forgotten. Feel better?"

She smiled and nodded.

"I have to admit, however, the thought of you burning your bra is an appealing one."

Skye could feel the color invade her face, burning her cheeks. "A gentleman would have forgotten I said that."

"I'm no gentleman." His mouth quirked with the effort to suppress a laugh.

"I noticed." Determinedly Skye began eating, refusing to let him see how he had embarrassed her.

"Did you enjoy yourself last night?"

Skye didn't understand the question, and glanced at him quizzically.

"Did you and your date have a good time last night?" It was a polite inquiry without a hint of jealousy or resentment. Apparently she'd misread him earlier; he really didn't care if she was with someone else or not.

"I tried phoning. You were out."

Darn, she'd forgotten his phone call. "Oh, last night . . ." Her mind worked furiously. "Yes . . . yes, I did. I was invited to a party." Another half-truth. John Dirkson had invited her, but Skye had never considered attending. She hadn't stepped out of her apartment all evening.

They played three games of backgammon after their meal. Jordan won the first two and showed no mercy. Skye won the third because she was tired of being Ms. Nice Guy and suffered no qualms about putting him off the board. She half expected Jordan to be angry, but when she replaced his man for the third time, she saw a glimmer of respect enter his eyes.

Afterward they sat talking while they drank several cups of coffee. They found their tastes were surprisingly similar in several areas. It was when they were discussing music that he questioned her about the hospital singer for the second time.

"What's her name again?" he asked with undisguised interest.

"Jane." A lump knotted her stomach.

"She's a talented lady."

"So she's been told." This was the very reason Skye didn't want him to know it was she. It embarrassed her to discuss her gift. And that was exactly what it was—a gift. She had done nothing to earn it and had always been ill at ease accepting compliments.

"Oh, dear, look at the time." She stood abruptly. "It's six already. I've got to be at church soon." But she had plenty of time; the evening service didn't start until six thirty.

"Church again?" He sounded as if he didn't believe her.

"Yes, would you like to come? I'd be pleased to have you meet our pastor. I know you'll like him. My brother and his family will be there, too."

Jordan stood and put his coffee cup in the sink. "Another time perhaps."

She wasn't disappointed. Skye was playing the piano for the service tonight, and he was sure to guess she was the hospital singer if he heard her.

Walking with Jordan to the small entryway, Skye could feel the muscles of her stomach begin to twitch. Was he going to try to kiss her again? Should she pretend she didn't want him to?

"Yes, I'm going to kiss you," he teased.

Her startled blue eyes flew open, and he gently gripped her arm, bringing her to his side. "You're very easy to read sometimes." The pressure of his grip moved from her arm to the back of her neck, slowly raising her head, decreasing the distance between their lips.

Was she that transparent? Skye wondered seconds before his mouth easily fit over hers. The urgency of his kiss parted her lips, and she succumbed to the tide of sweetness that swept through her.

Embracing was awkward: The unyielding cast of his broken arm pressed painfully against her ribs as his free hand moved down the curve of her spine. But the only sensation her mind registered was the rightness of being in his arms.

"While you're in church, say a prayer for me," Jordan said thickly, his voice slightly ragged.

Her voice wasn't any steadier. "I will."

The hand positioning her against him relaxed, as if he realized it must be uncomfortable for her. Skye shook her head but lowered her gaze, struggling against the magnetic pull of his eyes.

"What time does school let out these days? Maybe we can go sailing tomorrow afternoon."

"There's no school . . . it's spring break. Oh, Jordan, I can't." Regret filled her voice. "I promised Billy I was coming. Sally is making arrangements for me to take him outside the hospital for the day. I couldn't disappoint him."

"I wouldn't want you to. How about Tuesday?"

"I'd like that." She didn't even attempt to disguise her enthusiasm.

"I'll pick you up at ten."

Halfway out the door, Skye called to him. "Jordan."

He stopped and turned around.

"I *am* going to pray for you."

Something unreadable flickered in his eyes. "Do that," he said softly, and left.

On Monday Skye impulsively drove by and picked up her niece before stopping at the hospital for Billy. The two had met several times previously and seemed to enjoy each other.

"Hiya, Sprout."

Billy was in his wheelchair waiting. "Hi, Skye; hi, Janey." His eyes lit up eagerly.

"Okay, you two, we have the whole day ahead of us. Where would you like to go?"

"Chinatown," they shouted in unison.

"Chinatown," she moaned, as if it were some great tragedy, but a laugh lay barely beneath the surface. San Francisco's Chinatown was exciting. The largest community of Chinese people living together outside Asia, in many ways it seemed like visiting a foreign country.

Skye located a parking place with easy access to the well-defined area, and soon the three made their way down the crowded streets.

Billy insisted upon handling the wheelchair himself, but Skye found it necessary to help him several times as they moved up and down the narrow, hilly streets on and off Grant Avenue. Several of the stores had sidewalk displays, and Billy was able to investigate their wares without having to maneuver his wheelchair through the narrow shop doors.

They stopped to eat lunch in a nearby restaurant. Ushered by the waiter, they were given their own private dining room. Both children loved the privacy and took delight in teasing each other, especially over the chopsticks.

The food was delicious. Janey and Billy quickly devoured the traditional Chinese dishes, leaving Skye to sample the more exotic ones. The fortune cookies were the highlight of the meal as far as either child was concerned.

"What's yours say, Skye?" Billy wanted to know.

To appease them both she examined the tiny slip. The words seemed to reach out and slap her. beware of the stranger dark and bold. stay true to your love of long ago.

"It says—" She faltered slightly. "—it's time to take Billy back to the hospital."

They both objected, but not strenuously. Billy fell asleep in the car, and Janey was unusually quiet. Whether it was because she was exhausted, too, or as a thoughtful gesture so as not to wake Billy, Skye didn't question.

As the silence settled over the car, the message of the fortune cookie kept repeating itself in her confused brain. It was uncanny, inexplicable, and the words deeply troubled her. Was God using this silly fortune to warn her about Jordan? The words echoed through her mind a hundred times as she drove from the hospital to her brother's house. Although she'd made the proper responses when spoken to at the hospital, her mind was far from the matters at hand. It was something she couldn't explain or reason away. Above all else, Skye realized that nothing in her life happened by accident. God had a purpose in everything, no matter how minute.

Home looked good; her feet hurt after the extended hike. After hanging her jacket in the entryway closet, she went directly to the Bible set on the nightstand. For all her Bible study and all the verses she'd memorized over the years, she didn't know what to make of the message of the fortune cookie.

"Dear Jesus," she began silently, sitting cross-legged across the top of her bed. "I don't know why You allowed this message to come to me, or if it has any significance at all. I realize You guide me through life and I am trusting You. Thank you, Lord, for sending Jordan into my life. At first I didn't know how to handle the feeling he awoke within me. Although I find myself still unsure, I'm far less afraid. I'm asking You, Lord, to guide me in this relationship. I desire only Your will in my life."

Familiar with several books in the Bible, Skye read until she felt a soothing peace come over her spirit.

Because the situation was in God's hands, Skye forgot it, later fixing herself a light dinner. While she was washing the dishes her phone rang.

"Hello, Pollyanna. Been saying your prayers like a good girl?"

"Hello, Jordan." It felt good to hear the sound of his voice, and she didn't take exception to his greeting. "And, yes, I have been saying my prayers, including a few for you."

"I'm going to need them. Listen, Blue Eyes, I've got to cancel tomorrow. Things have gotten out of hand here in LA without me. I flew back this afternoon."

"Oh." Disappointment settled over her. Jordan had left the city. "That's all right," she assured him. Nervously her fingers looped a strand of ashen hair around her ear.

"It's not all right," Jordan said impatiently.

The doorbell rang, jerking her attention to the apartment door. "Jordan, there's someone at my door. Hold on . . . or do you want to hang up?"

"No, I don't want to hang up. Answer the door," he said, and sighed heavily in irritation.

Laying the phone on the small table beside her davenport, Skye rushed to answer the repeated buzz. If it was John Dirkson, she thought, she'd scream.

She didn't, of course. "Yes?" she said brusquely, hoping she sounded as unfriendly as she felt.

Indolently John placed himself between Skye and the door. "Hi, yourself. I'm just being neighborly. I wonder if you happen to have a tube of anchovy paste?"

"Anchovy paste?" Skye laughed. "No, John, I don't normally keep anchovy paste lying around."

"Maybe you should look," he persisted. "One never knows what lurks in the backs of cupboards."

"Listen," she said pointedly, glancing back into her living room, "I'm on the phone and it's important."

John beamed her one of the irresistible smiles meant to melt the defenses of the most determined woman. "I don't mind waiting." Before she could stop him, he had let himself in, sunk down on the davenport, and made himself at home.

Skye sighed in frustration. "Jordan," she began self-consciously, "it's my neighbor."

"So I heard," Jordan said in a voice that sounded very much like a snarl. "I want to talk to you, Skye. Get rid of him."

Skye turned her back to John and cupped her hand over the mouth of the receiver. "I tried," she whispered spiritedly. Jordan was out of sorts; Skye could feel his impatience. "I want to talk to you, too," she added so there would be no doubt where her preference lay.

His breath was expelled harshly. "All right, I'll phone back in ten minutes. Will that give you enough time?"

"Yes . . . yes, I think so."

Actually it took her only five minutes and a few choice words to show John exactly what she thought of his rude behavior. Because of his unfailing belief in his male charm, Skye's repeated rejection had fueled a challenge too blatant to be ignored. When she told him that if he bothered her again she would contact the apartment manager, John looked totally confused. Women didn't usually treat his attention lightly.

The phone only rang once. "Jordan?"

He didn't bother with a greeting. "Is he gone?"

"Yes, he's gone." She took the phone and curled up on the davenport. "And good riddance." She laughed lightly.

"As I was saying," Jordan began again, "I've had a change in plans. I've got to cancel tomorrow, but I should be in Frisco in about two weeks. How about dinner then?"

"Fine," Skye said shamelessly. She didn't even bother to look at her calendar; if other plans had been made, she'd cancel them. Being with Jordan was worth more than anything she could have scheduled.

"Oh, and while I'm thinking about it, give me the full name of that singer from the hospital again. I'd like to have Dan Murphy contact her. From the little I heard, the girl's got talent, exceptional talent."

"Dan Murphy?"

"He's the fellow who owns the radio station that employs yours truly."

"Oh." Skye had backed herself into a corner, forced to tell another white lie. "I told you her name is Jane, but honestly, Jordan, I don't think she's interested."

"You sound jealous." It was an accusation that rankled.

"That's ridiculous," she denied. "It's just that I find it disconcerting to have you phone me to ask about another woman."

They spoke for only a few minutes longer, the conversation suddenly stilted and unnatural. Skye replaced the receiver with a heavy heart. Her father had told her several years ago that *a liar is a fool who buries himself with deceit.* And here she was digging her own grave. Skye had always thought of herself as an honest person, yet somehow she had fallen into the habit of telling white lies. Had she been living a lie for so long that it had become second nature for her to utter half-truths indiscriminately? She had lied to herself and lied to God for eight years. *Darn you, Jordan Kiley,* she thought, *for what you're doing to me, and bless you, too, for forcing me into the light.*

* * *

Skye didn't hear from Jordan for the remainder of the week. She'd scheduled several projects for herself, including painting the kitchen and some spring cleaning, so her days were full and busy. Nonetheless, she couldn't help feeling disappointed that Jordan hadn't called. It had become of primary importance that she talk to him and explain her deception. She hadn't meant to lie; it had begun as a joke but had soon ballooned into a full-scale untruth.

The following Monday morning the children were happy and excited to be back in school. Skye had always loved children and was normally very patient, but by early afternoon she found herself snapping and fidgeting.

"How many times have I told you not to run in the classroom, David? How many?" she lashed out at the youngster from her desk.

Five-year-old David stared at her, his lower lip quivering. "I'm sorry, Miss Garvin, I won't run again."

Yelling was no way to deal effectively with children, and Skye immediately felt guilty. "I'm sorry, too, David. I shouldn't have shouted."

What had gotten into her to behave this way with the children? The answer was obvious. Misleading Jordan was weighing heavily on her mind, and she desperately needed to clear up things between them.

Tuesday night, after fulfilling her volunteer duties, Skye remained later than usual waiting for Sally. A melody had been running through her mind most of the day, so while Sally finished up a few odds and ends Skye sat at the piano in the reception room. Slowly her fingers moved over the keys, transcribing the melody into notes. The pencil held in her mouth was jerked from its location countless times as shew scratched out the notes and marked new ones on the music sheet. Finally satisfied, she set the pencil down, ready to play the piece through.

The familiar sound of Sally's footsteps echoed from the back of the room.

"Listen to this," Skye commanded without turning, not wishing to break her concentration. Her fingers played the first chords of the introduction, filling the silent room with vibrating sound. The song had a natural rhythm, and Skye stopped only once to change a single note. The music was bright and breezy, as her songs often were, with the kind of melodies that made people want to sing along and tap their feet. As the final notes faded, Skye smiled in satisfaction. A sense of accomplishment came over her. It was a good beginning, and the words were beginning to form in her mind.

"Sounds good, doesn't it?" she asked Sally, turning toward her friend.

But it wasn't Sally who stood behind her.

"Jordan," she whispered in disbelief.

"Hello, *Jane*," he said, and glared at her.

"Jordan . . ." Skye began, but stopped abruptly at the mistrust she saw in his eyes.

"You lied." His voice grated. "After all your pretty church talk, you out and out lied." With that, he walked out of the room.

Chapter Six

"All right, kid, tell Aunt Sally all about it." It had taken her perceptive friend only a day to notice something was wrong.

"Tell you what?" Skye sipped lackadaisically on her herbal tea, feigning confusion.

"What's wrong, and don't try to tell me something isn't. I can tell just by looking at you that you're upset."

Skye laughed lightly. "Do I actually look that different?"

Sally studied her shrewdly. "Yes, as a matter of fact, you do."

Crossing her eyes, Skye laughed, but her laugh held little genuine amusement. "I'm exactly the same person I was the other day."

"No, you're not," Sally disputed soberly. "That sparkle is gone from your eyes. No . . . not sparkle, the expectation is missing. Did you and this John have a spat?"

Skye lowered her head, her hair falling forward to frame her oval face. "Sally, I'm not dating and never plan to date John Dirkson. He *is* my neighbor, but I misled you by insinuating there was something more between us. I . . . I also misled Jordan

Kiley—but not about John—and when he discovered my game, well . . . no one likes to be the butt of a joke."

Sally paused, waiting for Skye to elaborate, but when an explanation didn't follow, she probed. "Can't you make it right?"

Miserably Skye shook her head. There was no way of contacting him, and even if there were, Skye had decided not to. God had sent him into her life for a purpose, and that had been accomplished. And she would always be grateful to Jordan for removing the blinders that had hidden the truth.

"Hey," Sally said, interrupting her thoughts. "Didn't you tell me you were going out to dinner with Jordan Kiley next Friday night?"

"That's been canceled." At least Skye felt sure it must be. If by chance Jordan did happen to show, she wouldn't be home. It was Janey's birthday, and she was having dinner with her family.

"That's too bad, Skye, but I think meeting Jordan has done you a world of good."

Her lips trembled slightly as she attempted a smile. "I think you're right."

Sally patted her hand. "Well, with Jordan out of the picture maybe I could interest you in a blind date."

How typical of the matchmaking Sally. "All right, you're on."

The contented grin of a Cheshire cat couldn't have shown more satisfaction. "Steve King is a perfect match for you," Sally elaborated. "He's an accountant at Andy's firm; I know you're going to like him."

Skye had heard these identical words at least twenty times. But an accountant? She somehow pictured a tiny, bespectacled man with a fastidious nature. Biting her lip, she glanced at Sally hesitatingly.

"You're not backing out already, are you?"

"No," Skye said, "I was just wondering if it'd be too forward to ask him to help me balance my bank account on our first date."

They looked at each other and burst into giggles.

Skye was in much better spirits Thursday evening and played and sang for the children with a free-flowing happiness. Finishing, she turned to smile at her audience, but the smile froze on her face. Standing in the back of the room was Jordan. Had it only been a few days since she'd last seen him? It seemed a lifetime.

His steel-gray eyes pinned her. Sally glanced from one to the other and with a quiet efficiency moved the children and their families from the room.

Jordan waited until the room was nearly empty before advancing toward her. The wild hammering of her heart rushed a fresh supply of blood to her already flushed face. Her fingers were trembling so badly she folded them awkwardly in her lap.

"Is it Jane or Skye?" he asked.

"Skye," she said in a breathy whisper. Nervously she moistened her lips. "Jordan, may I apologize? It was a stupid, childish prank. I . . ." She ran a shaky hand over her forehead, not sure if she should continue.

"Forget it," he said gruffly. "Is there somewhere we could go for coffee?"

Skye glanced pointedly at her watch, but if he'd asked her the time she couldn't have told him. "It's getting late."

"Is the cafeteria open?"

"Yes, but . . ." She hesitated. If she was honest with herself, she'd admit she wanted to talk to him and clear up this matter.

His hand cupped her elbow possessively while she led the way to the elevator. The cafeteria was deserted, the kitchen area closed. Coffee and a few remaining desserts were sold on the honor system; a bowl sat atop the counter to collect the change. Jordan paid for the coffee while she carried their cups to a nearby table.

"Have you ever thought of becoming a professional singer?"

His question was so unexpected, she widened her eyes and wondered at his game. "No. I've never given the matter much thought."

"You're very gifted. You realize that, don't you?" The compliment was issued almost as a challenge.

Jordan confused her. His question took her by surprise. Skye had hoped they could discuss their misunderstanding, not her singing ability.

"I'm not *that* talented," she insisted. His look was hard and unemotional, leaving her feeling as if she barely knew him.

"I want to tape some of your music. I have a friend who owns a recording studio, and I'd like to have him listen to you." He watched her as though he anticipated a wild burst of enthusiasm at the generosity of his offer.

She gave him none. "I'm not interested. I'm honored that you think so highly of my talent, but no thanks."

His gaze narrowed in disbelief. "Don't lightly toss away this opportunity, Skye." His gaze seemed to question her reasoning.

She sighed, releasing a jagged breath. How could she explain herself? Singing for the children was a joy; even an occasional solo with the church choir was a pleasurable challenge. But to make singing her life's work was out of the question. It didn't even tempt her.

She was given a respite by several nurses who entered the room. Their gaze rushed over her without notice and focused with interest upon Jordan. She couldn't blame them; even with his broken arm, he managed to suggest a latent animal grace, his appeal totally masculine.

Jordan didn't even notice the interest he was generating. Instead he continued to study Skye thoughtfully.

"This is a great opportunity. Are you sure you've thought this through?"

Nodding decisively, Skye said, "Quite sure."

Still he studied her as if he wasn't sure he should believe her.

Skye shifted uncomfortably. What a strange conversation this was. Glancing at her watch, she noted the time and quickly swallowed her coffee. "I need to get home," she said sadly. She had hoped to make things right between them, but it was clear Jordan wasn't interested.

His outstretched hand stopped her as she began to rise. The flint gray of his eyes pinned her to the seat. "I want you to reconsider. It wouldn't hurt anything to make up a demo CD. You have the talent to make it, but the choice is yours."

Without so much as a second thought she shook her head. "I'm not going to change my mind." She stood and deposited her Styrofoam cup in the garbage on her way out the door.

The sad puppy cried pitifully when Skye replaced the barrier confining him to the kitchen. He had been frolicking between her feet and chewing on the bright, fuzzy slippers she wore. Large chocolate pools of misery watched as she petted him and whispered soothingly.

She would have to hurry and change clothes or she would be late for Janey's birthday dinner. But every time she left sight of the pup, he would yelp and howl. Twice John Dirkson had been over to complain about the noise. Skye had difficulty keeping her temper the second time, but smiled sweetly and promised to do her best. Her relationship with John had been strained, and she wasn't sorry to hear he was moving at the end of the month.

With the puppy moderately quiet, she chose her most becoming new dress. The musky rose color accentuated the light tones of her hair, while the soft gathers at the waist emphasized her willowy suppleness. She'd finished fastening the button-loop closure down the front and knotting the tie when the doorbell rang.

Could it be Jordan? This was the night they had set their dinner date, but he had been distant and uncommunicative the day before. No, it wouldn't be him, but perhaps someday God would send him back into her life and she could make proper amends. She finished buckling the strap of her shoe and hobbled across her living room, one shoe on, one shoe off. It must be John to complain about the pup again.

It wasn't. "Jordan," she breathed, feeling stiff and nervous.

"Hello. May I come in?" he asked. His eyes widened in appreciation as he did an appraising sweep of her appearance.

Still suffering the effects of surprise, she stepped aside. "Of course; I'm sorry."

He moved past her into the living room, his eyes warm and amused as he watched her hobbling about with only one shoe.

"I didn't think you were coming," she began unevenly.

"Did I say I wasn't?" His eyes left hers momentarily and fell upon the puppy confined in her kitchen. "Your burglar alarm system?" he joked casually. "I see. Once warned, you attack the intruder, using your shoe as a weapon." A crooked smile turned up the edges of his mouth as he glanced at the high-heeled sandal in her hand.

"Of course not." Her step faltered slightly as she slipped the shoe on as gracefully as possible.

"Aren't you forgetting something?"

"What?"

"Your money? I'd hate to see you leave home without it."

"Why are you here?" she asked him breathlessly, confused.

"I thought we had a date."

"I . . . I didn't think you meant to keep it." Skye knew she wouldn't be able to maintain this pretense of self-possession much longer.

"Clearly you've made other arrangements." It was a statement full of irritation.

It would be easy to lie again, let him assume another half-truth. He would go then, and she knew with an unexplainable certainty that she wouldn't see him again.

"It's my niece's birthday. I was going to have dinner with my family. Janey's nine today."

"Ahh . . . Jane, that's where you got the name."

"My given name is Jane, too." She sat directly opposite him, pausing to buckle her shoe. "Jordan, listen. I don't remember how the whole thing started, letting you believe the singer was someone else. I've felt terrible all week."

"Let's forget it," he said tightly.

"I don't want to forget it, and I doubt that I'll be able to until I explain myself. I didn't mean to mislead you. I'm not even sure why I did. Maybe it was because I didn't want to talk about myself that first night. Or perhaps I wanted you to like me for myself, not for any talent I may possess. Can you understand that?"

His probing eyes swept over her. "Yes, I can."

"I don't want you to accept my apology. I want you to forgive me. There's a difference. I need your forgiveness, Jordan."

He stood and came to her side. Gently he brought her upright, easing her against his body. Kissing her hair, his hand gently stroked her arm. "I forgive you," he whispered huskily.

Skye's arms slid effortlessly around him, her mouth turning instinctively toward his. As his lips fit over hers a searing contentment stole over her. It felt so right to be in his arms. He shuddered against her, and Skye nestled her head upon his broad shoulder.

"Have dinner with me?" he mumbled into her hair.

"I want to," she admitted huskily, "but I can't. My family is waiting for me."

Raising her face, he kissed her again with an infinite tenderness, arching her toward him.

"You could come with me," she whispered. "Brad and Peggy won't mind." Her lovely mouth curved into an appealing smile. "Besides, I'm going to need help with the pup."

Jordan chuckled softly. "Scheming woman, aren't you?"

Her car had no sooner pulled up alongside the curb than Janey came rushing from the house and down the front steps. The screen door slammed behind her, only to be opened again a few seconds later.

"It's about time you got here," Brad scolded affectionately. Then he noticed Jordan, who came around the other side of the car. "So this is the reason you're late," he teased her in a brotherly manner.

"Don't embarrass me," she joked, but her eyes were serious.

"Would I do a thing like that?" he asked laughingly.

The two men shook hands after an informal introduction and walked toward the house talking companionably. Skye and Peggy rescued the pup from the backseat of her car while Janey squealed with delight over her birthday gift.

While the men sat in the living room talking, Skye helped Peggy finish the salad and add an extra place at the table.

"I hope you don't mind my showing up with Jordan unexpectedly like this," Skye said as she glanced into the living room and saw how well Jordan got along with her brother.

Peggy's smile was full of warmth. "Of course not," she denied instantly. "I was dying to meet him anyway."

"Is Jordan your boyfriend, Aunt Skye?" Janey quizzed as she lopped a fingerful of frosting from the cake.

"Hey, you!" Peggy cried. "Keep your greedy finger off the cake."

"Is he?" She repeated her question.

Skye wasn't sure how to answer. A contentment flowed through her, and unconsciously she found herself studying Jordan from the kitchen. Lean and powerful, he sat with his long legs stretched before him, exuding an aura of strength.

"Auntie Skye?" Janey grabbed Skye's hand as if to pull her attention back to herself.

"I'm sorry, cupcake." Skye broke her concentration. "Yes, I guess you could say he's my boyfriend." But she didn't want her niece to pursue the subject further. "How do you like the puppy?"

"He's wonderful . . . I think I'll name him Sampson. What do you think?"

"It's a great idea," Skye said, hugging her.

The meal was an enjoyable sharing time. Everyone participated in the laughter and teasing.

"I'm stuffed." Brad leaned back in his chair and patted his stomach.

"You better have room for dessert," Janey warned, not wanting to delay opening her gifts.

"I think I've managed to save a little room for cake. How about you, Jordan?"

"I've always got room for birthday cake." He purposely winked at Janey, who dissolved into delighted giggles.

Skye rose after Peggy, conscious of Jordan's warm gaze following her. "I'll help Peggy with the cake," she said, as if needing an excuse to leave.

They returned a few minutes later carrying in the cake with nine lighted candles and singing the traditional birthday song.

"Make your wish, princess," Brad prompted.

Janey closed her eyes tightly, then announced excitedly, "I wished for a baby brother."

Standing behind his wife, Brad laughed. "I don't know." His arms slid contentedly around Peggy's still-flat stomach. "I wouldn't object to another girl. It's not many men who can claim to live in a house full of beautiful women." Playfully he nuzzled Peggy's neck, making growling noises.

The gifts were opened, including the necklace Skye had bought with Jordan the first night they'd gone to dinner. Janey also got a new game and a pair of pajamas.

The adults moved into the living room, and when Skye brought Jordan his coffee, his arm circled her waist, bringing her down to sit on the arm of his chair. His grip held her there, his eyes smiling into hers.

"Where's Brad?" she asked, returning his warm gaze with one of her own.

"He's gone to phone for a taxi. My flight is leaving soon."

Skye's heart floundered at his casual announcement. "Already?" she asked hesitantly, and swallowed down her disappointment. She wanted to look away, afraid he would read her regret, but his gaze held hers.

"Come to the airport with me?" he asked.

"Okay," she returned lightly, although her smile wavered dangerously. "I . . . I can drive us."

A short time later they said their good-byes on the porch. Jordan and Brad grasped hands with the familiarity of good friends.

Skye hugged both Peggy and Janey. "I hope you had a very special birthday, cupcake."

"Oh, Auntie Skye, I really did," Janey assured her. "And I like Jordan a lot."

"I'd be more than willing to drive you to the airport," Brad offered, but the look he exchanged with Jordan showed he understood his wish to be alone with Skye.

Within a few minutes they were on their way. Brad, Peggy, and Janey stood on the porch waving; Skye focused her attention on the fading figures as long as possible.

Jordan was strangely quiet, as if there was something on his mind. Skye more than carried the conversation, babbling inanities that were totally irrelevant to anything.

The reality of his leaving hit forcefully when they approached the airport. Skye could no longer deny the tears burning for release. This was stupid; why was she getting so emotional? It wasn't like Jordan was heading off to war. A lone tear forced itself free and rolled down her cheek. Fiercely she brushed it away before Jordan could notice.

The security line seemed twenty miles long; Skye chatted continuously.

Stopping her abruptly, Jordan gently touched her wet cheek. "Why are you crying?" he asked.

"I am?" she questioned. "Oh, I always cry when I'm happy." She'd promised God and herself she wouldn't lie again, but her resolve crumbled under the first attack of pride. "I've never been so happy," she said in a kind of desperation. "Peggy's pregnant, Janey's birthday . . . and look at you, Oscar the Grouch, your arm is healing and . . ." A bubble of laughter quickly became a sob.

The line was crowded with people waiting to have their property scanned. Jordan stepped out and maneuvered Skye to a far corner offering them as much privacy as possible.

"I've listened to your Pollyanna chatter all the way here. Now I'll ask you again—why are you crying?" His hand tightly gripped her arm, the line of his jaw tight and controlled.

Everything suddenly went very still; the wall he backed her against felt hard and unyielding. Skye held her breath, concentrating on the top of his shoe. She didn't know what had gotten into her. She was normally a very composed woman.

"Skye," he groaned impatiently, and his finger lifted her chin to read her watery blue eyes. "Please tell me why you're crying," his low voice coaxed as he gathered her into his arms. Her softness molded against him, welcoming the comfort of his embrace. His hand rubbed her back in a soothing circular motion.

Held protectively, Skye accepted the solid strength and buried her face in his shirt.

"I'm sorry," she attempted in apology. "I'm being ridiculous." She could feel the gentle pressure of his lips kiss her hair.

"No, you're not." His own voice sounded strained and faintly raw.

"Oh, Jordan, I don't honestly know why I'm crying. I can't believe how stupid I'm being."

"I have to go, otherwise I'll miss my flight," he said impatiently. But he didn't relax his hold on her. When he did lift his head, an expanding frown darkened his expression.

Skye stared back wordlessly, but when she tried to pull away he caught her shoulder, fixing his gaze upon hers. With a fierce kind of gentleness, he cupped her face, his mouth seeking hers.

"I've got to go." The emotion in his voice was so ragged, it startled Skye.

A frail smile formed. "I know." Using the back of her hand, she wiped the remaining tears aside. She studied him, committing to memory every detail of his rugged face.

"I didn't mean to blubber all over your shirt." She wiped his chest, as if to erase the wet stains her tears had made.

His eyes regarded her with a languorous warmth. Glancing over his shoulder, he noted the long security line.

"There are things I want to tell you," he admitted with forced patience. "And now all I can think about is how long it's going to be before I can kiss you again." Quickly he checked the progress of the receding line and jerked his attention back to her. "If I fly back next weekend, will you be here?"

"Yes." Her voice sounded choked and small. Then, gaining verbal strength, she repeated, "Yes, of course I'll be here."

They began to ease their way toward the TSA agent.

"I have to go," Jordan said, gazing deep into her eyes.

"I know." Fresh tears misted over her eyes, and her mouth trembled in an effort to smile.

"I'll phone you," he promised, backing away from her.

"Okay, good-bye, Jordan," she finally managed to say, her voice a tortured whisper. She watched him disappear into the long Jetway that ushered him inside the plane.

She remained looking onto the brightly lit runway for several minutes after his plane had made its ascension into the night.

Skye knew Brad and Peggy had probably been waiting to hear from her, but she didn't feel like talking to them tonight. She had too many feelings to deal with. What had caused her to act as she had? She couldn't remember doing anything so stupid in her life. Anyone would have thought Jordan was going off to war instead of returning home. It was amazing he was interested in her at all. She had bungled this relationship from the beginning. She had teased him, promised and misled him, lied to him, ranted and raved at him, and now acted like a complete idiot.

A couple of hours later she sat on her bed reading from her Bible, sorting through her feelings, and discussing this relationship in prayer when the phone rang.

Jordan. It had to be him; no one else would phone this late.

"Hello." She didn't attempt to disguise the eagerness in her voice.

"You're home!" came the obvious observation. "Where have you been all night? I've tried phoning several times."

"Hello, Sally." She tried to hide her disappointment, but the unnatural dip in her voice revealed her letdown. "I was at my niece's birthday dinner." She didn't add that Jordan had gone with her.

"I should have remembered that," Sally chastised herself.

"Were you expecting a call from someone else? You sound disappointed."

"No, not really," Skye said. "What's up?" Sally wouldn't phone unless it was something important, not this late at any rate.

"I've got some marvelous news. I knew you'd want to know right away. You don't mind my calling this late, do you?"

Leave it to Sally to keep her dangling with anticipation. "You know I don't. Now, what's so all-fired important?"

"Dr. Warren was in this afternoon and he feels Billy has a slim chance of walking again."

"What? Are you kidding?" Skye gasped in disbelief. It wasn't a serious question. Sally wouldn't jest about Billy's future. The question was a natural outpouring of her own incredulity.

"A colleague of Dr. Warren's from back east—I think his name is Snell—has been doing some experimental surgery in cases like Billy's," she continued, listing the specific areas of the spine now operable under the new technique, but the technical terms flew over Skye's head.

"Yes . . . yes, but what does all this mean?" Skye interrupted.

Sally laughed. "I was getting to that. What all this boils down to is the fact that there's a possibility this new technique will work in Billy's case. Dr. Snell is flying here for some medical conference, and he's agreed to examine Billy and determine the feasibility of success. If—and it's a big if—Billy's found to be a low-risk candidate, he'll undergo the surgery."

"Oh, Sally, I've prayed for something like this."

"You're not crying, are you?" Sally accused, her own elated voice wobbling with suppressed tears.

"No, silly, these aren't tears, this is liquid joy."

Chapter Seven

Monday and Tuesday passed in a dull shade of expectancy. Even though her days and nights were full, Skye found several things she wanted to share with Jordan. Little things. She'd finally broken a seven-minute mile, a goal she'd set for herself a year before. And of course she wanted to tell him about Billy. And there was one thing he must know that was sure to displease him.

Wednesday afternoon Skye unlocked her apartment door, slipped off her shoes, and entered her bedroom to change clothes, a pattern so set it was almost like instinct. She flipped the switch to her radio, a sound to fill the silence. Funny, she'd never thought of music like that before. Music had been her panacea, filling the void in her life, offering challenge and purpose. Suddenly it had become a sound to fill the silence.

Later she lay with her head resting against the back of the sofa. Had she fallen in love with Jordan? Was all this longing for the sound of his voice and the coming weekend *love*? She cupped her tea mug with her long, slender fingers and sipped the tea absently. Her feelings for Glen had been so different from this. With Glen she'd felt cherished and protected. But Jordan drew from her something totally different. Something almost indefinable; a strong, fierce emotion. She shook her head to dispel her thoughts, unwilling to continue in this senseless vein.

Intent on reading her book, she tucked her bare feet beneath her and placed her mug down just as the phone rang.

"Hello," she said cheerfully.

"Hello, Skye."

"Jordan," she breathed, and her heart skipped a beat. "I'm so glad you called. I was beginning to think my watery charades had convinced you I was a candidate for the loony bin."

His laughter was full and rich. "The thought crossed my mind the first time you took off your shoe."

Skye tightened her grip on the receiver, as if it would make what she had to say easier. "I have some bad news and some good news; which do you want first?"

He didn't even pause. "I learned a long time ago to deal with any unpleasantness first."

"When I got home last week," she began hesitantly, "I looked on my calendar and I noticed that . . . that I've already got a date for this Saturday night. I . . . promised Sally I'd meet a friend of her husband's."

Jordan was silent for so long, Skye wondered if he was still on the line. "Jordan?" Her voice wobbled.

"Break it," he demanded.

"I can't. I want to, but Sally has gone to a lot of trouble, and I did promise . . . " she finished weakly.

Jordan's voice was sharp with anger. "I've already made my flight reservations, and frankly I really don't care about hurting your friend's feelings."

"It's not like a real date. I haven't even met this guy. Sally's been trying to fix this up for weeks. I can't let her down now."

The silence that followed felt oppressive.

"Just what do you expect me to do? Jump for joy?"

"No." The word came out squeaky and high-pitched. "I . . . I was hoping we could spend Saturday together, and as much of Sunday as your schedule will allow."

"You can't honestly expect me to come?" he asked forcefully.

"If you don't, I think I'll go crazy." She hadn't meant to reveal so much of her feelings, to admit quite that much.

He sighed heavily, and when he spoke, the irritation had left. "I think I would, too," he admitted huskily.

The stiffness left her shoulders. "We'll have a wonderful day," she breathed softly.

"Unfortunately it was the night I was looking forward to."

"Then I'll have to thank my guardian angel for looking after me," she said lightheartedly.

She could hear pages being flipped, as if he were consulting an appointment calendar. "What about Friday night?"

Skye had already made plans with the church youth group. "I . . . I kind of have something going that night," she said, more than a little apprehensive. "What time could you be here?"

"Around seven."

She sighed softly. "That'll work great. Eat a light dinner, because we're having hot fudge sundaes afterward."

"After what?"

"You'll see," she said, laughing lightly. "It'll be fun, I promise."

A male voice interrupted from the background. It sounded vaguely like Bill Malloy, the man Skye had met the day her car broke down.

"I've got to go," he groaned impatiently.

"Jordan, I have some wonderful news about Billy. I'll tell you Friday. Good-bye."

"Friday at seven," he said in a husky voice that sounded very much like a promise.

Skye had no sooner hung up the phone when it rang again. It was Janey. "Auntie Skye," she burst out excitedly. "Can you come over right away? I've got something to show you."

Skye glanced quickly at her watch; there was plenty of time before church. "All right, cupcake."

Brad and Peggy were doing yard work when she drove up. Janey saw her from down the street and came racing up the sidewalk.

"Come see," she yelled, running with all her strength.

Brad rose from the flower bed he was weeding to meet her. "Yes, come see," he encouraged with sparkling eyes.

Janey grabbed her hand, breathless from the run. "It arrived this morning. I was so surprised."

"Hey, you guys." Skye laughed, her brow furrowed. "What gives?"

Tugging fiercely at Skye's hand, Janey led the way around the back of the house. When Brad and Peggy followed, Skye glanced skeptically over her shoulder, thoroughly confused.

Once they rounded the corner, her gaze focused on a large brown doghouse. Built to resemble a miniature home, it contained white shutters beside two windows. SAMPSON was painted in book hand above the door. Squatting down, Skye could see that plush carpeting covered the floor except for a small space of linoleum in the kitchen area that was used for the dog's water and food dishes.

Sampson slumbered peacefully inside his new quarters. Skye petted the puppy with long, flowing strokes.

"Brad, it's a darling house. Where did you ever find it?" she asked over her shoulder.

"I didn't!"

Her eyes widened and swept his controlled expression, but

Brad only smiled back. Janey was no help, either. Obviously primed for silence, she pinched her lips closed with her fingers.

"Peggy?" Skye turned her questioning eyes to her sister-in-law.

"Jordan had it delivered this morning," Peggy said at last, recognizing Skye's frustration.

"Jordan did?" A warm bubble of happiness surfaced.

"Take some friendly advice," Brad said pensively. "Hold on to Jordan Kiley. He's a keeper."

Her smile was tremulous, but her eyes sparkled with a light of contentment and promise. "I think I will," she said.

"Aren't you going to tell Aunt Skye the best news of all?" Janey demanded from inside the doghouse. Sampson was cradled on her lap and looking disgruntled because his nap and his home had been invaded.

"What news?" Skye's attention swiveled back to her brother. "You got a job!" She really didn't need to guess further; nothing else could have removed the lines of doubt and worry that had furrowed his expression for weeks. He even seemed to stand taller, as if some heavy load had been lifted from him.

"I start Monday morning." A grin lit up his boyish face.

"And more money than we dared dream," Peggy interjected enthusiastically.

"The Lord works in mysterious ways. Funny, I never expected to get that job, let alone be asked to be the foreman." Brad opened the back door leading to the kitchen. "Come inside and I'll tell you all about it."

The three adults entered the house, leaving Janey contentedly behind, sitting in the doghouse.

The bus was loaded with thirty-five laughing, teasing junior high students. The festive mood intensified as Skye and Jordan climbed aboard with the bus driver.

"All right, kids." Skye stood in the front of the bus, calling them to attention. "Hold it down a minute while I go over the rules and introduce you to my friend. This is Mr. Kiley, and he'll be accompanying us tonight."

A chorus of hoots and welcomes came from the lively group.

Jordan acknowledged their acceptance with a casual wave of his hand.

"I see you had to twist his arm to come," one of the boys from the back of the bus shouted, referring to Jordan's broken arm.

Other jeers followed laughter. "Robert, be careful, I may have to twist your mouth as well," Skye said, returning the banter easily.

After reviewing the rules, Skye sat beside Jordan in one of the front seats of the bus. The driver started the vehicle and pulled out of the parking lot, while the eager bunch sang songs accompanied by Skye on the guitar. What they lacked in talent was more than compensated for in volume.

The theater parking lot was packed with cars and several other church buses. Some discussion followed on how to locate their bus after the movie.

"Just remember ours is the yellow one," Jordan offered.

"Cute, fellow."

"Funny."

"Who is this guy, Jeff Foxworthy?" came a sprinkling of wisecracks.

Although the Christian film's message was geared toward their charges, Skye prayed that Jordan would respond to the invitation to accept Christ as his personal Savior. At the end of the film the invocation was repeated by counselors at the front of the theater. Several teens and preteens went forward.

Skye tipped her head back to watch Jordan, but his expression was closed and unreadable. Sighing, she realized that for Jordan, placing his trust in Christ would not come easily.

Independence and self-reliance were so much a part of his personality, Skye wondered how long it would take him to recognize his need. From what she knew of him, Jordan would investigate Christianity thoroughly before making a commitment. Skye wanted him to know and love God as she did. There was no denying the growing attraction she felt for Jordan, and it was of primary importance that he share her faith.

Feeling her gaze touch him, Jordan turned, his eyes regarding her seriously. *I must be patient,* she told herself. *I must learn to let the Holy Spirit do the calling.*

Hot fudge sundaes waited for them back at the church. No one needed encouragement to dig in. Jordan and Skye sat opposite each other at one of the long tables. Although they sat among several teens, the numbers didn't lessen the sense of intimacy between them. Several times she found Jordan watching her curiously, but she avoided his gaze, joking with the kids around her instead.

Jordan finished his ice cream and pushed the bowl aside.

"You're not done, are you?" Skye asked incredulously. Jordan had eaten the vanilla ice cream but had left the chocolate syrup. Not waiting for his answer, she took his bowl and poured the chocolate over her ice cream. "I know, I know," she joked, "once on the lips, forever on the hips. But I'm going to splurge. I have a weakness for chocolate."

Jordan's smile seemed to reach out and touch her. "I have a weakness, too," he admitted, his eyes focused on her full mouth. "But my weakness lies in the area of blue-eyed blondes who sing like angels and hide cash from muggers in their shoes."

Her thick lashes quickly veiled her reaction, but his words brought a curious sensation to her heart.

Before she could find a witty comment to trade with him, the tables and chairs began to vibrate. Bowls of ice cream shimmied across the tabletop.

Someone yelled, "Earthquake." But no one moved, each paralyzed, their eyes filled with panic.

Skye had experienced several minor earthquakes in her lifetime, but nothing that seemed to be this strong. The crucifix suspended from the ceiling by two wires swayed as the room rocked. Several bowls had reached the end of the table and were ready to crash to the floor. Skye jerked herself upright to catch them, but in the rush lost her footing. She felt herself fall, the floor rushing up to meet her. Everything went black, although she was conscious.

Then it was over; everything was still. She remained frozen until she was roughly jerked into Jordan's arms.

"Dear God," he moaned into her hair, "are you all right?" Skye didn't care that his cast was biting unmercifully into her ribs. She clung to him as the only solid thing in a reeling world.

People began to move around; some of the girls were crying, still caught in the terror.

"I'm okay." Her first breaths came in gasps. "I must have hit my head. Everything went black for a couple of seconds, but I'm okay now."

Jordan's look burned her, his eyes a brilliant shade of silver. Urgently his hand pushed the hair away from her face, as if needing some reassurance she wasn't injured.

Besides the fright, no one had been hurt, and what had seemed an eternity wasn't any more than a few seconds—less than a minute, although it had seemed much longer.

In the aftermath everyone started to speak at once. Someone started singing a chorus of praise and thanksgiving, others joined, and soon the whole group was lifting their voices in gratitude to God. Everyone except Jordan, who remained detached.

Silently they rode home in her car. He had hardly spoken

since the quake. The radio was full of the news, stating that the quake had originated miles away, as was often, fortunately, the case.

Sitting beside him, Skye could see that his mouth was tight. She parked the car and turned off the engine.

"Are you sure you're all right?" he asked again gruffly. He didn't look at her; his profile, bathed in the moonlight, showed his jaw to be flexing.

"I'm fine," she insisted shakily.

Jordan expelled his breath forcefully. "Thank God."

"Yes, I do! Thank Him, that is." That Jordan should be so affected by what had happened brought an odd, breathless quality to her voice. She paused, unsure why she was asking him the question. "Would it have mattered to you if I'd been hurt?" Perhaps she needed assurance that this magnetic attraction was mutual.

His laugh was harsh. "Yes, it matters."

A puzzled frown marred her expression. What was wrong? He had been acting strangely ever since the quake. "Jordan, why are you so angry?"

He was silent for so long, Skye wondered if he'd heard her. "Jordan?" she repeated.

When he did turn toward her, his eyes were as hard as forged iron. "Maybe I don't like the way I feel about you. Maybe I wished I could put you out of my mind and find someone who lived in the real world. You Christians, you think reading the Bible and mumbling a few prayers is going to solve everything."

His words were so unexpected, Skye drew her breath in sharply.

"Well, I think it's time you woke up, Pollyanna. You could have been killed tonight."

"So what!" she spat angrily. "That isn't the worst thing that could happen to me. I might have blocked Christ out of my life. I might never have known God's love." *Or yours,* she added silently. "But . . . but you're right about one thing, Jordan Kiley," she said, her voice wobbling. "Maybe it is time I woke up." Angrily she jerked open the car door.

"Skye." The grim authority in his voice stopped her. "I wouldn't, if I were you."

"May I remind you this is the real world. I'll do darn well as I please." With a quickness born of anger, she jerked herself upright, ready to slam the car door.

"Skye, please." His voice was an odd mixture of fury and pleading.

Unsure, she paused, taking several breaths to release the tension.

Both were silent for several minutes.

Finally Jordan opened his car door and stood. "Invite me in for coffee."

Numbly she nodded.

Neither of them was interested in coffee, although Skye made the pretense of putting water on to boil. "All I have is instant."

"Fine," he muttered.

She stood with her back to him in the kitchen waiting for the kettle to whistle. With her thoughts a jumbled mess, she didn't want to face Jordan, not yet.

Suddenly he was there, behind her. Skye could feel his breath stirring her hair; then his hand cupped her shoulder, pulling her against him. Weakly she submitted to the potency of his unspoken command. Silently she turned, her arms sliding around him, his chest a cushion where she could hear the ragged pounding of his heart. His fingers tunneled through her hair, molding her head against him.

"I didn't mean that," he said at last, his voice raspy.

She lifted her face, her eyes meeting his. She understood his message.

His finger lightly touched her lips before lifting her chin to meet his descending mouth. The kiss began gently and fleetingly but deepened until Jordan shuddered and firmly closed his mouth over hers. When his tongue outlined her lips, Skye groaned and moved away slightly. They were tampering with temptations beyond their strength.

"Skye," he groaned into her hair. "I think you better make us that coffee."

Still dazed, she blinked her round eyes.

"Would you like me to do it?" He brought down two mugs from the cupboard, more in command of his senses than she.

"I'll . . . I'll pour, thanks." She was composed by the time she brought their coffee into the living room. "Before I forget, Janey needs your address. She wants to write you a thank-you note. It was thoughtful of you to buy her such a nice gift."

"My pleasure." He took the pen and pad from the coffee table and scribbled a few lines in bold, even strokes.

"How much time do we have tomorrow before your date?" Jordan demanded, and frowned.

"All day, really." She wasn't looking forward to this blind date. "Sally said I should be ready around seven thirty."

He nodded, his brows knitting together in an expression of disapproval.

"Can we go sailing tomorrow?" She didn't want to end the evening with another argument and hoped to steer their conversation away from any unpleasantness. "Brad and I share ownership in a small twenty-one-foot sloop. I think you'll like it."

Jordan grinned and gave an approving nod. "As long as it's understood I'm the captain and you're the crew."

"Yes, sir." She saluted him enthusiastically.

"I'll tolerate no insubordination," he said crisply.

"None, sir."

A grin twitched at the corners of his mouth. "I could get to like this. All right, your first command is to walk me to the door and kiss me good night."

"Right away, sir." She did as he requested, and by the time Jordan left the only thing cool was their coffee.

"If I take the wings of the dawn, and settle in the uttermost parts of the sea, even there your hand will lead me and your right hand will hold me."

"What are you mumbling?" Jordan's words shot past her in the brisk wind.

"Nothing," she mumbled. Prying her hand loose from the mast, she gave him a tiny wave of reassurance, then grabbed hold again in a death grip.

Once the sails were up, the sailboat immediately keeled, and Skye fought the sensation she would fall overboard. "Dear Lord," she prayed, "just get me out of this *alive.*" Her mind whirled with the wind. All she needed to do now was tie off the sails in an eight-knot. But how does an eight-knot go? Every sailor's daughter knows how to tie something so simple. How could she have forgotten? Everything fell into place suddenly, and Skye sighed in relief.

She crawled on all fours back to Jordan in the cockpit, her heart in her throat.

He seemed to be finding her escapades amusing, and there was no disguising the laughter in his eyes.

"We've got a good brisk wind," he said as she lowered herself to safety.

"A brisk wind?" she said incredulously. "I've seen hurricanes of less force."

"I thought you said you were an experienced sailor." His eyes were beaming with a wicked, teasing light.

"It was only a slight exaggeration," Skye said, defending

herself. "I sailed with Brad and my father several times. I may even have managed to raise the sails once or twice, but never in winds like this."

Jordan laughed and motioned for her to join him. Skye went readily; fitting into his arms seemed to come naturally. Expertly Jordan maneuvered the helm through the open waters.

"What were you mumbling up there? You looked very intent."

Lifting a strand of wind-driven hair from her face, she laughed. "I was talking to God, reminding Him that He said His right hand would guide me. I felt I needed it up there."

Some of the amusement left his eyes. "Do you always talk to God?"

"Sure, that's what's known as prayer." She smiled absently, enjoying the sensation of slicing through the water. It freed her spirit and lifted her soul.

"You really believe in this Jesus stuff, don't you?" His expression was thoughtful as he met her gaze.

"With all my heart." Her look, more than her words, stated the depth of her faith. "Is it so difficult for you to believe Jesus is God's Son?"

Jordan was quiet, as if turning the question over in his mind. Skye could see he was uncomfortable. "From the evidence that exists, Christ lived on earth. Whether He was who He said He was is another matter."

"Not if you examine the facts." Skye didn't want to be pushy. She had learned long ago that Christ was a gentleman who didn't barge into someone's life. He came only when invited.

"I guess what I don't understand is that you all seem to think God is so good, but look at all the evil and bad things that happen."

"That is difficult, isn't it? I think one of the hardest things for me to accept as a Christian has been the belief that everything that happens to me is for my good."

Jordan gave a small unpleasant laugh. "Don't try to tell me that injuring Billy was doing the poor kid a favor."

"No, but you're missing an important point. God didn't cause Billy's accident. He did allow it to happen, but ultimately it will be for Billy's good. A Christian must see that in every situation."

"Good grief," he responded mockingly. "You really are a Pollyanna. Wasn't that her game? The glad game? Finding something good in every situation?"

Averting her face, Skye could feel a lump forming in her throat. "I guess it does sound childish to you, Jordan, but I've put absolute trust in my God, and I believe that whatever happens to me or those I love is for the best."

Jordan sighed, his look pensive. "Then I think we should agree to disagree."

A brooding unhappiness settled over Skye. How could their relationship continue if Jordan differed so strongly with her religious views? With an upward sweep of her lashes, Skye glanced at him. His dark gray eyes were masked and troubled. Skye yearned to reach out and touch him, to answer the doubts that plagued him. The need crescendoed until she thought she would weep with the agony of it. She wanted to trust God, longed for that intense faith that would lift her above her own doubts. Instead she sat beside him weary and fearful that she hadn't explained herself well. Unexpectedly the sun broke through the heavy clouds, offering promise. Skye's spirits soared; she needed a promise, something to hold on to until Jordan recognized the truth. Smiling, Skye turned her face heavenward in silent communication. She was ready to trust.

"Hey, how about a sandwich?" she asked, feeling the need to lighten the mood. "I'm starved."

Jordan's gaze swept slowly over her face. "All right, how about a ham on rye with mustard, mayo, and pickles?"

"Yes, sir," she responded with a twinkle in her eye. "One peanut butter and jelly coming up."

The sound of his amusement followed her as she went below.

The mood became more serious as their discussion continued on other subjects. Although their opinions varied, and they were just as prone to argue over something as agree, their differences were not so far removed. Except for one—God and a personal relationship with Him.

Jordan's knowledge of music surprised Skye, and she noted how he cleverly steered the conversation to her singing.

"You have a marvelous talent," he reminded her. "I'd like for you to reconsider my offer and let Dan Murphy listen to you."

Skye laughed and dismissed his offer with a shrug.

"You can be persistent, can't you? Singing for money would take all the fun out of it for me. Besides, I already am a professional."

His eyes widened curiously.

"Teacher," Skye added.

"Do you enjoy teaching that much?"

Dragging her fingertips along the surface of the water, Skye straightened. "There are days I wonder, but then I've always loved children, and teaching is what I do best."

"You actually enjoy children?" He made it sound like a character defect.

"I'm a teacher, I'd better," she told him adamantly. "I think the younger the better. It's difficult for me to watch Janey grow up. I see her developing into a young woman and it tears at my heart. I don't want her to become independent and self-reliant. In the beginning it was almost as if Janey were my own child. She's named after me, you know." Skye laughed at his expression. "Poor kid, getting stuck with an ordinary name like *Jane.*"

His eyes held hers with mocking reproof. "There's nothing plain about you. But if you're so keen on children, why don't you have one?"

"I will, if I marry."

"In case you haven't heard, a girl doesn't need to be married to have a baby," he countered quickly, some of the teasing gone from his voice.

"This girl does."

"I see. It's like choking down your vegetables before being allowed to sample the delights of dessert."

Her eyes fell, avoiding his. "If that's the way you want to look at marriage, then I guess so. Do you find marriage so objectionable?"

His facial muscles softened, and the smile he gave her was warm and gentle. "No. As a matter of fact, I agree with you. I wanted to get married once, but the lady was more interested in a career than in a family—or in committing herself to one man, for that matter."

The woman had been mad, Skye decided, to reject Jordan's love. "Do you still love her?" The question popped out before she had a chance to censor it. Just thinking Jordan loved another brought a sharp pain to her midsection.

"No. Whatever I felt for her died long ago."

Skye risked a glance at Jordan and relaxed.

"Do you still love him?" Jordan asked unexpectedly.

"Who?"

"The one you've been eating your heart out over."

Confused and unsure of how to respond, Skye looked away. "Yes, I guess I do."

Jordan's eyes became grim and cold, and Skye realized she couldn't leave it there. "He was killed in a car accident eight years ago." Her voice was tight yet soft, indicating the emotion the simple words had cost her.

Jordan's expression softened, followed by surfacing compassion. "I'm sorry."

Her smile was weak. "So am I."

An hour later they docked the sloop at the marina.

"What about tomorrow?" Jordan questioned as they strolled toward her apartment.

"There's church in the morning," she announced casually. "I'm singing with the choir. Would you like to come?"

"Yes, I would," he stated softly.

His response surprised her in more ways than one. She'd expected him to complain because of their limited time together. "Wonderful," she murmured. Willingly Skye turned into Jordan's arms the minute her apartment door was closed.

"Take this with you tonight," he mumbled huskily as he possessed her mouth. Her tender lips felt swollen under the force of his kiss, but it didn't seem to matter. She understood his hunger.

Chapter Eight

"I enjoyed myself." Steve King stood in the hallway outside Skye's apartment. His gaze freely roamed her face, and Skye could feel the color surface; she always felt uncomfortable when people stared at her so closely. They had left Sally and her husband, Andy, following dinner. It was clear Steve expected her to invite him in for coffee, but Skye hesitated pointedly.

"Thank you. I had a nice time, too." Despite the fact her thoughts had been with Jordan the entire evening, still they had managed to enjoy each other's company.

Contrary to what Skye had expected, Steve was tall and good looking in a homey, down-to-earth manner. His mustache was an umbrella over a droll smile. He displayed an inherent sensitivity Skye found lacking in other men; his smile was warm and genuine, his laugh easy. She might even have considered seeing him again if it hadn't been for Jordan.

"There's someone else, isn't there?" He returned her keys to her open palm after unlocking her door.

Skye's blue eyes widened. "Is it so obvious?" she asked, feeling a twinge of guilt. "I'm sorry, it must have been a dull evening for you."

"Quite the contrary," he assured her. "I thoroughly enjoyed myself. I guess I should have known a lovely blonde like you would be spoken for."

"A lovely blonde like me?" Her smile was negated by a disbelieving slant of her head. "I won't argue; you're certainly good for the ego."

The masculine line of his mouth curved into a pleasant smile. "I mean it. If things don't work out for you with this other fellow, give me a call. Andy has my number." His eyes grew serious. Very gently he placed a fleeting kiss upon her unsuspecting lips before adding, "I'm very interested. Whoever he is, he's a lucky man." He opened the apartment door for her and retreated.

"Good night . . . Steve." She faltered slightly over his name. "And thanks again."

He turned and gave a friendly wave. "Good-bye, Skye." He spoke conclusively, as if he was aware he wouldn't be seeing her again.

The morning sky was a pale blue. The early-morning fog had dissipated, and the sun shone brightly. A thick covering of rich green leaves was making its appearance on the trees that lined the streets. Skye was up and dressed long before it was time to leave for church. She chose her outfit with care, having saved the powder-blue suit for a special occasion. And what could be more special than attending church with Jordan?

Her Bible lay on her nightstand, and she reached for it thoughtfully. If only she knew more, she chastised herself, maybe she could answer Jordan's questions intelligently and persuade him of the truth. A fragile smile formed. Did she consider herself more capable than the Holy Spirit? It was a ludicrous question. No, she had placed Jordan in God's hands;

now she must wait patiently and trust. It was an encouraging sign that he was willing to attend church with her.

She met Jordan outside at the steps of the church. Again Skye was struck by his basic masculine appeal. The dark suit fit him superbly, accentuating his wide shoulders and tapering to his slim waist and hips.

His eyes followed her as she approached, his gaze as appreciative as hers was of him. Skye felt elegant today, like a princess in a fairy tale. Certainly nothing to rival Carin Cain, the model she had attempted to imitate that first night with Jordan, but lovely in her own way. The thought crossed her mind that if she didn't strive for inner beauty as diligently as outer beauty, she would soon be vain.

Jordan's arm cupped her elbow possessively when they met. "Did you have a good time last night?" he greeted, his gaze probing hers.

"It was marvelous, just marvelous," she said, sighing, then giggled at the flint hardness that stole into his eyes. "Steve turned out to be a very nice gentleman, but I think I must have been rotten company, since my thoughts were with you. In fact—" She smiled broadly. "—it was so obvious, he told me you're a lucky man." Tilting her head and patting her hair, she continued, "And in this new outfit I tend to agree with him."

Jordan laughed, but then his expression grew sober. "You won't see him again." It wasn't a suggestion but a statement of fact.

Without argument she nodded and turned her attention to others who were beginning to file into the church. When she happened to glance up, she found Jordan watching her with a look of unbelievable tenderness.

"I have an irrepressible desire to throw good taste to the wind and startle these churchgoers by kissing the living daylights out of you."

A flood of color flushed her face, but her eyes shone with happiness. Jordan's gaze became obsessively attached to her lips.

The attraction between them was volatile, and, flirting with danger, Skye provocatively outlined the shape of her lips with the tip of her tongue.

Jordan paled, his gaze pinning hers. "Stop it, Skye," he murmured under his breath fiercely. Their eyes remained locked until Skye lowered her gaze.

It was unlike her to flirt quite so openly, but before she could consider her actions, Jordan's hand slipped around her waist, and they entered the church together.

The interior of the building was decorated with lilies, which surrounded the altar. A large flowing banner was suspended from the rafters behind the altar. Its announcement—he lives—was a reminder of the Easter season just passed.

Skye sat with the members of the choir in the front of the congregation and to the left of the altar.

The choir number was scheduled midway through the service, before the pastor's message. Skye was in the front row and stepped forward before the choir for her solo. Slightly nervous, she felt her stomach twitch with the first few notes, but as the song progressed she gained confidence, and her strong, clear voice rang through the church with a richness and clarity that was breathtaking. Her versatile voice had a three-octave range, and the difficulty of the musical score called upon the full range of her ability.

When the vocal presentation was finished, a hushed awe filled the church. As was the custom there was no applause, which suited Skye. If there were any appreciation for her talent, the praise should be directed to her Creator; He was the One who deserved the glory, not she.

Brad and his family found Skye and Jordan on the steps of the church after the service. The two men shook hands and chatted easily. Peggy winked at Skye knowingly while Janey skipped blithely up and down the stairs with her friends.

"It's good to see you, Jordan." Brad's arm was draped around Peggy's shoulders, holding her protectively close to his side. His smile fell on Skye. "Mom would have been very proud to have heard you today. You were great. I can't recall a time you sounded better."

Skye blushed becomingly. "God and I thank you." In her heart, she recognized she'd been singing to Jordan. The song was one of joy at the freedom and new life offered through Christ.

"I've been trying to persuade this stubborn sister of yours to let a friend of mine in the music world listen to her, but Skye won't hear of it."

Skye cast a pleading glance to Brad, but he quickly ignored the silent appeal. "You should, sis."

Peggy's apologetic gaze met Skye's. "You two leave Skye alone. Let her make her own decisions."

Skye sighed, grateful for Peggy's intervention. "Yeah, you two, leave me alone," she remarked with a half smile.

The men spoke for several more minutes while Brad described his new job eagerly.

"Are you ready to go?" Jordan smiled at her.

"He's flying home this afternoon," Skye explained to her family.

"Did you get my letter?" Janey wanted to know, leaping three steps at once to land directly in front of Jordan.

"Sure did, cupcake." He used Skye's pet name for her niece. "I'm glad you and Sampson like his house so well."

They bid their farewells, and Skye promised to stop by Brad and Peggy's later for dinner.

The ride to the airport was quiet and serene. Jordan's arm rested possessively around her shoulder, and when he tenderly kissed her temple, Skye turned and smiled at him peacefully.

"Tired?" Her small yawn prompted the question.

"No, content." It was so right to feel his arms holding her securely. Though another separation was inevitable, none of the agonies she'd experienced with their first parting remained.

She felt Jordan's eyes rest on her thoughtfully, but didn't turn to intercept his gaze. Gently the pressure of his lips moved across her hair.

When the car and driver he'd hired pulled along the curb at the airport, the driver stepped out to attend to the luggage.

Jordan turned Skye to face him, and stared deep into her cobalt-blue eyes, the tenderness unmasked and bare. "We never did have our talk," he whispered. "There never seems to be enough time to say all the things we need to say." He paused. "I know it bothers you that I don't believe in God the same way you do. All I ask is that you be patient with me." With that he slowly drew her into his arms.

He'd asked her to be patient, and Skye realized that she'd wait until doomsday for this man. She trembled, anticipating his kiss, then savored the moment with all the longings of her soul. Jordan shuddered, his breathing ragged and barely controlled. He rested his forehead against hers, as if fighting for command of his senses.

"You go to my head," he murmured heavily, the warmth of his breath fanning her flushed face.

"Good thing," she whispered. "I'd hate to think I was feeling this way alone."

Again, he folded her tightly into his arms. "I'll phone Wednesday evening." His own voice was as shaky as hers.

"I'll be waiting." Suddenly she was free. She felt cold and dazed without his arms around her . . .

"How you doing, Sprout?" Playfully Skye ruffled the crop of short blond hair.

"All right, I guess," he said without enthusiasm.

"Aren't you feeling well?" Concern knitted her brow; Billy so seldom complained. This subdued behavior was very unlike the gregarious youth Skye had come to love and admire. "Are you going to tell me what's the matter?" Gently she began to stroke his head, as if to ease his discomfort.

Indecision moved over his young face. "I . . . I overheard my mom and Dr. Warren talking," he began shakily, close to tears. "They didn't know I could hear them. They thought I was asleep. Dr. Warren told Mom there may be a chance I could walk again, but I'll need this new kind of operation." A solitary tear escaped and slid from the corner of his eye onto the white pillowcase. Embarrassed, Billy fiercely wiped his eyes. "My mom needs me to take care of her. Ever since Dad left, she's been so unhappy. She used to cry all the time—she still cries—but she tries not to let me know. I don't want to walk just for me. I need to walk for Mom. I'll be able to look after her then, instead of her looking after me."

Billy's unselfish concern for his mother brought tears shimmering to Skye's eyes. "Then we must pray very hard, Billy. But most of all, we must believe Jesus loves you and your mother and He knows what's best for both of you. We must trust Him to do what's right."

"Will you pray with me?" he whispered, almost as if he were afraid prayers were a sign of weakness instead of strength.

"Of course I will, every night, if you want," she promised.

The troubled face relaxed.

"If you're able to have the surgery, would you like me to stay with your mother? We could wait and pray together for you." Billy's sense of duty was so strong toward his mother, Skye knew this would help him.

A smile brightened his face. "Would you?"

"Sure thing, Sprout," she promised.

Later that evening, after Skye had sung and entertained the children, Sally joined her in the nurses' lounge for a cup of coffee.

"Dr. Warren has begun some of the testing on Billy," Sally announced.

"And?" Skye couldn't disguise the concern that heavily laced her voice.

"Thus far, it looks favorable, but everything rests on Dr. Snell's opinion," Sally explained with tight-lipped anxiety. Elaborating on the details the operation would entail, Sally was interrupted by a volunteer.

"Skye, there's a call for you on line one." Joyce Kimball stuck her head around the door frame. "I had it transferred in here. You can use the phone on the countertop."

"Thanks, Joyce." Setting her cup on the table, Skye moved to the phone. "I wonder who would be phoning me here."

Sally slouched indolently and batted her eyelashes teasingly. "I bet it's Jordan Kiley. He's fallen for you, my dear girl."

"Hardly." Skye dismissed the thought with a wave of her hand and turned her back on Sally's wicked gleam.

"This is Skye Garvin," she said hesitatingly.

"Hello, blue eyes."

It was Jordan, and the tender affection in his voice brought a tingling sensation to the ends of her nerves. But before she could express her surprise, Jordan continued.

"Are you free tomorrow afternoon?" The question was abrupt, asked in a brisk voice.

"Yes." She moistened her suddenly dry lips. "I can't think of anything offhand. Why?"

"Good. I'll pick you up after school; wait there for me. I haven't time to explain now. I'll see you tomorrow." As quickly as the conversation had begun it was over. Skye turned back to Sally, her expression showing her confusion.

"Jordan?" Sally asked with a know-it-all attitude.

Skye nodded, deep in thought. "He's coming tomorrow but . . . but he didn't say why."

"This sounds serious to me," Sally teased, twitching her eyebrows.

Still thinking about the brief conversation, Skye didn't notice the dramatic scene Sally was enacting until she glanced upward to witness a paper towel draped over Sally's head as she slowly marched up an imaginary aisle, singing in her loudest voice the reprise to the wedding march.

"Here comes the bride . . . tall, skinny, and snide . . ." Before she could complete another witticism, Skye threw a pillow in her direction and burst into laughter.

The afternoon beams of sunlight filtered through the window of Skye's classroom. Looping a long strand of honey-colored hair behind her ear, she stood from her position on the floor with the children and stretched. A warm sensation grew within her at the beauty of the unspoiled day. With the warm weather the children were anxious to be outside and rose eagerly when the bell rang announcing the close of another day. Within minutes her classroom was empty as the children exploded onto the playground.

When Skye returned to her desk to straighten a few papers, she caught sight of Jordan through her windows, walking across the school grounds, weaving his way among the children. Unbidden, her senses clamored at the sight of him, and she recognized anew the depth of her feeling for this virile man. His face looked drawn and tired, as if something were weighing on his mind, but the look they exchanged when their eyes met was anything but jaded.

He entered her classroom, his smile warm and disturbing. "Why is it none of my teachers was ever this beautiful?" he murmured.

Skye smiled contentedly, standing to greet him.

"On second thought—" His hand cupped her face, and he peered into her eyes. "—I may never have completed school if you'd been around. It would have been too tempting to flunk."

Unable to resist the temptation, Skye planted a tiny kiss at the corner of his mouth. More and more, touching him, kissing him, loving him, was becoming second nature.

"Are you ready?" his controlled voice asked.

"In a minute." Reluctantly she broke from his arms and withdrew her purse from the bottom drawer of her desk. "Do I have time to freshen up? I'll only be a few minutes." Her fingers rose unconsciously to her colorless lips before running through the tangles of her long curls.

"I don't see why you need fresh lipstick. I'm going to kiss it off within minutes anyway," he teased, the corners of his mouth curved in amusement. "But take all the time you need."

When she joined him again, she found him leaning against her desk, glancing through her students' papers and their still-awkward attempts at letters and numbers. He straightened when she entered, but the drawn look was back in his eyes before he could mask it from her.

A feather-light kiss brushed her lips. "Mmm, that tasted good." His head drew back slightly to examine her trembling mouth. "I'll have another," he said, and with a diminutive chuckle, he tenderly folded her into his arms.

"How did you know where I taught?" Skye asked, still descending from the delight of his kiss. The question had troubled her all day. She was sure she'd never mentioned it.

"You told me at one time or another." He dismissed her question. "Or perhaps it was Billy."

She relaxed. Billy knew, of course. Yet she couldn't help feeling a little apprehensive. Jordan's call last night had haunted her most of the day, and looking at him now, she could see he was equally troubled.

"Where are we going?" They were halfway across the school yard before she thought to ask.

Placing an arm around her shoulder, he glanced at her questioning eyes. "That depends," he answered cryptically. "Why don't we go to your apartment first? We need to talk. We'll decide from there."

Skye glanced again at the uneasiness she'd read in his eyes. *He's going to ask me to marry him,* she thought, *and he's nervous.* An overwhelming surge of love rose within her. Just as she knew his question, she knew her answer. She loved Jordan, and she wanted one day when the time was right to have his children. Together they would build a meaningful life. The differences in their beliefs would work themselves out. He wasn't a committed believer yet, but Skye had to believe that he was searching and that one day he would be.

All at once she was as nervous as Jordan and chatted all the way to her apartment. She put water on the stove while Jordan remained in her living room. She studied his profile anxiously, waiting.

"Skye, let's talk."

Instantly she moved into the living room and sat opposite him, her heart pounding wildly. She felt like a young girl nervously anticipating her first kiss.

"Yes, Jordan."

In a lazy, withdrawn manner he studied her, the pause lengthening. Skye had seen him use that expression only once before, and then, unexpectedly, a feeling of dread came over her.

"I was happy to be in church with you last Sunday and listen to your music. It gave me an opportunity to record you without your knowledge. Dan Murphy listened to the tape and would like to offer you a recording contract."

In a hurt, confused action, Skye quickly averted her face. Closing her eyes to block the pain, she pressed her lips tightly together. It hurt that Jordan had gone against her wishes in such an underhanded way. She would never have believed him capable of something like this.

"I'm . . . I'm not interested." She wanted to scream it at him, but instead remained outwardly calm and composed. Suddenly the living room became claustrophobic, and she jerked herself upright and stood before the bay window.

Jordan followed. "I don't think you understand what you're refusing." His gaze flickered over her as she stood, her back stiff and erect. "You've got it, Skye. Talent. Beauty. Appeal. You're superstar material, and I'll back you every way I can."

Skye looked at him with a sickening kind of disbelief and hugged her stomach, needing the warmth and protection her arms provided. Hanging her head, a numbness stole over her. And she'd thought he was going to ask her to be his wife. It was almost worth laughing over.

Jordan reached out to touch her, but she roughly pulled away, her indomitable pride taking over. "Please, don't touch me," she said, anger wobbling her voice. "What's in it for you, Jordan? Twenty percent?" she asked contemptuously.

The muscles along the sides of his jaw tightened and jerked. "That's enough," he returned.

"You're wrong. It's not nearly enough." Remaining another second in his presence was more than she could bear. "I think it's time you left." She could hear Jordan behind her and was caught by her arm and turned around so she had no choice but to face him.

"Skye, listen to me," he ground out.

Frantically she struggled against him, but it was useless to struggle; he held her helpless for several minutes until the wild, crazy tempo of their hearts returned to a normal pace. Only then did his grip slacken, but he still didn't release her. His fingers combed through her hair, easing it away from her face.

He cupped her face, drawing it upward, but she stubbornly refused to meet his gaze. "I wouldn't hurt you for the world. Skye, I love you."

Swallowing the painful lump in her throat halted her cry of disbelief. The heightened color of her face swiftly drained, leaving her deathly pale. From somewhere her proud anger responded.

"Sure you do." Her voice was thick with sarcasm. His lie slashed deep into her already wounded heart. Was he so desperate that he would go to any length to have her sign a contract?

"I deserve that." He laughed bitterly. "I don't blame you for doubting." His thumb moved slowly across her cheek. "Answer me one thing. Do you honestly believe I'd take advantage of you?" The lack of emotion in his voice gave his question all the more significance.

Her instincts told her she could trust him with her life, but logically she couldn't dismiss his repeated insistence that she become a professional singer. Unable to find the words to answer him and equally unable to trust herself to look into his eyes, she turned her face away.

Swiftly he brought it back, the steel gray of his eyes pinning her. "I had to know," he ground out angrily. "I didn't mean to fall in love with you. You crashed into my life with a force that sent me reeling. At first you were just a challenge—the girl with the witty façade who was hiding from the real world. But the more I came to know you, the more I realized that you were everything good I've ever dreamed a woman could be." His fingers dug into her shoulders. "Don't you know what it cost me to make that offer? I had to be sure. Can't you see that? I want a wife, not a career woman yearning after the glamour and glitter of footlights."

Risking a glance, and yet afraid to believe the fragile hope stirring within her, Skye found his dark gray eyes gleaming with intensity.

"You love me?" she whispered, unsure of anything at the moment.

"More than I thought it was possible to love anyone," he expelled with a shuddering breath.

Her lips trembled, and she bowed her head weakly to shield her eyes. "I want to believe you, Jordan," she whispered huskily. "I love you, too."

The response for each was as automatic as breathing, and Skye was crushed against the steel hardness of his torso.

Against her mouth, Jordan murmured, "Trust me, my love."

"I want to," she admitted, and her voice cracked.

Framing her face with his hands, he raised her eyes upward. "I need you, Skye. My world would be a dark hole without you now." He paused, a smile forming at the grooves of his mouth. "Who would have ever thought a funny little girl who hides cash in her shoes would steal my heart so completely? Skye Garvin, will you be my wife now and for all our lives?"

Wide blue eyes stared at him with all the yearnings of her heart. "I . . . I don't know . . ." Somehow the words wouldn't form. It was what she wanted with all her heart. Why was she hesitating?

Dark furrows ran across Jordan's forehead, drawing his brows together. Suddenly the reality of his love confronted her, and with a happy laugh she threw her arms around his neck, hugging him close.

"Yes," she said joyfully. As the excitement began to diminish, her expression turned serious. "It would be the greatest honor of my life to be your wife and bear your children."

Locked in his arms, Skye surrendered as he hungrily sought her lips, parting them with a desperate need.

A burning question remained unanswered. Skye ended the kiss. "Jordan, what would you have done if I'd agreed to sign the contract?" Her voice reflected the importance of the question.

Jordan cupped her chin. Indecision danced across his face, twisting his mouth into a cynical mask. "Exactly as I said. I'd have done everything in my power to make you into the superstar you have every possibility of being." He lowered himself onto the sofa; then his muscular arm circled her waist and he drew her onto his lap. Skye looped her arms around his neck, urging his mouth to hers. The moment was tender and serene, each of them absorbed in the magnificent gift of love God had granted them.

"I want to tell you about Glen," Skye whispered tautly, resting her head against his shoulder.

She didn't need to explain who Glen was; Jordan knew. His fingers began a comforting, stroking action down the length of her hair. "You don't need to tell me."

"But I want you to know." She sighed softly. "Glen was a wonderful Christian man. Dedicated, sincere, gentle, everything a woman could want. We fell in love when I was fifteen and he was twenty-one."

Skye could feel Jordan tense, the muscles of his jaw constricted. "You were hardly more than a child. You couldn't possibly have been in love." He dismissed her claim.

Tenderly her hand explored his jaw, caressing and gentle. This would be as difficult for him as it was for her. But it needed to be said.

"We knew. Brad and Glen were best friends, and Glen was always around. Neither of us openly acknowledged our love back then, but we knew. Without a spoken word Glen waited for me to grow up. I know he suffered wretchedly through my first dates and the junior and senior proms. But he need never have doubted. In my heart there was only him. I never considered marrying anyone else. The day I graduated from high school he gave me an engagement ring. I think Mom and Dad were shocked; as far as they knew Glen and I had never so much as dated. Neither of us wanted a long engagement, but my parents insisted I attend a year of college first. The request didn't bother us. We had our whole lives ahead of us. Then Glen decided to enter the ministry and enrolled in a Bible institute back east. We planned to marry the summer before he left, but my dad was having health problems, so we decided to wait until that Christmas." Unexpectedly her voice throbbed with remembered pain. "I . . . I never saw him again."

"Don't tell me, Skye." Jordan kissed her hair ever so gently. "I don't need to know."

"I want you to know." She smiled, loving him with a ferocity that paled in comparison with the love she had lost so many years before.

"About the time Glen began his studies, the doctors discovered my father had cancer. It was agony to witness this robust man waste away. I sat with Dad at the hospital for hours, reading him Scripture, holding his hand, anything to lessen the pain. Dad had always liked to hear me sing, so I started bringing my guitar. I played and created songs to amuse him. Then . . . then we learned Glen had been killed. He was driving home. He'd . . . he'd decided he was needed here in San Francisco with me . . . the car skidded on an icy patch in the road and Glen was killed instantly. Afterward my music was the only thing that kept me sane. I spent hours alone singing out my grief. Up to this time my voice had been normal, nothing spectacular. But it changed. As Dad got worse, I played more and more. Dying was agony. But death came sweet, gentle, and welcome. My new voice was God's gift. I could never exploit this talent. Since that time I've always used it as a means of bringing solace to others or to praise God."

Jordan's eyes filled with compassion as he viewed the tears that made wet paths down her cheeks. Carefully he brushed the hair from her damp face and tenderly kissed away each tear.

Chapter Nine

"Are you sure you don't mind?" Sally's eyes studied Skye.

"Of course not. I love Anne Marie," Skye quickly assured her, doing her best to conceal a smile of pure delight at having the baby for the evening.

"We shouldn't be late, and she'll probably sleep the whole time." Carefully Sally placed the sleeping infant inside the play-pen that was serving as a substitute crib.

"It's fine, Sally, don't worry. Even if she does wake, I won't mind. I don't see enough of Anne Marie as it is." Her warm blue eyes shifted from the slumbering babe to Sally.

"Jordan's not coming, is he?" Again Sally voiced her concern.

"No, but he'll probably phone. He does every night. You and Andy go and have a good time. Be sure and tell Andy I expect him to get this promotion."

"The phone number of the restaurant is in the diaper bag. Please don't hesitate to call if you need to."

"Yes, little mother." Skye mockingly rolled her eyes and eased Sally toward the front door.

"If she does wake, just warm her bottle and feed her. She'll go right back to sleep."

"Yes, Sally! You've already gone over everything at least twice." Opening the door, Skye ushered her into the hall. "I have your phone number, the doctor's phone number, the fire department's phone number, and on the off chance I spot a UFO, I have a phone number for them, too." The corners of her mouth turned upward in a teasing motion.

Sally giggled instantly. "I guess I am making a bit of a fuss. I really appreciate your taking over at the last minute like this. I don't know what we would have done."

"Nonsense," Skye said, dismissing the gratitude. "Didn't you say Andy was waiting in the car? Now scat." She grinned and shooed her friend away.

"All right, I'm out of here. We do appreciate it, Skye, more than words can say."

"Have a good time, and don't worry about Anne Marie."

"We won't," Sally promised.

Locking the door behind her, Skye tiptoed to the sleeping baby. Brown wisps of naturally curly hair framed angelic features. Sighing contentedly, Skye gently tugged the blankets around Anne Marie.

The two weeks had passed slowly. Jordan had been busy and unable to visit. Their only communication had been the daily phone calls, and these were often short, leaving them both frustrated.

Skye hadn't even been able to ask Jordan about a ring, and she wasn't sure how to broach the subject. There seemed to be so much to say and so little time to discuss the things that mattered.

She hadn't mentioned Jordan's marriage proposal to her family. She'd rather they did it together, not that it was going to be any big surprise. Skye could no more hide her love for Jordan now than Peggy could disguise her pregnancy.

She curled up on the sofa reading. It was quiet, peacefully so, especially since John Dirkson had moved. Yet her mind raced with a thousand anxieties. Dr. Snell had been to the hospital to examine Billy, and the surgery looked promising. But the strain of the unknown, the intense desire to do everything possible to help Billy and his mother, brought a worried frown to her forehead. Betty Fisher had been edgy under the strain of the uncertainty, relying more and more on Skye for support and comfort. These were the things Skye wanted to share with Jordan. She needed to express her own doubts and fears. She prayed continually for Billy and the success of the surgery, but her own burning desire to have Billy free from paralysis blocked her will from submission. She recalled the last painful days of her father's life and the desperate desire for his healing. He was healed, of course, but not in the way Skye had hoped. It was little comfort to a grieving daughter to realize her father was free from pain and cancer in heaven.

Thoughts of her father brought to mind something he had told her years before. With a burst of energy she crafted a bright, colorful sign that read:

WORRY
SERVES NO USEFUL PURPOSE
IS OF NO VALUE
AND DOESN'T CHANGE A THING.

With a revived sense of serenity she taped the sign to her refrigerator door, knowing she would see it often and be reminded of her father's wisdom.

Feeling as if a weight had been lifted from her shoulders, Skye placed the kettle on the stove to boil. She'd just finished adding the tea bag to the boiling water when Anne Marie woke. She was startled by the strange surroundings and the unfamiliar face and gave a loud cry of alarm. Gently cooing reassurances, Skye lifted the babe from the playpen and placed her over her shoulder. Patting her back, Skye hoped to urge her to sleep. While pacing the floor, Skye happened to glance out her window and observed a black car pull alongside the curb. Smoothly Jordan swung open the door and glanced toward her window, catching her eye.

A warm tingle of excitement raced through Skye, and she waved, her whole face brightening. Jordan hadn't figured on another visit until the end of the week, but nothing he did surprised her anymore. His job at the radio station, although he rarely spoke of it, was demanding and time consuming. She had learned their time together must revolve around his schedule.

Noticing the baby in Skye's arms, Jordan cast her a skeptical glance. Skye watched as his expression changed from puzzlement to one of amusement. The lines at the corners of his eyes broke into smiling crow's-feet as he moved from her sight and into the building.

Skye was waiting for him with the door open, her smile one of welcome and pleasure.

"You surprised me . . . It's good to see you." That was a gross understatement. Her heart beat urgently, anticipating his firm kiss. She wasn't disappointed. He closed the door with his foot and claimed possession of her mouth. Even with the baby in her arms, her pliant body bent toward him, yielding to his kiss.

"That alone was worth the hassle of getting to you tonight," he said, his voice low and disturbed.

Dazed and happy, Skye blinked her liquid blue eyes. She was forced to draw her attention back to the baby, who began to fuss in earnest.

"Anne Marie Avery, daughter of Sally Avery." She laid the crying baby on her arm for Jordan's inspection. "I would like to introduce you to the man I love, Jordan Kiley."

Anne Marie cried furiously, her reddened face twisting angrily while tears rolled from her squinted eyes.

"She doesn't seem to be impressed." Jordan shrugged, studying her.

"Give her time," Skye teased. "She hasn't woken up enough to appreciate your obvious male charm."

Anne Marie screamed at fever pitch and kicked with all the strength of her eight-month-old limbs, fighting Skye's attempts to change her diaper.

"What's wrong with her?" Out of his element, concern laced Jordan's voice.

"Nothing a dry diaper and warm bottle won't cure," she assured him, bringing a bottle from the supplies Sally had left. "Here, warm this; there's hot water in the kitchen. Just set the bottle in a bowl and surround it with the water."

In her dry diaper, Anne Marie's cries were no less frenzied. Jordan returned looking slightly unnerved. The room went from blustering cries to restful silence as soon as the bottle was placed in the baby's mouth.

Jordan sighed in relief and relaxed his lengthy frame in the chair.

"You look like you could use a cup of coffee," Skye said, watching Anne Marie greedily suck at the bottle. When she glanced up a few seconds later, she found Jordan's gaze lingering on her. His eyes were narrowed, expressing uncertainty, perhaps hesitation.

"Jordan, is something wrong?" she asked in a whisper.

His eyes cleared immediately. "No, I was just watching Anne Marie and seeing how very right you look with a baby in your arms." His look was tender. "We'll have beautiful children."

Their children . . . their child. A lump of wonder and joy blocked her throat. The deep womanly desire to bear children was one she had ignored for eight years; now it surfaced, and the longing to hold her own child swelled within her. Jordan was right; their children would be beautiful. God willing they would be dark, like Jordan, but their eyes a striking contrast of deep blue.

"Do you want a cup of tea?" he asked, breaking into her thoughts.

"I have one. It's sitting on the countertop in the kitchen, but it's probably lukewarm by now."

The time he was gone gave Skye a chance to gather her thoughts. Children were something they had barely discussed, and there were so many other things they needed to know about each other. Perhaps Jordan would prefer to wait a few years before starting a family. It was another question to add to the long list.

Anne Marie finished the bottle; her eyes closed, and she fell more than half asleep. When Skye gently withdrew the nipple from her lips, her tiny mouth continued the sucking action. She placed the baby over her shoulder and urged her to burp by rubbing her arched back in gentle, circular movements. The release came, and Skye placed her inside the playpen, covering her with one of the blankets.

Jordan returned with their steaming drinks.

"She's asleep," Skye whispered, accepting the cup he handed her.

By silent agreement, they sat together on the sofa.

"Have you missed me?" Jordan asked with a coaxing smile.

She studied the steaming cup of tea. "You know I have," she admitted freely. When he placed his arm around her shoulder she snuggled closer to his side. A contented happiness stole over her as his body pressed close to hers.

"Then I won't mind admitting how frustrated I've been these past two weeks." The words were issued in mild exasperation.

Shifting her position slightly, she slid her arms around his middle and rested her head on the firm hardness of his shoulder.

The gentle caress of his hand against her hair was comforting and at the same time arousing.

"What's worrying you, Skye?" Jordan asked quietly. The pressure of his lips touched the crown of her head. "The last few times we've talked, I've felt you were holding something back. It's the most frustrating thing in the world to hear your voice and realize you need me there. Won't you tell me what it is, sweetheart?"

A silence followed. Skye longed to tell him, pour out her doubts and fears, but she was afraid . . . afraid if he saw her lack of faith, it would hinder Jordan's budding awareness of God. Dare she bare her soul again? She had left herself exposed, and there was nothing left she could disguise from him any longer. Telling Jordan about Glen had left her naked, her heart, her mind, her soul.

"What . . . what makes you think anything is wrong?" she asked, her back stiffening slightly.

She could feel his smile against her hair. "Other than the sign on your refrigerator door, I'd say it was the hesitation and fear I sense in your voice."

Her arms tightened around his midsection, and she raised her face to look into the warm vibrancy of his eyes. Her fingers crept to his face, stroking the rugged jaw she had come to love so much.

"It's Billy," she whispered achingly. "His surgery is Monday morning. His whole life rests on the results." Her voice trembled slightly. "I'm so afraid. Does that make me sound like a terrible Christian?"

"No," he assured her softly, "it makes you sound very human."

"I am human, Jordan, and so weak. Billy's mother needs

me to be strong, she's so alone and frightened. I feel like such a phony spouting off assurances when I am really a quivering mass of doubts myself."

Jordan's arms tightened about her. "My dear, sweet Pollyanna, when will you learn you can't carry the world on your shoulders?"

"I don't know that I ever will. It seems worrying is a part of my nature, but I hate it. Sometimes I see myself as spiritually strong, and I confidently want God's will for Billy no matter what. But I don't have the faith to honestly trust God with Billy's fate. I want him to walk and run and play like a normal ten-year-old. That's the whole crux of the matter—*my* wants."

Jordan's finger lifted her chin as he gazed into her troubled eyes. "But don't you think that's what Christ wants? I'm confident Billy is going to be fine no matter what the outcome of the surgery. As for recognizing our lack of faith, that's good, too, because then we must rely on God, and that's what He wants."

Skye searched his eyes. This was Jordan speaking? This was the same man who had told her she was playing a Pollyanna game and wished to agree to disagree on spiritual matters? She immediately wanted to question him, but hesitated. Trusting Christ was new to him, and she didn't want to rush his faith or make him uncomfortable.

"What time is the surgery Monday?" he asked.

"First thing. Betty and I are meeting at the hospital at six. Sally and a couple of other nurses are planning to come later."

"I've got a conference Monday morning," he muttered, frowning. "What are Billy's chances for a complete recovery?"

"I . . . I'm not sure, but Dr. Snell told Betty there's a fifty-fifty chance he'll regain the use of his legs. But he also said there will be months of physical therapy, if not years. This is not some miracle cure, nor is it a simple procedure that's going to make everything hunky-dory. Even if everything goes according to plan, it'll be weeks before Billy can even attempt walking."

Jordan's fingers laced through the long strands of her honey-colored hair. "Would you like me to be with you Monday?"

"Oh, Jordan, yes. But your meeting . . . ?" She couldn't hide her desire to have him with her. She needed him; for the first time in eight years, she desperately needed someone to share her fears. Just knowing he would make the effort to come brought an indescribable peace.

"I can't guarantee it, Skye, but I'll try."

"I know you will." She'd been so preoccupied with her own worries, she suddenly broke contact with him. "Jordan, I'm sorry. Are you hungry? I didn't even think to ask. How about a sandwich?"

"Dessert?" His teasing eyes questioned.

"I have some peanut butter cookies," she said with a laugh.

"Cookies," Jordan said distastefully. "What kind of dessert is that?"

Skye blushed briefly. "The only kind you're going to get until things are . . . official?"

His gaze grew warm and possessive, and he reached inside his pocket and withdrew a small jeweler's box.

Skye's heartbeat tripped over itself as she accepted the package. Her blue eyes locked with his as she flipped open the plush velvet lid.

"It was my grandmother's," Jordan explained, his husky drawl a warm caress. "I had the jeweler clean it and adjust the size."

Glancing into the open box, Skye gasped with pleasure. A single diamond set in an intricate gold pattern sparkled back at her. It was beautiful, more beautiful than anything she had ever seen. Simple, yet elegant; antique in style, but unique. When she raised her gaze, Skye was speechless.

"I knew you'd like it," Jordan said simply. He took the box from her, removed the ring, and slipped it onto her finger.

Skye blinked through the wall of tears. "I've never seen a more beautiful engagement ring," she mumbled ardently, her voice weak with suppressed emotion.

Jordan watched her intently, his look almost physical. In the next moment Skye was crushed against his chest. His mouth settled over hers, taking freely of her softness in a devouring kiss.

"Skye," he whispered achingly, "this had better be a short engagement. I'm not going to be able to keep my hands off you much longer." His mouth burned hers in another passionate kiss.

Sliding her arms around his neck, she rested her head softly against his shoulder until their breathing had returned to normal. She raised herself slightly, turning his face toward her. "I want children. I don't want to wait to start a family." It was a crazy thing to say under the circumstances. Before questioning her actions, she opened her lips and kissed him hard and long.

Jordan moaned and broke the contact. "Unless you wish to start our family tonight, I suggest we stop this torture."

"Would you like a sandwich?" Skye asked apologetically. Her actions weren't helping either of them battle the temptations of their love.

"No, but fix me one anyway." Jordan helped her up and gave her rump a solid whack as she rose. "And no more teasing, understand?"

She nodded, her face a rosy hue. "But, Jordan, I wasn't teasing about wanting a family right away. I do want children."

His look darkened. "Skye," he said, his raw voice pleading with her, "fix me that sandwich."

Opening the refrigerator door, Skye scanned its contents for something appetizing. "Leftover roast beef okay?" She glanced toward Jordan.

"Fine." He was standing over the slumbering baby, his look warm and tender. "Do they always sleep this peacefully?" he asked, his voice startling Anne Marie, who woke with a feeble cry. Attempting to correct the damage, Jordan began whispering reassurances to her while casting a pleading look in Skye's direction.

Skye grinned at him, her eyes full of amusement. "You woke her, you take care of her."

The baby cried in earnest, and Skye laughed aloud at the frustrated, helpless look Jordan gave her.

"All right, all right." She set the sandwich makings on the countertop. "I'm coming."

The minute the baby was in her arms, the cries lessened. But it was obvious Anne Marie needed her diaper changed yet again; her blanket and her sleeper were moist and clammy.

"Can I help?" Jordan offered as Skye slid the safety pin through the gauze diaper.

"Give her your hand," Skye suggested as she snapped the legs of the sleeper together.

Jordan's gaze rushed over her skeptically before his hand smoothed the rumpled mass of her unruly curls. The taut muscles of his face relaxed as the baby cooed.

"For someone so little she has a good pair of lungs, doesn't she?" He bent forward again, and Anne Marie firmly gripped his little finger.

Both awake and alert, Anne Marie sat on Jordan's lap looking around curiously while Skye finished making the sandwich.

"I told you once she woke up she'd fall prey to your male charms. She hasn't been that content all night." She handed Jordan the sandwich and took Anne Marie.

"The kid's on her best behavior. She knows a prospective father when she sees one." He took a bite of the roast beef. "This is good."

"I'm on my best behavior, too," Skye joked. "I know a prospective husband when I see one."

They laughed, but when their eyes met, they locked, sharing promises they were both eager to collect.

Skye broke the contact first. "How did you know my ring size?" she asked. The ring fit her perfectly.

"I'm glad you reminded me." He pulled something from his pocket and extended his hand to her.

"What's this?"

"The ring I took the last time I was here. I needed to know your ring size and wanted to surprise you."

"Jordan," she said incredulously, "you didn't! Do you realize what you put me through? I knew the ring was on the kitchen countertop the last time you were here, and after you left it was missing." She flushed guiltily. "I couldn't think what might have happened to it. I've been looking everywhere."

A grimness settled over him. "I didn't think you'd miss it. I should have said something; I only meant to keep the ring a few days. As you know I got tied up and it's been two weeks. I can only imagine what you must have assumed. I would never steal from you, Skye."

"I know that," she said. "I've promised to be your wife, and with that commitment comes my trust. No matter what was missing, I would never believe you'd take anything from me."

A brooding look came over him. "You mean you trust me unquestioningly?"

Relaxing against the back of the chair, Skye gave him a full smile. "Always," she promised. "My faith came with my commitment to be your wife."

"I'm not worthy of this," he argued, setting his half-eaten sandwich aside.

Skye bounced Anne Marie on her lap, and the baby's glee filled the room. "It doesn't matter. I love you."

Jordan's sober voice contrasted with the playful sounds coming from the baby. "And I love you."

Standing, Skye transferred the baby to her hip. "I have something for you, too. It's not a diamond, but it comes from my heart." She left him momentarily, returning with a leather-bound book. "This was my father's. I want you to have it, Jordan."

He accepted the book, respectfully turning the pages. "It's his Bible." A troubled look darkened his face. "I can't accept this."

Skye didn't immediately speak. "After Glen was killed, my father tried to assure me God had another man for me. Bless his heart, it was little comfort then, particularly since I didn't want another man. I refused to believe him and built a wall around myself. If someone had told me even six months ago I would fall in love again, I wouldn't have believed them." She rushed on before he could stop her. "I owe you so much, Jordan. I don't think you'll ever realize how much. There's nothing I could give you that means more to me than this Bible, but I give it freely with all my love."

Anne Marie quieted as Skye laid her across her shoulder. Jordan's eyes burned with an intensity that seemed to reach out and touch her. The pressure of his hand brought her down beside him. He set the Bible aside and drew her into his arms. The taut muscle of his jaw flexed before relaxing. The kiss that followed was one of wonder, joy, and contentment; lovingly his hand remained to gently trace her face. "And with all my love, I accept." Tenderly she drew his hand from her face and kissed his palm, then rested against his shoulder in a comfortable and familiar position.

The alarm rang early the next morning. Skye groaned and buried her head beneath the pillow, attempting to escape the inevitability of rising to meet another day. Jordan had left only a few minutes before Sally and Andy had arrived for Anne Marie.

"Was Anne Marie good?" Sally had asked with a worried voice.

"Like an angel." Excitement burned within Skye; she could barely restrain the rush of words. "Jordan was by and . . ." But before she could explain further, Sally groaned.

"Oh, no, I knew something like this would happen. I'm so sorry, Skye, we ruined your evening."

Wordlessly Skye extended her hand, letting the sparkling diamond on her ring finger say it for her.

For the first time in all the years Skye had known her, Sally was speechless. "You're . . . engaged . . . Jordan . . . marrying?" she mumbled between gasps of amazement and undisguised delight.

"We've set the date for the last weekend in June, right after school lets out."

Impulsively Sally hugged her in a breath-denying squeeze. "I knew it the minute I saw Jordan Kiley. I said to myself, this is the man for Skye. I did, I really did. This calls for a celebration. Anyone for pizza?"

It was well past one before Skye went to bed, but her mind raced and she found herself unable to sleep. It had been hours since Jordan had returned to LA, but the lingering scent of his aftershave permeated the air, almost as if his presence had remained with her.

Skye had explained to Sally at least ten times that watching Anne Marie had been a blessing. Because of the baby's presence they were able to relax and talk, something that may have been denied them otherwise.

Now dressed and ready to face another busy school day, Skye downed a cup of orange juice while the contentment and excitement from the night before lingered.

Thick fog, so familiar to those in the Bay Area, misted the streets and clung to the earth. The weatherman forecast rain, and Skye pulled her new spring jacket from the closet. Folding it over her arm, something fell from the pocket—it was the uncanny fortune she had gotten the day she'd explored Chinatown with Billy and her niece. With a bubble of unsuppressed laughter she took the small slip of paper and threw it in the garbage. She had been undeniably silly to have allowed a fortune cookie to have troubled her. Her trust was in the Lord, none other. The flash of the diamond ring caught her eye, and she paused to look at it again. It was beautiful, incredibly so—a promise of love. She would never know a greater happiness than what she was experiencing this minute, she decided on her way out the door.

The whole day was like a teacher's dream. The children were well behaved, responding eagerly to the lesson plan and Skye's elated mood.

Betty Fisher was waiting for Skye in Billy's hospital room.

"Good afternoon, Sprout." Skye sat in the chair beside his bed. "Hello, Betty. Are we ready for the big day Monday?"

Billy nodded eagerly while his mother showed less enthusiasm.

"Dr. Warren asked me to come to his office this afternoon. He wants to go over the details of the surgery with me one last time. Could . . . could you go with me, Skye?" The hesitation in her voice showed that she really didn't want to ask, but her fear overrode her objections.

"I'll be happy to," Skye assured her quickly.

"Are you going to tell them, or do I get the privilege?" Sally asked as she strolled into the room, her eyes sparkling with mischief.

"I'll tell them," Skye said with a smile. "I think they're the only ones in the hospital who don't know." She cast a pointed stare at Sally, who feigned ignorance. "Billy, do you remember your old roommate, Mr. Kiley?"

"Of course he does," Sally interrupted impatiently. "Get to the good part. I've got to get back to work."

Laughing, Skye conformed to Sally's wishes. "Jordan and I are going to be married." She extended her hand to show Billy and Betty her ring.

Betty murmured her congratulations while Billy grinned with a know-it-all attitude. "I kinda knew you liked Mr. Kiley, Skye," Billy announced casually. "Every time you talked to him, your cheeks would get all red. Stacy McAlister's cheeks used to do the same thing when I was in school. That's how I knew she had a crush on me."

The three adults exchanged glances while Skye did exactly as Billy predicted.

Dr. Warren's office was within walking distance of the hospital.

"Do you want to wait out here, or do you want to come and talk to the doctor with me?" Betty questioned as they sat in the half-full waiting room.

"I'll stay out here," Skye whispered.

Betty immediately looked disappointed. "Okay," she nodded, putting on a brave front.

Skye was half tempted to change her mind, but she couldn't always be there for Betty to lean on, especially since she would be leaving San Francisco in June. No, it would be better if Betty started facing things on her own.

The nurse called Betty's name a few minutes later and she rose, sending Skye one last pleading glance. Skye winked, lending her emotional encouragement.

After Betty had left, she scanned through several magazines that lay on the end tables. An issue that was dated several months back caught her attention. The cover showed Carin

Cain's smiling face. Skye smiled secretly to herself. Of late she felt she owed the model a great debt. Flipping open the pages, she turned to the article and skimmed the contents that recounted the model's industrious career. The second page of the article showed several pictures. One in particular leaped from the page. It read: *Dan Murphy, well-known music magnate and longtime friend of Ms. Cain.*

Dan Murphy . . . Dan Murphy . . . Dan Murphy . . . the full-bearded man stared back at her while her mind screamed his name.

Her fingers trembled so badly, she thought she'd drop the magazine. A knot formed in her stomach and twisted painfully as she continued to stare at the picture. At first glance she wouldn't have known it was him; the full beard hid his features well. It was the piercing gray eyes staring back at her that betrayed him. The man she loved had lied to her.

Jordan Kiley was Dan Murphy.

Chapter Ten

Two nurses dressed in green surgical gowns briskly stepped across the family waiting area. Both women raised their eyes expectantly, only to be disappointed as the nurses walked through the room without pausing. It was too soon. They both knew it would be hours yet before they would receive word of Billy's condition, but they were looking for a miracle, anything to end the interminable waiting.

Billy had been wheeled on the long stretcher from his room to the surgical floor two hours before. Betty had broken into tears as she walked beside her son. Although drugged and woozy, Billy had attempted to assure his mother and sent a pleading glance toward Skye. But tears shimmered in her own eyes, and she looked away, unable to respond to his silent plea. Skye had wanted to be both supportive and encouraging to Betty, but her whole world had come crashing down on her and she was as desperately in need of emotional strength as Betty.

Now the two women sat together, yet very alone. Unable to boost each other's confidence, they didn't speak. Unable to comfort each other, they didn't touch. Unable to smile, they avoided looking at each other. The nervous uneasiness stretched between them to a fine, taut line.

As time progressed, every minute, every hour, became a battle waged against fear. Skye read her Bible, seeking solace, but the comforting words only skimmed the surface of her mind. The hurt of Jordan's deception blocked the comfort of God's words. She didn't know if Jordan was his name or if it was really Dan, and yet he was the man she had agreed to marry. A man she had insisted she could trust.

When a tall, blond-haired man entered the waiting area, Skye felt Betty stiffen.

"Bill." The name was wrenched from her in an outpouring of incredulity and relief. She sprang to her feet and locked her arms around him.

Skye recognized the stranger immediately. It could only be Billy's father. The sparkling blue eyes and broad forehead strongly resembled those of young Billy. Skye's throat constricted at the sight of the two entwined in each other's arms, tears streaming down their faces.

"I've been a fool. Can you forgive me?" he pleaded, his voice urgent. "I didn't know about the accident. I swear I'd have come home had I known."

Possessing a strength Skye would never have suspected, Betty calmly related the details of the accident and the events leading to the surgery. The fear that had sparked like electricity between them only a few minutes before was gone. This was what Betty needed to face the ordeal of Billy's surgery. Neither Skye nor anyone else could replace the presence of this man, her husband.

The scene was poignant and tender. The two needed privacy to speak, and after an awkward introduction Skye slipped unnoticed from the waiting room.

The small chapel was empty, she noticed gratefully. Here there could be no façade, and, staring into the distance, she allowed the acid tears to fall, burning her cheeks. She prayed again for Billy, her voice a hushed whisper, and for a long while afterward sat silently and meditatively.

"How could Jordan lie to me like that, Lord?" she asked as all the pain of his deception rushed forward. It was the same agonizing question she had uttered a thousand times during the past few days. It was ironic that he could have been so offended by her small deception and at the same time be grossly misleading her. From this point forward she knew she couldn't trust him or his love. With everything that had happened, she had to believe he'd offered marriage as a means of getting her to agree to sign a recording contract with his company. And all their talk about trust. Skye buried her face in her hands. If Jordan had any love for her at all, then he would have told her the truth.

How could she have been so wrong about him? Perhaps the hurt wouldn't be so intense if she hadn't bared her soul to him. The details of Glen's death that she'd shared had been a measurement of her love. Jordan couldn't possibly love her, she realized. Carrying the charade to this extreme proved his avowed love could only represent a shadow of what God meant their love to be.

After Glen and her father had died, Skye felt she would never again experience such deep emotional pain. Now she was forced to admit her error. No physical pain could possibly hurt this much. Straightening, she wiped her face dry and swallowed the lump in her throat. She knew what she must do.

The swish of air came from behind, indicating someone had entered the chapel. The tiny hairs at the base of her neck rose in recognition. It was Jordan. He had said he'd come, but Skye had half expected him to lie about that, too. She didn't turn around, wanting to delay seeing him as long as possible. The sound of each footstep advancing toward her was magnified a hundred times until Skye lowered her head to reduce the deafening noise. With her eyes shut tightly, she prayed for control and the strength to do what she must.

When Jordan sat beside her in the wooden pew, Skye jerked slightly with reaction. This was going to be worse than she'd imagined.

"I didn't mean to startle you," he whispered tenderly, and with familiar ease slipped his arm around her shoulder.

Skye couldn't tolerate his touch; it made things all the more impossible. Trembling, she broke the contact and stood shakily, her feet almost faltering as she left the chapel with him.

"We need to talk. Can we go someplace?" she asked breathlessly. Glancing briefly at him, she didn't quite meet his eyes.

Jordan's gaze made an appraising sweep of her face and the tiny lines of strain about her mouth. Her eyes held a troubled light.

"The cafeteria?" he questioned.

Skye nodded and led the way to the elevator, pushing the button to the basement floor. They made the descent silently, the only sound the almost indiscernible hum of the elevator. The large metal doors glided open and Skye stepped forward, walking directly into the cafeteria and finding a table while Jordan purchased two cups of coffee. Accepting the Styrofoam cup, Skye stared into the steaming liquid rather than meet Jordan's eyes.

"Are you that worried about Billy?" he asked suddenly, the charcoal gray of his eyes regarding her steadily.

"Not anymore." Her voice sounded shaky, and she was striving for a quiet firmness. "Billy's father came. I suppose you met him in the waiting room." She glanced briefly at Jordan. She wanted to memorize every line of his rugged features and at the same time erase his existence from her life.

"Jordan," she began shakily, clenching her drink with both hands and avoiding looking at him. "I have something important I need to tell you."

"Sure; what is it?" His hands gently cupped hers, his voice tender and concerned.

The hypocrisy of his concern gave her the courage to continue. "I've done some soul searching this weekend and . . ." She hesitated. Bile rose from her stomach, and for a moment she thought she might be sick.

"I've tried phoning several times. Where were you?"

She wanted to watch his reaction when she told him, but was incapable of looking higher than the knot of his tie. How silly it was to note how the dark blue silk sharply contrasted with the pale blue of his shirt. "The cemetery," she murmured, returning her gaze to her coffee cup.

Jordan removed the cup from her trembling fingers as her gaze followed his action. The finger lifting her chin brought her eyes level with his.

"What were you doing in a graveyard?" he asked, his voice tight and clipped.

"I had to talk to Glen," she said haltingly, her voice barely above a whisper.

His gaze narrowed, pinning her. "Glen is dead. You can't talk to a dead man."

"Glen is gone, I realize that," she said tightly, hoping he would see the subtle difference. "But his love for me is eternal, just as mine is for him." Rather than confront Jordan with what she'd learned, she'd decided to end it by putting forth an argument for which he had no response. She had no desire to listen to his explanations for fear they would only be more lies.

"Stop speaking of him as if he were a living, breathing person. The man's been dead and buried for eight years. It's time you owned up to that."

She ignored his words and spoke with a grim kind of calm. "I was kidding myself when I accepted your marriage proposal, Jordan. There will never be another man for me. I've heard of women who can only love one man in their lifetime. I didn't realize until this weekend that I was one of them."

When she glanced at him briefly she saw that the color had drained from his face.

"I'm sorry," she finished weakly.

"Yeah, sure. I bet you're real sorry." The aggression in his voice aroused the attention of others sitting nearby. Many stopped to stare at them curiously. Jordan ignored them. "I don't know what has gotten into you, Skye, but by heaven there had better be more explanation than this boloney." His hands gripped her wrists. "If what you say is true, then what was all that talk about wanting children?"

"I've always loved children. I guess it's only natural to want one of my own, but I could never desecrate Glen's love for me. I can't marry you, Jordan. I belong to Glen. I always will."

His eyes blasted her a look as frigid as the Arctic wind.

"I can't tell you how sorry I am," she whispered.

He released both her wrists at once, as if he found her touch repulsive. His face was rigid as though unwilling to show any emotion or reaction.

Skye could barely breathe, the tension mounting as the silence continued.

"Under the circumstances, I can't accept this," she said, sounding pitifully weak. She slid the ring from her finger and held it out to him.

An eternity passed before he accepted the diamond. His hand closed over the edge of the table, and he shoved his chair outward, jerking himself upright.

Skye watched him go, her breath so shallow it was almost nonexistent. Jordan weaved around the tables with long angry strides as if he couldn't remove himself from her fast enough. A second later he was out of sight and out of her life.

I should be grateful he's gone. I should consider myself fortunate that he's out of my life, her mind screamed, but her heart refused to listen.

"Heel, Sampson," Janey ordered, and without hesitation the dog returned to his mistress, his tail wagging and dark eyes eager to obey.

"Sit," she ordered next, and Sampson willingly complied, lowering his rump to the lush green grass.

"Good boy." Big, floppy ears waited for the petting and praise. Skye lowered herself beside the dog and Janey, who was now lying on her back examining the sky with a piece of grass clenched between her teeth.

"Are you two dog trainers ready for something cold to drink?" Peggy asked from the kitchen window.

"Bring some cookies, too," Janey instructed.

"Will do," Peggy agreed good-naturedly and joined the pair a few minutes later with a tray containing an iced pitcher, three glasses, and a plate of cookies.

"Have a cookie, Aunt Skye. They're chocolate chip and real yummy."

"No thanks, cupcake." Her appetite had been nonexistent for weeks. She ate only because it was a necessary part of life. As a result her willowy figure now bordered on gaunt, as Brad had pointedly remarked.

"When is Jordan coming to see you?" Blue eyes, miniature duplicates of her aunt's, waited for Skye's answer.

"He isn't," Skye said flatly, struggling to keep her voice steady.

"I thought Jordan was real nice. I liked him," Janey insisted before reaching for another cookie.

"I . . . I think he's nice, too," Skye agreed tautly.

"But I thought he was nice enough to be my uncle, and you said that . . ."

"That's enough, Janey," Peggy intervened sharply, watching Skye anxiously.

Skye smiled weakly in appreciation. She didn't want to think about Jordan or make further explanations; it only renewed the pain she was struggling to control.

"Janey, go inside and bring me my knitting." Peggy smiled gently at her daughter. "Thanks, sweetheart."

Janey bounced from her position on the grass with the fluid grace of a young fawn.

"Don't mind Janey," Peggy said, her voice suddenly sober. "She's been worried about you. We all have been. I wish things had worked out between you and Jordan. Janey doesn't mean any harm . . ."

Skye swiftly interrupted. "I don't mind, but I'm beginning to think the girl is ninety-five percent mother hen." The attempt at humor was accompanied by a feeble smile. Her thick lashes fluttered downward to hide the hurt and regret while her voice revealed everything. "I know it's difficult for you to understand, but it could never have worked between Jordan and me. There has to be a basic trust and honesty between couples—something sadly lacking in our relationship."

"But I can understand why he didn't want you to know the truth, especially in the beginning."

Why did Peggy have to defend him? She was experiencing so many doubts herself. It had been wrong to lie about loving Glen. Two wrongs didn't equal a right, but she'd been deeply hurt and assumed this was the best way to break the engagement.

"I do blame him," she said stiffly.

Peggy sighed, expelling her breath unevenly. "Brad found

out something yesterday I think you should know." She shifted uneasily, as if uncertain she should continue. "Jordan is responsible for Brad's job. Apparently the company owner is a friend of Jordan's, and he phoned, asking him to hire Brad. I'm glad Brad didn't find out right away. I'm sure he would have quit, but as it's turned out, the job is perfect for both sides. And I don't know what we would've done if Brad hadn't gone to work when he did. His self-worth, ego, and self-confidence couldn't take much more rejection."

A replica of a smile touched Skye's mouth. "I think I'd already guessed that. After we learned that Jordan was responsible for Billy's surgery and locating his father, there isn't anything that would surprise me."

Peggy defended him again. "His heart was in the right place. You have to admit that."

Skye's fingers curled around her glass of lemonade. "Perhaps. But Jordan was playing God. I don't think he would ever have learned to trust Christ with his life. His money could buy him anything he wanted. For that reason alone I know I did the right thing."

Peggy gave an exasperated sigh. "You're not making any sense."

Skye stood abruptly, impatiently. "Haven't you ever heard the Scripture about it being harder for a camel to go through the eye of the needle in one wall of Jerusalem than for a rich man to get into heaven? I think I fully understand what Christ was saying now."

Peggy's expression remained troubled as she regarded her sister-in-law. "How's Billy?"

Skye smiled, her first genuine smile of the day, a poignant catch in her voice. "He's doing terrific!"

During the past weeks Skye had carefully weaned herself from Billy. His progress had been phenomenal, and there was every indication he would walk again. Billy didn't need her anymore, and for her sake as much as his, she'd spaced her visits farther and farther apart. Whatever differences Bill and Betty had experienced before were working themselves out. From what she understood, they were working with a marriage counselor. For all Skye knew Jordan had his hand in that as well.

Skye changed into her jogging clothes once she was home. She ran more and more now, and a forty-mile week was not uncommon. Running dulled her senses until she was so exhausted, it didn't matter what thoughts her mind entertained. If anyone questioned her desire to pursue the sport, she explained that she was considering running a marathon. To prove her point she competed in the Bay to Breakers city run the third Sunday in May. She'd made respectable time, and was encouraged. At least running had helped her overcome the horrible apathy she'd experienced after last seeing Jordan.

The overcast skies didn't discourage her, and she set her pace, attacking San Francisco's hilly streets with a vengeance until her lungs burned and her calm muscles quivered. A loneliness beyond anything she'd ever experienced over all the years she'd lived alone came to prey on her mind. Before leaving Peggy's that afternoon, Janey had insisted on showing her the freshly painted bedroom being readied for the baby. Bright daffodil-yellow walls decorated with Disney characters met her. The bassinet was ready and filled with tiny sleepers and booties Peggy and Janey had lovingly prepared. Skye laughed and chatted for a few minutes, examining each piece while Janey beamed with pride. But as she left, walking across the street to her car, the tears came. They were a surprise then, and she quickly wiped them aside without Janey or Peggy noticing.

Now she understood. The reality hit her, hammering into her stomach. She would never marry. She would never bear a child. When she went to bed tonight and every night for the rest of her life she would be alone. There would be no Jordan with whom to share the intimate details of her life, no Jordan to listen to her silly songs. Her songs. She almost laughed. How very grateful she was to her music. It had been difficult in the beginning, when she'd felt bone-dry of any creative ability. All her efforts had been channeled toward presenting a cheerful façade. Now she was grateful for her time at the hospital; it helped fill the void. Sally had done her best to force Skye into the dating world and wanted to set up another date with Steve King, but Skye declined with the promise that she would, given time.

Completing her run, her lungs heaving, she slowed her pace to walk the remaining blocks to the apartment. The hot water of the shower soothed her upturned face, but not her heart. Without Jordan she would need to relinquish the deep womanly desire for a child. Peggy's rounding stomach was a knife twisting at her soul. The euphoric experience of being a mother would be denied her. She'd relinquished so much in her life, she thought bitterly: Glen, her father, Jordan, and now children.

She dressed and forced herself to eat half a sandwich. Although she had no desire to attend the Wednesday evening church service, she refused to allow any bitterness into her life. Her trust was in the Lord, she affirmed aloud.

Skye was grateful for one thing: Jordan had never returned her father's Bible. This was probably a subtle punishment that served its purpose in the beginning. Now she was glad he'd kept it. The time would come when he would be ready to accept Christ, and her father's Bible would be there. She prayed that when he read it he would remember her fondly.

For the most part, her anger at his deception was gone; the hurt remained deep and painful, but that, too, would pass with time. It would be very difficult to hate someone she prayed for, and she often found her prayers centering on Jordan.

The church was quiet and peaceful, offering solace. So much had transpired this day; emotions, awakenings, realizations. She wouldn't hide from her feelings again as she'd done after Glen and her father had died. Slipping into the wooden pew, she bowed her head in prayer. It was true she must relinquish Jordan and the desire for children, but the exchange was a fair one. Jordan had done so much for her, and she would always be grateful God had sent him into her life.

The pastor's words cut into her thoughts as the service began. The congregation sang a few choruses, and then Peggy and Brad slipped into the pew beside Skye. The Scripture lesson was on Matthew 19. Skye flipped open the pages of her Bible to the Gospel.

"Again I tell you," the pastor began, reading, "it is easier for a camel to go through a needle's eye than for a rich man to enter into God's kingdom."

Uneasily Skye felt her stomach begin to twist, and she sent Peggy a confused look.

Peggy shrugged, her eyes as perplexed as Skye's.

"To fully understand this verse," the pastor began to explain, "one must realize that the eye of a needle was the name of a gate, and it was possible for a camel to gain entrance, but first any cargo must be unloaded." He continued by making the comparison between the camel's cargo and our worldly goods. "Next the camel was forced to get down on his knees."

Skye's attention was pulled from the pastor as Brad began scribbling a note. Peggy intercepted it and added a message before handing it to Skye.

Speaking of going to my knees, would you take Janey this weekend? I want to be alone with my wife, the note read. Peggy's message was an added postscript. I hope you're listening to the pastor, and before you ask, no, I didn't have anything to do with his choice of topic.

Skye took her pen and scribbled a note back. *If you two don't quit writing notes in church, I'll report you to the elders. And yes, I'd love to have Janey.*

She rose early Saturday morning. She'd have to get her running in early since Brad was bringing Janey to her apartment around ten. She followed her normal course, which offered a variety of terrains: flat, steep, curvy. She managed the eight miles in less than an hour; rivulets of perspiration rolled off her body as she stepped into her building. She wiped the sweat from her cheekbones before stooping down to extract her key from a small compartment in the side of her shoe.

"Do you carry your whole purse in your shoe these days?"

The words struck her like a blow, depriving her lungs of oxygen. She straightened, slowly.

"Jordan," she managed. She wasn't ready to see him again; she needed time to school her reactions, to prepare herself.

He was dressed casually in dark corduroy pants and a charcoal-gray shirt that matched his eyes exactly. It was the first time she'd seen his left arm without the cast.

"Can I come in?" he asked. "Or will that defile your love for your dead boyfriend?"

Her back went rigid, her fists clenched tightly as she opened the door and stepped aside. Nervously she ran the back of her hand across her forehead before walking inside.

He followed her, closing the door. "I'm returning your father's Bible."

She nodded weakly. She'd rather he kept it, but to tell him that would reveal her love. Instead she mumbled, "Thank you."

He laid the Bible on the table in the entryway and hesitated before pulling an envelope from the Bible. "Your niece wrote me a very interesting letter."

She searched his face. "Yes, I know. She wanted to thank you for the doghouse."

"This didn't have a thing to do with the doghouse." He exhaled sharply. "She said you loved me." A muscle twitched in his jaw. "Is it true? Do you love me?"

Skye felt trapped. She couldn't lie to him, not again. "Yes." The lone word was wrenched from her.

"Why?" he demanded in a low growl. "Why did you lie?"

"You *lied* to me," she shouted. "I don't even know your name. Is it Jordan or Dan, Kiley or Murphy?" Her laugh was harsh.

He sighed wearily, the hard line of his mouth tightening. "Jordan Murphy. My mother's maiden name is Kiley. I gave the hospital the name Jordan Kiley because I didn't want to be recognized."

"Was it some kind of perverted game to play me for a fool? Did you want to see how far you could go?" Her voice was treacherously low.

"No, Skye—*no.*" He plowed his fingers through his hair in angry reaction. "It's true I didn't intend to tell you at first, but I didn't intend to fall in love with you, either."

Her gaze darted to Jordan, but she couldn't look at him long without revealing the effect of his words.

"If you loved me, then why continue with the charade? If you trusted me at all, why lie?"

"If you loved me, then why did you put me through this hell?" he countered quickly.

She lowered her gaze guiltily. "I was hurt and rightly so. I gave you an excuse that would make the cut quick and clean."

"Once you told me the girl's name who sang at the hospital was Jane. You allowed that charade to continue because you wanted me to like you for who you were, not for any talent you had," he said, and sighed heavily. "My excuse is the same. I wanted you to love me for who I am, not for anything I could do to advance your career."

"Really, Jordan . . ." She gave a small laugh that bordered on a sob. "Or do you prefer to be called Dan?"

His mouth thinned with displeasure. "Jordan."

"All right," she said stiffly. "And really that's a pretty weak excuse, seeing that I had no interest in a singing career, something I'd repeatedly told you. And yet you carried this whole thing to the extreme. When did you plan to tell me who you really were? On our wedding night?"

"I meant to tell you a hundred different times, but something always prevented me. I had every intention of telling you the night I gave you the ring, but you were so concerned about Billy, I didn't want to burden you further. I was going to tell you. Believe that, please."

Her weary blue eyes slid to him again. "It's more than the fact you lied. You're a very rich man. . . . You . . . you seem to think money can buy you anything."

"It didn't buy your love, did it?" he asked, his voice softening.

"No." Her hands gestured helplessly. "It's more than your deception. I'm afraid a relationship between us simply wouldn't work. We're too different."

"We're not different at all," he argued. "We share the same Savior."

The silence that followed was profound.

"Jordan," she whispered, almost afraid to believe what he was telling her. "You decided to make God a part of your life?

A hint of a smile tugged at the corners of his mouth. "It didn't come easy. The Lord had to bring me to my knees."

Suddenly the picture of a camel going through the eye of the needle in the wall of Jerusalem came to mind.

"You're right about my money," he continued. "In the past it bought me anything I desired. But it couldn't buy me your love. When we first met, I couldn't believe anyone could be so completely trusting in a Superior Being. You were too good to be true, and I kept waiting to find some flaw in your faith. There wasn't one. Soon I found myself falling hopelessly in love with you. When you declared your undying love for Glen, I was defeated. I couldn't fight a dead man. All the money in the world wouldn't buy me your love. It came to me then that I had all the money I needed or wanted, but it hadn't brought me happiness. Not knowing where else to turn, I read your father's Bible. It was the only way I could think to get closer to you. I even flew to San Francisco to talk to your pastor. I made a commitment two weeks ago."

"Oh, Jordan." Her voice wobbled as she bit down on her lower lip.

"I'll ask you again, Skye. I love you. I don't promise to do everything right, but I'm willing to be the best husband I know how to be with God's help." A humility entered his voice. "Will you be my wife?"

She floated into his arms, as if it was the most natural thing in the world. "Yes, oh, Jordan, a thousand times, yes."

She was crushed against him as he claimed her mouth in a devouring kiss that seemed to blot out all the hurt and anger of the past few weeks. Instinctively she wound her arms around his neck, arching against him. When he dragged his lips from hers and buried his face in the hollow of her neck, she could feel the uneven drag of his breath. Clinging to him, she closed her eyes while an overwhelming happiness stole over her.

"Thank you, Jesus," she murmured almost inaudibly.

Gently his hand caressed her cheek, then framed her face.

She couldn't speak as she gazed into his powerful face with all the love in her heart shining in her eyes.

Four months later Skye surveyed the dining room table carefully set for the Thanksgiving dinner. Mentally she checked every detail; she wanted this day to be perfect. She'd met Jordan's family on several occasions, but this was the first time they'd all gathered together.

Mrs. Somers, the housekeeper, was a jewel, and Skye couldn't have managed the large meal without her. The middle-aged woman had been with Jordan for years and welcomed Skye like a mother hen gathering a chick under her wing. Skye had felt awkward at first. Jordan didn't need her to keep his home, and she felt at loose ends with so much time on her hands. He didn't object when she began substitute teaching, but more and more she found herself involved in their church. Their outside activities would be curtailed soon enough, she decided.

One last glance revealed an elegant table set with fresh flowers and sparkling crystal. It was Thanksgiving, and her heart was full of praise for God's goodness to them both.

Jordan had to make a quick trip to the office, and while she waited for his return she wandered into the music room to play the grand piano. Her nimble fingers flew over the ivory keys with unquestionable skill; if anything, her love for Jordan had enhanced her musical talent.

How she'd come to love this room of their home. She recalled her first glimpse of the twenty-six-room mansion. Driving through the long driveway after their extended honeymoon in the Caribbean, the house loomed before her, elegant, imposing, and huge. At first sight Skye felt a tremor of apprehension.

Jordan had come around to her side of the car, opened her door, and lifted her effortlessly into his arms, prepared to observe tradition by carrying her over the threshold.

When Skye glanced at him, she discovered he was watching her reaction. "This is our home?" she quizzed softly.

"It's not as awesome as it looks," he assured her.

"I'd rather live in a three-bedroom rambler." Their happiness had been so complete during their honeymoon, and now she was faced with the realities of his wealth and position.

"I know. But things being as they are, will you take me as I am?" An unfamiliar quality entered his eyes. "Christ did, you know."

"Then I suppose I'll have to," she whispered, and planted a warm kiss on his open mouth before exploring the lobe of his ear with her tongue.

"I'm back." Jordan broke into her thoughts, walking briskly into the rose-colored room.

Skye lifted her hands from the keyboard, smiling at her husband with a happiness that was almost translucent. "Listen to this," she commanded as her fingers flew over the keys in a melody she hoped would express her love.

"It's beautiful," Jordan said, his eyes showing the special kind of awe he felt when he listened to her music.

"I'm trying to tell you something, and I honestly didn't think it would be this difficult."

His expression sobered. "You mean that you're pregnant? Did you honestly think I wouldn't know?" Suddenly, as if the thought had come to him all at once, he asked, "Everything is all right, isn't it? You're going to be okay?" His voice was deep with emotion.

"Of course I will." She quickly allayed his fears.

Drawing her tenderly into his arms, he held her close. "I love you, Skye. I didn't know it was possible to feel this deeply about anyone. You've become my life." His kiss was sweet and filled with passion. "How long do we have before my mother arrives?"

"Jordan," she said, giggling. "Not now . . . later," she whispered, her voice filled with promise.

She could sense his regret as he gently broke their embrace. "Did you know I owned your apartment building?" he asked unexpectedly. "I'm in the process of selling it. That's why I had to go to the office this morning."

"Jordan, no!" She was shocked. This man had a habit of saying the most astonishing things. "When . . . why?"

He chuckled, as if he found himself very clever. "It was the only way I knew to get rid of your pesky neighbor. I bought the building and raised his rent."

Skye's mouth must have dropped open.

"Careful, dear, someone might think you're imitating a fish."

"Jordan!" She could hardly find words. "Is . . . is there anything else I don't know?"

"I don't think so. Oh, yes, I hope the mechanic did a good job on your car. I threatened to have his certification questioned."

"You didn't?"

"Fraid so." He chuckled. "But don't worry, I'm learning a new way to deal with people. It's called love, Christian love."

Her fingers lovingly traced the line of his jaw. "Sometimes you shock me, Jordan Murphy."

He smiled deep into her eyes. "Oh my, you're beautiful."

She slid her arms around his neck and smiled with intense satisfaction. "Tell me that seven months from now. I'll need to hear it about then."

"A child," he murmured as if he was just beginning to fully comprehend this new life growing within his wife. "I have something beyond price: you, a child, and God's love. You've given me everything a man could ever want."

Jordan's arm tightened around her waist, and Skye happened to catch a glimpse of the dining room table. Thanksgiving: She now understood the full meaning of the word.

★★★★★

Love Thy Neighbor

Dear Friends,

Welcome to a vintage inspirational Debbie Macomber story. I wrote *Love Thy Neighbor* on a rented typewriter I set up on my kitchen table back in the early 1980s. Technology has certainly changed since then, hasn't it? It's hard to remember what our lives were like before cell phones, personal computers and the internet. I have a friend whose grandmother crossed the prairie as an infant in a covered wagon and before she died in the 1960s, she flew on a jet plane. Amazing, isn't it?

Yet it doesn't matter when a book is written; a good story remains a good story. I believe you'll enjoy *Love Thy Neighbor* despite the fact no one has a cell phone or a computer. Think of it as a time capsule: a look back to the way things were back then . . . once upon a time.

These days, I am connected on just about every bit of social media available. You can reach me at my website, debbiemacomber.com, or on Facebook, X, YouTube, Instagram and Pinterest. And as always, you can reach me via snail mail at P.O. Box 1458, Port Orchard, WA 98366. Choose any option—I do so enjoy hearing from my readers.

So, please, look beyond the obvious changes the years have made and simply enjoy this story.

Warmest regards,
Debbie Macomber

To Les Carr,
the best chauffeur
a teenage girl ever had.

Chapter One

Lesley Brown watched as her newest employee struggled to maintain her poise. Fifty-year-old Charlotte Lewis had been hired at Statewide Savings Bank last month and had proved herself capable of dealing with every aspect of banking. But today was her first day handling new accounts. The older woman looked red-faced and flustered. Frustration drove deep grooves into her smooth brow as she cast Lesley a pleading glance.

Lesley's natural reaction was to respond to Charlotte's silent plea, but that wouldn't help either of them. Every employee was left to deal with an impatient customer occasionally. Like everyone else, Charlotte would need to learn to react courteously and politely. Lesley realized this could sometimes be difficult, but she prided herself on the ability to keep a cool head and a calming demeanor.

Centering her attention on the loan application on her desk, Lesley ignored the raised voices from the other side of the room. With experienced skill, she ran down the printed form, checking to see that all the information had been completed.

"I'm sorry to bother you." Charlotte stood at Lesley's desk, her hands clenched tightly at her sides. "But Mr. Daniels has asked to speak to the manager."

"What seems to be the problem?"

"Actually, there are several. Mr. Daniels has recently moved into the area and wishes to open an account with a check issued from Indiana. I explained the bank's policy regarding checks issued from out of state, but he insists upon talking to someone in authority."

"I understand, Charlotte. Don't worry, you did the right thing." Lesley rolled back her chair and stood. Her high heels tapped against the tile floor as she moved across the room.

"Mr. Daniels." She extended her hand and introduced herself. "I'm Lesley Brown. Is there something I can do for you?"

His handshake was short and barely civil. "I want to speak to the manager." The dark eyes became narrowed slits.

"Mr. Fullbright is out of the office. I'm the assistant manager."

"I'll wait for Mr. Fullbright," he stated dismissively, and glanced at his watch.

"Mr. Daniels, I'm sure I can settle any problem."

His dark eyes ran over her. Boldly she met his glare. He was tall and lean, his jaw angular and sharp. But his eyes were what drew her attention. Dark and ruthless, they seemed to possess the sharpness of a hawk's. Lesley doubted that much escaped his notice. If it hadn't been for the contempt in his eyes and the tightly reined impatience about him, she might have thought him attractive. She noted he wasn't wearing a wedding ring. He looked like the type who would prefer to play the field than settle for one woman. Definitely not a man who would interest her.

As if aware of her censure, his mouth formed into an unyielding, hard line, his displeasure stamped on every feature.

So be it, Lesley mused. She didn't particularly care for the way he was arrogantly appraising her either.

"Mr. Daniels would like to open a checking account with an out-of-state check," Charlotte inserted, handing Lesley the check.

"I'm sure Mrs. Lewis explained that we must allot ten days for this to clear before issuing you checks for your account." The question was directed to him.

"She's explained that several times," he returned with marked patience, his tone sarcastic and dry. "But if you'd simply place a phone call, you'd be assured that the check is good."

"I'm sorry, Mr. Daniels, but that's not the way things are done. Coeur d'Alene isn't a vast metropolis; we move cautiously here. The check must—"

"When will the manager be back?" he interrupted her angrily.

"Mr. Daniels." Lesley could feel her own impatience rising. "Let me assure you Mr. Fullbright will say the same thing."

One corner of his mouth edged up in cynical amusement. "Now, that's something I doubt. I'll wait for someone with real authority."

"I assure you, in Mr. Fullbright's absence, I have full authority." Lesley could feel her calm façade evaporating with every sharp word.

"Still, I'll wait for someone who doesn't have the word "assistant" in their title," he declared in cutting tones that aroused the attention of customers, who turned to stare openly at the small group.

"I can see that it isn't going to do any good to explain the bank's point of view. If you prefer to speak with Mr. Fullbright, then you're encouraged to do so. Now, if you'll excuse me." Seething, she pivoted and stalked back to her desk.

Boorish, ill-mannered beast. Her fingers were shaking as she sat down and picked up her pencil. That man had a chip on his shoulder so big it made a California redwood look like an acorn.

The indignation persisted when Lesley pulled into her driveway that night. Her confrontation with Daniels had weighed heavily on her most of the day, and she sat quietly in the car an extra minute, enjoying the unexpected warmth of an Indian summer afternoon.

As Lesley slipped out of the driver's seat, she noted a sports car parked in the driveway on the other side of the duplex. She couldn't identify the make, but it looked fancy and expensive. Apparently the place had been rented. Swinging the long strap of her leather purse over her shoulder, Lesley wondered how long it would be before she met her new neighbor.

The duplex was in a quiet section of town, her nearest neighbors half a block away. Lesley didn't even bother to lock her front door. What did she have that anyone would want? Besides, if someone was determined to steal her things, they could rip out the door lock. In some ways her view of life could be looked upon as dangerously simplistic. But this was a small Idaho town, and she knew and trusted everyone.

At least once she was home she could remove the ambitious businesswoman façade and be herself. Changing into jeans and a red-checked, short-sleeved blouse, she slid open the back door to inspect her garden. Large tomatoes weighted the vines. Many of the green ones wouldn't have time to ripen before the first frost, and she picked several to take inside. The zucchini were still abundant, and she bent down to retrieve one. The pumpkin was large and turning orange. Dinner tonight would consist of a fresh vegetable salad, cheese and leftover roast.

She placed the vegetables in the sink and poured herself a glass of iced tea. Amid the loveliness of the afternoon, the world seemed filled with good things. The grass felt cool and welcoming as she sat, crossed her knees and leaned back to rest her weight on the palms of her hands. She chewed on a long blade of grass and tried to guess what kind of neighbor God had sent her.

Not that anyone could replace her sister, brother-in-law and niece. She was going to miss Terry, Robert and baby Lisa. The little family had become a big part of her life over the past year. Times like now, when she would normally have shared the tea with her sister, made it seem as if Terry was across the world instead of across town. But they had quickly outgrown the one-bedroom duplex after Lisa was born. It was so convenient living next door to one another that Terry had delayed the move for as long as possible. With mixed feelings, Lesley had helped her sister look for a house. They had hugged each other and cried when the last box had been loaded onto the rented moving van and the time had finally arrived for Terry and Robert to drive away.

But before Terry had climbed into the van, the two sisters had walked around the vacant apartment. Together they had prayed for whomever God would move into the duplex. The words of the prayer returned to Lesley now as she stared at the closed sliding glass door of her neighbor's apartment. Terry had promised to continue praying for Lesley's new neighbor. They prayed that whoever the Lord sent to the second half of the duplex would be someone special in her life. Now, alone on the grass, Lesley echoed that prayer.

Whoever had moved in would soon realize that the walls were paper-thin. Terry and Lesley often had to laugh because it was apparent, just from the sounds echoing through, what the other was doing. Countless times they had borrowed things from each other, shared the clothesline and weeded the communal garden. Water pressure had been a problem, but they'd learned to coordinate usage. Lesley would consider herself lucky to find someone as compatible as her sister.

The glass door that opened into the common backyard was closed, the drapes pulled. Lesley wondered who would want to keep the sun out on such a glorious afternoon. But whoever it was, Lesley felt God had specifically sent that family or person. Hadn't she and Terry prayed for just that?

The radio was playing softly in the background as she ripped the lettuce leaves apart for her salad. On an impulse, she pulled out an extra bowl and made two huge salads: one for her, one for her new neighbor. She would take it over as a way of introducing herself.

Adding a dab of gloss to her full mouth, she did a quick inspection of her five-foot-five frame and shoulder-length chestnut-colored hair in the bathroom mirror. No one was going to call a Hollywood producer, but she looked presentable.

She pushed in the doorbell and listened to the buzz.

Nothing.

Lesley rang the bell again. The fancy sports car was still in the driveway, but that didn't necessarily mean there was someone inside the house. She was about to return to her apartment when the door was jerked open.

In retrospect, Lesley didn't know who looked more shocked, Daniels or herself.

"You!" she gasped, her mouth dropping open.

"Well, if it isn't Little Miss Bank Executive." His voice was low and filled with mocking amusement. "Have you come to apologize and request my business?"

"Oh, hardly." She jerked the salad behind her back. Lettuce leaves fell onto the concrete step.

Purposefully she had returned to her duties that afternoon, forcing herself to concentrate on her work. Lesley had been unaware of how long, if at all, Daniels had waited for Ben Fullbright. "I'm here because . . ." She searched frantically for a plausible excuse. There had been some horrible, dreadful mistake. God wouldn't send someone like Daniels to be her neighbor.

"Yes?" He sounded bored and irritable.

"I'm your neighbor," she managed finally.

He started to laugh then—not a friendly, amused laugh, but one filled with irony, brittle with sarcasm.

Lesley could feel the hairs at the back of her neck bristle. Never had she felt such intense dislike for anyone. One demeaning glance from him assured her that the feeling was mutual. It took more restraint than she wanted to admit not to dump the bowl of salad greens over his head.

"What did you want?" he demanded, his gaze cutting into her.

"Want?" She stared at him blankly.

"You rang *my* doorbell."

He made it sound as if she'd tossed eggs at his windows.

"Yes, I did," she returned awkwardly. "I brought you dinner as a . . ." The word "welcome" wouldn't make it past the tight knot in her throat.

If possible, the dark eyes hardened all the more. "Let's get one thing straight right now. I don't want to be neighborly. You leave me alone and I'll leave you alone. You stay on your half and I'll stay on mine. Understood?"

"Oh, I understand all right—and concur. I wouldn't want to have anything to do with you if I were stuck in quicksand and couldn't reach a branch." Immediately Lesley recognized how silly she sounded. Under any other circumstances she would have burst out laughing, but there was nothing amusing about Daniels. Nothing!

She stalked across the yard and slammed her front door. Furious, she paced the small enclosure like a trapped panther. Not in twenty-three years had she met anyone she disliked more. He was awful, the epitome of everything she loathed.

Rands hugging her stomach, she paused in the middle of the living room floor, her foot tapping irritably against the worn carpet. A mistake had been made. Something wasn't right. God wouldn't present that bitter, hard, unreasonable man next door on purpose. All she had to do was stay calm and wait for him to leave. And that was exactly what she would do until God rectified the error.

Daniels' fancy sports car was gone the next morning when Lesley left for the bank. With *him* living so close, she decided her things were in imminent danger and locked the front door.

By the time she pulled into her usual parking space on the side street opposite the bank, she was feeling ridiculous. Daniels wasn't going to rob her. True, he was an unpleasant fellow, but they could learn to live in harmony. All she had to do was pretend the apartment was still vacant. That would be easy enough. He would probably be gone by the end of the month, anyway.

Lesley had been at her desk only a matter of minutes when Daniels strolled in. Instinctively she stiffened. Without being obvious, she followed his movements. First he went to a teller who smiled provocatively, obviously taken in by his charm. What charm, Lesley's mind tossed back instantly. The young teller pointed to Ben Fullbright's desk.

With even-paced strides, Daniels walked up to the bank manager's desk and introduced himself. Ben rose and they shook hands.

"Lesley, call on line one." Charlotte Lewis said from the desk beside hers. "Lesley," she repeated.

Lesley jerked upright. "Oh, sorry, what did you say?"

Charlotte repeated the information and Lesley reached automatically for the phone. It was a local resident requesting loan information, and Lesley was tied up for several minutes answering questions.

When she replaced the receiver, Lesley noted that Ben

Fullbright was standing behind the counter for new accounts and was completing the necessary information for Daniels.

The two men shook hands, then Daniels strode toward her desk. Lesley pretended an inordinate interest in the blank form. Although he stood directly in front of her, Lesley didn't glance up, hoping that Daniels would take the hint and leave.

"Miss Brown."

With exaggerated care, Lesley lifted her gaze. "Yes?" Her voice was barely civil.

"I thought you'd like to see these." He laid twenty-five freshly issued blank checks on her desk and riffled them with his thumb.

Closing her eyes and inhaling a deep breath enabled Lesley to hold her temper. "Statewide Savings does its best to keep every customer satisfied. I'm pleased we could be of service," she managed in a starched tone.

"Except that it took a true manager to listen to reason. I suggest you leave the decision making where it belongs."

"And I suggest you leave me alone before I throw this cup of coffee in your face," she informed him with a wide smile that conveyed the fact she wasn't kidding.

Challenge, mockery, and amusement all glittered from his dark eyes as he dipped his head in acknowledgment. "Good day, Miss Brown." A smile tugged at the corner of his mouth.

"Good day." Purposely she lowered her eyes to her desk. Her heart hammered wildly and her breath came in uneven gulps. Never had she disliked anyone so intensely. Lesley fumed with anger until she heard him turn and walk away.

During her lunch hour, Lesley had a date with Dale Wylie, a new-car salesman, at a local café for lunch.

"Hi, honey, how are things going?" He kissed her lightly on the cheek and slid into the booth, opposite Lesley.

Lesley's gaze followed Dale. "I wish you wouldn't do that."

Dale looked up from the menu with that innocent look she detested. "Do what?"

"Come in here and act like we're an old married couple," she told him forcefully. "We're friends, nothing more. I don't like you giving people the impression there's something more between us."

Dale laid the menu aside. Ralf the single women in Coeur d'Alene would give anything to have the urbane and good-looking Dale interested in them. Why he'd picked her, Lesley didn't know. They weren't the least alike, didn't share the same interests and often disagreed, especially about Lesley's strong religious convictions. Maybe he thought of her as a challenge. She'd given up trying to guess.

"My, my, you must have had a difficult morning." His blue eyes shone with sympathy. "Want to tell me about it?"

"I had a wonderful morning, thank you." She hid her expressive eyes behind the menu. She wasn't going to fool Dale, but talking about Daniels wouldn't do any good, either.

Gratefully, he didn't pursue the subject. Lesley doubted that he would: Dale's interest revolved around Dale.

"You'll be pleased to know I made a sale this morning."

"Congratulations. Anyone I know?" She laid the menu aside, genuinely interested.

"I don't think so. New fellow in town, Cole Daniels."

Cole Daniels! Lesley's hand tightened around the water glass.

"Interesting fellow, seemed to know a lot about cars. Paid cash."

She nodded, hoping he wouldn't notice the way she'd stiffened when he rolled off the name. So Daniels' first name was Cole. It should have been *Cold*.

"I know him," she said lightly, twisting the spoon with her fingers in nervous reaction. "Did he trade in that fancy sports car of his?"

"Sports car? No, he didn't, he walked into the showroom. He didn't have any wheels." Dale's mouth quirked briefly. "How do you know him?"

"He moved into the other half of the duplex."

Dale's look narrowed and he regarded her seriously. "I'm not sure I approve of the two of you living next to each other like that."

"What?" Lesley swallowed a gasp of resentment.

"Separated from the rest of the town like that," he hurried to explain.

"I'll tell you what," she began, deliberately setting the spoon aside and raising her eyes to his, "if you can figure a way to get him out of there, I wouldn't object."

"You wouldn't?"

"Not in the least. I find the man to be opinionated and irksome. Terry and I were such good friends, but I can't imagine Cole Daniels and me ever getting along."

"Well, in that case, I can't see much of a problem."

Men! Lesley felt like screaming. All they ever cared about was themselves. How could her sister be married and so happy?

"I'm not very hungry, Dale. If you don't mind, I think I'll skip lunch today." She started to slide out of the booth.

"I knew there was something wrong." Dale sounded pleased with himself for such keen insight. "You're not feeling well, are you? Headache?"

Her confirming nod wasn't a lie. Every minute she spent in Dale's company only made her head pound worse.

"Before you go." A hand on her forearm stopped her. "We'd better decide what we're wearing to Larry's party."

Could the day get any worse? "Larry's party?" she echoed. Maybe if she played dumb they could avoid another confrontation.

"The Halloween bash next weekend. I already told him we were coming."

"You did what?" she asked, her eyes spitting fire.

"Now, hold on, there's no need to get all upset." He patted her arm soothingly as if she were a recalcitrant child.

"I told you," she said in measured tones, "I have no intention of attending that party. I'm going to the one at the church. I thought I made that extremely clear."

"Let me explain before you become unreasonable," Dale returned calmly. "I'm not insensitive, I know this thing at your church is important to you. I want you to go, but there's no reason you can't attend both. You can give me a call and I'll swing by the church to pick you up. As I see it, you won't even need to change costumes."

"Everyone's dressing up as Bible characters. Can't you see how ludicrous it would be to go from church to Larry's?"

"Not necessarily," Dale inserted. "Who are you going as?"

"Lot's wife."

"Lot's wife? But she—"

"I know," Lesley interrupted. "I'm dressing up as a pillar of salt."

Amusement gleamed briefly from his eyes. "That sounds like a good idea, but you probably should wear something that will fit in at both parties."

"Dale." Lesley slid out of the booth and took a step in backward retreat. "Read my lips, because I have the feeling you never hear what I'm saying," she instructed. "I'm not going to Larry's party. Not this year, not ever. You know what I think of Larry O'Brien; I don't want to have anything to do with him."

"Lesley"—Dale murmured her name softly—"I'm sure you don't mean that."

What more did she have to say to reach this man? "I mean

it, Dale." Rather than argue further, she turned sharply and left the café.

The afternoon was another glorious one, but Lesley hardly noticed. What was the matter with her lately? Everything was going wrong.

Instead of going straight back to the bank, she strolled down the street, stopping in a couple of shops along the way to browse.

"He was so handsome. Mark my words, that man has broken a few hearts in his day."

Lesley picked up part of a conversation between a cashier and a housewife. Her interest sparked, Lesley stood behind a counter pretending to examine a sweater as she listened to the conversation.

"Said his name was Cole Daniels."

Hot color invaded her face. Was her ill-mannered neighbor going to haunt her all day?

"Tight-lipped, though," the woman continued. "Hardly said a word. Just paid for his purchase. I asked if he was from around here, and he said he wasn't."

"Did you ask where he's from?"

Lesley was more than interested and silently berated herself for eavesdropping so blatantly. She hadn't done anything like this since Terry was sixteen and standing on the porch talking to her dates.

"I asked, but he didn't say."

The check he'd deposited had been issued from Indiana; Lesley knew that much.

"He didn't seem inclined to talk about himself. Probably just passing through."

"Probably," the other woman agreed.

Silently, Lesley hoped they were both right.

The remainder of the afternoon proved to be uneventful.

At five o'clock Lesley walked out of the building with Ben Fullbright. He, at least, didn't mention Cole Daniels, and Lesley was more than grateful.

"See you in the morning." She gave Ben a small wave, waited at the crosswalk, then ran across the busy street to her parked car.

The car's interior felt warm and stuffy, unusual for late October. Lesley scooted inside and immediately rolled down the window. A cooling breeze flowed through the vehicle, whipping her hair across her face as she headed for home.

Her first impulse was to drive over to Terry's. She'd spent several days helping her sister unpack and settle in the new house. But Lesley hesitated. When Terry lived next door there was always an excuse to see each other, do something together. Things were different now, and should be. Terry, Robert and the baby were a family in themselves. And although it felt awkward not to share some of the things that had been happening with Terry, Lesley recognized it was for the best.

Since she'd skipped lunch, Lesley was hungry and pulled into a little mom-and-pop grocery store. The Walkers couldn't hope to compete with the large supermarkets, but their service was always friendly and warm. Both Paul and Martha Walker were strong Christian people, and Lesley liked to give them as much business as she could afford.

Absently she noted that there was only one other car parked in front of the store. She pushed open the glass door and smiled brightly. Her mouth froze. Cole Daniels was standing in front of the outdated cash register. Groceries lined the counter.

"Afternoon, Lesley." Paul Walker glanced up, a look of distinct relief touching his eyes. "Guess you could say it was providential, you stopping in today."

"Oh?" Her hand clenched the strap of her purse tightly.

"Mr. Daniels is here, and being new to the community and all . . ." Paul hesitated.

"What he really wants to know is if the check is good."

"You being from the bank . . ." Walker added.

The challenge in Cole Daniels' eyes was unmistakable. He stood tall and proud, almost daring Lesley to deny that he had enough money in his account to pay for his goods.

Self-consciously Lesley glanced from one man to the other. "Mr. Daniels opened his account with us today with a generous amount. I'm sure his check is fine."

Relief eased the age lines from the old man's weathered face. "No offense intended, but I can't stand to take a loss for this amount."

"I understand," Cole Daniels returned in a surprisingly sympathetic voice.

Cole left the market before Lesley. She made an excuse to linger, not wanting to see him again if she could avoid it, staying in the back of the store until she heard him leave.

After carefully inspecting the meat available in the small cooler, Lesley purchased a cube steak, julienned green beans and lettuce for a salad. She nibbled on a package of potato chips as she laid the few items on the counter.

"Seems like a nice fellow," Mr. Walker began.

"Who?" She was being deliberately obtuse. Cole Daniels had been invading her safe, secure world all day. She couldn't take much more of the irritating stranger.

"Daniels," Paul Walker said and gave her a funny look. "I hated to ask about the check, but he didn't have his name or address printed on it."

"I'm sure he will later." Lesley strove to sound nonchalant.

"I told him if he was going to buy that many groceries, it would be cheaper for him to go to a supermarket. I can't compete with their prices." His hands busily rang up her purchases on the antique cash register, then bagged her few items into a brown paper sack. "I didn't want to lose his business, but I hated to see him waste good money."

Paul Walker had to be the most unselfish Christian man she had ever known, Lesley decided. How many others who were working to keep a business going would have made such a suggestion?

"We don't get many strangers this time of year," he added.

Lesley agreed with a quick nod. "I know."

"How long is he staying?"

She motioned weakly with her hands. "He didn't say, but since he's rented the duplex and opened a checking account, I'd say he intends to be here awhile."

"Don't suppose you know what line of work he's in?"

"Not a clue." She paid for her things and lifted the grocery sack off the counter. "Wish I could be more help, but I don't know much of anything."

Paul Walker placed the money in the till. "I don't mean to be such a gossip."

The Walkers were nothing of the sort. "I'm sure you didn't," she assured him.

"Don't know what it is about the man." He paused to rub his chin with a thumb. "Sometimes the Lord gives me certain feelings about people. I took one look at him and could almost see the bitterness."

Lesley had felt that too.

"But more than that, I sensed he was running—not because he's in trouble with the law, but running scared from unhappiness and life."

Lesley noted that, as he spoke, a soft look came over Paul Walker's face. The old man hesitated. "Cole Daniels needs our prayers."

She couldn't agree with him more.

Chapter Two

Lesley carried her small bag of groceries into the house. Cole's new car was parked in his driveway. What had happened to the flashy sports car she saw yesterday? Had he parked it in the garage? She'd only seen it that one time. And although she wasn't much of an auto expert, she knew enough to realize it was no ordinary vehicle.

The house felt unusually warm and stuffy. Leaving the grocery sack on the kitchen counter, Lesley immediately opened the sliding glass door. She stood in the open doorway and unfastened the top button of her crisp linen business suit. Appreciatively, she paused to inhale the fresh, country-scented air. Slipping off her pumps, she flexed her toes and pulled her silk blouse free from her waistband. In a matter of minutes the transformation from rising bank executive to down-home country girl—complete with jeans—was complete.

Whistling, she cut the steak into thin strips, added a few vegetables and broth and left it to simmer in the slow cooker.

The garden fork was set against the back of the house. With the weather so unusually warm, it would be a good time to till under a portion of the garden. The work was strenuous, and she stopped several times to wipe the perspiration from her brow. Once she felt as if someone was watching her, but when she turned around, no one was there.

Rubbing the palms of her hands on the back pockets of her jeans, she stuck the fork in the ground and walked over to the side of the house to get the hose.

She could hear that Cole was running water. With a satisfied smirk she planned her small revenge. It seemed Cole Daniels was about to receive his first lesson in the problems the duplex had with water pressure. With a smile tugging at the corners of her mouth, she turned the faucet as far as it would go. Nothing happened at first, but soon an even flow of water ran from the tap.

She dragged the hose to the area she'd recently tilled and sprayed water over the grass and leaves she'd laid on top of the earth. Not more than two minutes later, Cole stormed out the back door.

"Just what do you think you're doing?" he demanded.

Startled, Lesley dropped the nozzle and swung around. "What do you mean?" she yelled back. If he hadn't been so angry, she would have laughed. Cole was dressed in jeans, his feet bare. His shirt was left open and clung to his wet torso. His damp hair was standing straight on end as if someone had electrocuted him.

Rands on hips, she met his furious glare. "Is there a problem?"

"You're darn right there is. I was in the shower when the water suddenly turned into a cold trickle."

"You can't blame me for that."

"Just whose fault is it, then?"

"The city, the landlord and in some ways the state of Idaho."

"Don't get cute with me, girl."

"Girl?" she fumed. "Well, listen up, bub, how was I supposed to know you were in the shower?"

"You mean to tell me I have to report to you every time I flush the toilet?"

"Now, that's just a mite different from washing clothes or taking a shower. We're going to have to work out a time schedule."

"No way."

"Fine with me." Ignoring him as best she could, Lesley swung around, picked up the hose and continued to douse the garden."

"Turn that off!" he shouted.

"No way," she returned in his own words.

Hands clenched at his sides, Cole raged across the yard, heading for the outside faucet.

"I'd advise you to stay away from that," Lesley shouted, "or you'll be getting a lot more than a cold trickle." She jiggled the hose a couple of times to prove she wasn't fooling.

"Threats, Lesley?" His voice was low and dangerous.

Goose bumps broke out across her forearms at the chill in his voice. "I'm warning you," she said with much bravado.

"Yes?" He took a step closer.

"Don't." She retreated, her resolve wavering. What was the matter with her? Show some mettle, her mind shouted. Straightening her shoulders, she faced him boldly. "We could compromise," she suggested, angry with herself for the way her voice wobbled. She wasn't some country hick he could push around.

"The solution is simple."

"Oh?"

"Turn off that thing, I'll finish my shower and then you can do as you please."

In a burst of temper, Lesley threw down the green garden

hose, stalked to the faucet and turned off the water. Hands placed challengingly on hips, she whirled around. "There. Are you happy?"

He made an indifferent sound as if what she did or didn't do wasn't of interest to him, and the irritating way he looked and spoke only served to fuel the temper stirring within her. Was she safe with this kind of man living next door? Paul Walker had sensed that things weren't right with Cole Daniels, confirming her own feelings.

"Before you go in, I think there's something you should know," Lesley warned.

"Yes?"

Lesley assumed the defensive stance her instructor had shown her. Her hands were positioned level with her face. Baring her teeth for effect, she glared at him. "I've had four karate lessons."

His robust laugh only angered her more. The man was despicable. She felt ridiculously close to tears and fluttered her lashes furiously at the smarting moistness. She never cried.

"Is that supposed to frighten me?" Cole asked.

"No!" she shouted, afraid the brightness of unshed tears might shine from her eyes. "But . . . I think you should know I can take care of myself."

The humor drained from his eyes. His entire demeanor changed, and Lesley couldn't understand why. A hard mask seemed to steal over his face. "Good. Finish those lessons. You may need them."

Lesley paused long enough to grab her purse and sweater and lock the front door. Then she drove straight to her sister's.

"Terry!" She burst in the front door, her voice urgent and confused.

Terry rushed out of the kitchen, the wooden door swinging after her. "What is it?"

"A man moved in next door."

Immediately Terry's expression relaxed. "Oh dear. For a minute you had me frightened. A man, you say. How interesting. Married?"

"I don't know." Her sister apparently didn't understand the situation, and from the look in her eye, the romantic side of Terry's nature had taken over. Lesley could almost see the little wheels in her sister's mind whirling a hundred miles an hour.

"Is he wearing a wedding band?"

"No." She swallowed a giant breath. "It's not what you think."

"He's old."

"No."

"Good. Young and handsome?"

"You could say that. Terry! Stop and listen to me."

"I'm listening," she returned with a distant look in her eye.

Only a year separated the two sisters, and when they dressed alike, it was difficult to tell them apart. Both had the rich chestnut-colored hair and sky-blue eyes that altered to a vibrant gray when they were excited or angry. High cheekbones and rosy complexion were a family trademark.

"I'm home." Robert announced and the back screen door slammed, hailing his entry.

Terry kissed her husband and wrapped an arm around his waist. "Lesley's new neighbor is a man."

"Interesting." Robert replied after he'd nuzzled Terry's neck.

"No, it's not," Lesley insisted. "I wish the two of you would listen to me. He's awful. Despicable."

"Unreasonable?" Terry added.

"Yes." Some of the apprehension drained out of her. Maybe Terry did understand.

"They're the best kind," Terry said knowingly. The baby let out a loud cry from the back bedroom. "Lisa's awake. Will you get her for me?"

Although she dearly loved her niece, Lesley didn't think Lisa could have picked a worse time to wake up from her nap.

"What's for dinner?"

Lesley heard Robert's question as she moved down the narrow hall to the bedroom portion of the house. What was the matter with everyone today? A strange man had moved in next to her, and Terry acted as if she'd been told Lesley had won the lottery.

Eighteen-month-old Lisa was standing, her tiny hands clenching the crib bars. When she saw Lesley, she gurgled happily.

"Hello, Lisa," Lesley said in the singsong voice the child loved. "How's Auntie Lesley's little girl?"

Lisa held up both hands, wanting to be taken out of the crib. Lesley lifted the baby into her arms, changed her diaper and carried her back into the living room.

Robert was reading the newspaper, his stocking feet propped against the coffee table. Lisa gave a cry of delight, and Lesley placed the little girl on the floor and watched as the baby ran to her father's arms. Robert scooted Lisa onto his lap. Together the two sat contentedly and read the paper.

Terry was in the kitchen frying hamburger. "Can't you see I'm upset?" Lesley said in an accusing tone.

"About your new neighbor?" Terry opened the refrigerator and took out a block of cheddar cheese. "I don't understand why. We prayed, didn't we?"

"Then God made a mistake."

Terry laughed. "Think about what you just said."

"I have. God would never move someone as horrible as Cole Daniels next to me. Obviously, whoever is supposed to be there got held up for some reason and this fellow will be moving on."

"Then there's no reason to worry, is there?"

Leave it to Terry to remain calm and sensible. "Yes, there is."

"Why?"

Lesley gestured defeatedly with her hand. "I'm not sure. But things aren't what they should be with this guy. He's so unfriendly, almost secretive. It's hard to explain."

"And you've got a creative imagination."

"I knew you were going to say that," Lesley cried. "I suppose you're going to bring up the time I thought someone was kidnapping Mom."

"The thought entered my mind." Terry sliced off a piece of cheese and handed it to Lesley. "This is a new smoked flavor; what do you think?"

"It's good," Lesley murmured absently. "Terry, *please* would you take me seriously."

Terry looked up surprised. "I am."

"You're not," her sister accused.

"What would you like me to do?"

"I don't know. But something. I . . . I don't trust this guy."

"Then lock your door."

"I have."

Lesley leaned against the counter, crossing her feet at the ankle. She hung her head, thinking over how much of the conversation with Cole she wanted to relate to her sister. The memory of her actions made her realize how ridiculous the whole thing had been.

"Maybe I should be more concerned." Terry broke into her thoughts, and her eyes flickered over her sister briefly. "But I've continued to pray about this neighbor thing."

"You have?" Lesley's head shot up.

"If you want to know the truth, I've been worried about you lately."

"Me?"

Terry stretched a piece of plastic wrap across the top of the cheese. Her gaze avoided Lesley's. "I know how you feel about

Dale and I know"—she took in a deep breath and hesitated—"That you're not seeing anyone else. So I started praying that God would bring a new man into your life."

"You're nuts! Do you mean to tell me that you've been praying that God would move a man in next door?" Gathering speed, her words seemed to stumble over her tongue. "And . . . and not just any man, mind you, but an unreasonable, mysterious boor?"

Lesley witnessed the silent laugh her sister struggled to disguise as Terry turned and pretended to stir the already cooked meat. "Nothing so dramatic," she said at last.

"What, then?"

"Well, I've continued to pray about the neighbor situation, that's true, but I assumed another girl would move in." She hooked a long strand of dark hair around her ear. "I don't know why. But I have been wondering about you and Dale."

"I don't want to talk about him."

Terry set the spoon on a dish at the side of the stove and turned. "Are you two fighting again?"

"I said I didn't want to talk about it."

Linking her hands behind her back, Terry shrugged. "See what I mean?"

Not willing to admit anything, but unable to ignore the taut line of her sister's mouth or the concern etched about her eyes, Lesley nodded.

"You need someone new in your life." Terry's voice was gentle, loving. "That's been my prayer. You can't be angry with me for that, can you?"

Dusk was purpling the sky when Lesley pulled into her driveway and shut off the car's engine. The conversation with her sister had been more disconcerting than she cared to admit. Her thoughts remained troubled as she opened the door. The aroma of stewing meat captured her immediate attention.

What was the matter with her appetite? No lunch and no interest in dinner.

The phone rang, jerking her attention beyond the kitchen.

"Hello."

"It's about time you got home. Just where have you been?"

"Evening, Dale." Lesley released a slow breath and ignored his question. "What can I do for you?"

"The party. I want you to know you're going to Larry's party with me or that's it. In other words, we're finished, through, over."

The decision wasn't even difficult. "Then so be it," she told him stiffly.

"Listen, baby, you don't mean that." Dale's tone grew coaxing and gentle. "What's the matter with a little fun now and then?" The sound of his laughter was slurred.

So, Dale had been drinking again. He was probably with Larry. She couldn't see fighting with him, especially over the phone. "We'll talk about it tomorrow."

"Meet me for lunch?"

"Okay." Reluctantly Lesley agreed. She didn't want to be subjected to another confrontation of wills. No matter how adamant she felt about Larry's party, Dale dismissed her feelings. Terry was right. This mixed-up relationship with Dale must end, and the sooner the better.

With growing concern over the craziness her life seemed to have taken on over the past couple of weeks, Lesley forced herself to eat dinner.

After doing the dishes, she set up the sewing machine on the kitchen table and brought out the white material she'd purchased for the church Halloween costume. The radio was playing mellow sounds, and soon Lesley found herself involved in the project, her troubles forgotten as she sang and worked.

A loud knock on the front door froze her actions. Removing

the straight pins from her mouth, she hesitated long enough to murmur an urgent prayer that her visitor wasn't Dale. Several times in the past he'd phoned her when he'd been drinking, but she'd never had to deal with him physically.

The doorbell chimed in short, impatient rings. Clenching and unclenching her fist, Lesley looked out the front window. Dale's car wasn't in her driveway. But unfortunately she couldn't see who was on her step. With no choice, she opened the door.

Cole Daniels glared at her irritably. "For someone who can take care of herself with her vast and intimate knowledge of karate, it took you long enough to answer the door."

Lesley decided to disregard his sarcasm rather than argue with him.

"What do you want?" she asked pointedly.

"What are the walls made of, anyway? Cardboard?"

"Are you trying to tell me the radio's too loud?" How could anyone object to the soothing sounds of mellow music?

"The radio's fine. I'll listen to that. It's you I can't take."

"Me?" She folded her arms across her chest in a pure instinctively protective habit. It was either that or slam the door in his face. What was there about this one man that could make her more unreasonable than any other? "Was that all?" Her voice was dipped in acid.

"Please." He pivoted and walked away.

Lesley closed the door and spun around. Her sister had been praying that God would send a man into her life? That ill-mannered beast couldn't possibly be him. She didn't need to be a devoted Christian to recognize that a mistake had been made.

Lesley lay awake for a long time that night, her heart heavy. She tried reading the Bible. A smile flickered over her lips. Terry had once told her that if she had trouble sleeping, instead of counting sheep she should talk to the Shepherd.

She liked to think of herself as a strong Christian. She'd been raised in a God-fearing home. From the time she could remember, Jesus had been a large part of her life. She had never done anything without first considering her Christian values. Maybe that was the problem—she hadn't really been exposed to certain things in life. But then, did she want to be? Everything seemed so muddled in her own mind.

Just when she felt she could sleep, Lesley rolled over, tugged the blankets to her shoulder and sighed a prayer. A noise interrupted the peaceful solitude. Her eyes shot open. What was it? Sitting up in bed, Lesley strained to hear the soft tapping sounds. A typewriter? Tossing back the covers, she wandered into the living room and then the kitchen. The sounds were more distinct now: definitely the sounds of a typewriter.

Cole Daniels was a writer? Maybe he was only doing a letter. She opened the refrigerator and poured herself a glass of milk. Sitting on the couch in the darkened room, Lesley pulled her long gown over her legs and wrapped her arms around her knees. After an hour of constant tapping sounds, she decided two could play his game.

Shoving her feet into large fuzzy slippers, Lesley jerked her coat off the hanger, opened the front door and stalked across the driveway.

He didn't answer her first polite tap. She waited and, like him, buzzed the doorbell, in short, impatient rings.

"Yes." He nearly took the hinges off the door when he pulled it open.

"I can't sleep with all that racket you're making."

"Racket?" He looked puzzled. "You mean my typing?"

"You've got it."

One corner of his mouth lifted in a movement that could have been considered a half-smile. "I'll try to hold down the voluminous roar."

"I'd appreciate that. Good night, Mr. Daniels," she said in a stiff, polite voice.

"Miss Brown." He closed the door even before she'd turned around.

Lesley had hung up her coat and returned to her bedroom when her doorbell rang a second time that night. Even Dale had the common decency not to come this late.

With a sense of dread, she opened the front door. "Now what?" she demanded.

Cole was leaning lackadaisically against the doorjamb, a pair of earmuffs dangling from his index finger. "I thought these might solve your problem."

Lesley's back went rigid. "And I assure you the only problem I have is you."

He shrugged as if to say the matter was out of his hands. "Then don't blame me if my typing keeps you awake, because I plan to do exactly that every day and every night until . . ." He left the rest of what he was planning to say go unspoken.

"Until what?" she prompted.

"Never mind." His eyes narrowed. "Good night, Miss Brown."

"Mr. Daniels."

Their eyes met and held: his dark, fighting to disguise his amusement; hers bright and angry.

Gently she closed the door and leaned against it, her hands behind her back. Never had she reacted this strongly to a man.

Lunch with Dale didn't go well the next afternoon—not that Lesley had expected it would. In the end she was forced to insist that she wouldn't attend Larry's party with him. Her decision was received with ill grace, but then she'd known from past experience that Dale was a poor loser.

After work, Lesley changed into her jeans with plans to wash her car. Before turning on the water, she decided to play it safe and let Cole know what she was doing.

Lightly she knocked on his door. The new car was parked in the driveway, but she never knew what to expect with him.

"What do you want now?" He threw open the door, and Lesley had to stifle a startled gasp. It didn't look as if he'd gone to bed. He was wearing the same clothes as the night before. A day's growth of beard darkened his face, and his eyes were narrowed and angry.

"I wanted you to know I was planning to wash my car."

He stared back at her blankly.

"The water pressure." Her eyes regarded him thoughtfully. "Are you all right?"

His confirming nod was swift and abrupt.

"Have you been writing night and day?"

He didn't seem to hear her. Instead he slouched against the frame of the door. Even in his condition there was an air of quiet authority about him.

"You must be exhausted." Lesley didn't know why she should care, but she did.

"Just leave me alone," he lashed out, and rubbed a hand across his face.

"Gladly," she returned in a tightly controlled voice. "I was only trying to save you from being stuck in a cold shower. But at this point it may be just what you need."

Something unreadable shot over his expression. Regret? Anger? Lesley didn't know. But when her gaze met his, a funny sensation raced through her: an awareness of him as a man, and not just any man, but a ruggedly virile specimen. The thought shocked her. She didn't want to think of Cole Daniels as a man. This was Terry's fault. She almost regretted having gone to her sister's yesterday. Their conversation had brought up more questions when Lesley had hoped to have some answered.

Lesley noticed that Cole's features had been darkened by the sun. Yesterday, when he'd come raging at her from the shower, she'd seen how deeply tanned he was, but in her anger the fact hadn't fully registered. The handsome features were marred only by the crinkling lines around his eyes.

Why would anyone who loved the outdoors so much choose to lock himself up in an out-of-the-way duplex? Nothing about Cole Daniels seemed to make sense.

Abruptly he turned away and closed the door. Lesley was left to face the nagging silence alone.

The rest of the week passed without incident. Lesley didn't once see Cole. Late at night she could hear the pounding typewriter keys, but she didn't complain about the noise and he didn't grumble about her singing. The unspoken agreement made for a fragile peace.

Halloween night, Lesley dressed in her costume. A large cone-shaped hat rested on top of her head. An empty salt canister hung around her neck, and the long flowing white gown reached the ground.

Lesley carried out a plate of homemade cookies to the car and returned to the house for the canister of lemonade. Munching on a cookie on her way out the door, she paused in mid-step and nearly stumbled off the stair. Cole Daniels was watching her with amused cynicism. His dark eyes surveyed her from head to foot, then back for a second disbelieving look. "My, my, what do we have here?"

"What do you want?" Lesley frowned. She liked it better when they didn't talk to each other. The fuse to her temper was never shorter than when she had to deal with him.

"Nothing," he denied. He was dressed casually in jeans and a sweater. Lesley was forced to admit he looked ruggedly handsome.

He slipped his hands into his pockets and leaned a shoulder against the doorframe.

"However, I'd be interested in knowing what you're up to." A slow smile moved across his mouth. "You look ridiculous."

Her blue eyes were wide and confused as Cole continued to stare at her flushed face with lazy interest.

"You know what your problem is, Cole Daniels?" Cool challenge narrowed her eyes. "You're suffering from a spiritual disease."

"A what?"

"You heard me. A disease. I've tried everything I know to get along with you. I want you to know that I'm praying for you." Without another word she jumped into the car, yanked it into reverse and backed out of the driveway.

Resentment burned through her blood. Even when she was halfway to the church, Cole's affront hadn't cooled. Maybe if she'd been paying closer attention to what she was doing, Lesley decided later, she might have avoided the accident.

A small dog darted into the street, and Lesley swerved to avoid hitting the animal. Her car jumped the curb and tilted headfirst into the ditch.

For a stunned, breathless second she didn't move. It had all happened so quickly. Lesley sat in a world of unreality. This couldn't really have happened—not to her, not on the way to church dressed up as a pillar of salt.

She didn't move for several moments, then gradually stretched her arms. Nothing seemed to be hurt. All she felt was numb.

Opening the car door, she climbed out to assess the damage, which seemed only minimal: a scratched bumper. Surprisingly, no one had rushed to her aid to make sure she was unhurt. But since it was Halloween, most kids were circulating or collecting candy on the more populated blocks.

A car approached in the distance. In the dark, it was impossible to see who it was.

She straightened and gave a small wave, hoping someone would stop and help her out of the ditch.

A horrid suspicion formed in her mind as the car drew closer. Cole Daniels.

He pulled up alongside of her and rolled down his window. "You all right?"

"Fine. Not a scratch on me." Nervously she laughed off his concern.

Cole tilted his head to one side. "Seems like you've got yourself into a mess here."

"I know." What did he want her to do, beg for his help? She'd rot first.

"I can see that you're probably suffering from . . . what did you say I had? Oh yes." He tipped back his hat with his index finger. "Spiritual disease. That's what you called it."

"B-but-" she stuttered.

"I want you to know I'll be praying for you." With that he rolled up his window and drove away.

Chapter Three

Lesley stared after Cole in shocked disbelief. "I can't believe that man," she muttered incredulously. As his car advanced down the street, Lesley became more scornful. He wouldn't really leave her, would he? All he wanted was the satisfaction of having her beg. But she refused to play his game.

Both arms hugging her waist, she shuffled her feet anxiously. "It's all your fault anyway," she shouted into the empty street after Cole, willingly placing the blame on him.

A couple of minutes passed, and still the street remained deserted. She could be stuck out here all night. Even the few houses in the immediate vicinity didn't have any lights on. The inhabitants were probably gone for the evening, so it wouldn't do any good to trek up and see about using the phone.

Another few moments, and Lesley looked around her helplessly. If Cole happened to drive by again, she'd be more apt to smile sweetly.

"Darn!" She kicked at the radial tire, stubbed her toe and wanted to cry with frustration. Everything was going wrong. Everything! What was she supposed to do? Walk down Harrison

Avenue garbed in a white sheet as a pillar of salt? That would cause quite a stir. She'd be the laughingstock of Coeur d'Alene.

A pair of headlights could be seen shining in the distance. Hope sprang as Lesley straightened and stepped into the middle of the street. When it looked as if the vehicle might turn, Lesley groaned and gave a shout.

"Here. I'm here." She waved her arm high above her head. "Don't leave, please don't leave."

The car seemed to hesitate, then came her way. Lesley heaved a giant sigh. As it approached, she saw that it was a tow truck.

The vehicle pulled up beside her. "Evening, miss, would you be needing help?" An older man was speaking with a soft southern drawl. He sounded like an angel.

"Yes, yes," Lesley cried eagerly. "You don't know how glad I am to see you. I was getting worried—there doesn't seem to be anyone home around here."

The gray-haired man climbed out of the truck's cab, grinning widely. He tipped his hat back with one hand as he surveyed Lesley's vehicle. "This doesn't look like it'll take much."

"Oh, good." Relief washed over her.

"I'll just attach the cable and haul her out. No problem."

"Wonderful," Lesley murmured and stepped aside as he climbed into his truck and backed it up across the road to position it to the best advantage.

On the street again, he regarded Lesley with curious eyes. "You always dress like that?"

"These? No, I'm on my way to church."

"Church," he repeated with a laugh. "On Halloween? You're likely to get mugged on a night like this."

Her good mood rejuvenated, Lesley responded with a light laugh. "I think I'll take my chances. But next year I'm not changing into my costume until I arrive at the church. I had visions of walking into town in this getup. Can you imagine the looks people would have given me?"

"Man said you'd be real eager to see me."

"Man?" Lesley repeated, slow comprehension seeping into her thoughts.

"Yeah, the guy that pulled into the service station. He said he saw someone in trouble but thought they were dressed funny and that I should be careful. That's why I came up real cautious like."

Cole Daniels, Lesley seethed. Of all the nerve. "I don't suppose this man was driving a new car."

"That's him," the tow truck operator responded without looking up, his gaze fixed on the rear bumper of her car. "Real knowledgeable about cars, too." He paused and wiped his hands on a greasy rag that hung from the back of his coveralls pocket.

"How do you mean?"

"Had this foreign job in the garage all week. Couldn't for the life of me figure out what was wrong. Then this guy in the new car pulls up while I'm working on it and listens to the engine running. Next thing I know, he walks over and moves a couple of wires, and bingo, that baby was purring like a well-fed cat."

"Nice of him," Lesley muttered caustically under her breath. Cole had no difficulty lending a stranger a helping hand, but it didn't seem to bother him to leave her helpless on a deserted street with an empty canister of salt hanging around her neck. Her neighbor was a real jewel, and when she saw him next she'd tell him exactly what she thought.

Lesley's little car came out of the ditch without a problem. She wrote a check to the tow truck operator and thanked him again.

Within a couple of minutes they were both on their way. As much as Lesley tried to put the incident with Cole behind her, she couldn't. He had left her like that on purpose. What kind of brute was he?

The church parking lot was full by the time Lesley arrived, which didn't help cool her indignation. Hurriedly she delivered the cookies and lemonade to the kitchen and was on her way to the recreation hall when she bumped into Terry.

"Where have you been?" Terry asked in an anxious, high-pitched voice. "I was beginning to get worried."

"Don't ask." Lesley responded with a half groan. "It's a long story."

"I love the costume." Lesley's sister took a step back to examine her.

"Thanks. What have I missed?"

"A few games. Bobbing for apples and the treasure hunt. Nothing much." A brooding look came over Terry's face. "Something's wrong. I think you'd better tell me about it."

"Not now," Lesley said with a sigh. "I'm too angry."

"I don't suppose this has something to do with your new neighbor?"

Lesley could feel the color invade her face. She'd never felt such intense dislike for anyone. All her life her parents had taught her to look for the good in every person and situation. But after tonight she could think of nothing to like about Cole Daniels.

"Yes, it's my neighbor," Lesley admitted after a meaningful pause. "I don't like him, Terry. The two of us seem to clash against each other. My life's going to be miserable until he leaves."

"Les?" Terry's blue-gray eyes probed hers. "I don't think I've ever seen you react this strongly to anyone. You've always been tolerant and good-natured."

"That's what I used to think."

A burst of laughter and applause erupted from the hall.

“Come on.” Terry glanced away from her. “If we don’t get going, we’ll miss the whole party. But promise you’ll tell me everything later,” she coaxed.

“I promise,” Lesley agreed reluctantly. She wasn’t looking forward to relaying the incident, mainly because she recognized that her role that evening hadn’t been entirely innocent. But if she was completely honest with herself, it wasn’t the fact that Cole had left her in the street alone, it was his parting words that irritated her. No matter how they felt about each other, if their roles had been reversed she would never have left him.

The recreation hall was alive with young and old alike as they gathered together for the All Saints’ Eve costume party. The gaily dressed youngsters had been divided into age groups and were involved in variety of games. A long table in the rear of the hall was full of carved pumpkins. Robert, wearing a badge that designated him as a judge, was closely examining each one. BRIBES ACCEPTED was sketched in large letters on the bottom of his badge.

“Come on, Robert may need a little help deciding.”

The two women weaved their way through the large crowd.

“We thought you might like our opinion,” Terry said as she slipped an arm around her husband’s waist.

“Nope, my mind’s set.” He was dressed as one of the apostles. A fake beard was glued to his face. A long brown housecoat was cinched at his middle, and he carried a fishing pole.

“Clever outfit,” Lesley commented, her bad mood dissipating under the shouts of laughter and the gay mood of the others.

“What about me?” Terry rotated slowly, her eyes smiling.

Lesley had been so caught up with her anger, she hadn’t noticed her sister’s outfit. Terry wore a long, draping white gown and a blue head scarf that flowed halfway down her back. Bare feet in sandals, she carried a ceramic pitcher.

"Martha from Bethany. Lazarus' sister?"

"Nope." Terry laughed. "I thought for sure you'd know."

Lesley shrugged in defeat. "I give up. Who are you?"

"The Samaritan woman who met Jesus at the well in the Gospel of John."

"You mean the one with five husbands," Lesley teased.

"Five husbands," Robert echoed loudly.

"That's the one." Lesley watched as her sister lifted laughing eyes to her husband. "So you'd better shape up or I'll move on to husband number two."

Lesley smiled, too. Terry and Robert were so much in love that she could almost be envious. It didn't seem fair that her sister should find someone so easily when she attracted men like Dale Wylie. Terry and Robert had met at church camp on Coeur d'Alene Lake their first year of college. Both were serving as counselors for the fourth, fifth and sixth graders for the summer. In the fall, Robert had gone back to Seattle Pacific University in Washington State while Terry attended the local community college. They wrote one another every day, and Terry lived for the holidays when Robert would be back in town. They were married two years later. Why couldn't she have met someone at summer camp? The thought was so ridiculous that it prompted one side of her mouth upward to form a lopsided grin.

". . . And you look ridiculous." Lesley picked up on the second half of Robert's statement.

"I look what?" she choked.

"You know, Les, you really do." Apparently, Terry must have noticed the outrage in Lesley's flashing blue eyes.

"That what Daniels said." She grew angry all over again.

"Is that what you're so hot about?" Terry quizzed her with open curiosity.

This was probably the first time in several years that Lesley was reluctant to share something with her sister. They'd always been close, but she felt a strange reluctance to tell Terry about Cole Daniels.

"That and more." She realized her attitude was absurd. Terry was her sister. So, as unemotionally as possible, Lesley related the events of the evening.

But to her dismay both Terry and Robert burst out laughing at Cole's comment that he would pray for her. Their amusement did little to ease her indignation. Lesley found nothing in her situation worthy of laughter. Pinching her mouth tightly shut, she moved into the crowd and joined the others in a song fest.

Later, the awards for the best costume were given, and Lesley won for the most original. Her smile was tremulous as she accepted the handcrafted bow and submitted to a series of picture taking. But the pleasure of the award didn't show in her eyes, and she felt drained and tired by the time the party broke up shortly before ten.

Robert and Terry walked out to the parking lot with her. Robert ran a hand along her car bumper. "It hardly shows. Of course, it's hard to tell without daylight. But by the look of things, you got off lightly."

"I suppose." Lesley knew she didn't sound grateful, but Cole Daniels had ruined her evening.

Terry gave her a funny look that Lesley chose to ignore.

"It's been a long week." Robert exchanged glances with his wife, but not before Lesley caught a glimpse of censure in their eyes.

"Yes, it has," Lesley agreed. "Tomorrow I'm going to look through the want ads and see about finding someplace to move. I can't take much more of that ill-mannered oaf from next door."

Lesley saw Terry open her mouth, then just as quickly close it.

"You might sleep on it," Robert advised.

"I might," she said more sharply than she intended. "I'll see you tomorrow." The comment was directed to Terry. The sisters did their errands and grocery shopping together on Saturdays.

"Night." Lesley scooted inside her car and started the engine.

"Night." Robert answered for them both.

Lesley noticed that her sister and brother-in-law were engaged in a lively conversation on the way back into the church. After a minute, Terry's head bobbed in agreement. Unconcerned, Lesley drove home. She would move. It was the perfect solution. There was no need to live this far out of town. But then she did enjoy the country life and having a large garden.

Lesley recalled how she and Terry had found the duplex shortly after Terry was married. She remembered the pride they had in painting the house and tilling the backyard for the garden. The closeness they'd shared as sisters had been enhanced because they lived so near to each other.

Now everything was different, thanks to Cole Daniels.

His car was in the driveway when she pulled up. Although she felt like slamming the car door, she exercised rigid restraint and allowed it to shut normally. She was reaching across her seat for the empty cookie plate and her purse when he spoke.

"I see you made it home safely."

Cole was leaning indolently against his door-jamb, his arms and legs crossed as he regarded her with lazy indulgence.

Lesley stiffened and swallowed back an angry outburst. "Yes, I did," she said tautly, her voice tight, "no thanks to you."

"I sent the tow truck." His mouth deepened into grooves as he fought to suppress a smile.

"Am I supposed to thank you for that?"

"A little appreciation wouldn't be amiss."

Hands on hips, she glared at him across the short distance that separated them. "Well, thank you very much."

"You're welcome."

"You . . . You left me standing out there in the dark and alone. I was worried sick. Because of you I missed half the party and the whole thing was your fault in the first place and—"

"My, my," he interrupted, the lazy smile evident in his voice. "You've worked yourself into a regular snit."

"Don't you dare say that word to me!" She pointed her index finger at him accusingly. "You left me there. Anything could have happened after you drove off." She could see that her anger was affecting him.

Cole straightened, dropping his hands to his side. "And just what was I supposed to do?" he challenged, an impatient edge to his voice.

"Help me!" she shouted.

"You needed a tow truck. I'm not Superman—I can't lift cars out of ditches."

"But . . . But you told the driver you thought I was dressed funny and he should be careful."

"From what I've witnessed tonight, who could argue?"

"You're the most despicable, selfish and hurtful man I've ever known. If I never saw you again I'd—"

"And you've got to be the most unreasonable, childish—"

"I don't have to stand here and listen to this garbage," Lesley shouted and whirled around. She stormed up the steps to her front door and turned the knob. Nothing. She tried again, pushing it in with her shoulder, forgetting she had locked it.

"Don't tell me I have to come over and hold your hand while you open the door?"

Lesley tossed him a look that left little doubt of what she was thinking. Her hand shook as she inserted the key into the lock. Cole Daniels had to be the most irritating man she had ever encountered. This little incident was the crack that broke the dam. She'd move. Tomorrow first thing she'd start looking for another apartment.

Still keyed up, Lesley jerked the cone from the top of her head and paced the living room floor like a wild, caged animal. The impatient tap that sounded from his side of the wall only fueled her anger. With purpose-filled steps she strode over and pounded right back. Take that, she fumed.

She changed out of her costume and climbed into a full-length purple velvet robe. Never had she reacted like this to any man, any situation. Not only did her personality grate against Cole's, he had the ability to make her say and do things that were normally foreign to her gentle nature.

The muted tapping sounds of the typewriter came through the walls. Did Cole feel the same way about her?

Lesley brought her knees up, hugging them against her stomach as she rested her chin on top.

Did she resent him because he'd taken her sister's place? The thought was too ridiculous to even consider.

The irritating blast of a car horn came from outside. Lesley stood and pulled back the center of the closed drapes to see what was happening.

A sinking sensation attacked the pit of her stomach and shut her eyes as frustration burned its way through her. This evening was going from bad to worse.

The car horn blared again impatiently as Dale and Frank drove onto the lawn, their tires digging deep into the damp grass.

Behind the small crack separating the drapes, Lesley watched as Dale climbed out of the passenger side of the car. He staggered a little, paused and took a long swig from the beer bottle he was carrying.

The doorbell buzzed and Lesley stared at the wooden door with terrified eyes. She wouldn't answer it.

“Come on, baby,” Dale cooed. “I know you’re inside. We’ve got a party to go to.”

Frozen in a standing position by the window, Lesley could hear her heart pounding in a wild beat. Nothing had ever sounded so loud. Dale was sure to hear it. Should she phone the police? Would Frank and Dale hear her movements inside the apartment and break down the door if she did? What did she have handy that she could defend herself with?

“Don’t let her get away with this,” Lesley heard Frank shout out the car window. “Put your foot down, man,” he added.

Dale jabbed the doorbell a second time, then started pounding furiously against the front door.

In desperation, Lesley hurried into the kitchen and phoned the police station. She couldn’t deal with two drunks, and there was no telling what could happen.

The officer who answered kept Lesley on the line for several minutes, taking down the necessary information. He assured her a patrol car was on the way.

When Lesley returned to the living room, she could hear angry shouts. Another glance out the window confirmed her suspicions. Cole was on the front lawn demanding that Frank and Dale leave. Frank had climbed out of the car and appeared to be the more sober of the two as he approached Cole, his look dark and angry.

The argument was fast becoming heated, the language more abusive. When Dale took a wild swing at Cole, Lesley gave a small cry of alarm. Cole ducked but took a punch in the stomach from Frank. Dumbfounded, Lesley stared as Cole stumbled a few steps before recovering enough to fight off Dale, who was attempting to hold him down so Frank could punch him.

More outraged than she could remember being in her life, Lesley grabbed the broom from the kitchen and stalked outside.

"Get out of here," she shouted at Dale and brushing him across the chest with the straw part of the broom. She repeated the action again and again, her revulsion fueling the attack.

Dale brought up his hands to defend himself, then tried to grab the broom out of her hand. He caught the bristly part and was pulling her to him when Cole laid him flat with one well-delivered blow. Frank was already on the grass, apparently knocked out.

"Are you all right?" Cole asked her breathlessly, his shoulders heaving. An ugly bruise was forming along the side of his face, and the knuckles on one hand were beginning to swell.

"I'm fine. What about you?"

He nodded and wiped the side of his mouth with the back of his hand.

A silence settled between them as they regarded each other.

Unsure, she lifted her hand, her fingertips lightly brushing the hair from his temple, and explored the darkening bruise.

Cole's smoldering gaze ran over her face, and their eyes locked. His look was gentle yet intense, and Lesley felt weak, as if her knees were about to give out on her.

A gentle smile touched his mouth. "Four karate lessons and you come at him with a broom?"

"I took the first thing that came to mind." There was a breathlessness to her response. "I didn't want you hurt because of Dale."

"Your friends?" His eyes narrowed slightly.

"Not likely." She shook her head self-consciously and looked away. "I went out with Dale a couple of times, but that was it."

Another car could be heard approaching, and simultaneously they turned to see who was coming. The police patrol car could be seen coming up the hill toward them.

"I called," Lesley supplied. "I didn't know what else to do."

Was she imagining things, or did Cole tense and take a step in retreat?

"I don't want to become involved." His eyes seemed to bore into hers. "Agreed?"

Numbly, Lesley nodded. Not become involved. But he already was. What he wanted was to avoid any contact with the police. But why?

By the time the two uniformed officers had parked their vehicle and approached her, Cole was inside the duplex, door closed and lights off. She cast one fleeting glance toward him, then turned her attention to the policemen.

The first one tipped his hat back with the end of his pencil. "Seems like you carry a mean broom, lady."

"Yes." Lesley swallowed tightly. "These two are drunk and disorderly."

The second officer picked up an empty beer can beside the car. "I think we get the picture. Looks like their car may have ruined a portion of your yard."

"Are you going to arrest them?"

"Looks that way. Any qualms?"

"None." Lesley's hand clenched the broom handle. "Throw the book at them."

"You'll need to answer a few questions."

The first officer returned to the police car and picked up the microphone to his radio.

"Would you mind coming down to the station and answering a few questions?" be asked, surveying the two men, who were sitting up. Dale was rubbing the side of his jaw and looked around confused. Frank was out cold.

"No," she agreed meekly, "I don't mind at all. Let me change and I'll be there in a few minutes."

"This one says a man slugged him." The officer glanced at Lesley.

"Ask him about ghosts and goblins—he probably saw those too," Lesley supplied. She wouldn't lie outright, but she owed Cole a debt of appreciation. "I'll be right back, Officer."

After an hour and a half at the police station, Lesley parked her car in the driveway to her apartment. Halloween wasn't a holiday she'd soon forget if as much happened to her every year. She felt bone-weary. It seemed that in the space of a few hours more had happened in her life than the past twenty years.

When her car door slammed, Cole came out of his duplex. His tall figure filled the open doorway, silhouetted by the light. "Everything go okay?"

"Fine." She wiped a hand across her face and sighed. "Frank and Dale are sleeping it off in the drunk tank." At his concerned look she added, "Neither one of them even showed signs of a struggle. I think you got the worse end of that deal." The bruise on his face looked angry and she squelched feelings of guilt. "Would . . . Would you like a cup of cocoa?" She wasn't sure why she issued the invitation. Tonight he had made her angrier than anyone or anything and only a short time later had rescued her from what could have been a nasty scene. The invitation was a way of extending her hand in friendship, her way of saying "Let bygones be bygones."

Cole hesitated, and Lesley tensed. He knew what she was saying. Now she almost regretted having asked. "Look, I didn't ask for your hand in marriage. A decision shouldn't be that difficult."

"You must be exhausted." He was offering her an excuse.

She refused it. "No, I'm too keyed up to sleep."

With a dignified just of her chin, she stood back and waited. She became fascinated with his strong profile as he stood in the open door. The contrast between Dale and Cole was all the more striking. There wasn't anything artificial about Cole. He was all male . . . and distant. Did he want to keep it that way?

His expression changed, softening somewhat. "Another time, perhaps."

Lesley sucked in a hurt breath. He was refusing her? She had extended an appreciative hand of friendship and he rejected it. It hurt. That was what surprised her. He turned her down and she felt like an insecure teen who hadn't been asked to the prom.

"Good night, Lesley." He turned back into his apartment and closed the door.

Was that regret she heard in his voice? Nibbling on the corner of her bottom lip, Lesley walked into her half of the duplex. Although dark and filled with shadows from a three-quarter moon, her home offered comfort and security.

Slipping off her shoes, Lesley flexed her toes in the carpet before moving into the kitchen and flipping on a light switch. Immediately the area was bathed in a soft glow.

She opened the refrigerator, took out a carton of milk and poured herself a glass. The package of hamburger caught her attention as she returned the milk carton.

Not giving herself the opportunity to change her mind, she slipped back into her shoes and marched over to Cole's front door.

He answered after the first knock, his expression thoughtful as his eyes fell on the meat.

"Here." She gave him the hamburger.

"Thanks, but I've already had dinner."

"It's not to eat," she announced primly. "Put it over your bruise."

A smile quivered at the corners of his sensuous mouth. "I thought you were supposed to use steak for that?"

"I didn't have steak, only hamburger," Lesley reasoned.

"I'm afraid I could only accept Choice, Grade A tenderloin beef. Corn-fed preferred." A teasing quality crept into his voice.

"Honestly," she admonished, quickly losing the fragile grip on her temper, "just take the hamburger. It'll make me feel better so I can get some sleep."

"And if you're asleep, you can't bother me," he added as if that was enough of an inducement for him to take the meat.

"Exactly," she said a trifle flippantly.

"'Tis done. Good night, Lesley, for the third time."

"Good riddance, you mean," she muttered with a brash air of unconcern.

His chuckle followed her as she turned and began to walk away.

"Lesley."

Expectantly she turned around.

His gaze flickered over her and she watched as a muscle in his jaw tensed. "Nothing. Good night."

Chapter Four

Lesley lay on her back, her hands supporting her head as she stared at the dark ceiling. Sleep was impossible.

The sounds of the typewriter had stopped, but Cole wasn't asleep either. She could hear his movements on the other side of the wall. It sounded as if he was pacing: walking to one side of the small living room, pivoting and strolling back . . . again and again and again.

Lesley closed her eyes, and the mental image of Cole formed in her mind. He looked troubled and weary; at least, that was how she'd seen him last. She wondered what he'd done with the hamburger. The thought was silly.

The pacing stopped and the night grew silent. But Lesley couldn't sleep. About three, she tossed back the covers and climbed out of bed. She never did have that glass of milk. Maybe it would help now.

The small lamp on the end table in the living room was all the light she needed. Holding the milk glass, she sat on the sofa and brought her knees up so she could slip the warm gown over her feet. The Bible she used for devotions sat beside the lamp.

Idly, Lesley flipped through the pages. Her parents had given her this purse-size edition when she turned sixteen. The pages were dog-eared, the edges worn from years of use.

Important pieces of her life were tucked away in its flap: the newspaper notice of her grandmother's death, a small card from Terry and Robert's wedding and Lisa's birth announcement.

Long ago Lesley had learned that if she couldn't sleep, reading God's Word had a soothing effect on her. Opening the book at random, she was surprised to see that it opened at Matthew, Chapter 22. Usually her Bible opened to Psalms, since that book was directly in the middle.

The bold-phrased lettering seemed to jump off the page at her. A soft smile touched her face. "You shall love the Lord your God with all your heart, with all your soul, and with all your mind." The greatest commandment. Lesley had read these words a hundred times, but the second part of the commandment caused a tightening sensation in her throat. "You shall love your neighbor as yourself."

Lesley closed the book and laid her head against the back of the couch. Love thy neighbor. Was this coincidence, or was God giving her a special message? But if He was sending her something with a profound meaning, it would be preceded by a blare from trumpets, or at least an angel's announcement. Not His word in the still of a sleepless night. Love thy neighbor, her thoughts reiterated. Cole Daniels had not been an error. God had sent him to her. Lesley didn't know why, nor did she question. For now she would trust. But sometimes that was the hardest thing to do.

"I just can't believe it." Terry looped a strand of hair around her ear and pushed the grocery cart ahead so another shopper could get by.

"I find Dale's behavior just as unbelievable," Lesley returned, placing several red Delicious apples in a cellophane bag.

"I didn't think he'd do anything like that. You're not still thinking about moving, are you?"

"No." Lesley looked up, startled for a moment. She'd forgotten she'd even threatened as much yesterday. "Not anymore." Although she hadn't told her sister about Cole's intervention with Dale and Frank, after last night she felt assured God had her exactly where she was supposed to be.

"Didn't your neighbor hear any of the commotion?" Terry feigned engrossment in the Delicious apples.

Amused at her sister's interest, Lesley successfully stifled a smile. Terry had an apple tree in her backyard, and the two had spent one whole weekend picking fruit and canning applesauce.

"I'm sure he did."

"And?" Terry prompted.

"And the police arrived." Her fingers gripping the handle of the cart, Lesley pushed it farther down the crowded aisle.

"But you don't think you'll move?" Terry sounded relieved.

"I did a lot of thinking about it last night and decided that maybe God hadn't made such a horrendous mistake after all."

"I'm sure He didn't."

"I'm even beginning to believe there's a reason God moved Cole Daniels beside me."

"I think there is."

Lesley paused long enough to turn around, her laughing eyes studying her sister. "Has anyone ever told you that on rare occasions you sound like a parrot?"

Terry batted her eyelashes wickedly. "Polly want a cracker."

They bath giggled like carefree friends and continued with their shopping.

After Halloween night, Cole avoided Lesley. She didn't see him for days, and once when she made up an excuse to knock at his door, he didn't answer. It was almost as if the duplex hadn't been rented. However, she knew he was there. And even though they didn't communicate, her awareness of him grew. She discovered that her early morning prayers often included Cole, and later recognized that he was dominating her thoughts more and more.

The first snowfall of the year came the second week in November. Lesley woke early and responded with delight to the fluffy white flakes that drifted to the earth like goose down descending from some glorious heaven. Her excitement dissipated with the knowledge that she had to dress and get into town. Although only a few inches covered the ground, the white powder was falling thick and heavy. She could have trouble getting out of the driveway.

After a hurried shower, Lesley dressed in dark wool pants and a thick pink ski sweater. The snow shovel was in the storage shed in the back of the apartment with the garden equipment. Tying a scarf around her neck, she next slipped on her knee-high boots and opened the sliding glass door to retrieve the shovel.

Halfway across the backyard, she noticed another pair of fresh footprints in the snow: a larger foot that made deep impressions in the fallen crystalline purity. Cole's, Lesley mused.

The shovel was missing. Blowing on her bare hands with her warm breath and rubbing them together, Lesley came around the side of the house to find Cole busy shoveling the snow from the driveway.

"Morning," she called, more than a little pleased to see him again. He looked well. His hair needed cutting, and the bronze tan that had caused her to wonder at his penchant for the indoors had faded. But he looked vibrant, fit and all male.

Cole stopped shoveling and straightened. "I didn't think I'd catch you up this early."

In other words, he'd been hoping to get away without seeing her at all.

A smile broke out across her face as she ignored his lack of welcome. "You don't need to do that." He was clearing the area behind her car so that she could back out safely.

He scraped the shovel against the cement and threw the snow aside. "I know that."

"Were you afraid that if I got snowed in, I'd be around to pester you all day?"

He paused momentarily. "You could say that."

That was a rotten thing to say. For days she'd taken pains to stay out of his way. If he didn't want to see her, that was fine. At least, that was what she'd been telling herself.

"Cole?" With an innocent lilt to her voice she called his name, mischief glittering from her eyes.

He glanced up expectantly just as Lesley threw the snowball and hit him squarely in the chest.

"How could I possibly bother you?" she challenged. "I haven't seen you in weeks." Her hands rested defiantly on slim hips; her eyes sparkled brightly.

For an instant Cole looked stunned. "So much for Christian charity," he murmured and tossed the shovel aside.

Lesley couldn't keep from laughing. Stooping over, she packed a second snowball. "You seem to think I'll let you get away with insulting me. Ha!"

Cole leaned over and formed his own snowball as a smile slowly made its way across his face. "How did I insult you?" he asked in a dangerously calm voice.

Her bare hands were freezing and she tossed her threat to the ground and rubbed the warmth back into her frozen fingers. "Peace?" she asked hopefully.

"Oh no, you started this."

"But . . . I don't have any gloves on."

"You knew that when you threw the first snowball."

"But . . ." For every step he took toward her, Lesley took one in retreat. "Would it help if I apologized?"

"It might," he said and advanced another threatening step. "And then again, it might not."

"You wouldn't."

"Don't challenge me, Lesley." His mirthful eyes pinned her.

"But you shouldn't have said that."

"Said what?"

"That I pester you."

"You haven't stopped since the day I first saw you."

"That's not true," she cried indignantly.

"You have no way of knowing, my blue-eyed temptress."

With bubbling laughter, she reached down, grabbed her snowball and threw it at him with remarkable accuracy. Intense satisfaction raced through her when she saw she'd caught him completely off guard. Pivoting sharply, she ran toward the house. Ten steps from her front door, Cole caught her.

Lesley let out a squeal as his hands gripped her upper arms and flung her around. Somehow she managed to elude him, but Cole made a diving catch for her that sent them both crashing to the snow.

Laughing and breathless, she tossed her head to and fro as Cole attempted to hold her face. "I'm sorry," she cried with bubbling exhilaration.

"I just bet you are."

"I'll never do it again, I promise."

Cole was lying halfway on top of her, his hands pinning hers above her head. Her deep smiling eyes met his as she heaved a giant breath from her lungs.

The warm, smoldering light clashed with hers, and they both went still. Slowly the laughter faded from him. Lesley noted that his gaze slid to her mouth, and it was all she could do not to moisten her lips in eager anticipation. He was so close that all she had to do was lift her head. His mouth hovered above hers for a timeless moment.

Lesley lowered her lashes, hungry for the taste of this man who had haunted her for weeks.

The hold on her hands relaxed and Lesley's gaze shot to Cole as he stood and brushed the snow from his pant legs. Resting her weight on her elbows, Lesley sat up and stared at him dumbfoundedly. When he extended a hand to her, she placed her bare one in his and was lifted from the wet snow.

Her eyes were filled with questions, but he ignored them. Cool and aloof, he pushed her toward the stairs into the apartment. "Get dressed or you'll be late for work."

"Yes sir," she tossed back saucily.

A hint of a grin sprang into his eyes and just as quickly disappeared. "I'll finish digging you out."

She stood, one foot resting on the porch, the other on the top step. "Cole."

He turned.

"Thanks."

"Why thank me?" he said in a husky voice. "I'm doing this for completely selfish reasons."

The words were meant to disarm her, and they did. With a sad smile, Lesley retreated into the warmth of her home.

Snow was a part of life in northern Idaho, but the first snowfall of the year created the usual rush on the service stations for snow tires and chains. Lesley bypassed the station where she normally did business and instead stopped in at Paul Walker's on her way home. After filling her gas tank, she stepped into the resort grocery.

"Howdy, Paul," she called out cheerfully. It was just after

four-thirty, and already the sun was beginning to set. Heavy clouds darkened the sky. "Looks like we're due for more snow."

"Seems that way." Paul was stacking jars of peanut butter on the shelf. "Anything I can get you?"

"How about a snowplow?"

He chuckled good-naturedly. "Haven't seen your neighbor in quite a while. Must be a week or so since the last time he was in. Buys most of his things here. Even had me special-order a few things I didn't have handy."

"Cole Daniels?"

"Only close neighbor you got up your way, I'd say."

Cole had continued to do his main shopping in this resort store? Groceries were 20 percent cheaper in town.

"In fact, if it isn't too much trouble, would you mind taking him a couple of things? He paid for them. No need to let them sit around here with you being so close and all."

"No," Lesley answered thoughtfully, "I don't mind."

"Good." Paul returned his attention to the peanut butter, and Lesley strolled down the narrow aisles picking up coarse salt and the latest issue of *TV Guide.*

Paul handed her a small sack marked "Daniels" after she paid for the gas and the couple of things she'd gotten.

Her thoughts were as heavy as the gray clouds that obliterated the sky when Lesley drove home. The hill had been sanded, which made the access up the hill to her place easier.

What did Cole do for a living? He was always there—at least, his car was. He seldom came out of doors. Sometimes she had the feeling he was hiding. But why, and from whom? She'd tried to tell Terry her suspicions on several occasions, but Terry had laughed them off, attributing such ideas to Lesley's overactive imagination. Rather than argue, Lesley said nothing.

Cole's lights were on when she pulled into her driveway.

After dropping off her sack in the kitchen, she walked over to his front door. He didn't respond to her first rap.

"Come on, Cole," she cried, half-angry. What did he think she was going to do? "I promise I don't have any snowballs."

The sound of his chuckle could be heard before he unlatched the lock and pulled open his door.

"Paul Walker sent this along." She gave him the small sack. The temptation to take a look had been almost overwhelming, but she'd resisted. Lesley hated to think of herself as the nosy type.

Frowning, Cole took the sack, looked inside, then glanced up at her. "Was there something else you wanted?" he asked dryly.

Why was it Cole had the ability to make her feel like a repentant child? "No, there's nothing else," she shot back hotly. She pivoted and marched down the steps.

"Lesley," he called out, stopping her.

She turned back, her eyes flashing angry signals at him.

"Thanks."

"You're welcome." She didn't feel the least bit gracious. She'd done him a favor, and Cole acted as if she'd purposely intruded on his privacy. "Next time I won't bother," she mumbled under her breath as she righteously marched back to her half of the duplex.

"Maybe you shouldn't," Cole called after her.

Lesley closed the door, the light and warmth of her home welcoming her. She wasn't angry with Cole, but more puzzled than anything. She didn't understand him, and the more she tried, the more confused she became.

Lesley opened a can of stew and let it warm on the stove while she changed into her wool pants and sweater. The phone rang as she reappeared in the kitchen.

"Hello," she answered and stirred the bubbling meat and vegetables.

"Hi, how's it going?"

It was her sister. "Fine."

"Have any trouble getting to work this morning?"

"No. Cole helped dig me out."

"That was nice."

"Neighborly, but I think he had his own interests at heart. If I was home, I might find out what he does with his time all day."

"Honestly, Les, are you still on that kick?" Terry asked and heaved a sigh. "I sometimes think you missed your calling in life. You should be working for the FBI."

"Maybe," Lesley decided not to argue.

"I got a letter from Mom and Dad today." Their parents wintered in Arizona every year.

"Oh, what did Mom have to say?"

"The usual. They're having a good time, Dad's golfing every day and enjoying himself. They wanted to know if all of us would come down for Christmas. Robert's going to see if he can get off an extra day, but you know what the post office is like this time of year. It looks doubtful for us. What about you?"

"I . . . I don't know yet, I'll have to check the schedule at the bank." The lights flickered, then dimmed. "It looks like I may be losing my electricity. What's happening your way?"

"Nothing yet, but you can bet if you go, we will."

"I'd better get off the phone and look for a candle. I'll talk to you tomorrow."

"Okay."

The soft buzz of the receiver told Lesley her sister had hung up.

Lesley was opening a kitchen drawer when the lights flickered a second time just before everything went completely dark. "Rats," she blurted out impatiently, fumbling to locate the flashlight in the kitchen junk drawer. Her fingers encountered something sharp, and she inhaled a pain-filled breath and jerked out her hand. The abrupt action pulled the drawer out of its socket and dumped the contents on the floor in a tremendous crash.

Something crashed on the toe of her slipper and Lesley cried out more from shock than pain.

Within seconds Cole was pounding on her sliding glass door. When she didn't immediately respond, he pushed it aside and flashed a light across the floor.

"Lesley," he asked anxiously, "are you all right?"

"I . . . I think so."

"What happened?"

"I was trying to find a flashlight and the drawer fell."

"Why are you sucking your finger?"

"Because it's bleeding."

"Let me see." He maneuvered his way through the mess on the floor and took her hand.

"It's fine. I think I caught it on the end of an open pocket-knife."

"Serves you right," he admonished gently.

A tingling warmth was spreading up to her elbow from his gentle but firm touch. He set the flashlight on the counter and turned the palm of her hand over to better examine the small cut. "It doesn't look too bad. Have any bandages handy?"

"The bathroom," she supplied.

The flashlight on the counter dimmed and within seconds had faded completely.

"Oh, great."

"No need to panic," Cole muttered with an edge of impatience.

"I'm not panicking," she denied. "I'll get mine. It should be down here somewhere." She took a tentative step and her foot encountered a spool of thread. "Oh," she gasped and flung her hands out to catch herself.

Cole wrapped his arms around her waist and caught her just as she started to fall. "It's dangerous just being around you."

Lesley's senses were clamoring at his nearness, and she required a couple of seconds to recover from the impact of being held by Cole.

Cole was just as affected. Lesley could feel the battle that seemed to be going on inside him. He tensed and inhaled deeply; his warm breath fanned the side of her face near her temple.

Lesley didn't swallow, didn't move. Instinct demanded that she turn into his arms, but she resisted. Her throat felt dry and scratchy.

"Lesley." He murmured her name softly. His arms turned so that only a few scant inches separated them. Gently a finger caressed her cheek and wandered to her lips in sweet, burning exploration.

Softly she moaned at the pure pleasure of his touch. "Cole." His name came in the form of a husky whisper.

His hand curved around the back of her neck, tilting her head up to meet his descending mouth.

Lesley released a slow sigh as she slipped her hands up to rest on the muscular curve of his shoulders. Her lips parted in response as he kissed her. Joyfully her heart burst into a wild, welcoming song.

The contact deepened as Cole pulled her tighter against him. The melody continued as he kissed her again and again in jubilant reprise. Lesley locked her arms around his neck. It felt so right, so good. She'd been kissed before, but not like this. Never had she wanted anything more than to be held by Cole.

Abruptly his hands closed over her wrists and firmly pulled her free. His fingers continued to grip hers.

Lesley's eyes had adjusted to the darkness, and she noted the harsh twist of Cole's mouth.

"That shouldn't have happened."

Was that regret she heard? "You kissed me," she whispered, her voice low and slightly shaky. "It's not that big a deal." She strove to sound flippant and unaffected.

"You don't understand." He raked his fingers through the tousled dark hair.

"No, I don't."

He lifted a dark strand from her face and kissed her again, lightly, brushing her lips with a sweet intensity that made her yearn for more.

"See?"

"See what?" she mumbled, still trapped in the rapture of his kiss.

"Once will never do. Kissing you, holding you will only make me yearn for more. I can't get involved with a woman. Not now. You couldn't possibly understand." His hands roamed up and down her back as if he couldn't bring himself to break away.

"No, I don't," Lesley admitted. "But I know that I like the feel of this." Standing on the tips of her toes, her hands on his shoulders, she pressed her mouth ardently over his.

Cole groaned and pulled her closer, kissing her long and hard.

Lesley broke the pressure and nestled her head to his chest, a gentle smile curving the corners of her mouth. She didn't know what was troubling Cole, but for now he cared more about holding her. A feeling of triumph filled her. Her mouth throbbed from his kisses, and his ragged breath stirred the short tendrils at the side of her face.

"Lesley, we've got to talk."

"No." She kissed his strong neck. "If we talk, you'll push

me away. And you've pushed me away for a long time, Cole Daniels."

"Be reasonable."

"How can I?"

His foot swung out and cleared a path so that they could move into the living room. The only light in the room came from the moon, and it was nearly impossible to maneuver in the darkness.

"Here," Lesley said, a smile evident in her voice.

"Let me lead. At least I know where the couch is."

"I know where everything is in this apartment," he muttered in a husky tone.

"How?"

"Don't you realize I can hear you? Some nights you drove me crazy. I'd picture you . . ." He paused and expelled his breath. "Never mind."

They sat, and immediately Cole looped his arm around her shoulder, bringing her close to his side. One hand slid around his ribs and she pressed her face to his solid chest.

"Cole," she said, not knowing where to begin, "tell me what you're doing here."

She felt him stiffen.

"What do you mean . . . doing here?"

"You don't have a job. How do you support yourself?"

"Because you allow a man to kiss you, does that give you the right to interrogate him?"

"No. Forget I asked, I don't care."

"Right now, with you in my arms, I don't either." The words were spoken so low that Lesley had to strain to hear him.

Afraid to ask anything more, Lesley didn't speak, content to be in his arms. After a while she realized by the even fall and rise of his chest that Cole had fallen asleep. Sometimes she wondered when he slept. No matter when she was up, early morning or late at night, so was Cole. Several times when she'd happened to catch a glimpse of him, she thought he was a man who had driven himself to the limits of his endurance. Now, in her arms, he slept peacefully.

Even when the lights came back on, Cole didn't stir. Lesley disentangled herself from his embrace, gently placed his head on a decorator pillow from the end of the sofa and covered him with a blanket.

She picked up the contents of the drawer and replaced it in the slot. Another hour passed before she ate the beef stew that had been simmering on the stove. Still Cole didn't stir.

In repose he looked like a lost and troubled youth. His forehead was creased in deep-grooved lines, his mouth tight, his body tense even in sleep.

Carrying her dish to the sink, Lesley turned, her hands gripping the edge of the counter behind her. As her gaze rested on Cole, a prayer came to her. Maybe someday he'd feel confident enough to share what was troubling him with her, but for now she must be content with the progress she had made. The thick wall of anger and bitterness he had erected against her and the world was gradually being lowered. Tonight was the beginning, just the beginning.

Lesley was running the water into the sink to do the dinner dishes when Cole stirred. He jerked himself upright and looked around.

Drying her hands on a terry-cloth towel, Lesley walked into the living room. "I must say this is the first time I've had that effect on a man."

He looked at her blankly, then bounded to his feet and ran his hand along the side of his head. "I should never have come here."

"But you did and I'm glad."

His eyes narrowed menacingly. "Just because I kissed you, it doesn't give you the right to—"

"I don't expect a thing," she assured him softly. "Are you hungry?"

"No." He sounded disconcerted, angry.

"Cole, what's wrong?" she probed gently.

"Wrong?" he snapped. "Everything's wrong. I was a fool to come here."

"But, Cole—"

"Listen, Miss Do Right," he said, pointing an accusing finger in her direction, "I knew you were trouble the minute I laid eyes on you."

"That's interesting," she countered evenly. "I felt the same thing about you." Not until tonight did she acknowledge that what they'd experienced was attraction, one so powerful and explosive it could disrupt their entire lives.

"I don't want you in my life. Can I be more blunt than that?" He stalked to the far side of the room, his back to her.

A lump was growing in her throat, making it difficult to swallow. "No, I don't think you can."

"Is it possible for us to live side by side and stay out of each other's way?" Still he kept his back to her.

"Yes," she mumbled. "Go on and go. I don't know why you're running, and I don't care. But I'll be here waiting when you're through."

He turned to her then, his eyes dark and tormented. She yearned to go to him and erase the lines of indecision and anguish, but she stood still and silent.

His hand gripped the doorknob, and she watched as his knuckles turned white. He didn't want to leave, but some force stronger than anything she could inspire in him drove him away and into the silent night.

Chapter Five

Lesley didn't see Cole for another week. Their meeting then was by chance. She'd gone down to the mailbox to collect her mail and saw a deer in the distance. It was unusual for the animals to come down this far, but already winter had been harsh and undoubtedly the small deer had been searching for food. Not wanting to frighten the lovely, tan-skinned creature, she moved cautiously, following it into the wooded area behind the duplex. To her surprise, she found that a bale of hay had been spread out and two other deer were eating from it.

Out of the corner of her eye, Lesley happened to catch a movement. She turned and saw Cole breaking apart another bale farther up the incline in the back of the property. Apparently he felt her presence and turned. Only a few yards separated them. Cole stopped and buried the pitchfork into the snow, his gaze never leaving hers.

"Hello, Lesley."

"Cole." She felt mesmerized by his gaze. He looked tired and she yearned to go to him. But she stood as she was, waiting, for what she didn't know.

"How have you been?"

She wanted to scream at him that she was miserable and that having him so close and yet so far away was hurting her unbearably. She longed to tell him that she knew he wasn't sleeping, because she wasn't sleeping either and could hear his movements. Some nights she pressed her fingertips to the wall because it was the only way she knew to communicate with him.

Lesley lowered her gaze. "I'm fine. And you?"

"Fine."

How could they lie to each other like this? She snapped her head up, suddenly angry. "If you won't be honest, then I will be. I'm miserable. I'd give anything to have the electricity go out again just so I could find that warm, vibrant man I was beginning to know." And love, her thoughts concluded.

A muscle twitched in Cole's jaw. "He doesn't exist."

"Don't tell me that," she cried. "I felt his arms around me, I know his touch and I . . . I gave him comfort. But when the lights came back—"

"When the lights returned," Cole interrupted angrily, "there was only me. I told you that night I should never have kissed you."

"But you did, and things have changed."

"They haven't," Cole argued. "They can't, I won't let them."

"You go ahead and try to deny it, then." The words trembled from her as she knotted her hands into tight fists. "Because I can't, and I've tried as hard as I can."

She turned and ran back to the apartment, her lower lip quivering as she slid the back door closed. Her whole body was shaking when she tossed the few pieces of mail on the table, her fingers biting into the back of the old kitchen chair.

Taking in several deep, calming breaths, Lesley put the teakettle on to boil. Would this be her fate, loving Cole? There hadn't been a time in her life that she felt more frustrated with anyone. And yet there was no reason she should love Cole: he was arrogant, stubborn, angry and hurtful. But the sensations he aroused in her were almost overpowering. There was something profound and intense about him. He was hiding from her and from the world. She might never know or understand him, but that didn't seem to matter to her heart.

When Lesley met her sister an hour later to do their weekly shopping, it was Terry who brought up the subject of Cole. They'd stopped in a local café for a quick lunch.

"Seen much of your neighbor lately?"

"Can't say that I have." Lesley attempted to brush aside her sister's interest.

"You know, for all the times you've talked about him, I've never seen him."

"I don't imagine you will. He's . . . private." She didn't know how else to explain it.

"Other than the first days he was in town, no one else has seen him except Paul Walker and you."

Lesley had mentioned the same thing only last week.

"I was wondering if you were safe up there with him."

"Very safe."

"But he could be an escaped convict."

Lesley didn't slough off Terry's sudden interest. "What makes you say something like that?"

Terry shrugged. "I don't know, but I started thinking about what you've been saying all these weeks and it doesn't add up, none of it."

"I'm not going to concern myself with it now."

"But he could be dangerous."

Now it was Lesley's turn to laugh. "Something isn't right with Cole Daniels, but I trust him implicitly. He'd never hurt me."

Terry set the fork she'd been fingering beside her untouched plate. "You're falling for this guy, aren't you?"

An immediate denial rose to Lesley's lips, but didn't make it past her nod of acknowledgment.

"Oh, Les," Terry groaned. "I was afraid of that."

"I'm a big girl now."

"Yes, I know, but I'd hate to see you get hurt."

"O, ye of little faith," Lesley said with a teasing smile. "Weren't you the one who was constantly telling me that we prayed about my new neighbor and that whoever God sent was—"

"Don't remind me," Terry interrupted, her voice filled with self-reproach. "But, Les, honestly, I'm worried about you."

"I don't know why you should be. If God sent Cole Daniels, then there's a reason. I don't know what it is yet, but I'm sure I will shortly."

"How can you sound so confident?"

Lesley fluttered her long lashes closed. "I'm not sure what Cole's running from, or if he's hiding at all. But I believe that he feels just as strongly about me."

Terry's round eyes brightened to a deeper shade of blue. "But I thought you hardly ever saw him and—"

"But I see the way he looks at me." Lesley glanced down at her chef's salad, idly fingering her napkin in her lap. "We've both been infected with the same virus."

"Love?" Terry made the word a haunting question. "But the kind meant to last a lifetime?"

"I don't know," Lesley returned sadly, "I simply don't know."

The conversation with her sister played back in Lesley's mind as she drove home. When she pulled into the driveway, she noted that something was different but couldn't put her finger on it until she'd taken the last bag of groceries into the apartment. Standing on the top step, she surveyed the area. Cole's car was missing. That was what was wrong.

Without meaning to, Lesley listened for his return the rest of the afternoon. Snow began falling again in soft feathery flakes that covered the ground. Several times Lesley found herself looking out the window. Not that she'd admit openly that she was watching for Cole . . . or anxious for him. Did he have car problems? Maybe he needed help.

Stop it, her mind shouted as she ran her fingers through the silky length of her hair. She was behaving like a worrisome mother. Cole could take care of himself.

About three, Lesley decided to bake cookies. She was ready to do anything to keep her mind off Cole. When she heard him enter the second half of the duplex, she released an unconscious sigh of relief.

Standing motionless in the kitchen, she heard him walk across the floor. Another pair of footsteps echoed and Lesley straightened. Someone was with him.

As quietly as possible, Lesley tiptoed into the living room and peeked out the window. Another car was parked in the driveway next to Cole's. Her eyes narrowed in concentration. She'd seen that car before, but where? She bit into the corner of her mouth. Red and flashy, it . . . She stopped, her mind spinning in deep-grooved channels. That was the car Cole had driven the first day she'd met him—the one parked in the driveway the day he moved into the duplex. Where had it been all this time? What had he done with it?

While she was still musing over these thoughts, the sound of raised voices filtered through the wall opposite Lesley's living room.

"Engstrom, be reasonable. The one who's going to end up getting hurt in this is you. Do you have any idea how hard Jennings is looking for you?"

The man had called Cole "Engstrom." Had he been using a false name all these months?

"He'd never find me here. Coeur d'Alene, Idaho?"

Cole made it sound like the end of the earth.

"Maybe."

The mystery man didn't seem to echo Cole's confidence.

"How's the report coming?"

"I'm finished."

"Good grief, you must have half killed yourself to do it in this time."

A short silence followed.

"Take it with you. See to it that . . ."

The timer on the stove dinged and Lesley yanked her attention to the kitchen. As quickly as possible she turned it off and took the cookie sheet out of the oven. The aroma of melting chocolate chips filled the small apartment.

Like a thief in the night, Lesley returned to the living room.

". . . low profile."

"As much as possible," Cole said, "but the girl next door has guessed something isn't right."

The other man laughed. "But you've always had a way with women. I wouldn't worry about her."

"I'm not."

Was that displeasure Lesley heard in Cole's cool tones?

"Do you want me to get back to you?"

"When you can."

"Listen, Engstrom. Don't take any chances. Your life won't be worth a plug nickel if Jennings gets wind of your whereabouts."

"I won't."

Lesley's knees felt wobbly and weak. She lowered herself onto the couch and covered her mouth with one hand. Cole didn't need to worry about her suspicions. He could handle her. After all, he had a way with women.

More than that, he was in danger, terrible danger. Tears filled her eyes, blurring her vision. The two men continued talking, but Lesley couldn't make out what they were saying. A few minutes later she heard the front door open, then close. When she'd gathered the resolve to stand up and look out the window, the sporty red car was gone.

Lesley didn't eat dinner that night, and breakfast held no appeal the next morning as she dressed for church. She sat through the Sunday school and the morning worship service, but if anyone had asked her what had been discussed, Lesley couldn't have told them.

She talked and chatted with friends and promised to come to a baby shower the women's group was giving Jenny Perkins the following Tuesday. She smiled at the appropriate times, spoke when necessary, but her mind was buzzing and the sick feeling that had attacked the pit of her stomach yesterday afternoon persisted the rest of the day.

On her lunch break Monday afternoon, Lesley stopped in the library. She wasn't exactly sure what she was looking for, but she had a name and would go from there. Without arousing the librarian's curiosity, Lesley took down from the shelves several volumes relating to the auto industry. Twice she'd heard people say Cole seemed to know a lot about cars. The one remark that struck a chord of response in her had been that of the tow truck operator, who'd said Cole had fixed the foreign car after just listening to the engine.

Flipping through the indexes of several books, Lesley drew a blank.

"Can I help you?" The gray-haired librarian asked her when she returned an armload of books to the counter.

"Not today. Thanks."

Lesley returned at five after the bank had closed, took down several more volumes and sat at a table, leafing through the back pages.

"If you'd let me know what you're looking for I might be able to help." The librarian tried a second time.

"I have a name of someone and I wanted to see if I could find it. Someone who may have been in the news recently." It was a stab in the dark, but she didn't know where else to look. If Cole was running from the authorities, his name would have been in the newspapers.

The woman's brow was wrinkled in a deep frown. "Locally?"

"No, I was thinking more on a national level. Possibly from Indiana." That was where Cole's out-of-state check had been issued.

"Possibly the personal names in the *New York Times Index* would be of help, but we don't have that reference book here."

"Could you find out for me?"

The woman looked unsure. "I can check, but it may take a few days. What's the name?"

"Engstrom."

"First name?"

"I'm . . . not sure." If Daniels wasn't his last name, who was to know what he'd used for his first name?

"I probably won't have the information until the end of the week."

"That's fine. Thank you."

November and December were heavy snow months in northern Idaho. Normally Lesley didn't mind. Idaho was sometimes called America's Switzerland, and the skiing was fantastic—some of the world's best. But Lesley's thoughts weren't on the glacial valleys or the pristine forests as she pulled into her driveway.

Everything was still and beautiful. The town below looked like something out of a fairy tale. The sky was already dark, and Lesley's nerves were raw. She couldn't stay in the apartment without pacing or having her stomach churn with nervous anxiety. What would she learn about Cole? What shocking thing was she about to uncover about the man she was coming to love so intensely, the stranger who lived next door?

With so much nervous energy pent up, Lesley charged out back and grabbed the snow shovel. Several inches more were forecast for the night. If she cleared the space behind her car now, it meant less work in the morning.

She had managed to shovel only a small portion of the area when Cole's front door slammed.

"Just what are you doing?" he demanded. His mood didn't appear to have improved.

Lesley straightened, one hand holding the shovel as she glared at Cole. She half expected him to look different, to have changed since their last meeting. He hadn't. One glance and her heart began to flutter wildly. The control he had over her was both dangerous and foolish. The stranger's words about Cole having a way with women sparked her indignation.

"What does it look like?" she shot back, slamming the blunt edge of the shovel into the compact snow on her driveway. Now, if she could only hold her tongue . . . But sometimes it was impossible to hold things back.

"Let me do that. It's too hard for you."

"It is not too hard for me." Her hand tightened its grip on the wooden handle.

"Don't be silly. I don't want you out here—"

"I'm sure that's true. You'd like to be rid of me all together . . . and it's not because you're attracted to me, either."

His laugh was mirthless. "What's that supposed to mean?"

Lesley swung around, intent on ignoring him.

"What's so important about doing this now? I was planning to do it in the morning. It doesn't make sense to do it twice."

"It makes perfect sense," she shouted, and tossed a shovel full of snow to the side. "Now kindly leave me alone."

"Lesley, please. Will you listen to reason?"

"Reason?" she echoed. "All these weeks I've watched you. It isn't normal, the way you live. A hundred questions demand answers."

"What are you talking about?"

"It doesn't matter. Go inside where it's safe and you don't have to deal with me."

"Lesley." He sounded exasperated and angry.

By this time she didn't care. "But then I could be easily silenced." She paused and placed a hand on her hip, her chin angled flippantly. "After all, you do have a way with women. I'm no problem." Realizing what she said, Lesley gasped and turned around.

His hand, biting roughly into her upper arm, turned her to face him. "What did you say?"

Pinching her lips tightly shut, she met his angry glare. "Nothing."

"Don't give me that."

"I just did." The acid sting of tears burned in her eyes. How could she possibly have fallen for someone like Cole Daniels?

"Lesley." He ground out her name impatiently.

She could feel the heat of his gaze studying her face, pausing to linger for a heart-stopping moment on her parted mouth.

Lesley struggled. At the first sign of resistance, Cole dropped his hand.

"Don't make judgments when you don't understand the situation." He ran a hand through his hair. His steel-sharp gaze pinned her as effectively as a vise. "What else did you hear?"

With a determined effort, Lesley lowered her eyes. "Enough, Mr. Engstrom." When she glanced up, she saw that Cole had closed his eyes, his mouth tight and controlled.

"Have you told anyone?"

Lesley shook her head. "Are you in any danger?"

"No."

He was lying, Lesley was sure of it. Hadn't the stranger said Jennings was after him?

"Are you in trouble with the authorities?"

"No," he said forcefully.

"Are you going to tell me what's going on?"

"Lesley," he pleaded and rubbed a weary hand over his face. "I can't. I could be putting you . . ." He didn't finish. Instead he took the shovel out of her hand. "Invite me in for coffee."

"All right," she agreed.

Stomping snow off her boots, Lesley led the way into the cozy, warm apartment. Cole followed her inside, sitting at the table while she placed the water on the stove to boil. For a second she stood, unsure, in the middle of her kitchen. She didn't know whether she should remain by the stove and wait for the water or sit beside Cole. Her first instinct was to wrap her arms around him and seek the comfort of his embrace.

Hesitantly Lesley stood with her back to him, her hands gripping the oven door to keep from turning and letting him see the doubts and anxiety in her eyes.

The scraping sound of the chair told Lesley that Cole was standing. The noise was followed by gentle footsteps moving behind her. A rough, calloused hand cupped each shoulder, bringing her back to rest against his solid length. His mouth found the sensitive area behind her ear and spread teasing kisses there. Tingling sensations shot down her back and arms.

"Cole," she moaned, close to tears, "don't, please don't."

He turned her in his arms, and Lesley struggled against surrendering to his stronger, more dominant will. Was she just another woman he was manipulating?

Some of the hurtful skepticism must have shown in her eyes.

"Can you trust me?" Cole questioned softly.

It would be so easy to fall completely captive to the power of his magnetism. She tucked her chin down and a cloud of dark brown curls fell forward, wreathing her face. "I don't know anymore. I don't even know your name and . . ."

A finger lifted her chin so that their eyes could meet. "It's Daniel Cole Engstrom." Something flickered from his eyes . . . doubt, regret?

Was it a name she should recognize? Lesley didn't. Her brow was marred with thick lines of concentration. "What should I call you?"

"Friend?" he murmured, then shook his head. "No, what I feel for you goes far beyond a simple friendship." His mouth was drawing closer and closer. "Lover?" he continued. "No, that's something for the future. Our future."

Her heart was pounding against her ribs like a sledgehammer. His hand curved around the side of her neck. His fingers weaved into the dark strands of hair and raised her head a fraction of an inch to meet his descending mouth.

Wave after wave of heat flowed over her. For days she'd longed for the warmth, the feel, the wonder of Cole's arms. His mouth moved over hers again and again, caressing her lips with persuasive mastery. And fool that she was, Lesley was a willing slave. Her arms circled his middle and she pressed herself to him, reveling in the scents of spicy after-shave and hard work.

When he buried his face in the side of her neck, it was all Lesley could do not to weep. Was she so spineless that Cole could wrap her around his finger with nothing more persuasive than a series of kisses?

The teakettle began to whistle, and reluctantly Cole released her, but his hands lingered on her shoulders for an extra moment. His thumb wiped aside a maverick tear and kissed her cheek.

Lesley's hands were shaking when she brought down the mugs. Why did he have to be so gentle? If he had been the least bit rough, she could have resisted him.

"What should I call you?" she asked again, her voice slightly husky as she placed his mug on the table. He still hadn't told her. Was this another game he was playing?

"Cole."

She nodded and sat opposite him. Both hands surrounded the hot mug, burning the sensitive area of her palms. Lesley almost welcomed the pain. Her gaze was centered on the steaming liquid.

"Can you trust me a little longer? Then I'll explain everything."

"And if I can't?"

His hand reached for hers, squeezing it. "I don't know, but I know you, Lesley, and I'm asking you to trust me for just a little while longer."

"Why should I trust you? Give me one good reason," she demanded.

"There isn't one. I know what you must be thinking."

"You couldn't possibly know."

"I didn't want to bring you into any of this."

"Into any of what?" she cried.

She saw that Cole was quickly losing the fragile grip on his patience. His jaw clenched and he expelled a long, impatient breath. "I knew the minute I saw you we were headed for trouble."

Lesley had known it, too.

"When I saw that you were the girl who lived next door, I should have packed my bags and left town. You're far too lovely for my level of concentration. And then when you dressed up for the Halloween party I knew there was no help for me. I might as well—"

"Don't talk to me like that, Cole." Pain seared her heart. She couldn't look at him. The thought that she was only another conquest was more than she could bear. Purposely, she lowered her gaze, but not before she noted the bewildered look in his eyes.

"Talk to you like what?" His voice was devoid of emotion.

It hurt to speak, the tightness in her throat was almost strangling. "I'm not like your other women. I don't want to hear meaningless phrases of love and devotion. Because I don't believe you. I can't. Not when everything you've done has been a lie."

She noticed how his hand gripped the mug. "I've never lied to you."

Lesley released a bitter laughing sigh. "You just did. I heard the man say that someone was after you. Jennings, I think his name was." She flipped her hand over in a gesture of helplessness. "I heard him say you were in danger, and yet when I asked, you denied it."

"I'm perfectly safe here," he answered forcefully. "No one knows where I am. Do you think I'd place you in a situation that could cause you harm? Do you honestly think that of me?" The lack of emotion in his voice made his words all the more profound. "What kind of man do you think I am?"

"I don't know what my opinion of you is anymore," she replied with taunting disdain.

An ominous silence followed. "Then there's nothing more I can say, is there?"

"No, I don't think there is."

Lesley remained sitting when Cole stood, his chair scraping against the linoleum floor. The front door closed softly, but the sound of it echoed across the room in ear-shattering decibels.

Love thy neighbor, love thy neighbor, love thy neighbor . . . A hundred times during the night the words were repeated in her thoughts.

Sleep eluded her. Never had she been more conscious of the man next door. Only a thin layer of wall separated them, and yet Lesley felt as if they lived on different planets. How could she believe him when he said the words she longed to hear? Everything about Daniel Cole Engstrom was a lie.

About two o'clock Lesley gave up the effort and crawled out of bed. Her Bible sat on the living room end table, and she curled up on the davenport reading through Psalms. Gradually her lashes began to flutter downward and she slept. Her night was spent on the sofa without a pillow.

The crick in her neck was painful when Lesley rose the next morning. Rotating her head seemed to ease the tension somewhat, but not enough for her to avoid favoring it. She dressed more casually than usual, in wool pants and a matching jacket.

The driveway was cleared for her car, and Lesley realized that Cole must have been up early to shovel it for her. The kindness made her love for him all the more potent.

Lesley was halfway to the car when she noticed that Cole was still at work, clearing the area around the mailbox. He turned just as she opened her car door. One dark brow quirked mockingly in her direction.

"Lesley," he began quietly, a serious note running through his tone. He stopped, but Lesley was sure he had wanted to say something more. A veiled look came over his face. "Have a good day."

"Thank you," she returned stiffly. "I will."

She didn't, of course. With so much of Cole dominating her thoughts and time, she made one mistake after another, until the bank manager gave her a peculiar look.

"Are you feeling all right, Lesley?" Ben Fullbright came up to her desk. His look was sincere.

"I may have a touch of the flu," Lesley returned with the hint of a smile.

"Do you feel you'd like to take the rest of the day off?" her employer inquired further.

"No, I'm fine. Thanks." Her hand tightened around the pencil until she was sure it would snap.

"Just say if you feel worse later."

"Thanks." She released a slow, impatient sigh. "I will."

About noon, her nerves stretched taut, Lesley couldn't stand it any longer. She couldn't work.

There wasn't a time in her life she'd felt more tired. Her neck ached and she wanted to go home.

Cole stepped out of his apartment the minute she pulled into the driveway. "Are you all right?"

"No."

He appeared to study the troubled, confused light in her eyes, his own look darkening. "What's wrong?"

"What's wrong?" she cried. "I can't even work. Nothing's right! I need answers, and I need them now."

"Lesley." He breathed in deeply as if to control his rising temper. "Trust me, for just a little while longer. Then I'll explain everything."

A protesting sob rose quickly to her throat and she shook her head. "I can't. I just can't."

The phone inside her apartment was ringing and Lesley pivoted sharply.

"Honey, please."

The endearment rolled off his tongue as if he'd said it a hundred times to a hundred different women.

Ignoring him, Lesley squared her shoulders and walked inside her apartment.

"Hello." Her voice was breathless as she spoke into the receiver.

"This is the library," the efficient voice returned. "The bank said I could contact you at this number."

"Yes?" Her heart was pounding at double time.

"We have the information you requested."

Chapter Six

Her purse still clenched in her hand, Lesley flew back out the front door, slamming it after her.

"Where are you going in such an all-fired hurry?" Cole shouted.

Lesley nearly stumbled off the top step, catching herself just intime. She hadn't expected Cole to be outside. "The . . . The library," she supplied on a breathless note.

"Is the place on fire?"

"No." Willing her pounding heart to be still, she opened the car door, climbed inside and started the engine.

"Then wait."

"No! I'm leaving and I'm leaving now."

Cole's look was bewildered, as if he couldn't understand a woman who was demanding answers one moment, then fleeing the next without a logical explanation. Lesley didn't care; he'd left her to face countless unresolved questions.

Although more outwardly calm, her hands were shaking as she gripped the strap of her purse and strolled into the library.

The woman who had helped her earlier was out to lunch but had left the information at the desk for Lesley.

ENGSTROM, DANIEL. His name was followed by a listing of dates and articles that showed Cole had been in the paper, at least *The New York Times,* on several occasions.

Briefly her eyes scanned the dates and articles. Cole was some kind of automobile executive. Although still reading, she walked across the library floor and sat at the table next to the shelves that contained the encyclopedias. Dynamic Engines Corporation kept appearing along with Cole's name. That was in Michigan. What was he doing with an out-of-state check issued from Indiana?

The information was scant at best. Wondering where she should search next, Lesley pulled out the latest edition of the business directory. He wasn't listed there, nor was he in *Who's Who in America.*

As she was returning the volume, she saw another book labeled *Who's Who in Finance and Industry*. Her fingers flipped open the pages and ran down the row of E's.

Engstrom, Daniel Cole. Her finger stopped as she sank back into the cushioned chair and continued reading: *AUTOMOBILE EXECUTIVE.* That she knew. *SINGLE.* Thank goodness. *EDUCATION: Bachelor of Science in industrial engineering at the Lawrence Institute of Technology. Master's in auto science. Degree in mechanical engineering from Chrysler Industries. MBA from the University of Michigan. Hired as an engineer for Dynamic Engines and promoted to the director of advanced engineering and finally chief engineer.*

Chief engineer! Lesley propped her head up with one hand pressed tightly across her forehead as the knowledge of his expertise washed over her.

Again she scanned the statistical information. Cole was thirty-four and had accomplishments men twenty years his senior would envy. But why hide himself away like this? For what reason? Should she confront him with what she knew? Or wait until he told her and see if his story jelled with what she'd learned?

Her thoughts muddled, Lesley walked outside the building and headed down the street toward her car.

"Hey, what are you doing shopping this time of day?" Terry pulled her car into the empty parking space beside Lesley's and rolled down her window.

"Oh, hi," Lesley responded with an absent smile.

"Hi yourself. What's up?"

"Up? What makes you think anything's up?"

"In addition to being your sister, I happen to know you, Lesley Joy Brown. Now, out with it."

"Cole Daniels is really Daniel Cole Engstrom," Lesley announced without preamble.

"What?" Terry gasped and jerked open her car door. "I think we need to talk." She unstrapped Lisa from the baby seat in the back of the car.

Fifteen minutes later they sat in their favorite café drinking coffee while Lesley explained what she'd learned from the library.

"I don't believe it."

"That's the tenth time you've said that," Lesley commented with an impatient snap to her voice.

"Sorry."

Lesley could tell Terry wasn't actually sorry. "Shocked" was a better word.

"What are you going to do about it?" Terry continued.

"I don't know. What do you think I should do?"

"Confront him?"

"Should I?"

"I'm asking, not telling." Terry turned her attention to Lisa, who was cheerfully eating a soda cracker, mashing it together with her chubby fingers.

"There are so many unexplainables with this."

"I've got it." Terry hit her hand across the plastic-topped table, directing the attention of half the café to their booth in the corner. "It's only logical."

"What?" Lesley leaned forward eagerly across the table. Nothing about this whole thing was logical.

"We're always reading about automobile recalls."

"So?"

"As chief engineer, wouldn't Cole—"

"Of course," Lesley interrupted. "He found out something that's wrong with the cars that would demand a recall. But D.E. is trying to hide this from the customers and has hired a hit man to do in Cole."

"What do you think?"

"I think we may have stumbled onto something," Lesley answered thoughtfully.

"What can we do?"

"Nothing." Lesley propped her chin on a palm. "We're going to have to trust the Lord with this one." Lesley took a sip from her coffee cup. "Cole keeps telling me that everything will be settled soon. I heard him say he was about to hand over the evidence or report or something."

"What are you going to do until then?"

"Thanksgiving's this week, and the bank's closed for the four-day holiday. I think I'll phone in sick tomorrow and stick around. At least, if anything happens, I'll be there to make sure Cole's all right. Let's hope the whole thing will be cleared up by the weekend."

Terry handed Lisa another cracker. The baby immediately glommed onto it, stuffing it into her small mouth. "You know, I feel like Nancy Drew all of a sudden—protecting the world from evil and upholding the cause of righteousness."

Lesley tossed her sister a disdainful look. "Honestly, Terry, that was Zorro."

The older sister wrinkled her nose. "Yeah, I guess you're right."

Lesley drove home slowly, wondering how she would react to Cole when she saw him. She was terrible at keeping secrets. Her friends knew her well enough to realize that if they wanted something kept quiet, it was better not to tell Lesley. It wasn't that she was a gossip, but anything that was meant to be kept to herself had a way of rolling off her tongue. Already, although she had the best intentions, she'd blurted out what she'd overheard.

The first thing she did when she walked into her apartment was phone the bank and tell Ben Fullbright that she wouldn't be in for the remainder of the week. Slight feelings of guilt invaded her resolve as she replaced the telephone receiver. The day before Thanksgiving was always busy at the bank, but she had to stick close to home for Cole's sake. She smiled, envisioning his reaction if he knew that she was calling in sick in order to stay at the apartment and protect him.

The light tapping sound on the other side of her wall reminded her of a high school drum cheer. She walked across the room and returned with her own message.

A moment later her doorbell rang. It was Cole.

"Hi." Her eyes avoided his.

"I've been waiting to talk to you."

"Oh?"

"Are you suddenly reduced to responses of one syllable?" He regarded her skeptically.

"No." Her eyes followed the worn pattern in the carpet.

Cole's index finger under her chin lifted her gaze to his. "I think we'd better talk?"

"Do you want coffee or Iacocca . . . I mean cocoa." She turned and hurried into the kitchen. Oh no! She'd nearly done it again.

Cole followed her, a hand on her shoulder stopping her as she held the teakettle under the faucet.

"What'd you say?"

"Nothing." She prayed he wouldn't question her further.

"Something about Iacocca?"

"No, silly," she said, desperately trying to brush off her blunder. "Cocoa, as in heated chocolate milk with melted marshmallows."

"All right, I'll have the Iacocca."

"The what?" She looked up, startled.

"All right, Lesley." Cole's hands gripped her shoulders and turned her around. "Are you going to say it, or am I?"

She felt like stamping her foot and groaning her frustration with herself. "I didn't want you to know that I'd learned."

"Exactly what do you know?"

"About the recall and everything."

"The recall?" His look was completely blank. "I think we'd better sit down and get this into the open." He took the kettle out of her hand and set it aside.

Lesley turned off the burner and followed him into the living room.

"Sit," he instructed, and gently settled her into the winged back chair that was positioned in the corner by the front windows.

Cole paced in front of her. Lesley's neck hurt to look up at him, but she wanted to watch his face, study the emotion that came from the dark, fathomless eyes. With a hand at the base of her neck she rubbed some of the tension from the muscles along the back of the sensitive area.

"What's wrong?" Cole looked down as if noticing her actions for the first time.

"I slept on the sofa last night without a pillow, and now my neck's killing me."

"Here, let me rub it for you," he offered and walked around behind the chair. His hands felt warm against her skin, and soon a tingling heat was spreading over her. Lesley closed her eyes to the potency of his touch. Her bones seemed to melt as his fingers gently kneaded the area.

"How does that feel?"

Was she hearing things, or did his husky voice sound as disturbed as she was feeling?

"Wonderful." The one word managed to make it past the sluggishness that affected her throat muscles. Feelings of languor, a tender dreamy state, took over her mind. "Oh, Cole," she murmured softly.

"Crazy woman, what were you doing on the sofa? You should have been in bed."

"I know," His gentle, massaging hands continued the slow rotating movements that eased the coiled tension from her. "But I couldn't sleep."

"Because of me?" The question was issued softly, in coaxing tones.

"Yes," she moaned softly. "Do we have to talk? Can't you just let your fingers work their magic?"

His soft chuckle caused her eyes to flutter open. "Did I just say something I shouldn't have again?"

"Again?" he prompted.

"I do that, you know."

His hands kneaded her shoulders, his thumbs finding the spot between her shoulder blades. "Yes, that's one thing I've noticed these last weeks."

It seemed important that she gather her resolve. Slowly she straightened, yearning for his touch, yet actively breaking contact. "I . . . It feels fine now. Thanks."

Cole moved around the chair and sat on the edge of the living room sofa. "You'd better explain what you know."

Lesley folded her hands together in her lap, as if laced fingers would lend her the strength to speak freely. "I found your name at the library today." He shrugged as if her knowing that didn't trouble him. "You're an important man, Cole Engstrom."

"But stupid." His eyes hardened and he seemed to look straight through her.

"Stupid?" she repeated.

Cole leaned forward and joined his hands. "Incredibly so."

"Is that why you're hiding?" Why couldn't he just come right out and explain? Was she going to have to pry every bit of information out of him?

That hard, chiseled look came over his face again, and he stared at her stonily.

"Cole?" she prompted.

Lightly he shook himself. "It's not what you think."

"There is no recall?"

A poor replica of a smile briefly touched his troubled features. "Honey, if you had any idea how carefully each car, each model, is investigated before ever hitting a showroom floor you wouldn't even suggest it. D.E. is proud of its record, and with good reason."

"But . . ."

"Lesley." He said her name in a sober breath. "Will you go out to dinner with me tonight?"

Lesley opened and closed her mouth, then nodded eagerly. "Is it safe for you to be seen?"

That intense look came over him. "Safe enough, but if I stay in that apartment another minute I'll go mad." He smiled then, one of those rare, earth-shattering, wonderful smiles that would disarm even the most hardhearted. "But then, the reason for my insanity could be attributed to my lovely neighbor."

"That's unfair, I've been more than—" Lesley stopped. How easily she fell prey to this man's games!

His eyes glinted with mischief as Lesley gave him a bemused smile.

"You like doing that, don't you?" she accused, feigning anger.

"It's easy to get a reaction out of you."

The words had a strange effect on her. Her reaction, as he called it, had a lot to do with her feelings for him.

"You ready?" Cole stood and extended a hand to her.

Lesley glanced at her wristwatch. "It's barely three."

"I know. I wanted to avoid the dinner crowd."

"You'll give me some answers?"

Cole met her narrowed gaze and nodded thoughtfully. "If you insist."

"I do," she said more forcefully than she meant to. Why did it seem that after every meeting she was left with more questions than when she started? But not this time, she vowed.

They drove to Post Falls, a small community to the west of Coeur d'Alene, and ate at a restaurant that overlooked the Spokane River.

"Tell me about Coeur d'Alene?" Cole asked after the waitress had taken their order. Apparently Cole was hungry, since he asked for the largest steak in the house. Lesley's own appetite was more modest, and she ordered salmon.

"Well," she said with a smile, "it's the largest city in the northern panhandle of Idaho and the county seat of Kootenai County."

"Kootenai County?"

"Yes. Try saying that three times without a breath." Her hand slipped around the chilled water glass. Lesley loved Idaho. She felt as if she'd been born and raised in some of the most beautiful country on God's earth.

"I love the lake," she continued softly. "It's been said that Coeur d'Alene Lake is one of the ten most beautiful lakes in the world. It has a hundred miles of forested shoreline with nature trails and scenic walks. This is God's country, Cole Daniels." She stopped, her eyes narrowing with frustration, when she realized what she'd said.

"Engstrom," Cole corrected.

"Yes," she mumbled and lowered her eyes to the white tablecloth. "I keep forgetting." He'd done it again. She had come expecting him to explain some of the things that had been happening, and he had quickly manipulated her into doing all the talking.

Cole chuckled, apparently noticing that she was on to his game. "I wish you could see your eyes. I can't recall seeing anything more expressive."

"Oh no you don't."

"Don't?"

"Change the subject again." Cole was clever. She'd say that for him. "Cole, don't do this to me, please." The last words were issued in a soft pleading tone that spoke of weeks of uncertainty.

"Can you trust me just a little while longer? Within the week everything will be out in the open," Cole said tightly.

"I think it's a matter of faith, all right, but of your trusting me."

"I got into this mess because I depended on someone else." The hard, masculine line of his mouth narrowed. "I won't be taken in so easily again."

"I'm not trying to take you in." Nervously her tongue moistened her lower lip. What kind of person did Cole think she was? "Do you think I'll run to the press? Is that it?"

"You could." The cynicism, the bitterness from whatever was happening to him vibrated in his words.

Hurt rippled through her. The pain of its aftermath brought stinging tears to the back of her eyes. With a determined effort, Lesley was able to forestall their flow. "I don't suppose you realize that the mining district just east of the city is still one of the largest lead-, zinc- and silver-producing areas in the world. Also, the Powder House Museum that was part of the original Fort Sherman is located at North Idaho College." She continued to ramble until her voice cracked. She inhaled a quivering breath and bowed her head.

"Lesley." Her name came on a low, pleading breath.

"It's all right," she said shakily. "Really. I understand. If it's trust you want, you've got mine. You may not have been around long, but I know one thing—you're not a criminal, Cole. I'll wait because that's what you want and seem to need from me."

A smile trembled from her lips when she raised her eyes to meet his. His gaze was glistening, his expression brooding and thoughtful, but he said nothing and she didn't either. Their meal arrived and they ate in silence.

Cole's knife sliced across the rare T-bone steak. "Do you know much about airbags?"

The question came so casually that Lesley didn't catch the importance.

"You mean the ones airlines hand out?"

"No," Cole mocked her softly. "I mean the ones in cars. Those little toys I tinker around with."

"Oh." Lesley took a sip of her coffee. "No, I can't say that I do."

"It's been estimated that air bags installed in automobiles could save up to two thousand lives every year."

"Why don't car makers install them, then?" Lesley hoped to appear as nonchalant as possible. She didn't know what Cole was telling her, but it obviously had great importance to him.

"Only Mercedes-Benz offers this safety measure as an option on their automobiles, but at the cost of eight hundred dollars, it's an expensive option."

"Yes." Lesley swallowed. "Yes, it is."

"It would mean quite a bit to highway safety if these devices could be made and installed cheaply in American cars, wouldn't it?"

"Two thousand lives." She quoted his own figures back to him.

Cole laid his knife across the top of the plate and pushed his chair back. His hand rested across his stomach. "That was one terrific steak."

"Mine too," Lesley echoed. Cole was kind enough not to comment that she had barely touched her meal.

He paid their tab and left a generous tip. His hand possessively cupped her elbow as he led the way out of the restaurant and into his car. He held the car door open for her, and his eyes rested on the dashboard momentarily, then flickered to her in an apologetic smile.

"I've only figured out the driver's side." He spoke absently. He closed her door and, puzzled, Lesley watched as he stared into space for a moment. The skies were obliterated. There wasn't a star in the heavens. Even the moon was invisible, tucked behind a thick layer of clouds. Still, she glanced upward, wondering what Cole found so fascinating.

He climbed into his side of the car and started the engine. Placing his hand along the back of the seat, he looked behind him, prepared to back out of the parking space. As he turned his head, their eyes met and held for a breathless second.

"You're an incredibly beautiful woman, Lesley Brown."

Lesley's gaze darted downward. Was this one of his lines meant to disarm her? If so, he had succeeded beyond even her expectations. "Thank you," she mumbled.

A finger lightly traced her chin and, following the delicate line of her face, traveled over her ear and down the side of her neck. The long, male finger entwined with the dark curls at the base of her neck. The gentle pressure brought her mouth within inches of his.

He bent forward and brushed his lips against the sensitive skin at the hollow of her neck. Lesley turned her head, thrilling to the delicious shivers that skidded over her skin.

His warm breath fanned her face. "Just a little while longer, I promise, Lesley," he murmured deeply. The searing kiss that followed his words stole her breath away as it sealed his promise.

One band continued to keep her close to his side as he leisurely made the return trip to the duplex. Lesley directed him down country roads and teasingly pointed out local landmarks.

When Cole pulled into the driveway, Lesley felt an eerie sensation run over her.

"Cole," she said and was shocked at the sound of her own voice. It was weak and uneven, yet brittle. "Something's wrong."

He was instantly alert, his cat eyes taking in the area with one sweeping glare. "Someone's broken into my apartment," he announced and pushed open his car door.

Chapter Seven

"No," Lesley cried and lunged for Cole's arm. She'd do anything to stop him from going inside the apartment. "You can't go in there. They could be waiting."

Cole didn't seem to hear her. He brushed her hand aside as if her grip were no more effective than a child's.

"Cole," she pleaded a second time.

He had apparently forgotten her presence until Lesley climbed out his side of the car and ran after him. With all her weight she pulled against his arm. "Cole," she cried frantically. "You could be killed."

He turned to her then, his eyes shining with an unnatural light. Hate. Never had Lesley seen anything more vivid in a man's eyes. Cole hated with an intensity that paled under every other emotion. His reactions were single-minded—even common sense was banished under the all-consuming drive.

Realizing nothing could effectively stop him, Lesley flung herself in front of Cole. His hands tried to push her behind him, but she clung to him, her own fear giving her strength beyond her normal capabilities.

"Lesley," Cole groaned and gripped her around the waist, holding her upright. His face muscles had relaxed and the intensity had waned. "If anyone was in there waiting, they could have killed us both several times over."

"Oh." She swallowed and loosened her hold.

"You put your life on the line for me." His face loomed bare inches from her own. "Why?"

"I . . . I didn't want to see you hurt." Her love had driven her just as his hate had him. But she couldn't tell him that, she couldn't give him another weapon.

Cole raked a hand through the dark hair that swept naturally over his forehead. "You can be the most exasperating female."

"Me?" she shouted incredulously.

He ignored her outrage and folded her fingers in his. "Come on, let's go see what damage they've done."

"Who?" Lesley wanted to know. "Jennings?"

Lesley felt the tremor that went through Cole as he tensed and glanced down at her. "No, that isn't his style. Jennings has others do his dirty work for him."

Cole pushed open the door to his apartment with one hand. It banged against the wall, and the sound vibrated through the room. One flip of the light switch and the area was flooded with light.

Lesley let out a sickened gasp at the mess that lay before her. The living room was in shambles, the furniture slashed and the stuffing pulled from the cushions. Something had been thrown through the television screen and the shattered glass was everywhere. Her gaze followed the path of destruction through the apartment.

Speechless with shock, they moved into the kitchen. The contents of the refrigerator had been dumped on the floor. Egg yolks and milk jelled on the linoleum. A bag of flour had been carelessly tossed across the top of the counter and stove.

"Oh, Cole." Lesley could hardly bear to look. In all her life she had never seen worse chaos. "We'd better phone the police."

"No!" he shouted.

"Yes," she returned stubbornly. "You can't let this kind of destruction go unreported."

"I know who did this and I know why. The police won't help."

"But, Cole," she argued.

"I thought you said you could trust me?" He made the shouting words a question. "Were you just lying to me?"

Lesley stared back at him dumbfounded, unable to answer.

"And why should I tell you anything? What right do you have to invade my life and demand answers to questions that are none of your business?"

"None," she answered in a soft, trembling voice. "None whatsoever."

Cole rammed both hands into his jeans pockets and shot a gaze at the ceiling. Neither spoke for several long moments.

"They didn't find what they were looking for. That's the reason for this." His hand made a sweeping gesture toward the kitchen and living room.

Lesley nodded, realizing that in his own way he was apologizing for his outburst. He was angry and lashing out at her. His reaction hurt, but it was understandable.

Avoiding as much of the egg and milk as possible, Lesley walked across the kitchen and took the broom from the narrow closet on the other side of the refrigerator.

"What are you doing?" he asked with a confused look.

"Cleaning up. It's got to be done." And if she was occupied, it would be easier to swallow back the questions that demanded answers. Who had done this? Why? And what were they searching for so desperately?

"Lesley," Cole groaned and took the broom out of her hand. "I'll do that. I don't want you to have to deal with this mess."

"But I want to help." Her voice wobbled treacherously. "You're always pushing me away—let me at least do this."

He didn't look pleased about it, but he managed a grin. "Any other woman in the world would have stormed off, and with good reason. I didn't mean to shout at you."

"I know," she supplied softly. "But I understand."

An unreadable expression passed over his face. His eyes seemed to caress her. Lesley swallowed tightly. The anguish, the mental torment he was enduring, was all there for her to read. Every part of her yearned to reach out and comfort him.

"Do what you can in there and I'll tackle the living room." Cole broke eye contact first, pivoting sharply into the other room. Lesley watched him for a few moments as he stooped over to pick up the glass, but soon concentrated on her own efforts.

"If we were still hungry, I might have been able to cook something out of this," she teased.

Cole made a disgusted sound and continued working.

With a soft smile lighting up her eyes, Lesley decided to dump the flour mess on the counter onto the floor before tackling that. With the broom she swept it off the counter. The white powdery substance filled the air until it was almost impossible to see. She coughed and waved her hand in front of her face. When the air cleared she glanced up to find Cole standing, hands on hips, watching her, his eyes filled with amusement.

Lesley brushed the hair from her eyes. Her hand came away caked with the fine dusting of flour.

"Here, let me do that," Cole muttered and took a step toward her.

"Don't you dare," she cautioned. "You'll track the flour everywhere."

"You come here, then." He pointed to the place where the carpet ended, where the living room met the kitchen.

Lesley did as he requested, attempting to brush the flour from her face and hair.

Cole sighed audibly. "You're only making it worse." He took a handkerchief from his hip pocket and made a show of unfolding it.

"That had better be clean," Lesley admonished with laughing eyes.

He laughed as he brushed the hair from her cheek and lightly ran the soft cotton cloth over her face. Although his touch was cool and impersonal, Lesley's reaction was overwhelming. Her teeth bit into her bottom lip. Immediately she regretted the telltale action and forced a bright smile onto her taut mouth.

"Thanks." She cast her gaze downward.

"Lesley." Her name was murmured in a soft tone, and when she glanced up she watched, amazed, as a nerve flexed tensely in his jaw. Her heart leaped at the tender look in his eyes.

Smiling gently, Lesley reached up and caressed his cheek, her hand lovingly stroking the proud line of his jaw. Cole's hand covered hers and directed it to his lips. Lightly he kissed her palm. The teasing gesture made her knees grow weak, and she locked her arms around his neck and fit her body to his.

Cole wrapped his arms around her and covered her mouth with hungry kisses that skyrocketed her to dizzying heights. The first taste of longing raced through her blood, catching her unaware. Frightened and more than a little unsure, she released her hold and levered herself away.

Cole relaxed his grip and expelled a long, shuddering breath. His eyes were still closed.

"I . . . I got flour on you," Lesley managed after a moment, her voice unsteady. Gently she brushed it from his shirt. Her palm could feel the rapid beat of Cole's heart and the labored breathing as he struggled for control.

"I'll get back to work," Lesley said and was surprised at the sound of her own voice. It was scratchy and weak.

Silently they worked in different rooms, at their separate tasks, but they were together mentally, even spiritually, in a way Lesley found unexplainable. She remembered stories her mother had told her as a child about the years Lesley's father was in the war. Months on end, and there was no word, no letters. Her mother didn't know if he was dead or alive, and yet somehow she did know, because the love they had for each other ran so deep that it spanned time and distance. At the time Lesley hadn't understood and must have looked puzzled. When you love, her mother had explained, then you'll know. Years later, Lesley discovered the same sensation for this mysterious man, working silently in the room next to hers. But they could have been continents apart and it wouldn't have mattered.

"You look very intense."

Cole's comment caught her off guard. "I was just thinking," she answered without meeting his eyes. The floor had been cleaned and mopped, the counters scrubbed. The transformation in the small kitchen was dramatic, as was the contrast in the living room where Cole was working.

"What will you do about the furniture? Almost everything will need to be replaced."

"I'm not sure it would be worth the trouble," Cole answered her thoughtfully. "I won't be around here much longer."

The rest of what he was saying faded into oblivion. Wouldn't be around here much longer, Lesley's mind echoed. He was leaving, within a matter of days. He'd pack his bags and without a backward glance be on his way. She meant nothing: a small-town girl who was a convenient distraction. Cole would leave without a thought, without looking back, and with him would go her heart. How could she have been so stupid as to fall in love with this man? Didn't she recognize in the library that a man like Cole wouldn't want anything to do with a nobody like her?

Lesley felt the shock vibrate through her. "Where will you go?" The question was squeezed out through the tight block of pain that formed in her throat.

"More questions?" His look seemed to sear right to her heart. Fresh pain washed through her.

For a moment Lesley stared at him blankly. She felt the blood drain from her face, her breath caught in her lungs, but she answered him with a short shake of her head. "No," she managed. Her hand was shaking visibly as she replaced the broom and mop in the narrow closet. She made a show of looking at her watch, but couldn't have guessed at the time.

"It's getting late. I'll say good night." Her eyes refused to meet his.

His hand on her shoulder stopped her as she stepped into the living room. His touch sent shock waves rippling over her skin. She shrugged her shoulder, breaking the contact. "Don't," she warned in a wavering voice. "Don't touch me." Each word was enunciated plainly so there would be no doubt about her feelings.

"You're angry." Cole sounded surprised.

"You know, sometimes your brilliant perceptions astonish even me," she returned flippantly. "Good night, Cole."

He looked so shocked that she almost wanted to laugh. With her head held high and her chin angled regally, Lesley marched past him. The short distance that separated their front doors was covered in a matter of seconds.

Lesley opened her front door, looked up and let out a bloodcurdling scream.

Chapter Eight

"Lesley." Cole shot into the apartment, nearly knocking her off her feet as he pulled her into his arms.

He stopped abruptly and looked around at the horrible mess that lay scattered before them. "How could they do this?" he muttered in a low, disbelieving voice.

The room was in shambles. Furniture was overturned. Photos of family and friends had been hurled across the room. Drawers were emptied and their contents spilled onto the floor. Lesley felt like screaming and weeping all at the same moment. But the only sound that came from her throat was an anguished cry like that of an animal caught in a hunter's trap. Her life lay sprawled before her. She felt vulnerable, as if she'd been violated.

Cole turned her into his arms, his hand at the back of her head holding it against the muscular cushion of his chest. "I'm so sorry," he murmured over and over again. "I never dreamed they'd do this to you."

Lesley welcomed the comfort offered in his embrace. It helped lessen the shock.

"Here." Cole cleared a path for her and righted the chair before sitting her down. "Let me get you something to drink."

Numbly Lesley shook her head. "No, I'm fine." This was a nightmare, some horrible dream that would vanish in the morning. She closed and opened her eyes, hoping the scene would miraculously disappear. But reality faced her. She couldn't sit idle while her home lay in shambles. Yet as hard as she tried to force herself to stand, she couldn't.

Cole was kneeling at her side, his look troubled and tender. "Are you all right?" He smoothed the hair back from her temple. "You're so pale."

"I'm fine," she murmured and brushed his restraining hands aside as she stood with trembling resolve. The first thing she picked up was the small Bible she used for devotions. Checking the inside flap, she noted that the contents had been undisturbed. It was ironic, since it seemed everything else had been destroyed.

The destruction in her half of the duplex wasn't nearly as extensive as in Cole's. It looked as if someone had come through her quarters searching for something. Drawers were opened and left dangling after their contents had been carelessly tossed aside. The scene was the same in the kitchen, bedroom and bathroom.

Cole set the furniture upright and bent over to pick up the broken pieces of glass that had once been her lamp.

Wordlessly Lesley wandered from room to room, surveying the extent of the damage. Hot color invaded her face at the thought of someone entering her bedroom and sorting through her personal items. With practiced care she carefully folded each piece and returned it to her drawers. Next she straightened the mattress on her bed and pulled back the covers and bedspread. The contents of her closet had been tossed on the floor. After examining each dress, blouse and skirt for damage, she replaced them one by one.

When she returned to the living room, Cole had finished cleaning as best he could and glanced up guiltily.

"Don't look at me like that," he said with a tight, pinched look about his handsome face. "Scream, yell, do whatever will make you feel better."

Lesley lowered her eyes and shook her head. What good would screaming do now?

The teakettle whistled, its shrillness piercing the heavy silence that filled the room. Without a word she moved into the kitchen and took the kettle off the burner. The whistle petered out to a soft whine.

Her hands shaking, Lesley brought down the instant coffee. She poured the boiling water into ceramic mugs and added sugar. Normally she didn't use the sweetener, but she felt she needed it now.

Cole accepted the cup from her and sat at the opposite side of the room watching her. A muscle worked in his jaw while his eyes were more narrowed and determined than she could ever remember seeing them.

"I want you to know I'll pay for everything."

Lesley looked up at him blankly. "Why?" she asked in a breathless voice that sounded strange even to her own ears. "You didn't do this."

"No." His fingers tightened around the handle of the mug. "But it's my fault. None of this would have happened if it hadn't been for me."

"I don't blame you." Lesley didn't know how she could be so calm, but she was amazingly so. She took a sip of the steaming liquid, and when she looked at Cole she was again jarred by the hate that seemed to exude from him.

"It might be a good idea if you moved in with your sister until after the holiday," Cole said, the words brittle.

"No," she answered forcefully. "I'm staying here. This is my home, and I'm not about to let a bunch of hoodlums dictate my life."

"These men play for keeps, Lesley. This isn't the time to stand on principle."

"I don't care," she shot back hotly.

"Honey, I know how you feel."

"You know how I feel?" She echoed his words in a low, taunting voice and laughed sarcastically. "If you knew how I felt you'd be screaming. You ask me to trust you. This isn't any of my business. But you made it mine the minute you moved next door. You could be anyone, or anything, but I don't have the right to question you. Now"—she inhaled a deep breath—"Now you want to send me away? Is it for my own safety or because you're afraid of what I'll do once I discover why you're hiding?"

Cole set his mug aside and stood. Lesley watched him as he strode back and forth across the floor. Pacing was something he'd done a lot in recent months. Lesley knew: she'd heard him.

"You know I'm an engineer," he said without looking at her.

"Yes."

"For years the idea of finding an effective and affordable method of manufacturing air bags has nagged at the back of my mind. I spent two difficult years of my life trying to come up with an idea that would work. Six months ago, I did it."

"That's wonderful, Cole." He didn't look as if he was pleased with his discovery.

He offered her a strange smile. "It's simple, really. The air bag fits into the car's steering wheel and is programmed so that at the moment of impact—" He stopped. "That's neither here nor there. You get the picture."

Lesley did and thought the idea was amazingly simple. "How soon will it be available in cars?"

"That depends. The patent is pending now. Two patents."

The words were heavy and dark. He turned to glance at her then, and the tormented look was in his eyes again. "Two patents from two different men, both claiming to have come up with the identical idea."

Lesley didn't need to hear the other man's name. "It's Jennings, isn't it?"

Thoughtfully Cole nodded, his brow marred by thick, creasing lines. "Yes, Jennings."

"But how?"

"Jennings was a friend. He knew about my idea, and once I got the prototype working and the bugs out of the system, I showed him. I was enthusiastic." He paused and wiped a hand over his face. "No, stupid," he corrected. "Jennings was smart, I'll say that for him. He waited until I'd figured a way to produce the air bags before taking everything. But I trusted him. We'd worked together for years, and I considered him a friend. He'd been having financial problems, but I never would have guessed he'd stoop this low. He stole my work and two years of my life."

"But surely you can prove it was you."

"It's not that easy," Cole ground out and clenched his hands together. "Jennings took all my papers and my notes. I've reconstructed everything as best I can, but as it stands now, it's my word against his."

"What about the man who came here? What's he got to do with this?"

"That's Peter Lansky."

"Friend?"

"I have no friends," Cole returned forcefully. Lesley wondered how he thought of her, but didn't voice her question.

"Lansky's my attorney," Cole supplied. "It was his idea to have me go into hiding until I could reproduce the evidence that would prove I was the inventor."

"But the check you came into the bank with was issued from Indiana."

"That was another of Lansky's ideas. He insisted I use the phony name and had the funds available from Indiana as a precautionary method."

"Against Jennings," Lesley muttered to herself.

"Right."

"But Jennings knows you're here if today is any indication."

"He knows," Cole reiterated.

"Then why didn't he . . ."

"Finish me off?" Cole completed the horrible thought for her. "I don't know. There was ample opportunity."

"They were looking for the report or whatever it was you gave Lansky?"

"It's the only thing they could be after, with one exception."

"What?" Lesley asked with a puzzled frown.

Cole straightened, his demeanor distant. "Me."

Lesley bit into the soft flesh in her inner cheek to keep from crying out. She couldn't bear to lose Cole. If Jennings were to hurt Cole, a part of herself would shrivel up and die with him.

"Now do you understand why it's so important for you to leave? It won't be long, I promise."

"Cole," she pleaded. "I don't want to go. You know I'd go crazy every minute of every day wondering what was happening to you."

"This isn't your battle," he returned forcefully.

"But I'm making it mine. We're in this together," she argued with him on a breathless note. If it wasn't safe here, they could leave, find someplace that was.

"Lesley." He came to kneel in front of her, taking her soft hands in his and raising them to his mouth. "Thank you. But I can't put you in any danger."

"But I'll be with you."

"That's the worst place you could be."

"I'll go crazy not knowing—"

"Only until after Thanksgiving. If I haven't heard anything by then, you can come back." He was coaxing and gentle, and Lesley doubted that there was anything she could refuse him.

"I don't like this."

"I know you don't, and to be honest, I'm not that excited about it either. There's a certain amount of comfort having you around."

"It's my four karate lessons, right?"

"Right," he chuckled, and kissed her briefly on her cheek. "Come on, I'll help you pack."

Lesley pulled the suitcase out from her closet. Ironically, it was one she had replaced only a half hour earlier. Cole sat on the foot of her bed as she filled the small case.

"I'm only taking enough clothes for two days."

"That should be enough time."

"Good." She snapped closed the lid of the small case. "Can I tell Terry why I'm suddenly descending on her doorstep?" At Cole's hesitation, Lesley added, "Give my sister some credit—she's bound to be suspicious if I show up with a bag in my hand."

"All right," Cole agreed, "fill her in, but only briefly. I don't want this out, you can understand that."

"Yes." She nodded, her head adding emphasis to her words. "Yes, I do."

They walked into the living room, and Cole helped her on with her coat, his hand lingering longer than necessary on her shoulders, bringing her close to him for a timeless moment. When he broke the contact, it was Lesley who opened her eyes and expelled a long, quivering sigh.

"I want you to have something," she said.

Cole watched her with a blank look as she moved into

the kitchen and took the broom out of the narrow closet. "It worked great on Dale and Larry."

Cole laughed as he accepted the weapon, gripping the handle tightly. "Here." He handed her a slip of paper with a number written boldly across it. "Call me if anything suspicious happens, even if you're not sure."

Mesmerized, Lesley stared at the figures. She had lived next door to Cole all these months and not known his phone number. "Okay."

"Let's go."

"Us?"

"Yes, I want to follow you into town. Jennings' men could still be out there."

A cold shiver of apprehension ran up her spine, and some of the anxiety must have shown in her face.

"Don't worry, it's only a precaution. I don't think they're still around, but I want to be certain. I'm not going to let anything happen to you."

After locking the front door, Cole placed the suitcase in the backseat of her car. Their eyes met when he straightened. His look: intense, worried. Hers: fearful and unsure.

"Honey"—his voice was a husky murmur—"Don't look at me like that. It's difficult enough to let you go."

She nodded, tears filling her eyes until Cole swam in and out of her vision.

He kissed her gently and held her close as if sending her away was the hardest thing he had ever done. "I'll be fine, don't worry about me."

"But I will every second."

"I know."

"I'll be praying, too."

"I could use a few prayers. If there's a God in heaven, I'll be awarded the patent."

If! Lesley's mind shouted back. If! She wanted to talk to him, explain. But now wasn't the time.

"I'll follow you as far as your sister's."

Lesley agreed with a feeble smile. She climbed into her car and started the engine. Cole followed her into town, waving a brief farewell as she turned into Terry's driveway.

"I can't believe it," Terry muttered, slowly shaking her head back and forth. They sat at the kitchen table, while Lisa was on the floor banging on a set of old pans with a wooden spoon.

"Why do I get the impression that this is a repeat of a previous conversation?"

"I can't help it." Terry shot back a half-angry glare. "It isn't every day I hear this kind of stuff. What did Jennings' men do to your apartment?"

"Dumped things, mostly. They were looking for Cole's report, and since they couldn't find it at his house, they must have assumed he'd given it to me. Most of the mess is cleaned up," she answered absently.

"Are you thinking of going to the police?"

"I don't know. I'm not sure what to do. Cole could be in terrible danger, but he definitely wants the police out of it."

"Can you blame him?"

"Yes," she returned loudly. "No," she finished weakly.

"It sounds to me like you're as confused as I am about this whole thing."

"For once, sister dear, we're in agreement."

"How much longer before Cole knows about the patent?"

"Apparently the judge hearing the case is making his decision soon."

"Shouldn't Cole be there?"

"Where?" Lesley looked up blankly.

"At the courthouse, wherever his case is being heard."

"Oh." Lesley took in a deep breath. "I guess not. His attorney seemed to think it would only place him in greater danger. Jennings would have open range on Cole if he'd stayed in Michigan."

"Is that so different from now? If this Jennings character knows that Cole's in Coeur d'Alene, isn't he in even greater danger?"

Lesley's finger made nervous circles around the edge of her coffee cup. "I don't think so. Oh, Terry, I'm really worried. My life has always been so peaceful and quiet. Who would ever have dreamed all this could happen?"

"Believe me, the next time you start complaining about something mysterious going on at your place I won't question or doubt or anything."

"That's encouraging," Lesley responded with a small, slightly high-pitched laugh.

Lisa banged loudly on an aluminum pan with her wooden spoon, causing both sisters to stop and smile. How safe and secure the baby's life was, compared to the harsh realities of what she was facing with Cole, Lesley mused.

"Lisa's making a joyful noise unto the Lord," Terry teased.

Lesley gazed lovingly at the baby.

The phone rang and Terry rose to answer it. "Hello. Yes, just a minute, she's here." She handed the receiver to Lesley. "It's Cole."

"Oh." Lesley hurried out of her chair. "Cole?" Her voice was thick with anticipation.

"I probably shouldn't have phoned, but I needed to hear your voice after all these weeks of living next to you."

"And complaining about all the noise I made," she added with a happy sigh.

"I'm finding it's incredibly quiet here. Too quiet."

"Don't say that." Lesley tensed, her hand gripping the telephone until she was sure her fingers had made permanent indentations in the hard plastic.

"Not to worry, it's not that kind of quiet. I'm finding that I miss your singing."

"But I can't carry a tune."

"You don't need to tell me that. I know, I've listened to you often enough."

Lesley laughed softly. "You must really be missing me, then."

"That just goes to show you how much."

They spoke for a few minutes longer. Cole's words were reassuring. Much of the terrible tension that had knotted Lesley's stomach all day lessened.

That evening the church was filled almost to capacity. The Wednesday before Thanksgiving was a time the congregation set aside to thank God for His continued blessings throughout the year.

Even after the church had emptied, Lesley sat in the pew, her gaze resting on the huge cross behind the altar. Her mind was filled with prayers for Cole. Mentally she pictured an army of angels surrounding him, offering him spiritual protection. His words "If there's a God" had shocked her. Until that time she wasn't certain where he stood with the Lord. The bitterness and hatred she had witnessed in him from their first confrontation was even more pronounced now. Paul Walker, with his spiritual insight, had sensed Cole's inner struggles at their first meeting.

For her peace of mind, Lesley rushed to the phone as soon as she returned to her sister's house, and dialed the phone number Cole had given her. She let it ring twelve times without an answer. With taut nerves, she hung up and dialed again: still no response. A flood of horrible, heart-stopping fear washed over her. Jennings' men had found Cole! He was hurt. He could be dying. She had to get to him.

Blindly she grabbed her coat and stumbled out of the kitchen.

"What is it?" Terry demanded, noting the pale, bloodless look on Lesley's face.

"Cole," she muttered, feeling numb. "He doesn't answer the phone."

"Les." Terry placed a restraining hand on Lesley's sleeve. "What are you going to do?"

"Go out there and find out if he's all right."

"Les, you can't."

Two pair of intense blue eyes clashed. "I've got to."

"At least wait until Robert gets home. Let him go with you."

"No."

"The Thanksgiving baskets will be delivered soon, he'll be back any minute." There was a desperate ring to Terry's voice.

"And he could be hours. For Cole's sake I've got to go now."

"Maybe we should phone the police?"

"No, that would be premature. Cole could be in the shower or outside or sleeping and not hear the phone. But I've got to be assured he's all right. I'll phone you the minute I know."

Indecision played across Terry's face. "I'll pray," she added. "And if I don't hear from you within forty minutes, I'm calling out the National Guard."

Lesley hardly heard her sister's words, she was so intent on getting to Cole as quickly as possible.

The car headlights illuminated the way as Lesley drove up the hill that led to the duplex. She pulled into the driveway and purposely left the car lights on, flooding the area with beams of light. Both sides of the apartment were dark.

Only an hour earlier, Lesley had been sitting in a quiet,

peaceful church, praying. Now she stood alone in a dark moonless night, facing . . . she didn't know what.

"Cole?" She cried out his name and waited.

Nothing.

"Cole, answer me."

"Lesley, is that you?"

Relief weakened her knees.

"You idiot, what are you doing here?" Cole questioned as he came around from the back of the house.

She ran to him and threw her arms around his neck, laughing to keep from crying. "I tried to phone and there wasn't an answer. I was frantic! Where were you?"

"In the back, breaking up hay for the deer."

"Why now?"

"It's dark, I figured it was safer at night. I'm not really into this cloak-and-dagger stuff, but it made more sense not to be a target in broad daylight."

"You crazy fool. . . . I didn't know what to think. Let me use your phone. Terry is worried sick. She didn't know what I was going to walk into once I got up here."

Cole turned off her headlights and followed her into the house. He turned on the living room lamp so she could see the dial.

"Yes, yes, he's fine. I'm fine, too." Lesley laughed at the relief in her sister's voice. "I won't be long," she promised and replaced the receiver.

Cole took her by the hand and led her into the long hall before pulling her into his arms and kissing her soundly.

Lesley looked up at him through thick lashes, her eyes warm with the effect of his touch. "Why are you kissing me here?" She glanced behind him into the narrow hallway.

Cole held her roughly against him, his chin rubbing back and forth across the crown of her head. "No windows," he muttered.

"Windows?" The word didn't make sense until she realized that they would have made an easy target standing as they were. Closing her eyes, Lesley accepted the comfort and warmth of Cole's enveloping embrace. "Have you missed me?"

"Like crazy," he whispered thickly.

"Want me to sing a few bars for you?"

"Nope." His breath felt warm against her ear as he took a small nibbling bite.

"The . . . The last time I was in your apartment you were saying something about not bothering to get new furniture because . . . Because you'll be leaving soon."

"Is that what upset you?" He grew still, but his hold didn't relax.

"Yes," she admitted honestly. How could he say how desperately he missed her one minute and speak of leaving her the next?

"Would you feel any better if I explained that I have no intention of leaving Coeur d'Alene without you?"

Lesley felt as if her heart were about to explode. "You don't?"

"I had no intention of falling in love when I moved here. Love was the last thing on my mind."

"You love me, honestly love me?" Lesley cried, spreading eager kisses over his face and neck.

A hand at both sides of her face stopped her long enough for him to kiss her quiet.

"I kept telling myself it would never work, especially not now. Not at the most difficult time of my life. I couldn't drag you into this mess. But there you were dressed as a pillar of salt for a church social. I should have been laughing at you, but I don't know when I've seen anyone more desirable."

"But you left me."

"Honey, I really didn't have much choice."

"I know," she murmured, teasing his lips with fleeting kisses. "I was pretty angry with you at the time."

"Once this thing with Jennings is settled, we'll leave Coeur d'Alene and be married."

"Married?" Lesley gasped and tightened her hold on his waist. "Oh, Cole, I love you so much."

"The hardest thing I've ever done is keep my hands off you. This is going to be a short engagement."

"Very short," she agreed.

"We'll fly into Boston so you can meet my parents."

"And then to Arizona so you can meet mine," Lesley added.

"And be married as soon afterward as possible."

"I'm not going to argue."

"The money I earn from the air bag invention will be enough to set us up for a lifetime. But it might be a good idea to set some of it aside in a trust fund for our children."

"Children?" Lesley repeated. "You do move quickly, don't you? I'm just getting used to the idea of being a wife and you've already made me a mother."

"We'll build a magnificent house on a lake."

Lesley laid her head against his chest, hardly able to take in everything he was saying. "This is getting better all the time."

"With a soundproof room for you to sing in."

Tipping her head back, Lesley laughed into eyes that were warm and shining with that special loving glow. For the first time she was looking at Cole and seeing past the pain and bitterness that had haunted him all these weeks. "I should be angry at that remark, but I'm too much in love to care."

"I didn't feel I had the right to ask you to share my life until I heard from Lansky, but I need you. My whole life can be in turmoil, but as long as you're by my side nothing else matters."

"That's the way I feel."

"I love you, Lesley Brown."

"And I love you, Daniel Cole Engstrom."

He continued to hold her around the waist as if he couldn't bear to release her. "Let's sit down. There's a lot we need to discuss."

A small burst of happy laughter erupted from Lesley. "And I was so sure God had made a mistake when He moved you beside me."

Cole looked down on her, his face frowning. "How's that?"

"Terry and I'd prayed about who was going to move into the duplex. When it was you, I was sure God had made a terrible error."

"After the first week, you'd nearly convinced me I had, too," he joked.

"What made you choose this apartment?"

They sat together on the couch. Cole looped an arm around her shoulder, bringing her head to rest against his shoulder. "The lake. I'd been driving for two days, not sure where I'd stop, having more or less decided to hole up in a small eastern Washington community. But the beauty of the lake seemed to beckon me. I stopped in at a real estate office and rented the duplex sight unseen."

"But God sent you," Lesley added confidently.

Cole didn't respond for a long moment. "If you say so."

Some of Lesley's happiness was dampened by doubt at Cole's tone. "You have a hard time believing as strongly as I do about Christ, don't you?"

"It's not that I don't believe. I guess I'm more agnostic than anything."

"Do my strong feelings bother you?"

"No," he responded in a straightforward tone. "Whatever you want is fine. The kids, too. If it's important to you, I'll go to church and the whole bit, but only because I love you."

Lesley vacillated. It was important to her—more than important: vital. Her relationship with Jesus had priority over everything in her life, including Cole. The thought flitted through her mind that if he agreed to come to church with her, she couldn't really expect more. Not for now anyway. That he was open-minded and willing was all she needed.

The phone rang, and Lesley could feel Cole tense at her side.

"It could be Terry," Lesley murmured reassuringly.

"Or Lansky," Cole added.

She watched his face as he picked up the receiver. "Yes." The lone word sounded clipped and final.

A play of emotions showed in his face. He looked for a moment as if someone had kicked him in the stomach.

Automatically Lesley reached for his hand, squeezing it. She was shocked at how cold it was. She watched as Cole went completely white, his face devoid of color as he laid down the phone.

"What is it?"

He looked at her, and she saw again the intensity with which he hated. "Lansky." His words were barely audible. "I know why Jennings didn't kill me when he had the chance."

"Why?"

"He didn't need to. The patent had already been awarded."

"Cole," she pleaded, "you're speaking in riddles. Tell me what happened."

"Jennings was awarded the patent," he said in a voice that was devoid of emotion. He sat and buried his face in his hands.

Chapter Nine

Lesley closed her eyes as the hurt and disappointment for Cole curled around her, cutting off her voice for a stunned moment. "Oh, Cole," she whispered, "I'm so sorry. Is there anything that can be done?"

He raised his head and looked straight ahead. "Not now, not legally anyway."

Just the way he said it shot a shiver of cold fear up Lesley's back. "Cole, what are you going to do?"

"Ruin Jennings," he replied without the least hesitation.

"And yourself in the process." Her voice was high-pitched, with a sharp edge of fear.

"Listen, Lesley, let's get one thing straight right now. My business life is my own. I do what I want, when I want. If you're going to be my wife, that's something you'll have to accept here and now."

"I don't understand." Her fingers were laced together until she was sure the fierce grip had cut off the flow of blood to her hands.

"Understand?" he repeated angrily. "What's so difficult about it?"

"Okay," Lesley murmured in a trembling breath, "maybe you'd better define what it is you want from a wife."

"A home." He sounded determined.

"Wouldn't a housekeeper serve as well?" How could she argue with Cole. He'd just heard the most devastating news of his life and she was fighting with him over a definition. "Cole." She said his name softly, not revealing any of her own anger and disappointment. "I'm sorry. These are the kinds of questions we can discuss later. For now we've got to trust God to see that justice is done."

"Trust God?" Cole spat the words back with bitter rejection. "God is righteous and just? Then I would have been awarded the patent."

Lesley placed her hands over her ears, unable to bear hearing his hostility. "Cole, please, don't say that. I know you're angry. You have every right to be. But there's a reason for this. God wouldn't have allowed it to happen otherwise."

"I'm being cheated out of millions of dollars. Doesn't that mean anything to you? We could have been set for life—no problems, no worries."

"Of course it matters. Not the money so much as the fact you deserve to have been awarded the patent."

"I might have won if they—Jennings' men—hadn't found the car."

"The car?"

"I had a prototype of the air bag installed in a sports car. I gave it to Lansky because he felt it was the evidence we needed to prove my case. But Jennings' men destroyed it. Apparently inside they found my road map and evidence that I stopped in Coeur d'Alene."

Lesley had wondered about the red car he had driven when he first arrived. Now she knew.

"Cole," she murmured and laid her hand over his. "Let's

sleep on this. It's been a blow, a terrible blow. You have every right to be angry and disappointed. I'll go back to Terry's and spend the night there. But tomorrow I'll be home and we can discuss things then."

He nodded, but Lesley wasn't sure he'd even heard what she'd said.

He walked her to the door. Lesley turned and wrapped her arms around him, allowing her love to flow from her as she murmured a silent prayer on his behalf. Cole crushed her to him and buried his face in her neck while he drew in deep, shuddering breaths.

"Do you want me to stay?" she asked in a low, gentle voice when he didn't release her.

He raised his face until their gazes met. The dark, haunted look in his eyes pulled at her heart. "No, I think I'd rather be alone, at least for a little while. There are some things I need to sort out within myself."

"Tomorrow's Thanksgiving. I'll be here early."

"Okay." His look was as absent as his word.

Lesley didn't sleep, knowing Cole probably couldn't either. Now she regretted having stayed the night with Terry. Cole might need her. But he hadn't encouraged her to stay; he wanted privacy until he had worked things out in his own mind. It was well after two o'clock when Lesley fell into a deep slumber, her mind filled with troubled prayers for Cole.

"Morning, sleepyhead," Terry greeted cheerfully as Lesley stumbled into the kitchen, arms stretched high above her head as she yawned.

"My goodness, what time is it?"

"After nine."

Wiping the sleep from her eyes, Lesley walked across the

small room and poured herself a cup of coffee. “I don’t suppose that was Cole on the phone?” The ring had wakened her.

“No, one of Robert’s cousins. They’re coming for dinner.”

“I hope you won’t be offended if I spend the day with Cole.” Lesley had been too exhausted and mentally drained to tell her sister Lansky’s news when she returned the night before.

“Why not bring him along? There’s always room for one more.”

“I . . . I don’t think so. Not this time. Cole got word yesterday that he lost the patent, so he’s not in any mood to socialize.”

“Oh, Lesley,” Terry groaned. “How awful for him.”

“He’s not taking it well.”

“Who can blame him? He’s being cheated out of years of work. Isn’t there anything anyone can do?”

“Apparently not, but I don’t think that’s going to stop Cole from trying.” Lesley pulled out the kitchen chair and sat, her hands supporting her head. Already a faint throbbing ache had begun. “It sounds crazy, but you know what Bible story kept running through my mind last night?”

Terry looked up expectantly. “No?”

“About Joseph. Remember how his brothers sold him into slavery and then he became Potiphar’s trusted servant in Egypt.”

“Until Potiphar’s wife wanted to seduce him.”

“But when Joseph refused, Potiphar’s wife went running to her husband with terrible lies about Joseph, and Joseph was sent to prison.”

“Unjustly,” Terry added with a curt nod.

“Yes, but even in those horrible conditions Joseph cared about others; his spirit was never broken.”

Terry pulled up a chair and sat across from Lesley. “What are you saying?”

Lesley wasn’t sure herself, or even why the story had stuck

so prominently in her mind. She saw Cole at a crossroads of his life. This whole thing with Jennings would make him either bitter or better, make or break him. But unlike Joseph, Cole didn't have a strong faith. Lesley's greatest fear was that Cole's spirit would be broken. "I love Cole." Her smile was wan as she lowered her gaze to the steaming coffee.

"I guessed as much. Is the feeling mutual?"

Lesley's hand tightened around the mug handle. "Cole asked me to marry him yesterday, and I agreed."

"That's wonderful news." Terry's voice seemed to contain the same reservations Lesley was feeling.

"It should be, but Cole asked me before he received word from his attorney. He was so different afterward. I don't know how he feels now, and I'm almost afraid to ask."

"If he honestly loves you, then it won't make any difference. Give him time," Terry advised. "He's only just heard the news. And give yourself time. Marriage is a serious commitment."

"I realize that," Lesley admitted, biting into the corner of her bottom lip. "I'm not so concerned for myself as for Cole. I'm afraid he's going to do something stupid."

"You're not going to feel right until you see and talk to him. So get dressed and get moving. And for goodness' sake, don't tell him the story of Joseph and Potiphar's wife. He won't be in any mood to hear it."

Lesley laughed lightly, but recognized the wisdom of her sister's words.

Cole opened the front door and greeted her with a fierce hug.

"How'd you sleep?" she asked. The question was silly. He wore the same clothes as yesterday and looked as if he hadn't gone to bed. Shadows darkened his cheeks, and the frown that drove deep grooves into his forehead appeared to be permanent.

"I didn't. What about you?"

Lesley shook her head, silently confirming she had slept no better.

"I talked to Lansky again after you left. There's a chance."

"But you said . . ."

"I haven't got time to explain. I'm catching the first plane out of Spokane."

Lesley felt her heart drop to her knees. For the first time she noticed the packed suitcases standing in the living room. Had he even planned to tell her he was leaving? Her gaze narrowed on the bags, and she must have looked as shocked as she felt.

"Honey, I was sincere about everything I said yesterday. You and I were meant to be together. You're the only good thing that's ever happened to me. I'm going after Jennings for us."

"But I don't want our marriage to start like this."

"Don't you understand?" Cole returned, and rubbed a weary hand over his tired face. "I'm doing this for our future."

"The only future I want is with you, but I don't need the fancy house on the lake and the huge trust funds for our children."

Cole knotted his hands at his side, his temper obviously on a short string. "But *I* need the house, the trust funds, the money. I earned them and I'm going to have them."

Lesley couldn't argue. He had done exactly as he said, and by all rights the money should be his.

"I'll drive you to the airport," she offered in a low, defeated voice. "How long do you think you'll be gone?"

Lovingly Cole gripped her shoulders and kissed her forehead. "I'll be back as soon as possible. Believe me, I don't want to stay away any longer than necessary. I want to see us married, settled and starting a family."

His words of promise rang in her ears as she stood in the Spokane airport and waved to his departing plane, a smile frozen on her lips. Tears filled her eyes and flowed heedlessly down pale cheeks as his plane ascended into the clear November sky.

* * *

The sights and sounds of Christmas filled the air. Lesley and Terry had volunteered to be in charge of the church Christmas program and worked long hours on the planned pageant. Although Lesley found it difficult to maintain her usual Christmas spirit, working with the children helped fill her time and keep her from worrying about Cole.

Although he phoned daily, Lesley hadn't seen him since Thanksgiving and her watery farewell in Spokane.

Following his attorney's advice, Cole had appealed the patent decision and was struggling to come up with the necessary evidence to prove his case. The patent and the appeal filled his life. Some days Lesley wondered why he bothered to phone her. He seemed to be living in another world, one far removed from her life in Coeur d'Alene.

As Christmas approached, he repeatedly promised to come to Coeur d'Alene for a visit. Every night she prayed fervently that he would. She was hungry for the sight of him and almost desperate to know that the love between them was as real to Cole as it was to her.

The Christmas program was scheduled for the Sunday school hour the morning of the twentieth of December. Like typical stage mothers, Lesley and Terry made sure every detail was as perfect as possible.

Everything ran smoothly, and over dinner at Terry's afterward they discussed the amusing antics of the cast.

"Did you see Jamie Lowell peek at the audience from inside the camel costume?" Terry asked, laughter dancing in her bright blue eyes. "I thought I'd scream."

"You did," Lesley reminded her. "That's what made Julie Palmer spill the gold."

"It was my opinion the three Wise Men were *men,*" Robert interrupted, sitting beside his wife and looping an arm around her shoulder.

"We ran out of boys," Terry informed him primly.

"But all in all, everything went very well."

"Even if we do say so ourselves," Lesley chimed in. The three had gathered together in the living room after a meal of roast beef and Yorkshire pudding, or what Terry insisted was Yorkshire pudding. Lesley and Robert remained somewhat skeptical.

"Heard from Cole lately?" The question came with deceptive casualness from Robert.

"Every day," she replied and focused her attention on the gaily decorated Christmas tree rather than meet her brother-in-law's questioning regard.

"He's still coming for Christmas, isn't he?" Terry quizzed.

"I hope so."

"Do I detect a note of doubt?" Robert raised thick brows with the question.

Lesley shook her head lightly. "Cole claims he's coming, but I don't know how. His schedule seems impossible. He's meeting with his attorney Wednesday morning in Detroit, then flying into Spokane, weather permitting, and renting a car there."

"Thank goodness he had the common sense not to have you come get him. Not on these roads."

She'd wanted to meet him, had pleaded with him to let her drive to Spokane, but Cole had refused.

Robert and Terry were having a small Christmas gathering with Robert's parents. With road conditions so hazardous, it wasn't a time to be traveling. Lesley had also been invited to the family gathering, but had declined. She wanted to spend as much of her time with Cole as possible. He couldn't stay long and planned to fly out again on the twenty-sixth.

The phone was ringing Wednesday afternoon when Lesley walked in the door.

"Hello," she answered breathlessly.

* * *

"Hi, honey."

"Cole," she cried, dismay creeping into her voice. "Where are you?"

"Detroit."

"Detroit," she echoed, her heart sinking. She closed her eyes at the painful rush of disappointment. "You can't make it." She made the announcement for him, her voice unbelievably calm.

"Honey, I'm sorry."

A thick lump was blocking her throat. "This really is a terrible time of the year to plan on any traveling." Her voice was soft and quivering. "Jesus did have to pick the coldest month of the year to be born," she said, attempting a joke. "Did I tell you it's snowing again? All the kids in town love it. A white Christmas. Everyone's dream." She continued chattering because if she stopped she'd burst into tears.

"Lesley." Cole's voice was husky with appeal. "You know how much I want to be with you."

"Yes." Her hand bit into the telephone receiver as a fresh wave of hurt and frustration rippled through her.

"It's been over a month since we've been together—the longest month of my life."

"Mine, too," she muttered, and to her horror a sob escaped. "I've got to hang up now . . . I'm baking cookies and the timer just rang." The lie was outrageous, but she had to get off the phone before she disgraced herself further. Cole's disappointment was as keen as her own, so listening to her tears wouldn't make it any easier on him.

"Lesley, I love you. Don't ever doubt that, not for a minute."

"No, of course not. Good-bye, Cole. And merry Christmas." Her hand covered her mouth as she attempted to hold back the sobs. The drone continued as she replaced the telephone, her hand gripping the handle until her fingers ached.

The bank closed at noon Christmas Eve. If Terry knew about Cole's call, she'd insist Lesley come with them to Robert's parents. But their plans for the holidays were already set, and Lesley preferred not to intrude on the family gathering. In the light of Cole's call she wasn't in a celebrating mood and decided to spend the time alone.

The soft Christmas music from the record player helped to lighten her mood as she fixed herself a special dinner of chicken cordon bleu and fresh spinach salad. The small Christmas tree was decorated with a hundred starched snowflakes she had crocheted in lace. The few presents her parents had mailed, and the one Terry delivered the day before, were stacked under the tree beside the one she had for Cole.

The inspiring notes of the *Messiah* filled the small duplex. Lesley hummed as she washed her dinner dishes, then sat with her feet propped up on the coffee table, her eyes closed. The music satisfied her loneliness.

The pounding on the front door nearly caused her to fall off the couch. Christmas Eve. Who would possibly be out this time of night? Her eyes flew to her wristwatch. It was after eleven.

"Lesley," the dear, familiar male voice shouted.

Cole. Her heart somersaulted as she rushed to the front door. "Cole!" Her arms flew around his neck and she spread a multitude of tiny kisses over his face. "You're here, you're here," she repeated again and again, her joy overflowing. "You must be freezing," she murmured and lovingly held his face with her hands. "Come inside."

He pounded the snow off his boots and followed her into the duplex. She watched him as he removed his thick coat and scarf. His face was red with the cold, his hair wet from the snow, but he looked marvelous . . . wonderful.

"Sit down, and let me get you something warm to drink. Are you hungry?" She took his coat and hung it where it would dry.

"The only thing I need to warm me is you." His arm crept around her waist and pulled her onto his lap. "It's good to see you, woman." Smiling, he wiped the moist tears of happiness from her cheek. For a breathless moment they looked at each other. It had been almost a month since he'd held her, touched her. Lesley had often wondered what she'd feel when she saw Cole again. Everything had happened so fast after he'd heard from Lansky. His declaration of love, his proposal seemed so distant.

"You really are beautiful, Lesley Brown," he whispered as his mouth settled hungrily over hers. Boundless joy raced through her as she gave herself freely to the mastery of his kiss.

Long moments later, her head resting against his broad shoulder, Lesley breathed in the fresh scent of woodsy aftershave and the tangy hint of spice. "How'd you get here?" Nothing mattered now that he was here and in her arms.

"The airport cleared enough for my flight to take off, but we were forced to land in Salt Lake City because of a new storm front. I would have phoned, but I didn't want you worrying and wondering."

"Cole, I wish you had."

"Sometime early this morning, we landed in Seattle and I drove from there."

"Seattle!" she gasped. "That's a good nine hours' drive."

"Twelve. Snoqualmie Pass was closed for two hours because of a snowslide."

Keeping her arm around his shoulder, she raised her face enough so that they could look at each other. "You went through all that trouble to get to me?"

"Nothing was more important than making it here for Christmas."

The warmth of his hold burned through Lesley's thin sweater. A rawness caught in her throat at the thought of what he had endured for her. "You do love me, don't you?"

"Had you begun to doubt it?"

"In some ways I think I had," she admitted in low tones.

"But not anymore?"

"Never again." Tenderly her fingertips traced the proud, determined line of his jaw. Cole was like that. When he wanted something, he was relentless until satisfied. Every day she prayed that the ordeal with the patent would be settled, because she didn't know if Cole would rest until it was.

"Are you ready to open your present?" he asked in a husky murmur as his teeth made biting kisses along the lobe of her ear.

"You brought me a gift?" He hadn't been carrying anything.

"Here." He reached inside his jacket pocket and handed her a small jeweler's box. "I didn't have time to wrap it."

"Cole, you didn't?" From the box size it wasn't difficult to guess what was inside.

"I would have preferred to have us shop for your ring together, but I thought, circumstances being what they are, you'd understand."

Slowly she opened the lid of the plush black velvet box. A huge solitaire diamond sparkled back at her. Lesley drew in a gasp of delight. "It's beautiful," she whispered, her breath stuck in her throat. "It's perfect. I couldn't have chosen anything more beautiful."

"Let's try it on for size." He took the ring out of the holder and slipped it onto her finger, the fit as perfect as the diamond.

Holding her left hand out for them both to examine, Lesley felt a sense of awe come over her. Cole's declaration of love, the proposal and all it entailed seemed real to her now.

"Since you're an engaged woman, it's about time you had a ring to prove it, wouldn't you say?"

"Yes." Lesley beamed happily. "Yes, I would."

Cole's restless hand moved caressingly up and down her

spine. "I'd like to set a wedding date, but I want this thing settled with Jennings first."

Lesley swallowed at the building tightness in her throat. "How much longer?"

A look of pain flashed across his face. Nwow, after the first moments of shock at his arrival, Lesley could study him more closely. He looked tired, but the weariness was more than physical. Losing the patent had taken its toll, had planted bitter seeds in his heart and mind. He'd lost weight; his face was thin, almost gaunt. His cheekbones were pronounced, and tiny lines fanned out from his eyes. His thick dark hair, needing to be trimmed, covered the back of his collar. His all-consuming drive was leading to physical neglect.

"I don't know how much longer." He raked a hand along the side of his head.

"A month, maybe two?" Lesley quizzed, praying it wouldn't be any more time than that. "A girl likes to know these things."

He kissed the tip of her nose. "By summer for sure."

"Summer," she gasped, doing her best to disguise her disappointment. "Cole," she said softly, not looking at him as she spoke, "would it be so unreasonable to leave the past buried and go on with our lives?"

"Yes," he answered forcefully. "The hearing for the appeal is scheduled the second week in January. Let's decide what to do after that?"

"Okay," she agreed. Maybe she was being selfish, but their future was together and she hated these separations. "Would you like me to fix you something to eat?"

"I'm starved," he answered. "I can't remember the last time I ate."

"Honestly, Cole, sometimes I think we'd better get married now just so I'll be around to take care of you."

"Now, that's a thought." But he was teasing, and they both knew it.

She rose from his lap and looked through the refrigerator for something to cook. "How does bacon and eggs sound?"

"Marvelous," he answered on the tail of a yawn. "I'm going to lie down for a few minutes."

Lesley watched as he stretched out on the sofa and closed his eyes. She recognized that he was almost instantly asleep and wondered how long it'd been since he'd seen a bed. Gently she closed the refrigerator: there was no need to cook anything. Fifteen minutes later she spread a thick blanket over him and lovingly brushed the hair from his forehead. He looked almost childlike in slumber. Her lips lightly brushed over his as she turned out the lights and tiptoed into her own room.

"It's beautiful," Terry breathed in awe as she examined Lesley's ring. "I bet you were surprised."

Terry didn't know the half of it. "I was."

"It's too bad Cole had to leave so soon."

"So soon" was right. Lesley awoke Christmas morning to find a message on her kitchen table. He had to get back to Detroit, and after checking with the airlines he'd found the only available space was on a flight that left at eight that morning. He signed the note with his love and the promise that they would spend every Christmas the rest of their lives together.

The engagement ring felt awkward on her hand the first few days, but Lesley soon discovered that having it meant more to her than any gift she'd ever had. At least she had some physical evidence of Cole's love and commitment to her.

"Did he have any news about the patent decision?" Terry asked anxiously.

"We should know something the second week in January.

Pray, Terry," Lesley pleaded. "The sooner this thing is settled, the sooner Cole and I can get on with our lives."

Never had the days of January dragged so laboriously. Lesley waited and waited. Then the decision came when she'd least expected to hear.

On January 15, Lesley was at her desk at the bank when Charlotte Lewis told her there was a call for her on line two.

"Lesley Brown," she answered in her efficient business tone.

"The appeal was denied." Cole announced in a flat voice that didn't disguise his frustration.

"No," she whispered as the meaning of what he was saying hit. "Oh, Cole." Lesley could feel the defeat and anger in his voice. But it was over, at last, and they could accept that and go on from there. "I know it's small compensation now, but at least you have the satisfaction of knowing the air bag you invented will save thousands of lives."

"Lesley, don't feed me platitudes. Not now."

She breathed in deeply. "What do you want me to say?"

There was a savage note to his voice. "I don't know."

"When will I see you again?"

He sucked in a ragged breath. "Let me sort things out here and I'll get back to you."

"Okay. I'm sorry things didn't go well. I love you," she whispered for his ears alone.

"Some days that's the only thing that keeps me going."

Lesley didn't hear from Cole for another week, one of the longest weeks of her life. Unable to contact him by phone, she wrote him long, chatty letters every night. She tried to offer assurances, but after the first few days she realized these would do little to comfort him.

The January snows melted, and February quickly turned to March and the promise of spring. Cole wired her a dozen long-stemmed red roses on Valentine's Day with a message of his love.

Lesley didn't doubt his love, but she recognized that his hate for Jennings was far stronger than any of his feelings for her.

With April came Easter and the return of her parents from Arizona. Cole had told her he'd fly in the weekend her parents returned, so he could meet his future in-laws.

Lesley picked him up at the Spokane airport. When he stepped off the plane she was shocked at his appearance. His features were strikingly gaunt, his dark eyes haunted. The smile on her lips wavered as he stepped into the terminal.

Tears blurred her vision as Cole approached. He set his briefcase on the ground and hugged her fiercely, burying his face in her neck.

"I've missed you," she whispered brokenly.

"I know, love, I feel the same way." His kiss was as urgent as his embrace. He smiled into her eyes and gently brushed a tear aside. "I like your hair."

Her hand reached automatically for the short curls. She'd had it cut last month.

"You look terrible," she replied honestly and brushed an imaginary piece of lint from his suit coat.

"But I'm making progress." He placed his arm around her waist, pulling her close to his side.

"Are you?" She didn't mean to sound so unsure. Progress—but at what price?

"Only a little, I admit."

"This battle can go on for years, can't it?"

He tensed and his hand tightened around her. "I won't let that happen."

"It's already happening," she murmured. "Cole, you're killing yourself over a stupid airbag. Is it worth it? Answer me, is your life worth less than some invention?" She knew she sounded angry and unreasonable, but she couldn't stand by and say nothing. Not anymore.

Lesley could feel him withdraw. He stopped mid-stride, and although he continued to hold her, he might as well have been miles away.

"Yes," he said finally, his dark eyes stony-hard.

"If I can't have justice, then I'll have my revenge, and that's worth more than anything . . . even you, Lesley."

Chapter Ten

"Even me," Lesley repeated, stunned. "Cole," she breathed, "look at what you're doing to yourself. I realize better than anyone how terrible this ordeal has been for you."

"You couldn't possibly know," he announced and savagely raked a hand through his hair.

"Maybe not," she conceded. "But I see what's happening to you. I hear the bitterness in your voice, I read the hatred in your letters. And then I look at what all this has done to you physically and I want to cry. What happened to the man who asked me to marry him? The man who wanted a home and family?"

"I still want that," Cole insisted. "But don't you understand, I'm doing this for us." His mouth was tightly pinched, and Lesley recognized that his temper was held on a taut rein.

"Then you're lying to yourself and to me."

They paused in front of the baggage carousel. Lesley centered her gaze on the variety of suitcases as they arrived instead of glancing at Cole, afraid of what his eyes would say.

"Nothing like this has ever happened to me," she continued,

"I guess you could say I've lived a sheltered life." She felt Cole's gaze roam over her face, and turned to offer him a weak smile. "In some ways I have you to thank for one of the biggest strides I've made in my spiritual life."

"I don't understand."

Lesley had doubted that he would. "Do you remember Halloween night when I told you I was going to pray for you?"

Amusement touched his mouth and Lesley wondered how long it had been since Cole had smiled, really smiled.

"I remember."

"Later you pulled up beside my car in the ditch and told me you were going to pray for me. I can't remember a time in my life I was angrier."

He chuckled and his hand affectionately squeezed her shoulder. "I'm rather proud of that comment."

Swallowing her pride, Lesley shook her head. "You should be. It helped me see what I was becoming." At his frown she elaborated. "Until I met you I was quickly becoming a self-righteous prude."

"And I changed that?"

Hands laced in front of her, Lesley smiled absently. "You helped me see that I was becoming so heavenly-minded that I wasn't any earthly good. I've never thanked you for that. Knowing you and loving you has helped me more than I could ever explain in mere words."

"But that's what I'm trying to tell you. Your love and support have made these last months bearable. I couldn't have done it without you."

Inwardly Lesley groaned, realizing that in the most important of matters she had failed him.

Cole retrieved his suitcase, and with their hands linked they strode to the parking lot.

"You'd better tell me something about your parents," he

suggested as she handed him the car keys. He unlocked her door, then walked around the front of the car and climbed into the driver's seat. "It's not every day a man meets his future in-laws."

"You don't need to worry. I think Mom and Dad are more nervous about meeting you." Her parents had arrived that Wednesday and planned a small dinner party for Cole and Lesley Saturday night. To say that her parents were curious would be an understatement.

The freeway leading from Spokane to Coeur d'Alene was particularly beautiful in the spring, when lush green contrasted with a pale blue sky. They sat not speaking, Lesley close to his side.

"Did I tell you Lansky warned me that marriage is often a three-ring circus?" Cole broke the silence.

"How's that?" Lesley looked over to him expectantly.

"First there's the engagement ring, then the wedding ring, and finally the suffering."

"Clever," she muttered, feigning indignation.

Chuckling, Cole pulled off to the side of the road and reached for her. He kissed her ardently; the hunger in him for her love was so overpowering it almost frightened Lesley.

"Why is it every minute apart is agony, and then the first chance we're together all we do is argue?" Cole asked her breathlessly, his forehead resting against hers.

"I don't know why. We're both dumb, I guess," Lesley said and rubbed her face along the slightly rough surface of his jaw in a feline action. "I love you, Cole, and it's hurting me just as much as you to be apart like this. Can't we forget Jennings?"

"I wish we could." He kissed the crown of her head and ran his fingers through the short dark curls. "No, I have to revise that. I wish I could, but I won't rest until things are set right."

Lesley released a long, slow breath, straightened and leaned her head against the back of the seat cushion.

"How's the apartment?" Cole asked, changing the subject.

"Fine." He'd kept his apartment in Coeur d'Alene and left Lesley his car, though she rarely drove it: there was little need, since she had her own vehicle.

As Coeur d'Alene Lake came into view, the faint stirrings of pride brought a sigh of contentment from Lesley. "Paul said to say hello, by the way."

"Paul?" Cole looked at her blankly.

"The grocer from Resort Grocery."

"Oh yes, Mr. Christian."

"Mr. Christian?" Now it was Lesley's turn to look confused.

"Yes. Paul used to place Bible verses in the bottom of my bags every week. I got quite a kick out of him. Nice old fellow."

"He's lived a hard life. When Paul was ready to retire and give his business to his son, they discovered Jeff had cancer. Paul mortgaged the business and spent the money on medical bills. Jeff died a year later."

"That's tough for any man."

"It was especially tough for Paul. Jeff was his only child, and they were as close as any father and son could be."

Cole was quiet as they approached the outskirts of town and turned off the familiar road that led up the hill to the duplex.

Lesley's gaze studied him as they drew closer. She loved this man, but she was losing him, might already have lost him.

"I love you," she whispered, feeling a crazy kind of desperation, not knowing what else to say or how to express herself.

"I could never doubt that." Cole's hand found hers on the seat beside him and gently squeezed it. Keeping his eyes on the road, he raised her hand to his lips and tenderly kissed her palm. "You'd have to love me to stand these past months."

Lesley felt all her hard-fought-for poise slip away from her. She had to talk to Cole, make him see the uselessness of this thing with Jennings.

When Cole parked on his half of the driveway, Lesley told him, "I put a casserole in the oven before I left. I hope you're hungry."

"That was a very wifely thing to do," he teased her affectionately.

"I was just practicing."

"Good."

"I only have three days to fatten you up and add some color to your face, and believe me, I'm going to take advantage of every one of those days." Three glorious days; she'd waited impatiently, circling the weekend off on her calendar. She'd felt like a child on Christmas Day when she awoke that morning, knowing Cole would be arriving.

"Honey," Cole said thoughtfully, stopping her from opening her car door. "I've been meaning to say something, but I didn't want to until it was necessary."

"Necessary? What?" A feeling of dread came over her. He was here; nothing else should matter.

"I can't stay as long as we'd planned. I have to be back early Sunday morning, which means I'll have to catch the plane tomorrow night."

With forced calm, her eyes wide with shock and hurt, Lesley turned and met his gaze. His eyes were pleading with her to understand. He didn't want to leave so soon, but it was necessary.

A tightening sensation gripped the muscles of her stomach into a cold, hard knot. The pain was so intense that she couldn't speak for several seconds.

"Don't look at me like that," Cole pleaded.

Numbly Lesley shook her head. "I can't help it." She opened her car door and blindly walked into her apartment, leaving the screen door open.

Cole followed her inside.

Lesley stood in front of the sliding glass door in the kitchen, her arms cradling her stomach. Her lungs took in deep breaths of oxygen as she struggled to hold back the emotion.

"I know you're angry and I don't blame you," Cole said from behind her. Gently he placed his hands on her shoulders as if he wanted to ease the hurt but wasn't sure how.

With a trembling smile she turned to face him. "Cole, sit down. We need to talk."

His eyes met hers, and he gently brushed a curl from her forehead. "This sounds serious."

"More serious than any discussion I've ever had." She led him into the living room and sat him on the couch while she remained standing.

"Do you remember what I told you about Paul?"

"Mr. Christian and his son?" His look spoke plainly of trepidation.

She paced across the floor. "Yes. I know this is going to be difficult for you to understand, but hear me out."

He attempted a grin. "Is it necessary for you to pace back and forth like that when you tell me?"

"Yes." She nodded curtly. "I'm afraid it is." Taking in a quivering breath, she continued. "Everything I've done in my life—all that I've experienced, each delight, every difficulty—has made me what I am today."

Cole looked confused.

"It's true I've never experienced great tragedy, but I've witnessed what has happened to others who have."

"The grocer."

"Yes, Paul. He's a wonderful, loving man because he has risen above the horrible pain of losing his son. There is no bitterness in his heart. When a family lost their only son in a drowning incident this summer, it was Paul who offered them comfort."

"That's understandable."

"I . . . I don't know anyone who can help you, and right now I feel terribly inadequate. I love . . . you." She faltered slightly, then regained fluency. "And because I love you, I can see what all this hatred for Jennings is doing to you. Your bitterness and drive for revenge have become an obsession, an angry monster that's consuming your life." She stood directly in front of him. "You invented a wonderful safety device that will save thousands of lives. Unfortunately, you'll probably never get the credit. But you have the personal satisfaction of this accomplishment. Isn't it enough?"

"No," Cole shouted, his face cold and solemn, his narrowed eyes darkened with emotion. He stopped and rubbed a hand over his eyes, then the side of his face, distorting his features. "I won't rest until I've seen justice."

"That will probably never happen. You've got to accept this and a whole lot more." She paused, knowing how difficult this would be for Cole and how hard it was for her to say these things to him. "You need peace within yourself. You've got to forgive Jennings."

"Forgive Jennings!" Cole spat in disbelief. "You're crazy."

"I've never been more serious in my life."

"Then you couldn't possibly understand what that man has done to me," Cole shouted. "To us."

"What Jennings did was wrong," she replied calmly. "I could never deny that. But what you're doing to yourself is far worse."

Cole bounded to his feet and stalked to one end of the room, his eyes blazing. "I can't believe you'd even suggest such a thing."

The smile that touched her eyes was troubled and sad. "It's the way I was raised. My parents brought up Terry and me in an atmosphere of love and forgiveness. We were raised in the church—"

"Here it comes." The shadows of pain darkened his eyes. "I

thought you just got done telling me I'd helped you get over being a self-righteous prude?"

"That doesn't have anything to do with this," Lesley defended herself, looking straight into Cole's shocked expression.

"But you're going to give me some holier-than-thou advice about forgiving the man who's ruining my life."

"The man you're letting ruin your life," she amended, hoping he would catch the subtle difference.

"Lesley, listen to me," Cole pleaded, fighting for control of his temper. "You're not making any sense."

With an aching heart, Lesley studied Cole: the roughly carved jaw, the thick creased grooves in his forehead, the tight line of his mouth. She would give anything to make herself clear, anything to help him understand.

"Today is Good Friday," she said at last.

A heavy silence hung in the room.

"What's that supposed to mean to me?" His expression was as hard as a granite wall.

"Unless you're a Christian, I guess it doesn't mean much."

"Then why bring it into the conversation now?" Slowly he walked to the far side of the room, his hard gaze pinning her.

"Because we were talking about forgiveness."

"Are we back on that subject again?"

Lesley's smile was tremulous. "I never stopped talking about it. When Jesus hung on that cross, He wasn't the pretty picture some artists have depicted. He was beaten so badly that He was unrecognizable as a man. He hung in shame between two criminals."

"Are you going to insist on giving me a Bible lesson?"

"Yes," she cried, her voice shaking violently. "Yes, I am, because maybe then you'll understand. Jesus was perfect . . . sinless . . . the Lamb of God."

Cole glanced away, a bored look on his face.

"When Jesus hung on the cross, He took every sin, every evil that was ever in the world—the past, the present and the future. He became so hideously ugly with sin that God the Father had to actually turn His back on Him. That was why Jesus called out and asked why His Father had forsaken Him."

"How much more of this do I have to listen to?"

"Not much."

His look was one of indulgent cynicism. "Good." He crossed his arms in front of his chest as if that could block out her words.

"Yet Jesus, in all his pain and torment, asked that God forgive." Lesley knew she wasn't reaching Cole, she doubted that anything she said would. Nonetheless she continued. "Don't you understand? If Jesus could show that kind of forgiveness for you and me, couldn't you find it in your heart to forgive Jennings?"

Cole's hands knotted into tight fists. For a long time he said nothing as he stood before her. He was so tall and hard, he might as well have been carved out of stone. "You ask too much."

Her eyes wide and shimmering with tears, Lesley slipped the engagement ring off her finger. "I love you, Cole, but my love will never be enough for you." She placed the ring in the palm of his hand.

"You don't mean this?" Cole's voice was as cold as the arctic wind.

"I've never been more serious."

"I won't come back." Cole's low words weren't a threat but a promise.

"I know that," she murmured and glanced down at the carpet. "God go with you, Cole."

One dark brow shot up with sardonic disbelief. "I'm taking the car with me. I'll contact the owner about the duplex. Whatever's inside can be given to charity. That's about as Christian as

I plan to get." He walked out of the house, looking back at her once, his gaze whip-sharp. "Goodbye, Lesley."

A hand over her mouth to hold back the threatening sobs, Lesley watched as he walked out of her half of the house and into his half. Not questioning her actions, she took the small devotional Bible on the end table and ran outside. If she tried to give it to Cole now, he'd throw it back at her. Carefully and as noiselessly as possible she placed it in the backseat of his car.

She was in the house by the time he returned. He glanced back at her once, his look uncompromisingly hard. Without another word he backed out of the driveway and out of her life.

Chapter Eleven

"Are you all right?" Terry asked as they walked down the church corridor from the Sunday school classroom to the sanctuary. Their footsteps echoed through the long hall.

"Why shouldn't I be fine?" Lesley decided to be obtuse. Three weeks and not a word from Cole. Not that she expected him to contact her.

"Don't play dumb," Terry hissed. "You're miserable, so admit it."

"Okay, you win," Lesley answered sharply. "I'm miserable. Does that make you happy?"

"No," Terry observed softly. "It makes me as brokenhearted as you."

"Well, don't be," Lesley responded in a falsely cheerful voice. "My relationship with Cole was doomed anyway. I only hastened the process."

"But you still love him."

Fresh pain burned through her heart. "That hasn't changed, but after my speech on God's love and forgiveness, I've got to look on the positive side of this situation and grow from it."

* * *

"Don't try so hard." Her sister squeezed her arm affectionately. "Give yourself time."

Lesley arched delicately shaped brows. "Time," she said with a sigh, "the great healer." But how much time would it take for the haunting memories to dissipate? How long would it be before thoughts of Cole didn't dominate every waking minute and before her life had order again?

Every time the phone rang, her heart pounded like a jackhammer. When she checked the mailbox, her fingers shook. Cole had written and phoned her so often. And now there was nothing. Nothing. Lesley was left to pick up the pieces of her life and go on. Although she accepted the fact Cole wasn't coming back, her heart waged its own battle. Time, she had to believe, would convince her heart, too.

"Is the other half of the duplex rented?" Terry whispered as they entered the vestibule.

"Not yet." The FOR RENT sign in the grass outside the duplex was a constant reminder that Cole was gone for good.

"Any nibbles?"

Lesley shrugged. "Not that I know of."

They slipped into the pew and waited for the morning worship service to begin. Robert joined them a minute later. Lesley bowed her head, seeking to clear her thoughts and prepare her heart for the pastor's message. As she raised her head, her gaze fell on her ringless left hand. Inadvertently she touched her bare finger. She felt naked without the engagement ring.

Terry's hand reached over and squeezed hers. "You're going to make it."

Lesley nodded. Yes, she would. She'd never stop loving Cole, her heart had decreed as much. But she would be stronger, better, because of that love.

The bright spring sunshine greeted Lesley as she drove home from work Monday afternoon. The time had come to get busy in the garden. She hadn't felt like working outside. The energy spent smiling and putting on a friendly façade drained her by the end of the long workday. She usually ate a light meal, read and went to bed early. Not that she could fall asleep so quickly.

The first thing Lesley noted when she pulled into the driveway was that the FOR RENT sign had been removed from the lawn. Apparently she was going to have a new neighbor. The place had been vacant for months with Cole gone so much of the time. It would be good to have someone close again.

Pouring herself a glass of iced tea, Lesley took a long swallow and set the tall glass on the kitchen table. The jeans she wore to work in the yard were a little large in the waist, prompting her to grab a couple of cookies from the cookie jar. They tasted stale, and after one bite she tossed them both in the garbage. Saturday she'd remember to pick up a fresh supply.

The sweatshirt was a faded red one she'd had since her college days. Lesley pushed the long sleeves up past her elbows as she walked out the sliding glass door into the backyard. The garden fork was resting against the back wall of the work shed. She successfully stifled a wince when she reached for it, refusing to look at the snow shovel, which forcefully reminded her of Cole and the fun they'd had in the first snowstorm of the season.

The earth was damp, which made the tilling easier. Lesley had finished the first long row of the garden when she paused to wipe the perspiration from her brow with the back of her hand.

She stopped in mid-action as she caught a glimpse of her new neighbor. It felt as if her heart had stopped beating, and all the color drained from her face. Cole. What was he doing back? Had he forgotten something? Had he come to torment her?

He stood framed in the doorway, watching her. Their eyes clashed, shocked sparkling blue against warm velvet brown. Mesmerized, Lesley watched as he pulled open the sliding door and stepped outside.

"Hello, Lesley." He was dressed in brown slacks and a tan sweater, looking so handsome it was almost impossible for her to breath evenly.

"Hello," she managed at last.

"I take it you're surprised to see me?"

Her hand curled around the rough wood handle of the garden fork. "Yes," she whispered. She wasn't ready for a confrontation with Cole. She needed more time to prepare, to school her reactions.

"You look well."

"I'm fine." How could they exchange pleasantries like polite strangers? This was the man she loved, and all that emotion had to be shining from her eyes for him to see. Why was he standing there? "How have you been?" she asked, her voice husky.

He shrugged one muscular shoulder. "Much better, actually."

"Good." She cast her eyes down at the partially tilled garden. "As you can see, I'm at it again." The toe of her tennis shoe parted the rich soil.

"Yes, I can." His smile was strangely enigmatic.

Lesley's nerves were pulled taut until they grated against one another. "What are you doing here?" she demanded, her voice quivering violently.

"You put the Bible in the back of my car, didn't you?" He answered her question with one of his own.

"Yes." She wouldn't lie. "I knew that I couldn't help you, but I thought my Bible might."

"You're wrong, I didn't appreciate it when I found it. The fact is, I went to throw it away. Purging my life of anything that had to do with you made sense at the time."

Lesley blanched. Tossing her Bible in the garbage would be like throwing away part of herself. But apparently that had been Cole's intention.

"This fell out of it." He handed Lesley a paper she'd used to mark her place.

Lovingly she fingered the long marker and nodded. "Thank you for returning it."

"There were other things inside the cover, too." His look was unreadable.

Briefly she nodded, unable to look at him.

"The card I sent with the Valentine roses, a death announcement. Some relative?"

Again she acknowledged him with a nod of her head.

"This book is important to you."

"Yes." She'd missed it terribly, and although she'd replaced it immediately after he'd left, Lesley had had difficulty finding familiar verses. The pages were still so new they stuck together, and the leather binding remained stiff.

"As soon as I saw the treasures you had stored in its flap, I couldn't understand why you'd given it to me, but I decided maybe I couldn't throw it away."

Lesley released an unconscious sigh of relief.

"But I wasn't about to return it personally, I'd already made myself perfectly clear. I wasn't coming back to Coeur d'Alene. I meant to mail it. Instead I found myself leafing through the pages. Soon I found myself reading the Gospels. You had several verses underlined in John. 'I came that they may have life, and may have it abundantly' was one that sticks out in my mind."

"John 10:10," she supplied.

"But Jesus wasn't talking about riches, was He?"

"No, He was talking about the quality of our earthly life." Her gaze slid to him again. A beautiful feeling of hope began to mount within her.

"Soon I found verses everywhere that spoke of forgiveness: Hebrews, Psalms, Acts. I read about the new life, the abundant life. For the first time in nearly a year I slept peacefully and uninterruptedly. I have peace within myself now. I can't say that everything's behind me yet. The hate and bitterness are lessening. I haven't forgiven Jennings for what he did. But I'm willing to try, with God's help."

Lesley stood immobile for only a moment.

"I love you, Lesley. You're the best thing that's ever happened to me. I want to share this new abundant life with you. Can we start again? Can we place the past behind us?"

The garden fork fell unheeded to the damp earth as she walked to Cole and slipped her arms around his neck. Brilliant tears of happiness shimmered in her eyes as she smiled up at him.

Very gently, Cole wrapped his arms around her, and kissed her with a fierce kind of tenderness. He released a shuddering sigh as he held her close, his lips moving back and forth against the side of her head, his breath ruffling her hair.

A happiness unlike anything she'd ever experienced stole through her. "Did the landlord explain about the water pressure?" she asked teasingly.

"No," Cole murmured and brushed the hair from her cheek. "But he had plenty to say about the occupant in the second half of the duplex. Apparently my new neighbor is a karate expert."

Laughter tumbled from Lesley as she tilted her head back to gaze into the powerful face of the man she loved, the man God had sent to her.

Six months later, Lesley came in the back door of her Detroit home and placed the two grocery sacks on the kitchen countertop. Pausing, she unzipped her short jacket and tossed it across the back of the kitchen chair.

A package of cookies was on top of the first sack. She opened it and dumped them in a red apple-shaped cookie jar, nibbling on one as she put the frozen foods in the freezer section of the refrigerator.

The sounds of Cole working in the basement brought a sigh of contentment from slightly parted lips. Even after several months of marriage, her husband's genius had the ability to amaze her. His work area was a collage of ideas. Most of his work centered on the automobile and parts she hadn't known existed. But his inventions extended into the kitchen, and he had her testing a few of his crazy ideas. If she wasn't so much in love, she would have complained.

"Cole." She pushed the button of the intercom. "Would you like me to bring you down a cup of coffee?"

"Sure." He sounded preoccupied, but then he usually did when he was in his workroom.

While she finished unpacking the groceries, Lesley plugged in the coffeepot. Ten minutes later she carried two steaming cups down the stairs.

"I hope you're ready for a break."

"In just a minute," Cole answered without looking up, keenly concentrating on his latest contraption.

A smile touched the corners of her soft mouth. She'd sat an hour waiting for his "just a minute" on more than one occasion.

"Cole," she said softly, "I've got something important to tell you."

"Go ahead, I'm listening."

Lesley rolled her eyes and sighed. "I was just thinking that maybe it would be a good idea for you to start working on a new type of car seat for the baby. I was looking at ones in the shopping center today, and they don't look all that secure. Do you think you might have a couple of ideas?"

"Sure," he mumbled, "no problem."

Lesley sat on a tall stool and took a sip of her coffee. Glancing at her wristwatch, she mentally calculated how long it would take to get a reaction. Five minutes, she guessed.

"Baby!" Cole exploded, and banged his head on the light fixture as he stood up abruptly.

Lesley shot a glance at her watch. "Very good. That only took you two and a half minutes."

Rubbing the back of his head, Cole looked at her and shook his head. "Did I hear you right?"

"As a matter of fact, I think you heard me perfectly." Lesley was loving this.

"A baby? So soon? Are you sure?"

"I saw the doctor this morning."

Cole took the coffee out of her hand and set it aside. He sat on the stool beside her, his hand tenderly resting against her flat abdomen. "Why didn't you say something earlier?"

Lesley brushed the hair from his forehead. "I wanted to be certain."

"But, honey, I wanted to build you that dream home on the lake before we started a family. I want to give you diamonds and smother you in furs."

Linking her arms around his neck, Lesley pressed an ardent kiss over his mouth. "Don't you know I'm already the richest lady in town?"

★★★★★